STORM RISING

STORM RISING

Book Two of The Mage Storms

MERCEDES LACKEY

DAW BOOKS, INC.

DONALD A. WOLLHEIM, FOUNDER

375 Hudson Street, New York, NY 10014

ELIZABETH R. WOLLHEIM
SHEILA E. GILBERT
PUBLISHERS

First Printing, September 1995

1 2 3 4 5 6 7 8 9

DAW TRADEMARK REGISTERED
U.S. PAT. OFF. AND FOREIGN COUNTRIES
—MARCA REGISTRADA
HECHO IN U.S.A.

PRINTED IN THE U.S.A.

Dedicated to Teresa and Dejah

OFFICIAL TIMELINE FOR THE

by *Mercedes Lackey*

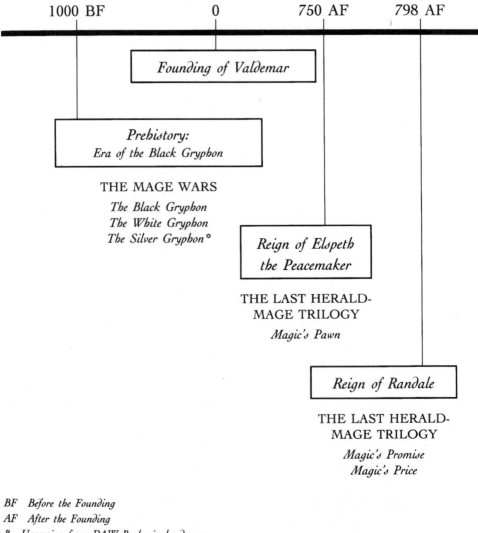

1000 BF   0   750 AF   798 AF

Founding of Valdemar

Prehistory:
Era of the Black Gryphon

THE MAGE WARS
The Black Gryphon
The White Gryphon
*The Silver Gryphon**

Reign of Elspeth
the Peacemaker

THE LAST HERALD-
MAGE TRILOGY
Magic's Pawn

Reign of Randale

THE LAST HERALD-
MAGE TRILOGY
Magic's Promise
Magic's Price

BF *Before the Founding*
AF *After the Founding*
* *Upcoming from DAW Books in hardcover*

HERALDS OF VALDEMAR SERIES

Sequence of events by Valdemar reckoning

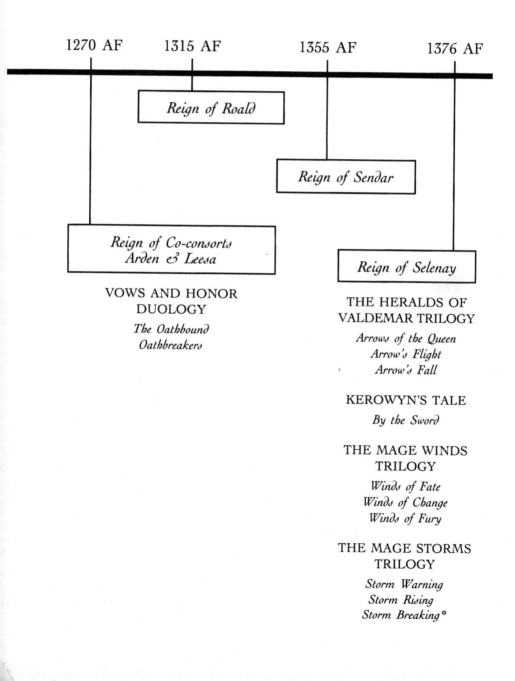

1270 AF   1315 AF   1355 AF   1376 AF

Reign of Roald

Reign of Sendar

Reign of Co-consorts
Arden & Leesa

Reign of Selenay

VOWS AND HONOR
DUOLOGY

The Oathbound
Oathbreakers

THE HERALDS OF
VALDEMAR TRILOGY

Arrows of the Queen
Arrow's Flight
Arrow's Fall

KEROWYN'S TALE

By the Sword

THE MAGE WINDS
TRILOGY

Winds of Fate
Winds of Change
Winds of Fury

THE MAGE STORMS
TRILOGY

Storm Warning
Storm Rising
Storm Breaking＊

One

Grand Duke Tremane shivered as a cold draft wisped past the shutters behind him and drifted down the back of his neck. This was a far cry from Emperor Charliss' Crag Castle—which, though outwardly austere, was nevertheless replete with hidden comforts. Even his own ducal manor, while primitive by the standards of Crag Castle, was free of drafts in the worst of weather. Tremane closed his eyes for a moment in longing for his own home as yet another breath of ice insinuated itself past his collar. It felt less like a trickle of cold water and more like the edge of a knife blade laid along his spine.

More like at my throat. That cold breath of air was the merest harbinger of worse, much worse, to come. That was why he had gathered every officer, every mage, and every scholar in his ranks here together, all of them crammed into the largest room his confiscated headquarters afforded.

Who did they say had built this place? A Hardornen Grand Duke at least, as I recall. His own manor boasted many rooms grander than this, and better suited to gathering large groups of men for a serious discussion. The tall windows, though glazed, were as leaky as so many sieves, and he'd been forced to block out the thin gray light of another bleak autumn day by having the shutters fastened down across them; and although fires roared in the fireplaces at either end of the room, the heat went straight up into the rafters two stories above his head, where it was hardly doing anyone any good. In happier times, this wood-paneled, vaulted hall with its floor of chill stone had likely played host to any number of glittering balls and entertainments. The rest of the time it had probably been shut up, given that it was a drafty old barn and impossible to keep at a reasonable temperature. Tremane glanced up at the exposed beams and rafters above him; they were lost in the shadows despite the presence of so many candles and lanterns on the tables that the air trembled and shimmered just above the flickering flames.

The massed candles must be putting out almost as much heat as the fireplaces; too bad none of that heat was reaching him.

Dozens of anxious faces peered up at him. He was seated on a massive chair behind a ridiculously tiny secretary's desk up on the platform where musicians had probably performed. It was uncomfortably like a dais, and he was well aware that such a comparison would not be lost on the Imperial spies in his ranks. Right now, though, that was the least of his concerns. The primary issue here was a simpler one: survival.

He stood up, and the murmur of incidental conversation below him died into silence without the need to clear his throat.

"Forgive me, gentlemen, if I bore you by stating the obvious," he began, concealing his discomfort at addressing so many people at once. He had never been particularly adept at public speaking; it was the one lack he suffered as a commander. No stirring battlefield speeches out of him—he was more apt to clear his throat uneasily, then bark something trite about honor and loyalty and retire in confusion. "Some of you have been involved in other projects at my request, and I want you all to know our current situation as clearly as possible, so that nothing has to be explained twice."

He winced inwardly at the awkwardness of his own words, but there were some nods out in his audience, and no one looked bored yet, so he carried on. Officers formed the bulk of his audience, massed at three long tables in front of him, dark and foreboding in their field uniforms of a dark reddish brown—the color of dried blood. Some wag had once made the claim that the reason the field uniforms were that color was to avoid the expense of removing stains after a battle. As a sample of wit, it had fallen rather flat; taken at face value, it might just have been the truth.

To his right and left, respectively, were his tame scholars and the Imperial mages; the latter in a variation on the field uniforms, looser and more comfortable for middle-aged and spreading bodies. The former, as civilians, wore whatever they wished to, and were the sole spots of brightness here. He addressed his first summation to mages and scholars both, rather than to the officers. "Although the Imperial forces have not met with any active opposition since we pulled in our line and took a fortified position here, we are still in hostile territory. Everything to the west of us was completely unsecured when we broke off all engagements, and I would not vouch for Hardornen land to the south and north of our original wedge. Hostilities could break out at any moment, and we must keep that in mind when making plans."

Grimaces from the scholars and mages, grim agreement from his officers. The Imperial wedge meant to divide the country of Hardorn into two roughly equal parts, to be divided still further and conquered, was now an Imperial arrowhead, broken off from the shaft and lodged somewhere in the middle of Hardorn. And at the moment, he only hoped it was lodged in such a way that it could be ignored by the populace at large.

"We have been cut off completely from Imperial contact ever since the mage-storms worsened," he continued, giving them the most unpleasant news first. "We have not been able to reestablish that contact. I must reluctantly conclude that we are on our own."

There were not many in his ranks who knew that particular fact, and widened eyes and shocked glances told where and how the news hit home. They took it rather well, though; he was proud of them. They were all good men— even the Imperial spies among them.

Are any of them still in contact with their overseers in the Empire? I'd give a great deal for the answer to that little question. There was no way of knowing, of course, since anyone who was an agent for Emperor Charliss would be a better mage than he himself was. Charliss was too canny an old wolf not to cover that contingency.

Another draft of cold licked at his neck, and he turned the fur-lined collar of his wool half-cape up in a futile attempt to keep more such drafts away. It was the same dulled red as the uniforms of his men; he wore what they wore. He had a distaste for making a show of himself. Besides, a man in a dress uniform covered with decorations made far too prime a target.

"The mage-corps," he continued, turning to nod at the variously-garbed men seated at the table nearest him, "tell me there is no doubt but that the mage-storms are worsening rather than weakening. As you have probably noticed, they are having an effect on the weather itself, and they will continue to do so. That means more *physical* storms, and worse ones—" He turned a questioning glance at his mages.

Their spokesman stood up. This was not their chief, Gordun, a thickset and homely man who remained in his seat with his hands locked firmly together on the table in front of him, but rather a withered old specimen who had been Tremane's own mentor, the oldest mage—perhaps the oldest man—in the entire entourage. Sejanes was nobody's fool, and perhaps the mages all felt Tremane would be less likely to vent his wrath upon someone he had studied under. In this, his mages were incorrect. He would never vent his wrath on anyone telling him a harsh truth—only on someone caught in a lie.

Sejanes knew that, and looked up at his former pupil with serenity intact. "You may have noticed what seems to us of the Empire to be *unseasonable* cold, and wondered if we are simply seeing weather that is normal to this clime," the old man said, his reedy voice carrying quite well over the assemblage. "I assure you all, it is not. I have spoken with the local farmers and studied what records are available, and this is possibly the worst season this part of the country has ever encountered. Fall struck hard and early, the autumn storms have been more frequent and harsher, and the frosts deeper. We have made measurements, and we can only conclude that the situation is going to worsen. This is the effect of the mage-storms upon an area that was already unstable, thanks to the depredations of that fool, Ancar. The mage-storms themselves are growing worse as well. Put those things together—and I'd just as soon not have to think about what this winter is going to be like."

Sejanes sat down again, and Gordun stood up; about them, looks of shock were modulating into other emotions. There was remarkably little panic, but also no sign whatsoever of optimism. That, in Tremane's opinion, was just as well. The worse they thought the situation was, the better they would plan.

"We've flat given up on restoring mage-link communications with the Empire," he said bluntly. "There isn't a prayer of matching with them when both of us are drifting—it would be like trying to join the ends of two ribbons in a gale without being able to tie a knot in them." His face was set in an expression of resignation. "Sirs, the honest truth is that your mages are the most useless part of your army right now. We can't do *anything* that will hold through a storm."

"Just what does that mean, exactly?" someone asked from the back of the room.

Sejanes shrugged. "From now on, you might as well act as if we don't exist. You won't have mage-fires for heat or light now or in the dead of winter, we can't transport so much as a bag of grain nor build a Portal that'll stay up through a single storm. In short, sirs, whatever depends on magic is undependable, and we can't see a time coming when you'll be able to depend on it again."

He sat down abruptly, and before the others could erupt with questions, Tremane took control of the situation again.

"The latest mage-storm passed three days ago," he said. "I have been taking reports since then." He leafed through the papers he had read so often that the words danced before his mind's eye. *Give them some good news.* "The last of the stragglers from that engagement outside Spangera trickled in right before it passed. Every man's been accounted for, one way or another. The preliminary palisades were finished just as the storm hit, so we are now all behind *some* kind of wall or other." He let them digest that bit of good news for a moment, as a palliative to all the unpleasant information they'd had until now. The shutters behind him rattled in a sudden gust of wind, and the candles flickered as another draft swept the room. This time it was a puff of warm air that touched him, scented with wax and lamp oil.

Shonar Manor, the locals called this place; he'd chosen well when he'd chosen to make it the place where the Imperial Army would dig in and settle down. This fortified manor he had taken as his own had no one to claim it, or so he had been told; Ancar had seen to that. Whether he'd slaughtered the family, root and branch, or simply seen to it that they were all sent into the front lines of his war with Valdemar, Tremane did not know. Nor did it matter, in truth, except that there would be no inconvenient claimants with backers from the town to show up and cause him trouble. The walled city of Shonar itself could hardly hold a fraction of his men, of course, even if he'd displaced the citizens, which he had no intention of doing. They were much more useful right where they were, forming a fine lot of hostages against the good behavior of their fellows—and in the meantime, providing his men with the amenities of any good-sized town. In fact, they were being treated precisely as if they were Imperial citizens themselves, so long as they made no trouble. For their part, after their first alarms settled, they seemed satisfied enough with their lot. Imperial silver and copper spent as well as any other.

From the reports Tremane had gotten since the last mage-storm cleared, it was a good thing for everyone that he *did* get all his men together before it broke.

"The scouts are reporting a fair amount of damage in the countryside this time," he said, turning over another page without really reading what was written there. "This time it's not just the circles of strange land appearing everywhere. Though we've a fair number of those, and they're bigger, there *are* fewer of them emerging—but we have something entirely new on our hands." He regarded them all with a grave expression; they looked up at him expectantly. "I'm certain that at one time or another each of you has seen mage-made creatures; perhaps some of the attempts to recreate the war-beasts of the past like gryphons or makaar. It appears that the mage-storms are having a similar *changing* effect on animals and plants, but with none of the control that there would be with a guiding mind behind the magic."

"*Monsters,*" he heard someone murmur, and he nodded to confirm that unpleasant speculation.

"Monstrous creatures indeed," he acknowledged. "Some of them quite horrifying. *So far* none of them have posed any sort of threat that a well-trained and well-armed squad could not handle, but let me remind you that this last storm hit us by day. What is relatively simple for men to deal with by day may become a much more serious threat in the dark of night."

What if the animal trapped had been something larger than a bull, or smarter than a sheep? What if it had been an entire herd of something? He sighed, and ran his hand through his thinning hair. "This," he pointed out fairly, "is going to do nothing for morale which, as most of you have reported to me, is at the lowest point any of you have ever seen in an Imperial Army."

He turned over another page. "According to *your* reports, gentlemen," he continued, nodding in the direction of his officers, "this is also to be laid at the feet of the mage-storms. I have had reports of men being treated by the Healers for nothing more nor less than fear, so terrified that they cannot move or speak—and not all of them are green recruits either." As the officers stirred, perhaps thinking of an attempt to protest or defend themselves, he gazed upon them with what he hoped was a mixture of candor and earnest reassurance. "There is no blame to be placed here, gentlemen. Your men are trained to deal with combat magic, but not with something like this—certainly not with something which is so random in the way it strikes and what it does. There is nothing *predictable* about these storms; we do not even know when they will wash over us. That is quite enough to make even the most hardened veteran ill-at-ease."

Yes, the one question none of us will ask. What if the mage-storm changes not only beasts, but men?

He smiled a little, and his officers relaxed. "Now, as it

happens, this is actually working in our favor. My operatives in unsecured areas tell me that the Hardornens are just as demoralized as our men. Perhaps more so; they are little used to seeing the effects of magic close at hand. And certainly they are not prepared for these misshapen monsters that spring up as a result of the storms. So, on the whole, they have a great deal more to worry about than we do—and that can only be good news for us."

In point of fact, active resistance had evaporated; it had begun to fade even before the last mage-storm had struck. He watched his officers as they calculated for themselves how long it had been since a serious attack had come from the Hardornen "freedom fighters" and relaxed minutely as he saw *them* relaxing.

"Now—that is the situation as it stands," he concluded, with relief that his speech was over. "Have any of you anything to add?"

Gordun stood. "Following your orders, Your Grace, we are concentrating all our efforts on getting a single Portal up and functioning. It will not remain functional after the next storm, but we believe we can have it for you within a few days, with all of us concentrating on that single task."

May the Thousand Little Gods help us. Gordun by himself could have created and held a Portal before these damned storms started. Will we find ourselves wearing skins and chipping flint arrowheads next?

He nodded, noting the faintly surprised and speculative looks his officers were trading. Did any of them have an inkling of what he was about?

Probably not. On the other hand, that is probably just as well.

Finally, at long last, it was the scholar's turn; he did not even recognize the timid man urged to his feet by the sharp whispers of his fellows, which argued for more bad news.

"W–we regret, Y–your G–grace," the fellow stammered nervously, "there is n–nothing in any r–records to g–give us a hint of a s–solution to the s–storms. W–we l–looked for hidden c–ciphers or other k–keys as you asked, and there was n–nothing of the s–sort."

He didn't so much sit down as collapse into his seat. Tremane sighed ostentatiously, but he did not rebuke the poor fellow in any way. Even if he'd been tempted to—the man couldn't help it if there was nothing to find in the records, after all—he was afraid the poor man would faint dead away if the Grand Duke even looked at him with faint disapproval.

These scholars are hardly a robust lot. Or perhaps it is just that they are neither fish nor fowl—neither ranked with the mages nor bound to the army, and thus have the protections of neither.

Odd. That wasn't anything he would have taken much thought for, in the past. Perhaps because he knew they were on their own, he was taking no man for granted, not even a scholar with weak eyes and weaker muscles.

"Gentlemen," he said, even as those thoughts were running through his head, "now you know the worst. Winter is approaching, and much more swiftly than any of us thought possible." As if to underscore his words, the shutters that had been rattling were hit by a sudden fierce gust that sounded as if they'd been struck by a missile flung from a catapult. "I need your help in planning how we are to meet it when it comes. We need shelter for the men, walls to protect us, not only from the Hardornens, but from whatever the mage-storms may conjure up. We cannot rely on magic—only what our resources, skills, and strength can provide." He cast his eyes over all of them, looking for expressions that seemed out of place, but found nothing immediately obvious. "Your orders are as follows; the engineering corps are to create a plan for a defensive wall that can be constructed in the shortest possible time using army labor and local materials. The rest of you are to inventory the civilian skills of your men and pool those men whose skills can provide us shelter suitable for the worst winter you can imagine. Do not neglect the sanitation in this; we are going to need *permanent* facilities now, something suitable for a long stay, not just latrine trenches. Besides shelter, we will need some way to warm that shelter and to cook food—if we begin cutting trees for the usual fires, we'll have the forest down to stumps before the winter is half over." Was that enough for them to do? Probably, for now. "You scholars, search for efficient existing shelters, ones that hold heat well, and some fuel source beside wood. If you find anything that looks practical, bring it to my attention. Mages, you have your assignment. Gentlemen, you are dismissed for now."

The men had to wait to file out of the great double doors at the end of the hall, suffering the cold blasts penetrating the hall as one of the shutters broke loose and slapped against the wall. The Grand Duke was not so bound; his escape was right behind the dais, in the form of a smaller door at which his bodyguard waited, and he took it, grateful to be out of that place. The short half-cape did nothing to keep a man warm; he wanted a fire and a hot drink, in that order.

The guard fell in silently behind him as he headed for his own quarters, his thoughts preoccupied with all the things he had not—yet—told his men.

The mages probably guessed part of it. They were not simply cut off, they had been *abandoned*, left to fend for themselves, like unwanted dogs.

The Emperor, with all the power of all the most powerful mages in the world at his disposal, could (if he was truly determined) overcome the disruptions caused by the mage-storms to send *some* kind of message. Tremane had never heard of a commander being left so in the dark before; certainly it was the first time in his own life that *he* had no clue what Charliss wanted or did not want of him.

There could be several causes for this silence.

The most innocent was also, in some ways, the most ominous. It was entirely possible that the mage-storms wreaking such havoc here could be having an even worse effect within the Empire itself. The Empire had literally been built on magic; distribution of food depended upon it, and communications, and a hundred more of the things that underpinned and upheld the structure of the Empire itself. If that was the case—

They're in a worse panic than we are here. Civilians have no discipline; as things break down, they'll panic. He was enough of a student of history himself to have some inkling what panicking civilians could do. *Rioting, mass fighting, hysteria . . . in a city, with all those folk packed in together, there would be nothing for it but to declare martial law. Even then, that wouldn't stop the fear or the panic. It would be like putting a cork on a bottle of wine that was still fermenting; sooner or later, something would explode.*

Tremane reached the warm solitude of his personal suite, waving to the bodyguard to remain outside. That was no hardship; the corridors provided more shelter from the cold drafts than half of the rooms did. Fortunately, *his* suite was tightly sealed and altogether cozy. He closed the door to his office with a sigh. No drafts here—he could remove his short winter cloak and finally, in the privacy of his quarters, warm numb fingers and frozen toes at a fire.

The second possibility that had occurred to him was basically a variation on what he, himself, had just ordered. The Emperor *could* have decreed that literally everything was to be secondary to finding a way for the mages to protect the Empire from these storms. There would be no mages free to try and reopen communications with this lost segment of the army. The Empire itself might be protected, but that might very well be all the mages could manage.

But the Empire would hardly spend such precious resources as Imperial mages on the protection of client-states. No, only the core of the Empire, those parts of it that were so firmly within the borders that only scholars recalled what names they had originally borne, would be given such protection.

Which means, he mused, feeling oddly detached from the entire scenario, *that the client states are probably rearming and revolting against Charliss. If the Empire itself is under martial law, all available units of the army have been pulled back into the Empire to enforce it. They won't be spending much time worrying about us.*

No, one segment of the Imperial Army, posted off beyond the borders of the farthest-flung Imperial Duchy, was not going to warrant any attention under conditions that drastic.

But no one born and raised in the Imperial Courts was ever going to stop with consideration of the most innocent explanations. Not when paranoia was a survival trait, and innocence its own punishment.

So, let us consider the most paranoid of scenarios. The one in which our enemy is the one person who might be assumed to be our benefactor. It was entirely possible that these mage-storms were nothing new to Emperor Charliss. He could have known all along that they were going to strike, and where, and when. In fact, it was possible that these storms were a weapon that Charliss was testing *on them.*

Tremane grew cold with a chill that the fire did nothing to warm.

This could be a new terror-weapon, he thought, following the idea to its logical conclusion, as his muscles grew stiff with suppressed tension. *What better weapon than one that disrupts your enemy's ability to work magic, and leaves land and people beaten down but relatively intact?*

There was even a "positive" slant to that notion. Perhaps this was new Imperial weapon that was *meant* only to act as an aid to them in their far-distant fight, and it simply had a wider field of effect than anyone ever imagined.

But far more likely was the idea that, since no one knew precisely what the weapon was going to do, it was tested out here, in territory not yet pacified, so that any effect on Imperial holdings would be minimal. Tremane and his men were nothing more than convenient methods by which the effectiveness of the weapon could be judged—

Which would mean that they are watching us, scrying us, seeing how we react and what we do, and whether or not the locals have the wit to do the same. This lack of communication was a deliberate attempt to get them to react without orders, just to see what they would do.'

If this happened to be the true case, it ran counter to every law and custom that made the Army the loyal weapon that it was. It would be a violation of everything that Imperial soldiers had a right to expect from their Emperor.

For that matter, being left to fend for themselves was almost as drastic a violation of that credo.

In either case, however, this would *not* be above what

could be done to test a candidate for the Iron Throne. Other would-be heirs had been put through similar hardships before.

But not, his conscience whispered, *their men with them.*

That was what made him angry. He did not mind so much for himself; he had expected to be tested to the breaking point. It was that the Emperor had included his unwitting men in the testing.

There was no denying that, for whatever reason, Charliss had abandoned them. There had been time and more than time enough for him to have sent them orders via a physical messenger. This silence was *wrong,* and it meant that there was something more going on than appeared on the surface. It was the Emperor's sworn duty to see to the welfare of his soldiers in times of crisis, as it was their sworn duty to protect him from his enemies. They had kept their side of the bargain; he had reneged on his.

It would not be long before the rest of the army knew it, too. In a situation like this, they all were aware they should have been recalled long ago. Since there was no way that a Portal could be brought up that was large enough to bring them all home, Charliss should have sent in more troops to provide a corridor of safety so that they could *march* home. And he should have done all this the moment the mage-storms began, when it became obvious that they were getting worse. Then they would not only have been safely inside the Empire by now, they would have been on hand to deal with internal turmoil. That meant a kind of double betrayal, for somewhere, someone was going shorthanded, lacking the troops he needed to keep the peace because the Emperor had decided to abandon *them* here.

Or rather, it was more likely that he had opted to abandon *Tremane* and, with him, his men. He had probably written Tremane off as the potential heir because he had not achieved a swift victory over Hardorn, and had chosen this as the most convenient way to be rid of him.

And if I cannot contrive a way to bring us all safely through the winter, they will suffer with me.

That was the whole point of his anger. He had been

schooled and trained as an Imperial officer; he had been an officer before he ever became a Grand Duke. This callous abandonment was counter to both the spirit and the letter of the law, and it made Tremane's blood boil. It represented a betrayal so profound and yet so unique to the Empire that he doubted anyone born outside the Empire would ever understand it, or why it made his skin flush with rage.

The men would certainly understand it, though, when they finally deduced the truth for themselves and then worked through their natural impulse to assume that anything so *wrong* could not be *true.* And at that point—

At that point they will cease to be soldiers of the Empire. No, that's not true. They will be soldiers of the Empire, but they will cease to serve Charliss.

He sat down in the nearest chair, all in a heap, as the magnitude of that realization struck him. Revolt—it had not happened more than a handful of times in the entire history of the Empire, and only *once* had the revolt been against an Emperor.

Was *he* ready to contemplate revolt? Unless he did something drastically wrong, it was to him that the men would turn if they revolted against Charliss. Was he prepared to go along with that, to take command of them, not as a military leader, but as the leader of a revolt?

Not yet. Not . . . yet. He was close, very close, but not yet prepared to take such drastic action.

He shook his head and ordered his thoughts. *I must keep my initial goals very clearly in mind. I must not let anything distract me from them until the men are secured to face this coming winter. That is* my *duty, and what the Emperor has or has not done has no bearing on it.* He set his chin stubbornly. *And to the deepest hells with anyone who happens to get in my way while I am seeing to that duty!*

He rose and went directly to his desk. The best way to ensure total cooperation among the men was to make things seem as normal as possible. So—to keep them from thinking too much about the silence from the Empire, he should keep up military discipline and structure the changes he planned to make to the military pattern.

He wrote his officers' orders quickly but carefully. He had already recruited a half-dozen literate subalterns to serve as scribes and secretaries since it was no longer possible to replicate written orders magically—and they would have to be able to read his handwriting in order to copy it. Now he was grateful for the "primitive" but effective and purely mechanical amenities of this manor. Nothing here had been affected by the storms. His lights still burned; his fires still heated. His cooked food arrived at the proper intervals from the kitchen. The jakes performed their function, and the sewage tunnels carried away the result without stinking up the manor. Somehow he was going to have to find men who could manage these same "primitive" solutions for an entire army.

We need men who don't need magic to get things done. Leather workers, blacksmiths—farmers, even—break all the work of running the camp down into what is and isn't done by magic, then scour the ranks for those who know how to do those jobs with ordinary labor. Now, how to see to it that these men were given the appropriate recognition so that they would volunteer their abilities. . . ? Well, that was a simple problem to solve. *Promote them to "specialist" rank, with the increase in pay grade.* There was nothing like an increase in pay to guarantee enthusiastic cooperation.

He put the cool, blunt end of his glass pen to his lips for a moment, and felt his lips taking on a wry twist. *Money. There isn't much in the coffers at the moment. Well, that makes the plan that much more important.* Money was the other constant in the Imperial Army, and had been, from time immemorial. *Small wonder, given that our history claims we began as a band of mercenaries.* Regular pay was the foundation of loyalty when it came to the individual Imperial fighter. Troops had been known to rise up and murder commanders who shorted their pay; an Emperor had been dethroned for failing to pay the army on time and another had been put in his place because he had made up pay and even bonuses for the men directly under his command out of his own pocket.

Of course, there had never been a situation like this one,

with troops abandoned so far from home, and cut off from all supplies. Under circumstances like this one, his men *might* be understanding . . . or they might not. It was best to be sure of them for now.

He sanded the inked orders and took them to the door of his quarters, where one of his bodyguards took them away to the corps of secretaries to be copied and distributed.

"I do not want to be disturbed under any circumstances," he told the guard, who nodded and saluted, and when he went back into his room and closed the door, he also locked it. The guard would think nothing amiss in this. Locking his door was nothing new; he often required privacy to think and plan. There was no one of higher rank here to question that "need" for absolute privacy.

This time, however, he needed privacy to act, not to think. And it was just as well that he had made a habit of privacy. No one would know what he did here, tonight.

Thanks to the Little God of Lust that my aunt was his devotee. If it had not been for his aunt, and her own need for secrecy. . . . He sat down at his traveling desk and reached beneath it, straining a little to touch the spot behind the drawer that held his pens, ink, and drying sand. The place he needed to reach lay just past the right-hand corner of that drawer. . . .

He felt the tiny square of wood sink as he depressed it, and he quickly removed the pen drawer, taking it out of the desk and placing it on top, out of the way. His aunt had been a woman who was very protective of her secrets—and absolutely ruthless in that protection. If he had removed the drawer first, pressing the key-spot on the bottom of the desk would have resulted in a poisoned needle through the finger-tip. Within an hour, he would have been dead. The poison on that needle was known to persist in potency for two hundred years, and as for the mechanism, he was certain it would outlive him. He reached into the cavity that had held the drawer and felt for a similar spot in the back of the cavity and on the right-hand side.

Another square of wood sank beneath his questing finger, and he moved his hand to the left side of the cavity. In this case, had he not removed his hand immediately but continued to press at the spot, it would have triggered a second mechanism, and the secret drawer he was trying to free would have locked into place. Unless you knew the way to reset it, nothing short of hacking the desk to pieces would allow one to reach that hidden drawer.

That second drawer, the secret one, half the height of the original, had slid a bare fraction out of the back of the cavity. He pried it completely out, touching *only* the top edge, and brought it out of its hiding place into the candlelight. It, too, was trapped; this time with a slow-acting contact poison that was a natural component of the wood forming the bottom. He was *very* careful not to touch the bottom, only the sides. The inside was lined with slate to insulate what it held from the poisonous wood.

All of this was quite necessary, for within this drawer was an object that meant death without trial if it was ever found in his possession. Or rather, it *had* meant a death sentence. Now, well—unless there was an Imperial spy in his army with the rank and authorization to carry such a sentence out, it was—

It is less likely. I will never say "unlikely" when it comes to the power of the Emperor.

More precious than gold, more magical than jewels, more potent than drugs. It was the pure, crystallized essence of power. He took it from its nest of silk with hands that were remarkably steady, given the deadly danger it represented.

It was a completely accurate copy of the Imperial Seal, identical in every way, mundane and magical, with the original. It had been obtained at incredible risk—although the actual *cost* had been minimal, for he had made the copy himself. He could never have bought this; there was not enough money in the world to pay a mage to make this, and not enough to bribe an Imperial secretary to let it out of his keeping long enough to make that copy.

He set it carefully on the desktop, and the memory of the first time he had placed it on this very desk overlaid itself on the present.

To this day, it was the single most daring act he had ever

accomplished. He was still not entirely certain what had possessed him to even contemplate such a mad action. Although he had not known it at the time, it was Emperor Charliss' policy to assign each of the potential candidates for the Throne to a stint within the Imperial Secretariat, so that they would know what the duties of their underlings were— and where the opportunities for bribery and espionage among those underlings lay. During *his* tour of duty, the Imperial Seal had come into his hands for two entire days, as he followed Charliss on a Royal Progress through newly conquered lands. Charliss had been preoccupied with the machinations of a local satrap and had immersed himself in dealing with his twisted and involved plots to defraud Emperor and Empire of their rightful portions and authority. He'd sensed possible treachery, and had entrusted the Seal to Tremane while he dealt—personally and magically—with the "problem." He'd had no other thoughts on his mind, and it might have been that he had forgotten that Tremane was a mage.

But Tremane's skill, while not the equal of the Emperor's, was still sufficient to copy the Seal. By sheerest accident, he'd had the time, the materials, and the Seal itself, all at once, all readily at hand. The temptation had been too great; he'd bent to it and had made the Seal during one long, feverish night of work.

Once he had made it, however, he had almost destroyed it in panic. Only one thing had prevented him from doing just that: the existence of this desk.

He'd inherited it from an aunt with numerous lovers— many of them dangerous to know, all of them married to other women. She'd had the drawer built to conceal missives too hazardous to keep, but too precious—emotionally or with an eye to later blackmail—to burn. It was the only place remotely safe enough to hold something as risky as a copy of the Imperial Seal.

Since that time, the desk and its burdensome secret had always traveled with him. He had used it only once, just to be certain that it *was* identical in every way to the original, and then only to seal a document the Emperor had already approved and signed, one of an entire stack of similar documents that Charliss had signed and sealed without glancing more than once at each.

Now, however, Tremane was about to forge a document that the Emperor would definitely never approve of.

On the other hand, in order to reach him to bring him to justice, once the deception was discovered, the Emperor was going to have to come to *him*. Or, at least, his minions were.

That was hardly going to be an easy proposition, all things considered. There was a great deal of disturbed and hostile territory between him and the Emperor.

It was also going to be some time before Tremane was found out, and during that time conditions were only going to worsen, which would further protect him from Imperial wrath.

Besides all that, there was no telling if Charliss could manage to track Tremane down in the first place, much less put through a Portal to haul him back for justice—or send troops across the unsettled countryside of Hardorn to accomplish the same goal.

In either case, he would prove he *could* reach them—and there would be questions about why he had not evacuated the troops if he could pursue Tremane to bring him to book for his actions. Charliss would have no excuse not to bring back the rest of the army as well as the errant Grand Duke.

If he does come after me, I would just as soon it were an overland trek. I have a notion that I could manage to escape from custody during a mage-storm if I put my mind to it. He shook his head again; he was allowing himself to be distracted by speculations. He must keep his mind on his immediate goals.

Especially since he was going to need intense concentration and a very steady hand for the next few hours.

He wrapped a scarf around his forehead to keep sweat out of his eyes; not that he was too warm, but he knew from past experience that he was going to be sweating from nervousness. He had to be able to see clearly, and he didn't want any drops falling on his pages either; Imperial scribes did not *sweat* over their work. Setting aside the secret drawer and the pen drawer, he selected a new glass pen and picked out one very special bottle of ink. While this bottle was not going to land him in any trouble, it might have caused some raised eyebrows if anyone had known that Grand Duke Tremane possessed a bottle of the special ink used for official Imperial documents, ink made with tiny, glittering flecks of silver and gold in it, to mark the letters as coming unmistakably from the hand of an Imperial scribe.

First, though, he took out a piece of paper and a silverpoint pencil, and worked out the exact wording of the document he intended to forge.

It wasn't terribly elaborate—but it wasn't every day that someone came to an Imperial storage depot, authorized to empty it and the Imperial pay coffers of every scrap, bit of grain, and copper coin. The wording had to be such that it would cause no one to question it during the time he and his men were there.

This was the plan. He had one chance to ensure the survival of *all* of his men this winter—if the storage depot was fully stocked, as he expected it to be, there would be enough supplies there to see them all through, not only until spring, but possibly even well into summer. If the coffers were full, the men could be paid for long enough that he would have the time to win their personal loyalty. Even if there was no place for the soldiers to spend the money locally, their morale would be buttressed simply by having it to spend later. So now it was time.

This was the Portal he had targeted for reopening, the one leading to the storage depot lying nearest them. Fortunately, it was *in* his duchy, and he'd had to fight the temptation to use it to flee homeward, leaving his men to loot the depot and then fend for themselves. But his duty lay here; his duchy was in good hands, and there was no one there he had any real emotional ties to. And frankly, when his raid was complete, he would be much safer here than there. *Here* was a known quantity. The mage-storms may have left his home duchy a chaotic wreck, and holding a Portal open long enough to move more than just a raiding party through could be impossible.

This was a small Portal, able to a take only a few men at

a time, and the mages doubted that they would be able to hold it open for more than a few hours. He would not be able to use it to bring more than a scant fraction of the troops home—but he *could* use it to bring everything they needed back here.

He had a select group of experienced and trusted men from his personal guard ready to move the moment he alerted them. They were all huge; as his bodyguards, they towered over him. Before joining his guard, they had all worked as stevedores or in similar occupations. The Portal wasn't even large enough to admit anything bigger than a donkey; what they brought out would have to be moved with the help of those tiny beasts of burden and their own muscles.

Once he had the wording worked out, he dipped his pen carefully in the special ink, and began tracing the glittering letters on the snow-white vellum.

The very act of writing with such ink on such a surface brought back more memories—of overseeing the Imperial scribes, of writing such documents himself during a brief stint as an Imperial scribe, when he had been brought to court by his father at the age of sixteen.

All the discipline drilled into him at that time came back, steadying his hand, and sending his breathing into the calming patterns that enabled the scribes to work, bent over their desks, in a state of meditative concentration for hours at a time. This did not, however, keep him from making mistakes.

An Imperial document would be flawless. There would be *no* mistakes, no blots, no misspelled words. He could not permit the tiniest discrepancy between this document and the genuine ones that would have been presented ever since the depot opened.

He made and destroyed half a dozen copies before he had a perfect one. As he waited for the ink to dry, he threw the rest, and his faint original of the wording, into the fire. He watched them burn, making sure that they were all reduced to ashes before turning back to the next and most difficult part of his forgeries.

Ordinary red sealing wax would become something extraordinary before he was through with it.

He lit the tip of the brittle, gold-dust impregnated wax at his candle and dripped it carefully onto the vellum, at the very base of the document. While it was still hot and viscous, he pressed the Seal into it, and mentally twisted the energies about the Seal and the wax together, activating it. The metal of the Seal grew warm in his hand, and the wax beneath it glowed, first white, then yellow, then the red of iron in a fire.

Carefully, he raised the Seal from the vellum as the glow faded.

Impressed into the wax was something that deceived the eyes, but not the touch. His fingers told him that the wax impression was a sketchy bas-relief, but his *eyes* told him quite a different story.

What he *saw* was the Wolf Crown, rising out of the wax of the seal as if made from that wax, scintillating with gold dust and a hint of rainbow. Was it an illusion? Not exactly. Nor was it exactly reality. It lay somewhere in between the two.

He laid the Seal back in the drawer and sat where he was, catching himself with both hands on the desk as he went momentarily giddy with exhaustion.

He had not expected that, and it took him completely by surprise. Was it the effect of the mage-storms, or only that he was much older, and under much more strain, than he had been the last time he'd used the Seal? There was no way to tell.

And it didn't matter. If he was lucky, he would never have to use it again.

If I am wise, I will never use it again!

Nevertheless, luck and wisdom had very little to do with the traps Fate might hold for him. He put the Seal back into its hiding place, and put his forgery in with several other, perfectly genuine "contingency" documents that the Emperor had supplied him with when he traveled out here. No one knew exactly what documents he had, nor how many of them there were. When he took this one out of the stack, there would be no way that anyone could say that this one had not been among them originally.

He rested a while after that; no point in unlocking the door directly; someone might sense that magic had been at work here, and he wanted to wait for those energies to fade. Besides, it gave him a badly-needed chance to rest.

Only when the last of those energies had dissipated past *his* ability to detect them did he rise, unlock the door, and tell his bodyguards to summon his escort.

While there was still daylight left, it was time to make one of his periodic rounds of inspection, and survey his small and desperate kingdom.

Tremane never walked out of his personal stronghold without an escort of half a dozen strong, superbly-trained bodyguards. Of course, at least one of these men was in the pay of the Emperor. He didn't let it bother him, but rather set himself to winning, if not their complete loyalty, then at least a moment's hesitation when the time came for them to raise the assassination knives. *That* was his best defense against Imperial agents among those he was required to trust.

As he had told his generals, the preliminary defensive wall, a wood-and-daub palisade, had just been completed a few days ago. This palisade contained not only the Imperial camp, but the entire town within its protection. The local populace was *quite* happy to have them here now, although they had not been too pleased to see them at first. A few attempted incursions by what creatures the mage-storms had left behind had shown them that they could not possibly defend themselves against these weirdling beasts, so bizarre and unpredictable.

The palisade had been easy enough to construct; dead trees had provided the framework, which was filled in with wickerwork and then covered with a particular mix of mud that hardened to a rocklike state when dried. The wall was about a hand's breadth thick, and able to withstand a certain amount of punishment in the way of direct mass impact. It was enough to keep out "dumb" beasts, but Tremane was not about to take the chance that it would have to stand up to more than that. If conditions in the area outside the palisade worsened, there could be mobs of people roaming the countryside, looking for loot, food, or shelter. Tremane was not about to risk the lives of his men against a mob when a well-made wall would take all the risk out of the situation.

Nor were unruly mobs the only possible danger. The war-monsters of ancient legend had been able to take down simple palisades—or go over them—and those war-monsters had been created by magic. With more magic loosed in the land, it was possible that chance could recreate something like them. While it was still possible to build before real winter struck, his men were building; building a *real* wall, one that was constructed of sturdier, and less flammable, materials.

Normally they would have erected a second palisade of wooden tree trunks behind the wicker-and-daub construction, but the sheer size of the camp and the fact that the town was part of the camp made that notion prohibitive. He did not want to denude the countryside of trees, which was what such a palisade would require.

However, there was an abundance of limestone and other materials for making cement, so that was precisely what his walls were being made with. In one huge shelter the men cast molded bricks of cement and put them aside to dry and cure. When they were ready, they were taken to the perimeter for the next step.

Two brick walls were under construction there, behind the "protection" of the wickerwork wall. Construction proceeded in stages, with a team of men devoted to each section of the new wall. When the two brick walls were much taller than the tallest man in the ranks, rubble and earth were packed down between them, and a brick "cap" built over the rubble filling.

It would take an organized force to get over that, but Tremane wasn't done with his project even then. He planned for a curtain wall to be built on top of that, giving his men a protected walkway to use to patrol the perimeter, a protection only real siege engines could breech. Emotionally, he would have liked for the walls to be taller, but practicality

told him that there was no real need for them to be that tall.
No mere beast, however twisted by magic, could possibly
come over the single-story wall—and if anything else came
at them, it would be the men and their weapons that kept it
back, not a wall.

Still, he found the three-story wall around his confiscated
manor very comforting, and he would have liked for that
same comfort to be shared by his troops.

Four out of every five of the men were working on the
walls, and even with the wretched weather they had been enduring, they were making good progress. There was certainly
no shortage of hands for what would ordinarily have been a
very labor-intensive job. He'd broken up the long stretch into
a hundred sections so that each team of men could see real
progress being made. It gave them heart, gave them a reasonable goal to reach.

He took a tour of the brickworks, then went out to where
the men were laying a course of bricks. Those who were real
masons supervised the trickier bits; the rest laid bricks and
spread mortar, bending to the work as if they, too, realized
they might be grateful for such protection before long.

But even if Tremane had not personally felt a need for this
wall, he would have had the men out doing *something* constructive. The best way to keep them from getting into trouble was to keep them busy—too busy to make up rumors and
spread them, too busy to think of anything other than the
good, hot meal waiting for them at the end of the day, and
the warm bed to follow that.

The duties varied, and the men were rotated out through
all of them unless their skills were particularly needed on
one specific job. Those not actually laying bricks or making
them were cutting stone, building molds, crushing stone,
carrying bricks, or mixing cement and mortar.

And when the wall was complete—which looked to be
sooner than he had hoped, for the men worked with a will
and a speed he had not expected—he would put them to
building winter quarters as soon as the design was determined. That could not come soon enough, and he hoped that
somewhere among all of the books he had dragged with him

on this journey there would *be* a design. Something that could concentrate and hold heat, something to take a winter a hundred times worse than any he had endured. He had to plan for the worst, then assume that his imagination was not up to the reality and add to his plans.

Perhaps—I wonder if I can't build the kitchens onto the barracks, and use the waste heat from the ovens and stoves to heat the barracks. . . .

The thin, gray light filtering through the clouds made everything look faded and washed out, as if all the life had been leeched out of the world. Although there was no wind, the air was chilly and damp, and he was glad of his uniform cape.

There was a certain nervousness in the way the men moved, nervousness that had nothing to do with the inspection. Perhaps rumors were spreading about the newest monstrous creatures showing up in the countryside. If that happened to be the case—the men could be even more eager to see the wall completed than their commander was! *I would not be unhappy if they acquired a sense of urgency on their own. Fear is a powerful motivator, and the more motivation they have, the faster the walls will go up.*

He made a point of watching the men work at each section and complimenting the team leaders on their effort. At least the Hardornen rebels were no longer a factor. Where they had gone, Tremane had no firm answer, but he had some guesses and one of them was probably very close to being correct.

The rebels were, in the main, Hardornen farmers; the rest were young hotheads playing at being virtuous heroes. The former had crops to get in, and the latter were not numerous enough to make a head-on attack on a fortified town.

That was his optimistic guess. His pessimistic projection was far different, and he could not even begin to guess how probable it was.

There might be something out there that had eluded his own patrols; something that was concentrating on the Hardornens, who were not as well armed or armored, and not as accustomed to fighting eldritch creatures as the Imperial forces were. The Imperials were ensconced in one place, behind a wall; the Hardornen rebels had been in concealed camps scattered everywhere. It would be much easier for a clever, powerful creature to take men in a series of scattered camps than to pry the Imperials out of their protections.

On one hand, even the pessimistic guess allowed for a certain relief. If mage-warped creatures were out there picking off the Hardornens, then neither the Hardornens nor the monsters were attacking *his* men. But if that *was* the case and it was not simply that now that the Imperials were bottled up in one place, soldiering farmers had gone back to their farms, then sooner or later Tremane and his men would have to deal with whatever it was that was giving the natives trouble.

He hoped the reason for their current state of "peace" was just the harvest and the coming winter. He truly did. One thing that his scholars *had* managed to unearth was a series of chronicles and fragmentary tales from something called the "Mage-Wars." He did *not* want to have to face some of the creatures described in those faded pages. Even the names were ominous—makaar, cold-drakes, basilisks. . . .

Perhaps some of those stories, which had thoroughly rattled his scholars, had leaked out to the men. That would account for the nervous haste—and yet the careful attention to detail—with which the wall was going up.

Try not to think of it for now. Wait until you have a chance to talk to those scholars. Perhaps there are physical defenses against those creatures suggested in the chronicles.

He only hoped that the defenses did not prove to be chimeras. Any defense that required more magic would be useless.

He completed his inspection and moved on to the troops on active patrol duty. There were always patrols coming in and out through the newly-constructed east gate; in spite of the fact that the walls were not yet up, he wanted them to be in the habit of coming and going by that route.

He was just in time to see one of his speculations made flesh.

Shouting and excited cries at the gate in one of the completed portions of the wall drew everyone's attention. Men ran toward the gates, where the shouting took on a tone of alarm; more men dropped their tools and ran to see what the matter was.

Tremane did not hasten his pace, however. The alarm trumpets had not sounded, so whatever it was that was causing the uproar, it was not an attack, and it would wait until he got there. The Commander did not, *must* not run, unless there was an attack in progress. No matter how he felt personally, he must maintain the dignity of his position, must show through his calm that he was in command of every situation. Panic, and even the appearance of panic, was contagious.

Now the gate, which had been standing open, darkened with a rush of people, both uniformed Imperial soldiers and civilians. At first, it only appeared that one of his patrols had run into some hostile farmers, but when he arrived at the gate itself, it was just in time to see stretcher bearers carrying away three badly-wounded men, and the too-quiet, covered forms of two dead.

The civilians were not under guard; it appeared that whatever had injured and killed, it had struck his men and the civilians indiscriminately.

Could it be that his worst guess was the correct one?

Heart in mouth, he looked for someone to interrogate, but the leader of the scouts found him first. "Commander, sir!" the man said, appearing right under his nose, snapping to attention and saluting smartly. "Reporting an encounter, sir!"

Tremane returned the salute just as crisply. "Report, scout leader."

By this time a cart drawn by a pair of sweating, nervous ponies had come into the compound through the gate, where a crowd of onlookers had gathered to await it. There was a tarpaulin draped over the back of it, hiding whatever it held. Someone unhitched the ponies and led them away before they bolted, which they threatened to do at any moment. Whatever was under the tarpaulin had them in a state of near-hysteria.

"We were on patrol, just past the ford across Holka Creek, when we heard shouting," the scout leader said. This was not a man Tremane knew personally; he fit the mold of the semi-anonymous Imperial officer candidates, so nondescript that they could all have been brothers of a particularly undistinguished house. Everything about them was average: height, weight, appearance. Except, of course, for their intelligence, which was much, much better than average, and their ability to apply what they learned, which was quite exceptional. The young officer continued, his words crisp and precise. "We investigated, and we found six of the locals defending against *that*—"

"That" was revealed as the men pulled the tarpaulin off the cart, showing that it was filled with a creature so bizarre that he would never have believed a description. In general, it was spiderlike; hairy with a round thorax, a rust-brown in color. It had *far* too many razor-taloned limbs, no discernible head, and a lumpy body which had been liberally feathered with arrows.

"It had already killed two horses and three men; a couple more of ours charged in before I could stop them and were wounded," the scout leader continued. "I ordered a withdrawal into safer range, then we kept hitting it with arrows until it dropped over."

"Good work," Tremane commended absently, unable to take his eyes off the monstrosity in the cart. Had it been a spider? If so, how did it get so large so fast? And if not, what *had* it been?

"Have any of the locals ever seen anything like this?" he questioned the scout leader, as they circled the cart, examining the dead beast. It stank, smelling vaguely of musk and stale sweat. No wonder the ponies had been afraid of it; the scent alone would have driven them half crazy. The rust-brown limbs were also furred, but thinly.

The scout shook his head. "No, Commander, it was as new to them as it was to us. They're very grateful to us, by the way."

So here it is; something deadly the mage-storms conjured up. Exactly what I was afraid of. Are there more of these things? I hope not.

"Take it to the scholars," he ordered. "Perhaps they can

make something of it. And send word to the town, as well; there might be a priest or someone else who can identify what it is—or was."

The scout leader saluted and marched off to attend to his orders. Tremane turned away from the bizarre scene and headed for the main camp site. He still had an inspection to complete.

He walked along the rows of tents, surrounded by his guards; the few men in camp left off what they were doing and jumped to their feet, saluting smartly as he came in view. The tents were closer together than was usual in an open camp, arranged in neat rows, with the ground between kept immaculately cleaned. He noted a number of makeshift ways to keep warm already cropping up; straw or hay mattresses under the sleeping rolls, quilts made of two blankets with more hay stuffed in between. Canvas tents were no real protection against the cold; they barely screened against the wind. The more money a man had, the more blankets he'd bought, but that was no kind of solution.

The tents, despite their makeshift contents, were up to an inspection; he nodded his approval to the officer in charge and moved on.

He completed his inspection with the latrines—which had already been replaced with an efficient, if involved, system that sifted and dried the waste and turned it into grain-sized dry granules which were eagerly sought after by the local farmers for fertilizer. He didn't ask how it worked; he had a similar system on his own estate, and he had never wanted to know how *it* worked, either.

There are some things a man is not meant to know.

At least they wouldn't need to worry about their water supply being contaminated. He did *not* want to think about a plague of dysentery in the dead of winter. If even half the men survived something of that nature, he'd count himself lucky.

But as he turned his steps toward his headquarters, he found himself thinking about his estate, and his people, and wondering how they were faring. Were things better there than here? Could they be worse?

Absently, he returned the salutes of the men that he passed. He had been trying to keep thoughts of his home out of his mind, but they kept intruding.

At least I have no Duchess to worry about. For once, prudence has paid a dividend in having one less person to fret over.

Marriage had not seemed particularly wise once he became a candidate for the Iron Throne. He had not dared to marry for affection; his wife would have become nothing more than a target, a way to manipulate him, and he would put no woman he cared for through that kind of experience. He would not wed for pure expediency; his wife might well have been set upon him as a spy, or be in and of herself an attempt to manipulate him. He had kept all of his affairs strictly commercial, choosing comely and willing women from those on his estate, and setting them up with the husbands of their choice and a proper dowry after both of them tired of the situation. It satisfied the needs of the body, if not the heart, and he took care that there were no children to complicate the issue.

So although he had great affection for the land and the people of his estate taken as a whole, he had no particular concern for any single person on that estate. He felt warm fondness, in the way that a young man might have fondness for a favorite horse or dog, but nothing more passionate. He had always felt that the love of his heart was somewhere out there, distant, untouched. Gaining emotional attachment for his immediate surroundings . . . well, he hadn't deemed it to be of strategic advantage in the development of a Grand Duke or a potential Emperor. Prudence dictated that one should never extend himself past his ability to predict outcomes.

It was altogether fortunate, given the effect of these mage-storms, that his family had maintained a tradition of conservatism where the management of the estate was concerned.

People called us old-fashioned and sometimes laughed at us, but we'd never depended on magic to run the estate. Water was pumped by hand or by windmills, water mills ground the grain, transportation was by well-maintained roads, using horses and mules, ridden or driven. So of all of the lands claimed by the Empire, Tremane's duchy was probably one of those that was better off than most at the moment.

As for Kedrick, he's young, but he's sound, or I wouldn't have left him in charge in the first place. His current heir, a young cousin, was as well-schooled in the management of the estate as Tremane could manage before he left. Now he had plenty of incentive to do the job right; if he failed, he'd starve right along with the others.

I did everything I could for them. It will have to be enough. I certainly can't manage anything more at the moment.

Though if he could get back, *with* the troops, the duchy could certainly support that many more mouths to feed. It would be impossible to pry him out of his little kingdom with his own private army. That might be a thought to tuck away, for later consideration.

And as I recall, there was a scarcity of eligible young men round about there. It wouldn't be a bad thing, to tie the men to me by marriage. . . .

Once back at the manor house, he dismissed four of the men and went on to his rooms with his usual two trailing along behind him. He stopped at the office where his chief aide sat behind a desk laden with lists. Young Cherin looked up at Tremane's footstep; the aide could easily have been the older sibling of the scout leader. Brown hair, brown eyes, sun-browned skin, square and unremarkable face; he was neither ugly nor handsome, but at least Tremane did remember his name, which had not been the case with his last aide. The poor boy had been so self-effacing that Tremane often forgot he was in the same room. He was so good at being inconspicuous that Tremane eventually sent him off to his spymaster for special training.

"Have you any reports for me?" he asked as the young man looked up, then jumped to his feet with a crisp salute.

"No, Commander," was the prompt reply. Tremane sighed; he'd hoped that at least one of his people would have some ideas for meeting the coming winter. But perhaps he was asking too much, too fast.

"Carry on, then," he replied automatically. The youngster saluted again and returned to his work; lacking anything else constructive to do, Tremane went back to his own suite to sit at his desk and leaf through the old reports listlessly.

A word caught his eye; *Valdemar*. It was nothing much; just a report that the Valdemarans had been working frantically on a way to block out the mage-storms themselves.

He hadn't thought much about the report at the time he'd first read it, but now as he reread it, he began to wonder about some of his earlier assumptions.

I was so certain that they were the source of the storms, he mused, staring at the fire in his small fireplace and listening with half an ear to the sounds of his men drilling in the courtyard below his office window. He found that sound rather comforting in its ordinary familiarity. *I was so certain that this was some strange new weapon that Valdemar had unleashed upon us. But according to this,* they *have been suffering as badly as we have. Their Queen doesn't have the reputation for being ruthless that Charliss has. So would she turn something like this loose on her own people just to eliminate us?*

She might, of course. Just because Selenay did not have a reputation for being ruthless, it didn't follow that she was *not* ruthless. She might simply be a very good actress. She could be mad, too; that was hardly a novelty among royalty.

What was more, Valdemar did not depend on magic for anything. It didn't even *have* magic as Tremane knew the art. So the only hardships that Valdemar was suffering were those caused by the storms interacting with the physical world—

But there, his reasoning broke down, as he thought about the creature his men had brought in. *Only? Not a good choice of words. There was nothing "only" about that monster.*

And as a counter to the rest of his arguments, there was the entirely random nature of the storms and their effect. Why would *anyone* who was sane—and he had seen no reason to think that Queen Selenay was insane—unleash something whose effects were so completely unpredictable? If you had a weapon and you knew what it did, of course, you used it. But if you had a weapon and you had *no idea* what it was going to do—well, there was no sane reason to use it, not when it could harm you as badly as it harmed your enemies.

Now his head hurt, and he rubbed his temples with the heels of his hands. He hadn't *liked* sending that assassin in to destroy the alliance Valdemar was making. Something had told him at the time that he might be making a mistake, but he had persisted in order to make the mage-storms stop.

But they didn't stop, did they? In fact, they got worse.

Could he have made a major error in judgment? Granted, the alliance hadn't been disrupted, but at least one of the more important mages had been eliminated. Since the storms hadn't started until after that Karsite priest had arrived in Valdemar, it made sense that he was one of the prime forces behind the mage-storms, *if* they were indeed originating from Valdemar. With him gone, they should have stopped.

What if Valdemar was not perpetrator, but fellow victim?

His head hurt worse than before. If he'd had better spies—but he didn't. He'd done his best to break up the alliance with Karse, and it hadn't happened. He'd tried to scatter them, leaving them as disorganized as a covey of quail scattered by a beater. But they *weren't* disorganized, and his assassin hadn't even made an appreciable difference in their level of efficiency. Furthermore, and this was the important point, the mage-storms continued, increasing in frequency and in power.

So what if I was wrong?

He brooded on that for a while, feeling sicker and sicker the longer he thought about it. If that was the case, he had ordered the assassinations of people who could have been his allies against the storms.

Nothing like burning your bridges *before* you reached them.

I haven't heard from the assassin, and that fool of an artist would contact me if he thought he was in the tiniest danger. He shifted his position in the chair as his back began to ache and his legs to twitch restlessly. *The fool must have gotten caught, though I can't imagine how. He's probably dead by now. Even the Valdemarans wouldn't keep an assassin alive. They're probably working out ways to pickle his head and send it to High Priest Solaris in Karse.*

In fact, given the evidence from Valdemar, the assassin must have been caught before he did any damage. Only that would account for the seamless way in which Selenay and her allies were presenting themselves.

He botched the assassination, then he botched his attempt to escape. That's what I get for relying on operatives someone else puts in place.

He shook his head and checked in a desk drawer for a headache remedy. Like the Hardornens, he had other things to worry about besides far-off Valdemar. At the moment, there was nothing they could or could not do to him or the Imperial forces. And there was nothing he could do to or about them.

It was far more important to deal with the immediate survival of his own troops.

I must have those plans for winter quarters. Should I step up the patrols? What are we going to do about food supplies if the plan can't be carried out?

Could he get his men to help the locals make a really *efficient* harvest? There was always grain left in the fields, but if he sent his men out to glean behind the harvesters, there would be that much more—

It might not seem like much, but experience had taught him that many small gains often added up to a large total. If he could just find enough of those little gains, he might have enough to ensure his victory against his real enemy.

Not Valdemar, but the mage-storms, and what the storms gave birth to. *Concentrate on one enemy at a time. I can't afford to divide my attention or my resources. . . .*

Frantic pounding at his bedroom door woke him. He had taken to leaving a single lamp burning, not because the darkness disturbed him, but because he might be awakened at any hour. He raised himself up on one elbow, instantly alert. "Enter!" he called imperiously. Keitel, Sejanes' apprentice, burst in the moment he spoke the word. Behind him trailed his aides with more lamps and his clothing. Only one thing could have brought Keitel and the aides here at this hour, in such a state of excitement.

"The Portal?" he asked, reaching for his trews and pulling them on.

"It's up, Commander," the skinny youngster blurted, every hair on his head standing up in a different direction. "Sejanes sent for the men—he said to tell you the Portal's unstable, he doesn't know how long he can hold it open, but that you'll have the time for what we need most."

"Get back to him, then; he'll need everyone to keep it open, including you." Excitement chased the last sleep-fog from his mind. The youngster nodded, hesitated for a moment, then fled the room. Tremane pulled on the rest of his clothing, his aides handing each piece to him as quickly as he donned the last. From his bedside table he took the packet of papers he had ready and stuffed it into the breast of his tunic. He jumped to his feet, stamping hard to settle his boots in place, and turning that motion into a leap of his own for the door. His aides and guards sprinted down the hall behind him; from their panting he was amused to think they were finding it unexpectedly difficult to keep up with "the old man."

Didn't pay any attention to the amount of time my swordmaster spends training me, obviously. The few guards and the like that he passed stared after him with eyes wide and mouths agape. The Commander never ran—

Except when time is against us. If Sejanes said that the Portal was unstable, he was not exaggerating for effect. Tremane cursed as his boot soles slipped and skidded on the stone floors; this would be a fine time to slip and break an ankle!

The manor was built around a central courtyard, and it was here that the mages had set up their working area. Tonight the courtyard was ablaze with light, torches in every available sconce—and in the center of the courtyard, doubling the illumination, was the Portal.

To Tremane's experienced eye, the instability was obvious; instead of a clean curve, the edge of the Portal wavered and undulated like a ribbon in a breeze. It should not have been giving off as much light as it was, either; that was a sign of wasted energy.

The mages surrounded the Portal, each adding his effort to the whole. To the untrained eye, the Portal itself, a dark hole, laced with lightning and surrounded by white fire, could easily have been a living thing. It had a feeling of *life*; in this case, a rather sinister life, and the movement of its edge added to the effect. To the trained eye, however, the Portal was an inferior specimen of its type. It was the kind of structure a group might build as their first effort at such an undertaking.

As Tremane and his escort came through the doorway and slowed to a walk, the mages surrounding the Portal managed to exert a bit more control over their creation. The boundary stiffened into a proper curving arch, and the dark, energy-laced center faded, replaced by a view of a loading platform and a warehouse wall.

The rest of the handpicked men entered at a quick-march from another door, then took their places on the cobblestone courtyard with drill-team precision. Tremane straightened his uniform tunic and took his place at their head; his aides and all but two of his guards fell back. There were no wasted orders or movements. As they had all rehearsed, the men moved in behind him as he strode toward the Portal and through it.

He had expected the usual disorientation of a Portal-crossing, but this was much worse. As his feet touched the floor of the warehouse Portal-platform on the other side, he staggered and went to one knee. His men were similarly disoriented as they came through, wavering to one side or another as if they were drunk or faint. One or two clutched their stomachs and turned pale.

He fought back nausea and regained control of himself by

hauling himself erect, closing his eyes, and locking his knees until his dizziness passed.

He opened his eyes again as soon as his stomach and balance settled. He and his men stood precisely where he had expected them to be; on a wide loading platform in front of the permanent Portal, under a clear night sky. Two steps down took them to the walkway, and a ramp ran from the walkway to the large wooden loading doors that were directly before them. The walkway led to the office, and predictably there was a light in the office window. This *was* an Imperial depot; there would be a clerk on duty, no matter what the hour. Tremane pulled his packet of forged and genuine papers from his tunic.

"Stay here until you see the loading doors open," he told the men, then motioned to his guards to follow. He didn't think about the fraud he was about to perpetrate, or he might have shown some sign that not all was correct. He simply walked briskly to the office and pulled open the door, confronting the startled clerk inside with a bland and impassive expression.

He dropped his papers on the desk in front of the middle-aged, stoop-shouldered man, and stepped back, folding his arms over his chest. This place had the familiar look and smell of every Imperial office—the precise placing of desk, stool, and filing cases, the scent of paper, pungent ink, and dust, with a hint of sealing wax and lamp oil.

The clerk gingerly picked up the top paper and read it through; he examined the seal, his face reflecting growing bewilderment, and then read the second. By the time he reached the end of the stack and looked up at Tremane, his face was stiff with shock.

"S–sir—" the clerk stammered, "—s–surely this can't b–be right—"

"I have my orders," Tremane said flatly. "You have yours."

"B–but—these orders—they s–say—you're t–to strip the d–depot—"

Tremane allowed his expression to soften a little. "Friend, with all the Portals down, it's going to be impossible to get supplies in or out of here. We had to make an extraordinary

effort just to get *this* one working, and it won't last past the
next storm, if that. Shouldn't the supplies go to men who
need them, before they rot or get spoiled by vermin?"

The direct appeal, one to the clerk's good sense and logic,
had the desired effect. The man faltered, looking from the
papers to Tremane and back again. "But if there are no supplies here, there's nothing for us to do—"

"That's why the last papers authorize you to take indefinite leave," Tremane explained patiently. "Strange things are
occurring, and you are stationed out on the edge of the Empire, alone and unsupported. There is no reason for you to
suffer this isolation when you could be sent home during
this crisis. If the warehouse is empty, there will be no need
to guard or staff it. Your Emperor knows that you must be
anxious about your families, and he knows that without Portals it will probably take you some time to make your way
to them. Hence, he has given you indefinite leave."

The clerk picked up the last paper and reread it, his face
clearing. After all, it *did* authorize Tremane to pay him a full
year's salary as discharge pay—him and every other clerk
here. "There's just the four of us, Commander. Standard
depot—and we're all clerks, no—"

"That's quite all right; I brought my own men," he interrupted. "Let's just get those doors open and move out those
supplies while we still can."

"Yes, sir!" The clerk jumped to his feet, knocking over his
stool in his haste, and hurried over to unlatch the winch that
operated the huge loading doors. By clever use of mechanical
contrivances, this rather undersized and scrawny individual
was able to open doors even the strongest guard would have
had difficulty hoisting.

As soon as the doors opened, the men poured in. This, too,
had been rehearsed, since every Imperial depot was built to
the same pattern. They went straight to the most important
items of food and rough-weather supplies. Once those were
through the Portal, they would move to items of lower priority: uniforms, bedding, and blankets. And once those had
been carried off, they would proceed to strip the depot for as
long as the Portal held. Imperial depots were notorious for

containing equipment so antique and out-of-date that even a historian would have been hard put to determine the function. Among these, there might be items useful to them in a time when magic had ceased to work. And if nothing else, such items could be converted to their component parts.

Meanwhile, Tremane ordered the clerk to get him the records and to open the lock room at the back of the office containing all records and the Imperial gold stores normally held to pay for deliveries from civilian merchants and for pay shipments to the troops. Out of that, he counted out the discharge pay for the four clerks, putting the small, wafer-thin gold coins up in pay packets and neatly labeling each with the man's name and his own seal.

"As of this moment, you are free to go," he said kindly as he handed the clerk his particular packet. "We can carry on from here. If you have a stable, help yourself to mounts and baggage animals on my authority."

"Thank you, Commander," the clerk replied, his face now full of eagerness. He shuffled backward, toward the door, as he spoke. "I've got a long way to travel—perhaps I ought to make an early start of it—"

He could not back out of there fast enough, and Tremane thought he knew why. Every Imperial clerk indulged in a certain amount of graft; reselling Imperial supplies and the like, recording that he had paid more for deliveries than he'd actually given out. This man wanted to get out of reach before Tremane compared the lists of what *should* be there with what actually *was.*

Little did he know that Tremane didn't care. Of course the mice would have nibbled the crust; most of the loaf was still there, and that was what mattered.

He had his own reason for wanting to be rid of the clerks. When—or if—the authorities *did* descend on this place, if there was no one here, that would confuse the situation still further. Somehow the authorities would have to decipher where the clerks had gone before they could find out whose seal was on the pay packets—assuming that the clerks *kept* the packets. He intended to take his papers with him when he left. All the authorities would have was a looted warehouse, with no idea who was responsible. Unless, of course, one or more agents managed to get "left" behind.

Even if that happened, it would still take the agents a long time to reach the capital and the Emperor. They might not make it. Conditions could be bad enough here to prevent even an experienced agent from reaching his contact. All of the spymasters relied on Portals and mage-crafted messengers to get information to and from their agents. Without those, an agent might not even know who his contact *was!*

Meanwhile, his guards were taking the gold through and handing it over to the custody of his *other* guards, to be placed under double guard and lock in the strong room. Gold was heavy; the men could not move much at a time. But, as he had hoped, there was enough there to pay his entire army for a year. That would give him the time he needed to win their personal loyalty.

Once the gold was all across, he directed his two guards to join the rest of the men in stripping the warehouse to the bare floor, walls, and ceiling. There were even stores of lumber here, and if he got the chance, if the Gate held long enough, he'd take those.

They had been at this task for long enough that the vital supplies were all through; now the men just made a human chain, passing boxes, bundles, crates, and barrels through without bothering to check what was in them. He had clerks of his own that could inventory the mass of supplies at leisure.

While they worked, Tremane helped himself to the warehouse records. What he found there confirmed his fears and his hopes; the personnel here had been in disarray for weeks, without orders, contact from their superiors, or any sign that the Empire still existed. They had no idea what was going on; all they knew was that the Portals suddenly went dead, and that there were strange things going on outside the safe walls of the fortified depot. What he found indicated a certain amount of panic on their part, and he didn't blame them. In their place, he'd have been panicking, too.

The huge warehouse echoed strangely as the contents were emptied; the torches his men placed to light their way made oddly-moving shadows among the racks and shelves. He wished there might be time to loot the small stable that was surely attached to this post—but on the other hand, the four clerks would probably need every beast there, just to get themselves and their own goods home safely. *It wouldn't do to be greedy,* he chuckled inwardly.

The Portal showed no signs of deteriorating, and this warehouse was more than half emptied. As he checked on the progress of his men, he caught sight of another door where he had not expected one, and he stopped dead to stare at it.

Another door? Could it be possible that this depot was a *complex* of warehouses?

He ran across the dusty floor and wrenched the door open. Enough light came from the torches behind him to show him a sight to make his heart leap.

Grain. Tin barrel after barrel of grain—meant for horses, for cavalry, but perfectly edible by humans.

And here was the answer to the dilemma of how to keep both town and garrison alive. This would buy him the loyalty of the town, especially if the winter ran long and hard and supplies ran short. The farmers had been complaining that the weather had been bad and the harvest poor, and he had been assuming their complaints were nothing more than the usual. Every farmer he had ever known had complained about the weather and the harvest—they always did, and never would admit to having a good year.

But what if this time the complaints were genuine? He had seen the weather and the state of the fields for himself. How could he have thought that the harvest would be *normal?*

Because I didn't dare think otherwise, or I would have given up.

Quickly he hailed half of the men over to this new storehouse, telling them to haul the grain but leave the hay bales that would also be here for the very last. Hay was not a priority, but if there was time, why not take it, too?

I need more men. It was a risk, bringing still more men— men who had not been checked beforehand—across an unstable Portal, but the gain was worth the risk. Almost certainly some of these would arrange to be left behind. There *would* be agents among them. He didn't care.

He ran out to the Portal and sent a message across with one of the guards; Sejanes was no fool and he should know how many more would be safe to send across.

He went back to the men—but now it was to join them in a frenzy of hauling. He joined the line, working side-by-side with one of his own bodyguards and a man whose name he didn't even know for certain. When the man cursed him for clumsiness when he dropped a box, and cursed him again for being slow, he kept silent. It was more important to get one more box across that Portal than it was to maintain the distinction of Commander and subordinate. He sensed, rather than saw, more men making a second line; at the time he had his own hands full and sweat running into his eyes.

He had never done so much hard physical labor in his life. His muscles and joints begged him for the mercy of a rest, his lungs burned, and his throat and mouth were as parched as if he were crossing the desert. There was no rest; his line was down to transporting the lumber at the back of the warehouse, but the other line still had grain to move.

There was light outside now; at some point dawn had arrived, and he had missed it. How had Sejanes managed to hold the Portal up so long? The poor mages would be only semiconscious for a week after this!

His line broke up at that point; there was nothing more to move. Half of them went to the sides of the warehouse to try to get the few large objects—dismantled siege engines—that could not be hauled by a single man. The rest joined the grain line, but now the grain line was actually hauling hay bales!

At just that moment, a whistle shrilled from the Portal; the signal that the mages had held it as long as they could. Tremane had drilled his men in this, too; every one of them dropped what he was holding and sprinted for the Portal at a dead run. The new men who had not been drilled took their cue from the rest. He joined them; as they reached the outside they formed into four running ranks, since the Portal was only large enough for four abreast to cross at once.

Those four ranks continued to race for the stone arch that marked this side of the Portal.

Despite his care, he knew that when he called for more men, he had allowed many agents to cross over, and now some of the men would deliberately lag behind, to remain when the Portal collapsed. There would be agents of the Emperor and of his own personal enemies among them. That would be fine; no one else knew that his orders were forged.

In a way, he wished them no ill, for if this Imperial depot had been left so completely on its own, that did not speak well for conditions in the Empire as a whole. They would have to somehow find transportation, work their way across several client states, and only then would they reach anything like solid Imperial territory. Faced with such a situation, he would give up and find a place to wait out the situation; they might well do the same.

And as for the rest who lagged behind—they had worked with a will, and he could not find it in his heart to condemn them for snatching the chance to stay on home ground. Without a doubt, the Empire would need them as much or more than he would.

And every man who stays here is one less mouth to feed—as well as one less agent that might turn to sabotage in the absence of other orders.

He was one of the last men through, and the instability in the Portal was directly reflected in the effect the crossing had on him. He landed on the other side in a tumble, unable to stand, his head reeling, his stomach racked with nausea. He lay on his side in a helpless heap for a moment until someone dragged him clear.

He opened his eyes and regretted doing so; the courtyard was spinning around him and the bright sunlight lanced into his skull like a pair of knives thrust into his eye sockets. He closed his eyes again, hastily, and simply lay where he was, waiting for the sickness to pass.

"It's coming down!" someone shouted, voice hoarse with exhaustion.

"Let it go—we can't wait any longer!" That was Sejanes' voice; the old man must have counted noses and come up short. "They'll be all right over there—drop the pattern, before it burns us all away!"

He opened his eyes again, just in time to see the Portal collapse, folding in on itself until it was a single point of bright, white light that burned for a moment, then crackled out.

The illness had passed enough to let him rise; he found that he was in a corner, dragged there by some wise soul on this side of the Portal. That was a help, for with the aid of the wall he was able to get to his feet and lean against firm support until the rest of his equilibrium returned.

Finally, when he thought he could present a reasonable front, he walked slowly out into the courtyard full of collapsed men, collapsing mages, and heaps of supplies.

The guards he had left here were still standing; he sent one of them off for help. "Stretchers and stretcher bearers," he directed. "Everyone down should be taken to his own quarters and given full sick leave for at least one day. Have the Healers look at them." He looked around the courtyard at the supplies still there, and frowned. They had emptied two warehouses—why wasn't this courtyard stuffed with supplies?

The guard correctly interpreted that frown. "As soon as things started coming across, Sejanes sent for more men to move the supplies by wagon out to storage, Commander," the man said. "They'll be back shortly."

Tremane's frown cleared. "Good. And the clerks are making inventories?"

"Yes, sir. Everything is as you ordered, Commander, except—" the guard could no longer suppress his grin, "—except that Sejanes held the Portal open longer than even *he* thought possible. Commander, you did it!"

Now, for the first time in weeks, he relaxed enough to reply to the guard's grin with one of his own. "Now, let's not tempt the Unkindly Ones with our hubris. We were lucky. We have no idea how long those supplies sat there, or what condition they're in. Half of them could be useless."

The guard nodded sagely. "Indeed, Commander. Shall I send for your sedan chair as well as the litter bearers?"

Tremane was about to refuse—he had scarcely used his sedan chair a handful of times in the past year—but a sudden wave of dizziness made him reconsider quickly and nod. "Do that. I'll be over by Sejanes."

He managed to get as far as his old mentor before *needing* to sit down, and he succeeded in seating himself on a box without making it look as if he had collapsed. The old man was in about the same shape as Tremane—which in itself was remarkable, given the strain under which the mages must have been laboring. Sejanes lay flat on his back on the cobblestones, and acknowledged Tremane's presence with only a wave of one hand.

"Well, old man," Tremane said, "we did it." He was rewarded by a thin smile and a weak twinkle in the old mage's eyes.

"We did. We've bought the time you needed, my boy. And I hope you're prepared to reward your hard-working mages—"

"I'm having you all moved into the best quarters this place affords," he interrupted. "There's no reason for you to be bivouacked with your units anymore when your units can't use your services. And to head off any question of favoritism, I'll make it known that after the great personal sacrifice you have all made in this effort, you've all been rendered invalids, or the next thing to it. Therefore, you need special consideration."

"You won't be far wrong, boy," Sejanes replied seriously. "We won't be up to much but bed rest for days."

"Then bed rest is what you'll get," Tremane promised. After a few silent minutes, the haulage crew returned, and with them, his aides. He hailed his chief aide Cherin over and put him in charge of the mages.

"Put them in the infirmary for now," he said. "And find a way to reshuffle my officers so that we can get quarters in the manor for every mage who worked on the Portal. I want them all moved in before the end of the week. They're going to be invalided out of field service for now."

Cherin looked at the mages, still lying where they had collapsed, and seemed more than convinced. "There're some store rooms could be made into barracks, Commander," he offered. "We could take your bodyguards, put 'em in there, shuffle the pages and messengers into *their* barracks, put the aides in the little rooms the boys have been in, and that'll give you rooms for each mage and still let the aides have private quarters."

"And it puts the boys back in a common room where the page-serjeant can keep an eye on them. That's good," Tremane agreed, with a wry, yet appreciative smile. "Those little imps have been unnaturally good lately, but I don't have faith that the spell is going to last. See to it."

The aide saluted. "Sir!" he replied and marched off to begin the shuffling.

"You're a good lad, Tremane," Sejanes said gruffly, and closed his eyes.

At about that time, the sedan chair and its four carriers arrived, and Tremane decided it was time to let his aides do the work of getting everything organized. He gave each of them assignments and ordered them to have reports on his desk when he woke up. He climbed stiffly to his feet and took his place in his chair. The four carriers raised their poles to their shoulders and marched off to his suite as he lay back and closed his eyes.

I would like to sleep for a week. He wouldn't, though. He'd wake up as soon as his body had recovered enough to allow him to function. By then he would have some idea of what, precisely, they had looted from that depot.

He did know this much; even if, as he said, fully half of what they'd taken proved useless, he still had enough to see his men through a winter out of a Northman's nightmares. His men—and possibly even the town as well.

The future looked a hundred times brighter than it had yesterday. And as dark as things were at the moment, that was enough.

Two

A stable was hardly the place one normally took lessons in protocol, but neither Karal of Karse nor his adviser were precisely "normal" as an ambassador and his tutor.

It was a cold gray day; the sky was a solid sheet of low-hanging clouds. On the whole, the stable was not an unpleasant place to be on such a day, especially not for a young man who had begun life as a horseboy. It was no ordinary stable either. This was the foul-weather shelter for all Companions now resident at the Herald's Collegium and Palace at the Valdemar capital of Haven. The stalls were mostly empty; those that were filled were preternaturally silent, since Companions seldom acted or sounded much like horses.

But in every other way, this building, as no other place in all of Haven, reminded Karal of home. The warm scent of hay, the dusty aroma of grain, the rich odor of leather (as much a taste as a smell); all those comforted him and made him relax. Although the air outside was cold, inside, sitting next to a huge brown-tiled stove, Karal was as comfortable as he would have been in his own room.

"All right," Karal said, rubbing his tired eyes. "Explain to me how the followers of all these religions manage not to slaughter each other over their differences one more time."

That warm fire behind the iron door of the stove at his back crackled cheerfully, and the relative gloom of the stable was actually rather restful to his aching eyes. It was too bad Florian wouldn't fit into his suite at the Palace, though. A hot cup of tea would have been very nice right now.

Of course, a hot cup of tea might have put him to sleep, which was not a good idea at the moment.

His adviser shook his white head until his mane danced. *:It's really very simple, Karal. The single rule that each of them* must *obey if they wish to continue practicing in Valdemar is "live and let live." You can proselytize as much as you wish, but you may not persecute, harass, intimidate, or otherwise make a nuisance of yourself. The secular laws of Valdemar take precedence over the dictates of every religion. No matter how deeply your religious feeling is offended by something allowed according to the religious practices of your neighbor, you have no right to force him to live by your rules, and no right to try to. If you can't live by that, then you are escorted to the border and left there.:*

Karal tried to imagine something like that being effective in Karse and failed utterly. *His* people would simply ignore the law and revel in their holy and God-given right to persecute, harass, intimidate, or even murder those who did not agree with them. If *their* God, in their own narrow interpretation of His Writ and Rules, said that something was wrong, then it was wrong for *everyone*, whether or not anyone else agreed even with that particular interpretation. Karsites had been cheerfully slaughtering each other over interpretations of the Writ and Rules almost as long as they had been killing those outside their borders and religion. Things had been different once, as he had found from his reading, but the current state had been holding for generations. Since Vanyel's time, in fact. Or, as Ulrich would have pointed out—since the time that the Son of the Sun had been elected by the Sun-priests and not by Vkandis Himself. "It seems too simple to work," he replied wearily.

Florian scraped a hoof on the floor, which Karal had learned was the equivalent of a shrug. *:I suppose it works largely because it was established as a law back when there were fewer people in Valdemar and all of them were of the same religion. At that point, of course, no one saw any reason why such a law shouldn't be in effect. If you plant a tree early so that it has time to grow, the roots are too deep for a later storm to tear it up.:*

A cat from the stables strolled by—a perfectly ordinary black-and-white, and not one that bore the vivid markings of a Firecat. Karal held out his fingers to the mouser, but his majesty had other things on his mind.

"That sounds like another Shin'a'in proverb," Karal observed, turning a little so that his right side could benefit from the warmth of the stove. Was it his imagination, or was it too early in the autumn for it to be so cold? "You've been tromping around An'desha too long."

Florian "chuckled"—more of a whicker. The fact that Karal was talking to a blue-eyed white horse might seem very odd to anyone from beyond the borders of Valdemar. The fact that he was talking to a Companion—or, as he would have said a year ago, a "cursed Valdemar Hellhorse"—would have been sheer blasphemy to many still in his own land of Karse. But Karal had learned more about Heralds and their Companions in that last year than he had ever dreamed possible, and now he relied on Florian's advice in the ways of Valdemar as surely as he relied on his friend An'desha's advice in the ways of magic. Both were equally opaque to him although he was familiar with the effects of magic if not the practice of it. As for the ways of Valdemar—they were all as odd as this surface congeniality among religions.

"I guess I'd be safe to assume that any time I have to deal with a priest *from* Valdemar that they're going to tolerate me, even if they don't like me." At Florian's nod, he shrugged. "At least, that's easier than waiting for holy assassins to waylay me in the hallway."

:Holy assassins are going to come from outside Valdemar, if they come at all, and Kero has had a particular watch out for that sort for some time.: "Kero," of course, was Herald Captain Kerowyn, the only Herald in all of the history of Valdemar who was also the Captain of a mercenary Company. She was in charge of Valdemar's less conventional defenses—the ones that the Lord Marshal did not want to know about officially. She was also one of the—former— Great Enemies of Karse, and had been rumored to eat Karsite babies on toast for breakfast.

Karal could vouch for the toast, and Kero swore she didn't

touch babies, Karsite or otherwise, before lunch at the earliest.

Florian did not actually "speak" to him; the Companion's "voice" echoed inside Karal's head. They called it "Mind-speaking" here. The locals took it for granted that Heralds and Companions talked to each other just like two human friends. One Herald could mention an appointment with a thought, and his Companion would round the corner a moment later, to bear the Herald on his way. It was odd, still, to see a Herald and Companion walk by, and witness the Herald suddenly breaking up in laughter at some silently-shared joke while the Companion whickered merrily. Heralds spoke with their minds and Companions answered, and none of it was considered the least bit unusual.

This was a magic that Karal had never even known existed before he came here—largely because in the past the Sun-priests did their best to eradicate children "Gifted" with such things. "Witchery," they called it, and hunted it out ruthlessly until Solaris took the Sun Throne.

Other Heralds had the ability to talk with each other as they did with their Companions. Some could move things without touching them, or see things at a distance. Others could see into the future or the past, and some had even stranger abilities.

All these things could be accomplished with the magic that Karal was familiar with, of course, but this was *not* the magic he knew. Sun-priests often had the ability to work "true" magic; the false priests used it to create "miracles" to deceive the gullible. Because such a power could be controlled, the Sun-priests had incorporated those with the ability to perform magic into their ranks, rather than destroying them.

The Valdemarans had the "witch-powers"; they called it "mind-magic," or "Gifts," and they were something that was inborn, though skill in them could be honed with training and practice.

Karal had gotten used to it, to a certain extent, although it never ceased to amaze him how casually the Heralds accepted these powers. And it would have been so very easy for those powers to be misused, as the power of true magic had been misused in Karse. Yet here—there were the Companions.

The only place to find training in mind-magic was at Herald's Collegium, and the only way to be accepted into the Collegium was to be Chosen by a Companion. Thereafter, the Companion acted as best friend, mentor, conscience, and sometimes stern taskmaster. The fact that the Companions happened to look like horses—always white, always blue-eyed—was incidental. Florian told him once that the initial reason Companions came in that particular "shape"—rather than, say, a dog or a cat—was because a horse was not only ubiquitous and hence invisible, but because a horse was weapon, fellow fighter, and transportation all in one. In Karsite mythology, as a sort of mirror image of the reality, the Heralds, in their all-white uniforms, were the "White Demons," and the Companions the "Hellhorses."

Florian had been "assigned" to him by the other Companions when he first arrived as the secretary to his mentor, the ambassador from Karse, Master Ulrich. Florian had assured him many times that he had *not* been "Chosen" to be a Herald, which was normally what happened when a Companion sought out a particular human and spoke to him in his mind. No, in this case, Florian was simply an adviser, someone who could steer him through the complicated tangle of life in the Kingdom of Valdemar without having an agenda of his own to pursue. Karal had no reason to mistrust the Companion's seemingly altruistic nature; after all, he had it on very trustworthy authority that Companions were the same as Karsite Firecats—particularly wise humans who had opted for rebirth in this rather odd form, the better to guide and advise those who held great power in their lands. Not being human, or having human concerns, made it possible for them to take the long, dispassionate view of things. That was the theory anyway. As Florian had once said, being solidly ensconced in a material body had a tendency to skew one's outlook sometimes. "And," he'd added obliquely, "it also depends on how many times you've been around."

Whatever *that* was supposed to mean.

Karal was graced—or burdened—with a Firecat, too, although he was not certain why. However, as wise as Altra was, he knew no more about Valdemar than Karal did. Both were somewhat handicapped when it came to understanding the land that had been Karse's enemy for centuries—as, once again, he was learning.

He dropped his head down into his hands for a moment, putting his cold fingertips against his aching temples. It helped, but not enough.

:*You are tired,*: Florian said with concern. :*I am not certain I should continue to drill you without some rest.*:

"I'd like some rest, too, but I'm meeting the *entire* Synod, or Assembly, or whatever it is they're calling it, tomorrow afternoon, and if I don't have the proper addresses down, I'm going to mortally offend someone." Karal sighed and massaged the muscles at the back of his neck. "I never *wanted* to be the Ambassador of Karse," he added mournfully. "I had my hands full enough being the aide. I was a *secretary*."

Florian didn't answer for a moment; he looked away, as if he were considering something. In the silence, Karal clearly heard mice scuttling around in the hay stored overhead. That was probably why the tomcat had not lingered for a scratch. :*I hesitate to suggest this—it means you would have to trust me much more than you already do—but there is a way around this particular problem.*:

"What?" Karal asked eagerly. He was perfectly willing to consider anything that might help at the moment. The "Holinesses," "Radiances," "Excellencies," and other titles were all swimming in his poor, overheated brain and would not stick to any particular "uniform." He had no idea how he was going to master them all by tomorrow. Like so many things, this meeting had been sprung upon him with little warning.

:*If you'd let me inside your mind, let your barriers down, I could look through your eyes, see who you were talking to, and prompt you,*: Florian replied hesitantly. :*I can show you how to let those barriers down easily enough. The problem is, I'll see more than surface thoughts if you did that. I'll know whatever you're thinking, and you tend to think*

*about several things at once. You might not want me that—
hmm—intimately in your mind.:*

Well, that was something of a quandary. *Did* he want
Florian to know what he was thinking? Some of it wasn't
going to be very flattering. He had already encountered some
of the religious leaders of other sects here, and they had
made it very plain that there was no love lost between them
and the representative of Vkandis Sunlord—even if, or *especially* if, that representative was a field-promoted secretary.

Now, it was true that the followers of Vkandis Sunlord had
wrought terrible things against the followers of other religions in the past. But that *was* the past, in days when the
Son of the Sun had been (to put it bluntly) a corrupt and ve-
nial tool of other interests than Vkandis'. High Priest Solaris
had put an end to that, to the war with Valdemar, and to the
insular and parochial attitude of those under her authority
regarding those who lived outside the borders of Karse.
Things were different now, and there had been Sun-priests
spilling their blood to save Valdemar to prove it. Furthermore, Karal was hardly old enough to have done anything
personally to anybody under the old rule—despite the fact
that some of these old goats seemed to hold him personally
responsible for every slight and every harm worked upon
their people and possessions since the time of Vanyel.

So Karal's innermost thoughts were hardly likely to be
charitable.

On the other hand, if he couldn't trust Florian with those
innermost thoughts, who *could* he trust?

"I think I had better accept that offer," he told the Companion. "But you ought to know you're likely to share in my
headache as well."

:I don't mind,: Florian told him. *:Not at all. Now, this is
what you do; it's easy, really. You know how it feels when I
talk to you?:*

He nodded.

*:Think of that, then imagine that you are reaching out a
hand to me. When you "feel" me clasp it, your barriers will
be down.:*

It was actually quite easy to imagine just that, since

Florian had never been a "horse" to him. He closed his eyes and stretched out an imaginary "hand" to his friend, and almost at once he had the uncanny sensation of having another "hand" enfold his. He opened his eyes, and for a moment experienced a very curious double image, the "Florian" he knew superimposed over a young man about his own age, thin, earnest, with dark hair and eyes, dressed in Herald's Whites.

The second image faded quickly, but Karal had to wonder. Was that what Florian *had* been—before?

:That's excellent!: Florian applauded. *:Can you sense the difference?:*

"Yes," he answered at once. "Now it's as if you're standing right at my shoulder and whispering in my ear."

:I'm seeing things through your eyes now. Mind you, I wouldn't advise it for the inexperienced. It's rather disorienting.: Florian chuckled, and Karal "felt" the chuckle at the same time that he heard the whicker.

:You're working so hard,: Florian continued wistfully. *:I only wish I could do more to help you.:*

"You help me a lot" Karal replied with feeling. "Just knowing that I have a real friend here helps more than I can say."

A light footstep at the door alerted him to the fact that he was no longer alone with Florian in the stable. "Only one?" An'desha asked as the Shin'a'in Adept entered the stable. "If I didn't know you didn't mean that literally, I would be sorely hurt." The teasing tone in his voice told Karal that he wasn't particularly serious.

As An'desha neared, Karal noted that he looked better than he had in days. Both of them had participated in a magical ceremony at the Valdemar/Iftel border that had been much more powerful and traumatic than either of them had ever dreamed possible. The end result of that was a temporary "breakwater" running from the northernmost tip of Iftel to the southernmost end of Karse, a breakwater that disrupted the mage-storms as they moved across the face of the land, broke them up and dissipated their energies harmlessly. It wouldn't last forever—for as the storms increased in power and frequency, they were tearing away at the new protections—but it bought them some time to come up with a better solution.

Of the two, An'desha had been the most exhausted, for he had been the one doing most of the work. Karal was not a mage; his mentor Ulrich had said once that he "had the potential to become a channel," but no one here knew what Ulrich had meant, until he was needed at the Iftel border.

Channeling must be instinctive, rather than learned. That was what other mages had said, once he described what had happened. He had recovered quickly, once they all returned to the capital of Haven and the expert care of the Healers. An'desha's recovery had been much slower.

An'desha's complexion was closer to the healthy golden tones of his Shin'a'in ancestors now, rather than the pasty yellow he *had* been sporting. There was more silver at the roots of his hair, which was hardly surprising, considering how much magical power he'd been handling. Handling the extremes of mage-energy bleached the hair and eyes to silver and blue, so Karal had been told. That was why An'desha's lover, the Tayledras Adept Firesong, had hair as white as snow before his eighteenth birthday, as it was to this day.

Karal had been told that An'desha had once been something called a "Changechild," a creature with a body that seemed part-animal, part-human; changed into that form by the spirit of an evil Adept who had taken possession of An'desha's body and twisted it into the form *he* chose, that of a cat-man. Mornelithe Falconsbane had eventually been driven out and destroyed, and by some miracle—literally a miracle, according to those who had been there at the time— An'desha's body had been returned to the form it had once held. With one exception.

An'desha's eyes were those of a cat's, still: green-yellow, and slit-pupiled. Now, though, they were growing paler, more silvery blue than greenish yellow. Again, that was the effect of all the magic An'desha had handled in setting up the breakwater.

Those were the outward signs of change. There were other signs; a calm that had not been evident before, an air of relaxation. *Confidence.* An'desha knew what he was now, and was comfortable with the knowledge. He also knew what he was not.

He was *not* Falconsbane, though he shared that evil creature's memories.

"I'm glad you know I did not mean to exclude you," Karal said with a welcoming smile.

"And I know what you meant—you are glad to have one *Valdemaran* friend. I am as much a foreigner and lost among these crazed folk as you." An'desha winked at Florian and dragged a short bench over from beside the stove. He was wearing clothing that marked him as foreign as Karal's Karsite robes, a cross between Hawkbrother garb and the quilted winter clothing of his own Shin'a'in nomads. "Firesong is complaining of the cold and swearing he will freeze to death before the first snow. Darkwind reminded him that his home Vale has winters worse than any in Valdemar. Firesong, of course, retorted that *he* never had to go out into such barbaric weather, and Elspeth chose to point out that he showed up at Darkwind's Vale riding *through* a snowstorm. *He* claimed it was because he represented his Vale and thus he *had* to make a dramatic appearance, and Darkwind said he was just posing. This became a contest of exaggerations, and no one noticed when I left." An'desha was laughing, so the "argument" must not have been that serious. "Firesong is looking for pity, and he is not going to find it from a Herald and a Tayledras scout, I fear."

"Nor from you?" Karal teased.

"Nor from me." An'desha stretched out his booted foot toward the stove. "If he seeks it, I shall only tell him what he told me so very often; too much sympathy makes one look for excuses, not answers. If he does not like the weather, perhaps he should consider making a Veil to cover Haven and turning it all into a Tayledras Vale."

"Ouch! A hit, indeed." Karal chuckled, and Florian whickered his own amusement. "Poor Firesong! All hands are raised against him today."

"It is only the weather that makes him irritable," An'desha said matter-of-factly. "In that, I cannot blame him

too much. Grim, gray, gloomy, and chill! I hope that the
farmers are able to get their harvests in, or we all shall be
wearing tighter belts come spring."

"I don't know. I haven't heard that things are any worse
than previous years, but no farmer anywhere admits to a
good yield," Karal replied. "I *have* heard that things have improved, now that the breakwater is up." That gave him an
opening he'd been looking for. "An'desha—you were outside
the Iftel border. Did you see anything when I went in?"

"How do you mean? I saw a great deal, both with Mage-
Sight and my own two kitty-slit eyes." An'desha pointed to
them, then crossed his legs gracefully and leaned forward a
little. The wood of his seat creaked as he moved.

Karal thought carefully and phrased his question as clearly
as he could. "Did it seem to you that the magic barrier at the
border actually . . . *recognized* me in some way?"

"Oh, there's no doubt of that!" An'desha told him firmly.
"It touched and tested you before it allowed you to pass
within. I Saw it myself. Short, then longer tendrils." He
frowned a little as he concentrated. "The area you were in
brightened, and I Saw things—it is hard to describe—I saw
the energies touching you, and I knew from some of—of
Falconsbane's memories that they were what he called
'probes,' ways to test someone. Though *what*, precisely, you
were being tested for, I cannot say."

"But why did it recognize me?" Karal blurted. "Altra was
very firm about that, remember? He said the border would
only recognize *me* of all of us. So why me?"

"It wouldn't have been only you," An'desha pointed out.
"He said that it had to be a Karsite Sun-priest of a particular
kind. Ulrich would have been the first choice. And obviously, Solaris would have served as well."

"But what is the connection between the magic at the border of Iftel and a Karsite Sun-priest?" Karal asked, frustrated.
"And just what *is* Iftel? No one can get in or out, except for
a very few, all of them selected traders and Healers, and you
couldn't get one of them to talk if you tortured him, which
is the point, I suppose. I've asked Altra—*when* he happens to
show up, which isn't often since we got back—and all he

does is switch his tail and tell me that I'll find out when the time is right."

:I can't help you; I'm as baffled as you are,: Florian admitted. *:Sorry, but there it is. Neither Altra nor Vkandis Sunlord have bothered to confide in this insignificant Companion.:*

"I suppose we'll just have to be patient. Frankly, if your Vkandis is anything like the Star-Eyed, I'm afraid He's probably going to insist that you figure it out for yourself." An'desha shrugged. "Deities seem to be like that. If I were one, I'd have a little more pity on my poor, frustrated, thick-headed followers."

Karal had to laugh at that, and reflected again how much he himself had changed. A year ago such a joke would have had him white with shock at the irreverence, not to say blasphemy.

An'desha smiled. "Good. Finally, I've made you laugh. You should be laughing more; you look as if haven't had a good laugh in days. And why haven't you been spending any time down at the Compass Rose with Natoli and the other students? I was down there last night. They've been missing you."

"I'd like to," Karal replied wistfully, "but I don't have the time. I'm doing my old job and Ulrich's, too. And having to learn all the things he knew about protocol without having the leisure to learn them over the course of a year or more." He shook his head as Florian's ears dropped sympathetically. "It started almost as soon as we got back from the border, and it hasn't let up any. I can't just be a place-holder, An'desha, I have to be a *real* envoy, whether I'm ready for it or not."

:Too true.: Florian nuzzled him, and he absently patted the Companion's nose. And got another curious overlay of someone clasping his shoulder, and he patted the comforting spectral hand in thanks.

"Take today, for instance. *Please* take today," Karal continued. "I hadn't even finished my breakfast before a page brought me a message from our border. There's a Herald down there trying to arbitrate a dispute between some

Holderkin and a set of Karsites who style themselves 'border-riders.' Neither party would accept a Herald, so it got thrown back in *my* lap and it had to be answered immediately."

"Did you?" An'desha asked with interest. "Could you?"

"In this case, at least, yes." He made a sour face. "I happen to know more than I'd like about the border-riders. They aren't much better than bandits; back in the old days, they had a habit of keeping two sets of clothing, Valdemaran and Karsite, and raiding farms on *both* sides of the border. Now that Karse is at peace with Valdemar, they can't do that anymore, so they've settled down to the odd cattle theft, or helping themselves to everything in a house when the family is away at the Temple Fair." He frowned, then took a deep breath and grinned a little. "They tried abducting the odd Holderkin girl, but often as not they couldn't tell the girls from the boys, and in either case they generally wished they'd stuck their hands in a wasps' nest instead when the family came boiling out, looking for blood. With no protection from the guards on our side of the border, and a kidnapped brat screaming blue murder, they didn't get away with *that* very often."

"So what was the dispute this time?" An'desha asked.

"The usual; cattle the Holderkin swore were theirs. Knowing what I know, I pointed out that the Herald should check the ear-notches to see if they were fresh. Holderkin don't notch the ears of their cattle because they hold them in common at each Holding; Karsites do, when the cattle are still calves, because cattle theft is in our blood, I'm afraid. If the notches were fresh, the cattle had been recently stolen, and there you have it."

:Oh, do tell him the outcome, it's rather funny,: Florian prompted.

Karal chuckled. "I got word back that *most* of the cattle had freshly-notched ears, but on just about a third of them the notches were clearly done when the cattle were young. It seems that the Holderkin were not above trying to get a little revenge by claiming the *whole* herd instead of just the ones that had been stolen."

An'desha laughed. "You should tell Talia; she'll be amused, I think."

"I shall; really, I think you're right. She certainly has no great admiration for her own kin." He sighed. "I just wish all the things I'm asked to settle were so easy to solve. Tomorrow I'm supposed to meet with the heads of nearly every sect and religion in Valdemar, and settle some disputes between the splinter sect of Vkandis that took root up here in Vanyel's time and some Sun-priests that came up from Karse during the war with Hardorn. I'm afraid I'm not going to make anyone happy with my decisions this time."

An'desha made sympathetic noises. "That is not something I would care to deal with. I remember—" He paused. "I have noted that in matters of religion logic, facts, and reason bear little weight when measured against emotion. It does not matter what *is,* when people are convinced that the very opposite is *what should be.*"

"I wish that were less true. I could pile up a hundred facts in favor of a particular argument, and all would be dismissed in favor of 'but that is not what I believe.' I am afraid that my age is going to tell against me as well." He eyed An'desha's silvering hair enviously. "Perhaps I ought to have you impersonate me. Or better still, have Darkwind do it. They would respect silver hair more than black."

"Oh, why not go the whole way and ask Firesong to do it?" An'desha laughed. "I can just see the faces of those stolid priests as Firesong sweeps in, wearing *his* version of a Sun-priest's robes."

"Oh, glory!" Karal had to laugh at that idea. Firesong's clothing was never less than flamboyant. "And once he began to talk, he'd have them all so tangled in logic and illogic, and dogma and cant, that they wouldn't even remember their own creeds!"

"It is entirely likely," An'desha agreed. "And it is a pity you wouldn't dare. I believe he would probably have a wicked good time of it if you asked him to."

"Now *there* is a 'White Demon,' for certain," Karal chuckled. "I think he gets more enjoyment out of twisting people around and playing with them than any other pursuit."

"I would not say he is *that* manipulative," An'desha temporized, "But there is a streak in him that makes him want to prod at people simply to get a reaction, and the more dramatic, the better."

"He certainly has a talent for drama, whether being at the center of it or inducing it," Karal agreed, and sighed. "Well, Florian seems to have solved the problem of how I am to remember who goes with what title tomorrow, so I shall be able to get a *little* rest tonight."

"I came here thinking you would go to the Compass Rose with me," An'desha said, looking hopeful. "Don't you think that just for once the Court can do without you at dinner? They were baking sausage rolls at the Rose this afternoon, and I'm told that the new yellow cheese is excellent."

"Demon! You know I'd do anything for good cheese and sausage rolls!" These were the closest foods Karal could find to the homey fare at the inn where he had grown up, and An'desha knew it. He cast an imploring glance at Florian. "*Could* I be absent, just this once?"

Florian was not proof against what the Companion had called "Karal's lost-puppy eyes." With a shake of his head, Florian gave in without a fight. :*I'll see that it's arranged,*: he promised, :*even if I have to tell an untruth and claim you're with me. But you'd better go now, or something else is likely to come up to prevent you from going at all.*:

The Compass Rose was a tavern unlike any other in all of Haven, and possibly all of Valdemar. It wasn't so much the food—which was quite good, but by no means up to the demands of a gourmet—or the drink, which was just about average. It was the clientele.

The Palace grounds actually hosted three Collegia; Herald's, Bardic, and Healer's—but there was a fourth unofficial Collegium there as well. If one looked into almost any given classroom, there would be *four* uniform colors in evidence. A gray uniform meant that the student in question was a Herald-trainee, a rust-brown tunic identified a Bardic student, and a pale green robe betokened a fledgling Healer. But a *blue* uniform was an "unaffiliated" student. More often than not, these were merely the offspring of courtiers who preferred to have their families with them rather than back on the estate or holding. Classes at all three Collegia were open to them, and they were required in these days to wear a blue uniform, although that had not always been the case. But there was always a group of students who came from common blood, who were there at the Collegia, receiving the best education possible in Valdemar, because of merit or exceptional intelligence. They usually had a sponsor, either in the Court or one of the three Circles of Heralds, Bards, or Healers.

Most of *these* were divided into two groups; pure scholars and "artificers."

The latter were the people who would go out into Haven and beyond, to invent and build—bridges, mills, roads, cunning devices which would allow one to navigate or survey the land accurately—the list of possibilities was as endless as the imaginations of those who were doing the inventing.

And most of *these* spent their "leisure" time at the Compass Rose.

So did their Masters, the teachers at the three Collegia, and those artificers who resided in Haven itself. And "leisure" time was relative, for at any given moment in the Compass Rose you could find people working out the difficulties in the gears of a new mill or a student project—planning an irrigation system or arguing over the results of the last exam—

Or finding a way to integrate magic with logic and avert the peril of the mage-storms.

The students and teachers at the Compass Rose had been just as responsible for the creation of the magical breakwater as any of the mages whose talents and powers built it. If it had not been for them, in fact, there probably would never have *been* a "breakwater" at all. The entire concept was a new one, and mages were accustomed to using only the old, tried, and proven ways of doing something.

When Karal had first arrived in Haven, he had been introduced to the daughter of the Herald who had been their guide through Valdemar to the capital, a young lady named

Natoli who was one of those "student-artificers." She had taken him to the Compass Rose, for she had known that among people who are accustomed to questioning everything, a "hated Karsite" was likely to be given the benefit of the doubt until he proved himself. That had been a lucky chance, for when the mage-storms first began wreaking havoc upon Valdemar, it occurred to Karal that the inquisitive and analytical minds of those same people were the ones best suited to taking the problem apart and perhaps coming up with a new answer.

Sometimes the most vital part of solving a problem was simply getting people to think about it.

For the first time, mages and artificers spoke to one another, and a new synthesis resulted.

Unfortunately for Karal, he hadn't gotten to see the aftermath of that synthesis since his duties had kept him away from the Rose, his friends there, and from Natoli. He was afraid now that she would be angry with him for deserting her for so long. Matters had been tending in the direction of something more than mere friendship, and now she might be thinking that he was getting cold feet over the idea.

A crowded tavern was not the best place to explain himself to someone who was possibly hurt and angry—but it was better than not seeing her at all.

It was that, and not the sausage rolls and cheese, that really took him to the tavern tonight.

He couldn't tell if An'desha was aware of that or not. The Shin'a'in was very good at keeping his thoughts to himself when he chose, and the subtle differences in his eyes made his expressions a little harder to read than most people's. On the other hand, An'desha was Natoli's friend, too, and she might have confided in him.

If nothing else, he thought, as the two of them wound their way through the streets of Haven to where the tavern lay, wedged in between a warehouse and a clockmaker's shop, *it will be good to be just myself for one evening, and not His Excellency, the Karsite Envoy.* It had gotten dark early, in part due to the heavy overcast, and the chill, damp air, though windless, had gotten colder yet. The darkness seemed very thick, as if it were swallowing up all the light. He was glad both of his heavy coat and the light from the streetlamps.

They turned a corner and were finally on the cobblestone street in the merchant district. The Compass Rose stood in the middle of the block. As usual, the Rose identified itself by the hum of conversation long before they reached the doorstep. Rumor had it that the clockmaker who shared a wall with the tavern was deaf; Karal certainly hoped so, or the poor man would never get any sleep at night.

From the sound, the Rose was full, which was the usual case on sausage roll night. The tavern boasted both a carved door and a carved sign bearing the compass rose of its name, both illuminated by torches. Karal hung back, feeling suddenly shy, as An'desha reached for the brass handle and opened the carved wooden door.

Cacophony assaulted them the moment the door swung wide, and Karal felt a twinge of nostalgia. It was as if nothing had changed—the room was exactly as it had been the first time Natoli had brought him here.

Table after table was full of students—eating and talking at the same time, gesturing with rolls or a piece of cheese, making mechanical arrangements out of the cups and plates, much to the disgust of those who were trying to use those cups and plates. The tables themselves were covered with rough brown paper, because the students tended to draw on them to illustrate some point or other, whether or not the surface was suitable for drawing. There were one or two of the Masters out here, usually with a tableful of their own students, prodding them through an assignment. The rest of the Masters were in the back room, a room reserved for them alone. A student "graduated" when he (or she) was invited to take his meal back in that hallowed sanctuary; there was no other special ceremony marking the ending of his life as a student and the beginning of his life as a professional. Here there were Masters, but no apprentices nor journeymen.

The roar continued for a moment as the door closed behind them with a thud, and Karal let his ears get used to the noise and his eyes to the light. The Rose was one of the few taverns where the light was as important as the drink, since so many here were working on projects as they ate. In fact, the lighting in the Throne Room at the Palace was dim by comparison. After coming in from the thick darkness outside, the glare of light took some getting used to.

But as they stood there, and Karal tried to see if Natoli and her cronies were at their usual table, the uproar began to subside, as people saw who was standing in the doorway, and turned to poke neighbors who hadn't yet noticed. As Karal shifted his weight uneasily, the roar faded into absolute silence.

No one moved. Then, off to the right, a single person stood up, a person who had been sitting with her back to the door. She turned and peered across the sea of faces to the doorway.

It was Natoli. And for a moment, Karal considered bolting back outside. *She's upset with me, and everyone knows it . . . I've hurt her feelings, and now they all hate me. Oh, glory, what am I going to do?*

"Karal?" she said clearly, and her strong, handsome face lit up with a welcoming smile. Natoli was not "pretty"—but her face had such character written in every line that you never noticed. "Havens, they finally let you take a night off! It's about time! Get *over* here! Look, everybody, it's Karal!"

The place erupted again, this time with cheers of welcome, a few playful catcalls, and offers of beer, food, or both. As Karal and An'desha waded through the crowd on their way to Natoli's table, he was staggered often by the hearty back slaps and playful punches his friends aimed at him. It occurred to him then that sometimes being Natoli's friend could be as hazardous as being her enemy!

He didn't manage to get across the room without being loaded down with food and an overfilled mug that slopped every time someone slapped his back. He kept apologizing, but it didn't seem that anyone noticed. Or perhaps they were just used to stray beer going everywhere.

Natoli's table was crowded, as usual, but also as usual there was always room for one or two more. People edged over and places were made for him and An'desha, one on either side of Natoli. As he sat down, Natoli helped herself to one of the many sausage rolls that had been thrust at him and offered him a plate of cheese in return.

He shared his bounty with anyone who didn't have food in front of him, and in the course of getting everyone settled again, he lost all of the apprehension he'd felt.

"You looked like a Bardic student in front of a hostile audience when you came in," she said, quite matter-of-factly. "Problems?"

"I suppose I was afraid that you would all be upset with me for not coming here before this," he said, a little shyly. "You might think *I* thought I was too good for you, now that I'm the Ambassador. Or—something."

She raised a hand and mimed a cuff at his ear. "Be sensible. Father's a Herald, remember? Just because I don't stick my nose into Court, that doesn't mean I don't know what's going on. They've had you tied up with more meetings and business than any one person has a right to be burdened with, and we all knew it. *I made sure* everyone knew that."

He relaxed at that. "I didn't want you to think that I'd forgotten who my friends are."

"Ha." She applied herself to her meal with a grin. "You've been working, and we haven't exactly been idle. Even if everyone else in Valdemar thinks that the crisis was solved, *we* know we only put it off for a while. We're still trying to work out a solution. Master Levy thinks there won't be *a* solution; he thinks we're going to have to come up with one make-do after another, because he thinks that the problem is getting too complicated to actually solve in the time we have."

"Do the mages know that?" he asked, feeling a chill. *More temporary solutions? Doesn't that leave us open to mistakes and the results of mistakes?*

"The mages know," An'desha confirmed. "At the moment they're trying to let their minds lie fallow while they track the current patterns of mage-energy for Master Levy's crew to analyze. I think some of them are hoping that if they don't *try* to think about a solution, one will spring forth from the back of their heads, fully formed."

Natoli snorted but didn't comment otherwise.

"Well, that's not necessarily bad thinking," one of the others pointed out. "I'm not talking about wishful thinking—it's just that if you try too hard to put all the facts together, sometimes they won't fall into place. Come on, Natoli, *you* know that even happens to us!"

"I suppose you're right," Natoli admitted grudgingly. "There *is* Cletius and the bathtub, for instance. It's just that some of these mages are just *so* certain that they can vibrate their way to answers that it makes me want to drown them all."

"Let's talk about something else," Karal urged. "Something that has *nothing* to do with mages or mage-storms or the Empire. What's exciting?"

A red head at the end of the table popped up. "Steam!" he exclaimed. "*That's* what's exciting! There's no end to what we can do with it! Who needs magic? Steam will save the world!"

"Don't go too far overboard," Natoli warned. "There're problems with steampower that we really ought to consider before we have people riding all over in steam-driven carriages. You have to burn things to heat water, and that makes smoke, and what happens when we start putting more smoke in the air? There's already a soot problem in Haven from all the heating and cooking fires."

"But you won't need heating and cooking fires if we heat everyone's house with the hot waste water from the steam-driven mills and manufactories," the other argued. "In fact, we should eliminate most of the soot problem that way."

"Not if you replace every one of those cookfires with one heating the boiler in a steam carriage," someone else put in. "Natoli's right about that. We really need to think about what we're doing before we launch into something we can't stop."

"Wait a moment," Karal interrupted. "Steam *carriages?*"

"One of the Masters came up with a water pump for draining mines that was steam driven, and someone else realized that the same principle could be used as the motive power for a carriage, by basically adding wheels to the whole affair rather than having a stationary boiler," Natoli explained. She snatched a stick of charcoal out of someone else's hand and began to draw on the paper covering the table in front of them. "You see—here's the boiler, in front of the firebox; pressure builds up in here and you vent it into the cylinder— the piston gets driven back—that turns a wheel—"

As she sketched, Karal began to see what she was talking about. "But why steam carriages at all?" he asked. "Aren't horses good enough?"

Natoli's eyes sparkled, and he realized he had uncovered her secret passion. "But these go *faster* than horses, Karal," she said. "They never get tired, they can pull more than horses can without hurting themselves, and the only time they have to stop is when they run out of fuel or water."

"Huh." He could think of places where that would be use- ful. In the mountains, where the roads were cruelly hard on carthorses. Or any time you needed to send something very quickly somewhere. Supplies, perhaps, or soldiers. Of course these things would be limited to places where the roads were good, which was quite a limitation, when you thought about it. Using them on a regular basis meant that the roads would have to be improved and kept in repair, and that could get rather expensive. . . .

"We're thinking about putting them on rails or in grooved tracks," Natoli continued, waving a sausage roll in one hand as she spoke. "Like the coke carts at the big iron-smelting works. The only problem is that takes a lot of metal, so where do we get all that metal? And if you used cut stone, it would wear out rapidly from the wheels. Every time you solve a problem you bring up twenty more." But she didn't look particularly discouraged. "The point is, we know we can use large versions of this in places where windmills don't work and there isn't any water for water mills. We can use the waste heat to heat houses, or even the Palace. Wouldn't *that* be a sight!"

"Wouldn't it be a sight as you get in everyone's way dig- ging up the Palace and grounds to lay all your pipe," An'desha pointed out sardonically. He pushed a fall of his long hair back from his forehead, showing his pale eyes crin-

kled in smile lines. "I can't see the Queen holding still for
that! Especially not in the foreseeable future."

"Oh, I didn't mean right now," Natoli said airily, waving
her hands in the air. "I just meant eventually. After all, it's
not as if it hasn't been done. Think of the mess it made
when all the new indoor privies and the hot and cold water
supplies were put in. That was in the first couple of years of
Selenay's reign, and I don't hear anyone complaining about it
now!"

"A point," An'desha acknowledged. "I'd like to see you
folk find some other source of heat than a fire, however.
Fires are not very clean."

"Some magical source, maybe?" Karal said without thinking, and blushed when every eye on the table turned toward
him. "I don't really know what I'm talking about, I'm just
speculating—" he stammered. "Don't pay any attention to
me, I'm just babbling."

"But your babbling makes some sense," Natoli responded,
her eyes lighting up with enthusiasm. "A practical application of magic! That might be the answer to my chief objec-
tion as well."

The talk turned to possible magical sources of heat then,
and An'desha held center stage as he speculated on how this
might be accomplished in such a way that the mage would
not actually have to be there to make the source work. It led
into talk of binding magical creatures, small ones that
thrived on fuel of one kind or another, and it was clear to
Karal that An'desha was in his element. Karal was able to
watch Natoli to his heart's content, as her face grew ani-
mated during the heat of the discussion, and she tossed her
hair with impatience or excitement.

"So," An'desha said, as the door of the Compass Rose
closed behind them, shutting off part of the noise, which had
not in the least abated. "Feeling rested and relaxed?"

Karal paused and took stock of himself and blinked in surprise. "Why—yes!"

An'desha laughed. "Good. That was what I hoped would
happen. Now are you wondering why I pulled you away after

Natoli left?" He started off down the street in a fast walk, and Karal followed.

"A little," he admitted, sniffing in the cold and damp, "Though I must admit once she left I got a bit bored when they all started talking about mathematics and drawing on the tables again."

"Because you and I are going to go to the *ekele*. Firesong is up to his eyebrows in some discussion involving the Tayledras, the Shin'a'in, and k'Leshya at Haven, so he won't be there. *I'm* not taking part because I've been told I'm not Shin'a'in enough to satisfy the envoy. He doesn't like half-breeds."

"Hmph, I'm not surprised. He seems to dislike all sorts of people," Karal growled. "Well, I don't like *him*, so we're all even."

Karal walked on in silence, seeming lost in thought, then turned to An'desha. "What did you have in mind when we get there?"

"You are going to soak in the hot spring, and you are going to have a nice, relaxing cup of Shin'a'in tea, and then you are going to go to your suite and sleep." It was too dark to read An'desha's face, but his voice told Karal he was not going to be argued with. "As I recall, you made the same prescription for me a time or two, and turnabout is fair play."

"So is that why you have turned into my counselor?" Karal asked, and he wasn't entirely being facetious. The events of this afternoon and evening had proved to him that An'desha had achieved an inner peace that he found enviable.

If only I could be so sure of things again!

"The turnabout? Oh, it is a part of it," An'desha said, with serene warmth in his voice. "You have done good things for me, with good reason and without. You have been kind when you could have been neutral. There is a saying from the Plains: *Every gift carries the hope for an exchange.*"

Karal mulled that over, but his thoughts about the Shin'a'in proverb were eclipsed by marveling over An'desha's calm.

That was part of the problem he had with the entire situation. He was not only acting as envoy, but as a priest—and a priest should be utterly sure of himself and his beliefs. Either a priest or an envoy should be sure and calm.

But he was being required to determine what was heresy for those of his faith here in Valdemar, and *that* was where his beliefs were collapsing around his ears. How could he make a judgment on what was heretical, when he had seen evidence with his own eyes that what he "knew" was the Truth was only truth in a relative sense?

Take the very existence of An'desha's Star-Eyed Goddess, for instance. For a Sun-priest, there was *one* God, and one only, and that was Vkandis—yet he had ample proof that was beyond refutation that the Star-Eyed existed and ruled Her people right alongside Vkandis Sunlord.

To even think that was rankest heresy by the standards of the Faith as he was taught it. But he had been taught *the old ways* and things had changed drastically since.

He'd already deferred the decision once, which had only made both parties angry at *him*. He suspected that this was the reason why he was being confronted by all the heads of religion in Valdemar. They weren't going to accept a deferred decision again.

Perhaps in his new-found confidence and serenity, An'desha could act as *his* adviser as he had once acted as An'desha's.

"Would you mind listening to a problem of mine?" he asked, as they walked side-by-side up the deserted street, toward the Palace.

"You listened to mine often enough," An'desha replied. "It only seems fair. I won't promise an answer, but maybe I can help anyway."

He explained the predicament he was in; his own uncertainty, and his unwillingness to label *anything* heresy. "I don't know now if there *is* a wrong or right, in anything. And I am put in the position of being the person that is supposed to know! It all seems so relative now," he ended plaintively.

But An'desha only chuckled. "If I were to turn and stick my knife in you now, *that* wouldn't be 'relatively' good or bad, would it?"

He had to laugh. "Hardly!"

"Work from that, then," An'desha suggested. "You've *been* reading all those old books that Master Ulrich brought with him, the ones written back before the Sunlord's priesthood went wrong. You have a fair idea what was considered heretical then, don't you? And what's more, since you have those books, and since Solaris approves of them, you can cite sources to *prove* the position you're taking, right?"

Fog rose from the damp cobblestones all around them, but it seemed that the fog in his own mind was lifting. "Well, yes, literally chapter and verse. That's true," he said slowly. "I think the problem is that I know what I wanted to say, but I couldn't think of a way to make it stick."

"You probably still won't be able to make it stick," An'desha warned. "The people you're dealing with are like that new Shin'a' in envoy that replaced Querna; hidebound and dead certain they're right."

"True, but if they don't like *my* decision, I can tell them to appeal to Solaris, and as long as I follow what Master Ulrich was trying to show me, I think she'll back me." His cheer was mounting by the moment. "I don't much care if they don't like me afterward. There are so many people in Valdemar now who don't like me that a few more won't matter."

"That's the spirit!" An'desha applauded. "Good for you. *Now* are you ready for that soak?"

"I'm soaked in trouble anyway, why not add hot water?"

"Careful with that kind of talk," An'desha grinned. "You'll make it start raining again."

Karal's backside and face were both numb. His shoulders ached; he maintained an expression of calm interest, but inside, he was yawning. *All we do is talk!* he thought, taking a covert glance around the Grand Council table, and seeing nothing but the same expressions of stolid self-importance he had seen for days. *We never actually do anything, we just talk about it!*

The Valdemaran "Grand Council" was new; an institution formed so that Queen Selenay could attend to the problems that were strictly internal to Valdemar in a forum where every envoy, Guild functionary, Master artificer, and their collective secretaries did not feel urged to put in their *own* bits of advice. She had been getting nothing done, and every busybody in her kingdom had been privy to Valdemar's internal problems. The old Council Chamber had gone back to the use for which it had been built, and one of the larger rooms in the Palace, formerly a secondary Audience Chamber for the reception of large parties, had been turned over to the new function.

Of course, everyone involved had his own ideas on protocol, which meant that the Queen and her advisers had to come up with some seating arrangement that would suit everyone. A new table had been constructed in the form of a hollow square with one side open, like an angular horse shoe. Around it were placed enough seats for everyone who might conceivably want to have a hand in the situation with the Empire, the mage-storms, or both. The table sat squarely in the middle of the otherwise empty room, and on the platform that had once been the dais was a huge strategic map of Valdemar, Hardorn, Karse, Rethwellan, the Tayledras lands to the west, the Dhorisha Plains, and south as far as Ceejay. The gryphons, when they attended, actually sat (or rather, lounged) in the hollow interior of the table, with the rest spaced evenly along the outside. No one sat at the "head" of the table, for there was no head or foot, and so everyone could feel he was equal, superior, or whatever his pride demanded.

Although the room was well-provided with lights, both along the walls and from a chandelier hanging from the ceiling, it was cold. Two ceramic-tiled stoves, one at either end of the room, had to make shift to heat the whole place. The white marble floor and white-painted walls and ceiling added to the impression of cold. Karal always dressed warmly for these meetings, and kept the pages busy refilling his cup of hot tea which he mostly used to warm his hands. Nor was he the only person to resort to such measures to keep warm; he noted that Firesong actually had the forethought to bring a handwarmer and a heated brick which he put inside a special footstool. He cast envious glances now and again at both, as he wriggled his toes in an attempt to keep them from turning into little blocks of ice.

Prince Daren acted as the Queen's voice on the Grand Council, leaving Selenay free to rule her country and not sit in on meeting after endless meeting. Meetings at which, it seemed to Karal, very little was accomplished.

That's not fair, actually, Karal thought, looking around again. *No one has ever done anything like this before. We're all having to come to terms with each other, and that takes time. We have to learn to work together before anything can happen.*

All this, obviously, meant that the Seneschal, the Lord Marshal, the heads of the three Circles, and any other Valdemaran official that normally sat on the Council often ended up attending double meetings when the Grand Council met. And any other Valdemaran functionary who wanted to look important (or actually felt he might be needed) helped to round out the field. This, of course, meant that every single meeting since the breakwater went up consisted of one person after another pontificating on how he and his special interests had been affected, what would probably happen next, and what *he* thought should be done about it. Typically, those with the most important and relevant information generally said the least.

There should be a way of cutting this nonsense out. It's taking up time. Maybe a maximum word count, enforced by cudgel?

Karal really would have preferred to be off doing something constructive, even if all he was doing was making copies of energy-flow maps for the artifiers. At least that would be accomplishing more than just sitting here trying not to fall asleep, a job that grew more difficult as the time crawled by.

So far today, at least eight people had made long speeches that were only variations on "as far as my people can tell, this breakwater business is working and everything is back to normal," and the one currently droning on was the ninth. He was the particular representative of dairy farmers—and *only* dairy farmers—and they had already heard from grain growers, shepherds, vegetable farmers, fruit growers, professional hunters, the fisher folk of Lake Evendim, and poultry farmers. Each of them had gone on at length about why *his* particular group had suffered more than any other from the mage-storms, though what this was supposed to accomplish, Karal didn't know.

Why can't the farming folk find one *person to represent them all? And why can't he be someone who'll give us hard information instead of whining?*

He cupped his hands a little tighter around his tea and resolved to find out where Firesong had gotten the footstool with the heated brick in it.

They can tell the people who sent them that their complaints and troubles are on record, I suppose, he thought vaguely. *As if that makes any difference to this group. I suppose it must make people feel better to know that someone at least* knows *that they are having hard times.* It would have been much more useful for all these farmers and hunters and herders to have compared the damages this year with those of previous bad years—during the time when Ancar's magic in Hardorn was causing ruinous weather all over, for instance. Then all the foreign envoys would know how things stood here in comparison to the way they *should* be, and could offer advice or even help-in-trade if it looked as if help really was needed. They could *all* compare notes on the damages across the region, and see if there were any differences. The plans being worked out by Master Levy's artificers and the allied mages were all based on information mainly gathered in Valdemar. They were all assuming that patterns in Valdemar were similar to patterns outside Valdemar. But what if they weren't?

He'd tried suggesting that, but the people he'd suggested it to had said that gathering such information was going to take a great deal of time, and could he justify such an undertaking? He'd tried to point out why it would be useful, but no one seemed to find his arguments convincing.

Finally, the man stopped droning. It took Karal and the others a few moments to realize that he had actually ended his speech, rather than simply pausing for breath as he had so many times before.

Prince Daren nobly refrained from sighing with relief, as he consulted his agenda. Though still as handsome as a statue of a hero, the Prince was showing his age more and more lately; there were almost as many silver hairs among his gold as An'desha sported. The stress of the past several years was beginning to tell on both of Valdemar's monarchs. There were strain lines around his eyes that matched the ones around the Queen's. Like the Queen, since he was also a Herald, he wore a variation on the Herald's Whites.

"Herald Captain Kerowyn, I believe you are next," the Prince-Consort said, and although the gentlemen and ladies now seated about this square table were too well-trained to show relief in their expressions, people did begin sitting up a little straighter, and taking postures that showed renewed interest. Kerowyn at least was not going to stand there and drone about nothing; whatever she reported was going to be short, to the point, and relevant.

Kerowyn, who was the same age as Daren, nevertheless remained ageless. Her hair, which she always wore in a single long braid down her back, was already such a light color that it was impossible to tell which hairs were blonde and which were silver. And any new stress lines she had acquired would be hidden by the weathered and tanned state of her complexion, for Kerowyn was not one to sit behind a desk and "command" from a distance. She had begun her military career as a mercenary scout in the field, and that was where she felt most at home. There was not a single pennyweight of extra flesh on that lean, hard body, and every Herald-trainee knew to his sorrow that she was in better physical shape than any of them. When she wasn't drilling her own troops, she was drilling the Herald-trainees in weapons' work, and heaven help the fool who thought that because she was a woman, she would be an easy opponent. She had been sporadically training Karal, and he knew at firsthand just how tough she was.

She stood up to immediate and respectful silence from everyone at the table, Valdemaran or not.

With one hand on her hip and the other holding a sheaf of papers, she cleared her throat carefully. "Well, I don't need to go into the obvious. What we're calling the breakwater is obviously working. The mages tell me that what's happening is that rather than reflecting the waves of force as they come at us to somewhere else, this business they've set up is breaking them up and absorbing them to some extent. That's good news for us, but Hardorn is still getting the full force of the waves."

Chuckles met that, and she frowned. "As a strategist, I don't think that's particularly good for us, my friends. If the situation in there was bad before—and it was—it's worse now. We may see the Imperial forces in Hardorn getting desperate, and desperate people are inclined to desperate acts. I might remind you that they may be blaming *us* for all these mage-storms. They've made one attempt to break up our Alliance. They may decide to act more directly."

The pleased looks around the table evaporated. Even handicapped, the Imperial Army was vastly larger than anything the Alliance could put together, and everyone here knew it. The members of the alliance had been fighting the renegade King Ancar of Hardorn, separately and together, for years before the Eastern Empire came onto the scene, and their forces were at the lowest ebb they had ever been. The attrition rate had been terrible on both sides, for Ancar had been perfectly willing to conscript anything and anyone and throw his conscripted troops into the front lines under magical coercions to fight. He had intended to take Valdemar and Karse, even if he had to do it over a pile of his own dead a furlong high. Ancar was gone now, but. . . .

"Now, one way to make sure they don't come after us is to take the fight to them," Kerowyn continued matter-of-factly. "You know what they say about the best defense being a good offense. My people tell me that the Imperials pulled everything back and they've concentrated in one spot, around a little town called Shonar. Looks as if they are making a permanent garrison there. That makes them a nicely concentrated target. Their morale is bad, and it looks as if they've been cut off from resupply and communication with the Em-

pire. They depend on magic; right now, they don't have any.
My best guess is that they're doing their damnedest just to
get dug in to survive the winter. The questions I have for all
of you, are—do you think we should take advantage of that,
and are you prepared to back a decision to go on the offensive when that means taking what troops we have right into
Hardorn?"

Half of the people at the table began talking at once; the
other half sat there with closed expressions, clearly thinking
hard about what Kerowyn had just said. It was fairly typical
that the people who had begun babbling were the ones who
were the least important and the least knowledgeable so far
as a decision like this one was concerned—representatives of
farmers and herders, tradesmen and Guilds, priests and the
like. The rest—the actual envoys, the Lord Marshal, the
Seneschal—were the silent ones, and Karal was among them.

On the other hand, he was inclined to think—*why not?*
Why *shouldn't* we hit these people while they are in trouble?
The Shin'a'in envoy, Jarim shena Pretara'sedrin, began to
speak as Karal was considering that.

"This is our chance," he said fiercely. "Let a few bad winter storms take their toll, then let us strike while they are
freezing and starving! Let us wipe them from the face of the
world! If we destroy this army now, the Empire will never
again dare to send a force against us. Let us take our revenge,
and let it be a thorough one!"

And for once, on the surface and at first impulse, Karal
was inclined to agree with him. *They murdered Ulrich,* he
thought angrily. *They murdered Ulrich and poor Querna,
they injured Darkwind and Treyvan and others, and they
didn't even come at us as honest enemies! They sent an
agent with vile little magic weapons to assassinate whoever
happened to be in the way, with no warning and no prov-
ocation. Don't they deserve to be squashed like bugs for
that? Don't they deserve to be treated the way they treated
us—as insignificant and not even worth a fair fight? Doesn't
Ulrich's blood cry out for revenge?*

But it was that last thought that stopped him because *revenge* was the last thing Ulrich would have wanted. What

was being proposed meant that vengeance was enacted, not upon the perpetrator, but upon people—soldiers—who had no idea what evil had been wrought here. Ulrich had once commanded demons—and gladly renounced that power when Solaris decreed it *anathema*. The demons were the next thing to mindless, and too often, like a hail of arrows loosed at random, they killed those who were innocent along with those who were guilty.

These soldiers, far from home and desperate, were not the real enemy. The real enemy was the one who had commanded those magical weapons, and the one who had sent the assassin. They had caught the original assassin, after all. What would be the point of going after anyone else now—unless, perhaps, they in their turn specifically targeted the commander of these forces, assuming he had been the one who had ordered the assassin to strike in the first place.

Others joined Jarim in calling for action, or opposed him, cautioning that it might be better to let the full force of winter take its toll before acting. But Karal sat and clasped cold fingers before him, wondering what had happened that he was no longer able to see things involving humans as day or night, good or evil.

He knew when it had begun; something had changed when he entered the barrier at the border with Iftel, and it had continued to affect him in the days he had spent recovering from the experience. He had the feeling, always humming in the background like the blood in his veins, that he had been welcomed by something extraordinary. Karal lived in a time of wonder and strangeness, yet the feeling he had was not, at any time, that of being a spectator. He was a *part* of it all, an active player in whatever game the fates set the board for, and that feeling itself was beyond anything he'd prepared for.

I can't help it; present me with a situation, and I have to think about both sides of it. I can try to suppress it, but I cannot shut off the way I think. Once knowledge is gained, there's no going back to ignorance. I think about what the other feels. I can't stop it, and I don't think Vkandis Sunlord, Solaris, or Altra would want me to. Or Ulrich, far away in Vkandis' arms.

Ironically enough, it had been Ulrich himself who had planted the seeds of this change, back when he and his mentor had first crossed into Valdemar. Ulrich had asked a slow but steady progression of perfectly logical questions that had ultimately forced him to see his former enemies as people, and not as a faceless horde. Because of Ulrich's patient coaching, he now knew, at the deepest level of pure reaction, that the impersonal and evil army of nameless demons that lay across the border of Karse was nothing of the sort. It was Heralds and Companions, farmers and townsfolk, soldiers of the Queen and ordinary citizens; people very like those he had known all his life.

Now he could no longer see an enemy impersonally. The great and mindless "they" were nothing more nor less than people, and he saw them that way. While the others spoke of wiping out the Imperial Army, *he* saw ordinary fighting men, suffering unseasonable cold and demoralizing doubt, wondering if they would ever see home again. He even imagined faces, for the faces of fighters came to look much alike after a few seasons in the field: tired, unshaven, with lines of suppressed fear and dogged determination about the eyes and mouth.

"They" were just doing their jobs. They didn't know anything about Valdemar. Conditions in Hardorn had been so dismal when they first crossed the border, they had been welcomed as liberators. Ancar had abused his people to the point that they were happy to see even a foreign invader, if that meant that Ancar would be deposed. Now the Imperials were probably wondering why the welcome they'd gotten had turned so sour. Things they had come to depend on were no longer working, and by now word must have filtered down that no one had any contact with their headquarters back home. Strange and misshapen beasts had attacked them, and they had seen a "weapon" at work that no one understood.

If any of them had the slightest notion that their superiors had assassins working in Valdemar, a few of them might even be horrified. Certainly, since the professional soldier generally had the deepest contempt for the covert operator, they probably would be a bit disgusted. But it was unlikely that any of them knew or even guessed what had happened in Valdemar's Court, that one of their leaders had assassinated perfectly innocent people.

So why should perfectly "innocent" soldiers suffer for the action of what was probably a single man?

They were already under more privation than they had any right to anticipate.

They're far from home and all the things they know. They have no idea if they will ever find their way back again. They may not even be able to retreat in a conventional way. They must be afraid—how could they not be afraid? And winter is coming, more mage-storms. The storms created some terrifying creatures here before we built the breakwater. What can they possibly be making in Hardorn?

Since he was alone and far from home himself, he couldn't help but have some fellow feeling for them. Perhaps it was foolish, but there it was.

For that matter, it was only presumption on their part that the assassination orders originated with someone commanding the forces in Hardorn. There was no real reason to assume that was actually true.

After all, Talia and Selenay's old nemesis, Hulda, had been getting *her* orders directly from the Imperial capital, possibly even from one of Emperor Charliss' personal spymasters. Charliss was accustomed to sending in operatives who worked at an extreme distance, for with the magics the Empire used routinely, distance was no object. So who was to say that the assassin hadn't been sent directly by Charliss or someone just below him, and had nothing to do with the forces in Hardorn at all?

The Imperial Army itself had never done anything overtly against Valdemar; they had only moved to take over a disorganized and demoralized country after its own ruler had been killed—

—by Valdemarans. Valdemar *assassins*, not to put too fine a point upon it.

Don't we have trouble enough right now without adding to it by attacking the Imperials directly? We should be con-

*centrating on the next step after the breakwater, not trying
to get an army of our own halfway into Hardorn to attack
someone we don't even know is our enemy!*

The general din seemed to have died down a bit, and he
saw an opening. With shaking hands, which he disguised by
keeping them clasped on the table in front of him, he
spoke up.

"I'm not certain going after them is a good idea," he said
quietly. "We should be concentrating all of our effort on the
mage-storms; the breakwater isn't going to hold forever—in
fact, if the storms change their pattern drastically, it won't
hold at all. The Imperials haven't done anything we can
prove, and they are going to have all they can take with the
results of the mage-storms over there. Why don't we just
leave them alone, at least for now, and see what happens?"
Stunned silence met his suggestions, and he added into the,
deathly quiet, "Our resources are limited, and things might
get even worse. Who knows? They have so many mages with
them—they know things we don't—they might turn out to
be valuable allies."

"*What?*" Jarim sprang to his feet, his face scarlet with outrage. Karal felt his heart stop, then start up again, and he
knew that he had gone pale by the cold and stiff way his face
felt. "Are you *mad?* Or are you so much of a coward that you
won't even face what these Imperial jackals have done to
you? They slew *your* mentor, *your* envoy! Are you a fool,
boy? Or—are you a traitor?" He put one hand on his knife
hilt and drew the blade with a single swift motion. "Those
assassin blades somehow mysteriously never touched you!
Foul piece of *sketi*—have you been the traitor in our midst
all along? By the Star-Eyed, I swear I—"

Karal kept himself from shrinking back only by iron will
and the knowledge that Daren and the others wouldn't let
Jarim actually *do* anything to him. Darkwind rose malevo-
lently and grabbed the Shin'a'in's wrist in a grip of steel,
roaring to drown out whatever Jarim was going to say.

"Stop that, you fool! Where are your senses! Drawing steel
in the Grand Council, threatening the Karsite Envoy, are you
trying to break the Alliance apart all by yourself?" He shook

the man's arm, rattling the startled Shin'a'in's teeth. Karal was impressed; Darkwind did not give the impression of being stronger than any other normal man. Evidently there was a great deal about this Hawkbrother that was not obvious.

The Shin'a'in was so startled that he dropped the knife, which clattered to the table. Firesong snatched it up before Jarim could reach for it.

"The boy is only pointing out alternatives—*as is appropriate*. He *is* a priest, he *is* supposed to think beyond the obvious, and he *is* supposed to suggest peaceful possibilities rather than ones involving war!" Darkwind turned to glare at everyone around the table, and some of the representatives of other gods had the grace to look chagrined, since they had been doing nothing of the sort. In fact, they had been calling for war as enthusiastically as Jarim. "He is absolutely right; in regard to what has happened here, we have no proof as to the origin. We have speculation, but no *proof*. For all we know, our real enemy could be someone we are not even aware of, someone who set all of this up to make it *look* like the Empire was the perpetrator!"

"Oh, that's hardly likely," the Lord Marshal scoffed. "Who would this nebulous enemy be? Some hypothetical evil shaman from the North, beyond the Ice Wall?"

"Not likely, I will grant you, but possible—and we have not even discussed the possibility. I remind you, before any of you accuse our own Council members of duplicity, that *outside* influences should be the first consideration. A history-proven means of destroying vital alliances is to sow dissension among its members, *from outside, by duplicity!*" Darkwind met the Lord Marshal's eyes squarely, and it was the older man who dropped his gaze. "Furthermore, as a mage, I concur with his priority. You've all accepted the breakwater as the solution to the problem of the mage-storms, but it was never meant to be more than a stopgap measure to gain us time."

"Now that is completely true and irrefutable," Firesong drawled, toying with the Shin'a'in dagger. "Forgive me, Herald Captain, but this breakwater of ours is rather like its namesake—and the more storms that come to wash away at it, the faster it will erode. It is more like a levee made of sand than one made of stone. I know it seems to you as if this is a good time to strike at a *possible* menace, but believe me as a mage of some talent—they will have all they can handle and more as the mage-storms wreak havoc in Hardorn. If they are very, very lucky, the monsters that are conjured up will be stopped by walls and enough arrows. If they are not—" He shrugged. "—well, let me remind you that the breakwater may stop mage-storms, but it is no barrier against hungry creatures capable of decimating an army. What comes to dine on them might well move in to dine on *us* before all is said and done. As mages and artificers—" he bowed ironically to Master Levy, "—we should be searching for the next level of protection against the storms. As military leaders, *you* should be searching for ways to hold off whatever might come at us *through* the Imperial Army. The likelihood is that, if you do not, it may be our Alliance that will be smashed like a particularly inconvenient bug."

He held the dagger out to the sullen Shin'a'in, hilt first; Darkwind released the man's wrist, and Jarim took the dagger and thrust it back into the sheath. He sat down again, his face still rebellious.

Karal drew a breath of relief; at least this crisis was over, for the moment anyway. Kerowyn had simply stood there through all of it, her own expression a study in passivity.

Finally, she spoke. "On the whole," she said carefully, "I must admit that more energy should be put into finding another solution to the mage-storm than anything else. I wanted to point out the possibility that the Imperial Army *might be* vulnerable at this time. I do not want anyone to think that I am certain of that. After all, as Karal rightly pointed out, nothing is certain but those facts that we can verify for ourselves. He is also correct in pointing out that a great deal of what we think we know is only speculation. *Probability* is not fact, and I for one prefer not to send troops into battle while the home fronts are unprotected."

She sat down amid heavy silence. Prince Daren cleared his throat. "In that case," he said, with remarkable aplomb, considering that moments before, one of his allies had been stopped just short of declaring blood-feud on another, "Perhaps the next to speak should be Darkwind k'Sheyna."

Darkwind seized the verbal "ball" that had been thrown to him, and proceeded to take over the meeting. The Hawkbrother did not have his bird with him, but he stood as if he was so accustomed to the weight of the forestgyre on his shoulder that he was always ready for it. He, too, sported the all-white hair of a Tayledras Adept, for he had been Elspeth's original teacher of magic, before he became her partner and beloved. He was a typical Tayledras; strongly handsome, rather than the sculptured beauty of Firesong. He tended to much less flamboyant clothing than his fellow Hawkbrother, but when he spoke, it was with authority, and people listened.

Karal simply sat very still during most of the rest of it. It was all to the good that Darkwind managed to get across the fact that the breakwater was *temporary,* and get the attention of the allies centered on that rather than anything else, though he did not seem to Karal to be getting the urgency of the situation across to them. But Karal could not ignore the smoldering glances of Jarim, or the dismissive glances of many of the rest of the people at the table. Once again, his youth was speaking against him. People assumed that because he was young he was inexperienced. And Jarim clearly assumed that because he was not ready to rush out and slaughter every Imperial that came his way, he was, at the least, a coward.

Well, Darkwind and Firesong seem to think I've got a point. Maybe I ought to work through them instead of trying to make my points myself.

But if he did that, he'd just look ineffectual, and how would *that* serve Karse?

When the Grand Council broke up, it was with very little accomplished and nothing really settled.

As usual.

He returned to his suite feeling as if he had failed in his duty.

As he closed the door, shoulders slumping beneath his

elaborate black robes, a patch of golden sunlight in the middle of the floor rose up to greet him.

:You look as if you could use a friend,: Altra observed, as what had been golden light resolved itself into a huge cat, cream colored, with reddish-gold mask, paws, and tail—and vivid blue eyes. *:Did the meeting go badly?:*

Karal managed to dredge up a ghost of a smile and sagged into a chair as Altra padded across the floor and sat regally down at his feet. At least it was comfortably warm in here, with the sunlight streaming in the windows and a fire in the fireplace. The Valdemarans took good care of their guests, and sometimes it seemed as if the one commodity that Valdemarans treasured above all others was warmth. He had a suite of three rooms, including his own bathroom—not the same suite he had shared with Ulrich, which would have been too painful to return to. That suite had been given, ironically enough, to Jarim. "It didn't *end* badly—but if you were paying any attention to the meeting, you'll know I was within a hair of having Shin'a'in blood-feud declared against me."

The Firecat blinked. *:I was eavesdropping a bit, and I must say you're certainly talented. No Sun-priest has had Shin'a'in blood-feud declared against him in the entire history of Karse.:*

Karal just sighed at this display of Altra's rather sardonic sense of humor. "It's not funny, cat. I guess the important thing is that this all proves that I am in far past my depth, here, and I might as well admit it. It's one thing to have Solaris send a piece of paper making me the envoy, but it's quite another to get people to *accept* me as the envoy."

Restlessness overcame his lassitude and weariness. He lurched out of his chair and began pacing. "I'm too young, I'm inexperienced, and if I was a place-holder, neither of those things would matter. But I'm not just a cipher. I'm supposed to be making decisions here; I'm supposed to be representing Karse's best interests. But how can I *possibly* do that when I'm young enough to be the *son* of half the people in the room, and the *grandson* of the other half?"

He was so frustrated and so very, very tired! His repressed

emotions boiled over and came pouring out of him in a tor-
rent of impassioned words. At least Altra was listening,
rather than cutting him off. "The worst thing is, I know I'm
too young, and *that* shows, too! Altra, these responsibilities
are driving me mad! I don't want to sound as if I'm whining,
but I am *not suited* to this! I thought this would only be for
a few weeks—that Solaris would send someone else, someone the others would listen to. When we were trying to
catch the assassin, it was reasonable to have me as the envoy. It was even reasonable when I was only interacting with
the people on Selenay's internal Council—after all, Darkwind and Elspeth and a couple of the others know that I have
a good idea now and then and are willing to listen to me because they know me. But now I'm supposed to be dealing
with all of these other allies, and they all look at me and see
a—a child!" He turned toward the Firecat and held out his
hands, imploring Altra to see the dilemma he was in. "Altra,
I can't do the task I was given, and there is nothing that is
going to make that possible, short of aging me twenty years
overnight. I'm doing my best, but this is akin to asking a
blind man to sort beads by color. Trying to do what no one
will let me do is going to drive me insane without helping
Karse!"

Altra had remained silent during this entire outburst.
When he finally subsided, Karal bitterly expected the Firecat
to deliver a crisp lecture on growing some backbone. After
all, that was what he had done on similar occasions in
the past.

But Altra did nothing of the sort. He curled his tail tightly
around his legs, and sat so quietly that not even a hair
moved. His eyes had grown very thoughtful and were looking far away, to some place Karal could not even begin to
imagine. His introspection was so deep, Karal wondered
if he was actually *communing* with something—or Someone—else.

After waiting a few moments for a reply, Karal took his
seat again, dropping heavily into his padded armchair with a
thud. Altra did not seem to notice.

Huh. This is different. He's never acted like this before. . . .

Then, suddenly, without any warning whatsoever, the Firecat leaped straight up into the air—

—and vanished into the patch of sunlight he had appeared out of.

"Oh, now *that's* an informative answer," Karal growled to the empty air in disgust. "Thanks a lot!"

Somewhere out there, Natoli and the others were collating energy patterns, An'desha was helping them analyze the patterns, and Master Levy and his mathematicians were plotting courses. He suspected that Firesong's warning about monsters being created in Hardorn had been taken to heart, and Kerowyn's folk were inventing monsters and ways to deal with them. Somewhere in this very Palace, others were getting actual work done. Somewhere out in Haven, or beyond, artificers were trying to find a way of getting people and supplies in and out of an area quickly, perhaps involving some of Natoli's beloved steam machines.

And I am sitting here waiting for yet another Grand Council meeting. He sighed glumly and then sat up a little straighter as he realized that the Shin'a'in envoy, who had just entered the room himself, was heading, not for his own seat, but straight for Karal.

Oh, glory. Now what? A challenge to personal combat?

He made himself smile, and rose in courtesy as Jarim reached him. "Greetings, sir." *Now what do I say? "I trust you realize we are still on the same side?" Or—"Are you still desirous of examining my liver at close range? I fear I cannot oblige you—"* He settled for a neutral and polite, "How can I serve you?"

"You can serve me, Envoy, by accepting an apology," the Shin'a'in said brusquely—and grudgingly. But at least he was saying it, which was an improvement. "I overreacted yesterday. My people are protective of their own."

And mine are not? Is that your implication? "I understand, sir," he replied smoothly. "Please, *you* must understand that I am trying to think of the best use of our admittedly limited resources. I am trying to suggest what is useful for the Alliance as a whole. Your people never encountered the armies of Ancar of Hardorn. My country and Valdemar are low on fighting men and the wherewithal to supply them; your people are mighty warriors, but they do not send folk off the Plains very often, and they would be at a bad disadvantage. The Hawkbrothers are no use as an offensive military force, and Rethwellan has sent all it can afford. I frankly would rather that the Imperials were slowly whittled away by magic-born monsters than that *any* fighter of the Alliance perish in ridding us of them. We must survive the mage-storms ourselves, after all, and—"

"Yes, yes, I see your point," Jarim interrupted. "But it should be obvious that we are going to have to eliminate these interlopers while we have the chance. They have a long history of conquest, and no border has ever stopped them before. It is pure folly to think that they will allow anything to stop them now, save such a fierce resistance that it is clear even to them that they have met their match in us! The only way to do that is to strike now, strike hard, and remove every trace of their forces from Hardorn. Then and only then will the Empire respect us enough to let us alone!"

He was getting wound up again, and nothing Karal had said had made any difference to him. His *words* said "we," but it was obvious to Karal that what he wanted was personal revenge on the Empire for daring to murder a Goddess-Sworn Shin'a'in.

By now most of the others had arrived, and all of the Grand Council were listening closely to this exchange, obviously waiting to see how he would answer.

But any answer other than the one that Jarim wanted—full agreement—was only going to start another argument. So instead of replying directly to Jarim's statement, he turned to Elspeth, who happened to be nearest to him.

"How long do the mages believe the breakwater will remain intact?" he asked earnestly. "Has anyone an estimate?" It was one question that no one had asked yet—but it was important, because an answer might make it clear that there was no time for personal vengeance—or, indeed, any revenge at all.

"Good question," the Princess replied, arching an eyebrow at Darkwind and Firesong, who edged closer at her signal. "Do either of you have an answer—or even a guess?"

"I would prefer to err conservatively," Firesong replied— earnestly, for once, rather than flippantly. He cast a glance at Karal that looked appreciative. "I would not trust it to hold for more than four months at the most. Through the winter—perhaps. Not much beyond."

"I would give it until summer, but that is certainly no more than six months away at best," Darkwind said, nodding. "Now, given that winter fighting is difficult at best and suicidal at worst, that means we will lose the breakwater before we have any chance at attacking the Imperials."

Karal noticed that Prince Daren was also giving him a look of both appraisement and approval. Evidently he had impressed the Prince-Consort. Jarim looked startled; his eyes widened with shock. "I thought that it would last longer than that," he objected. "You only just put it up!"

Firesong shrugged. "The breakwater loses a bit more of itself with every storm, and the storms are coming more and more frequently. There is a mathematical progression to them. We *told* you that. The erosion is accelerating. Pity, but we knew when we set it up that all we were doing was buying time, and we tried to make that as clear as possible to all of you."

Firesong can say that, and say it insolently, and get away with it. Jarim respects him; I think he might even be a little afraid of him. Today Firesong was wearing stark and unornamented black, a costume that accentuated both the gold of his Tayledras skin and the vivid silver-blue of his eyes— which only served to remind Jarim that the Hawkbrothers and the Shin'a'in were related—and the silver of his hair, the reminder of the power he wielded. Firesong was very good at choosing the best costume for the purpose. Today he was obviously in the mood for intimidation. It was a talent Karal wished he had.

Prince Daren stepped forward at that point, and took over

the discussion. "Ladies and gentlemen, would you all take your seats? Firesong, would you repeat what you have been saying to everyone? This is important, very important, and I want to make sure there are no misunderstandings."

Daren went to his own seat and sat down, effectively beginning the meeting.

There was some shuffling about as people found their accustomed chairs, and Firesong not only stood up, he stood in the hollow center of the table where the gryphon Treyvan was, with one hand on the gryphon's shoulder. The gryphon twitched an ear-tuft a bit.

"Some of you were part of our earlier Council when we first learned how we could, *temporarily*, protect the Alliance lands and Iftel from the battering we were taking from the mage-storms," he said gravely. "This we did, and as you are all aware, it was successful. But it was still a *temporary* solution. Like a shoreline breakwater from which this protection takes its name, it absorbs the force of the waves of the mage-storm, but at a cost to itself. It is eroded, a little more with every battering that it takes. It *will* come down, collapsing under the repeated battering that it is subject to. Just because you are not feeling the effects of the mage-storms, that does not mean they are not continuing to move in on us. Even if you, yourselves, do not feel the force of one of these storms against your body, somebody out there *will*. They bring pain and misery and destruction. They are still coming at us, and the frequency and force are increasing as time goes on. We can measure this force, and we are doing so. I estimate that the breakwater will collapse in about four months' time, Darkwind gives it a slightly longer six months. Once again, all that we did was to buy our Alliance time to concoct another solution—one that could involve magic, since our magic is no longer being disrupted by the storms. We told you this was temporary at the time we did it, and we meant it."

That was just about the longest speech Firesong had ever made, and his words were given added impetus when the gryphon nodded with every salient point.

"I have sssseen the effectsss frrrom the airrr, frrriends.

They leave the earrrth rrriven in placesss. We sshould be concentrating on the brrreakwaterrr'sss replacement," the gryphon added. "And, frrrankly, on what we can do if we cannot *find* a replacssement in time. If you thought thingsss werrre bad beforrre—"

He left the sentence unfinished, hanging in the air like the threat that it was.

Although Karal distinctly remembered that this point was made before anyone left Haven to set up the breakwater in the first place, the fact that it was not the permanent solution still seemed to come as a complete surprise to many of the officials and envoys, Jarim among them.

"Well, why didn't you put a permanent solution in place?" snapped the head of the dairy farmers.

Firesong leveled a look at the man that should have melted him where he stood. "Oh, and you wanted us to wait to *find* one?" he asked, then continued. "This phenomenon was as new to us as it was to you; completely unprecedented, and we still don't fully understand it. As I recall, the mage-storms created a few killer cows before we put a halt to them," he said icily. "*As* it happens, we did the best we could at the time, to save the rest of you from as many of the effects as we could while we tried to put together something better. Would you rather we had let the storms rage across the landscape, turning more cattle into monsters?"

Perhaps the man had seen one of those "killer cows," for he paled and looked shamefaced. "Well, no—but—"

Someone else interrupted with another shouted accusation, which Firesong met with equally devastating wit and logic. Accusations and counteraccusations flew for a moment, until it was finally driven home to even the most hardheaded at the table that the mages and artificers had not somehow "cheated" them—that they had done what they could at the time. "Like a barricade of sandbags holding back floodwaters," was Elspeth's analogy.

The uproar settled into silence, and it was Jarim who was bold enough to break it.

"Well, if this is only temporary, then what *are* we going to do?" he asked testily. "Have you people made any progress at all?"

What does he want us to say? They've already told him everything they know!

Darkwind sighed, and Elspeth patted his shoulder. "Well, candidly, not much," he said wearily. "We don't have enough facts yet—"

"Why not?" Jarim interrupted. "Why haven't you made any progress?"

"We have made *plenty* of progress! It is only magic we use, were you expecting miracles?" Firesong shot back testily. "If you want miracles, speak directly to a God. Or a Goddess." That last was a shrewd hit on Firesong's part, since Jarim, unlike Querna, was *not* Sworn to the Star-Eyed. He could pretend to no special communication with his deity, no more than any other Shin'a'in had.

Karal closed his eyes and just let the words wash over him, as Darkwind and Elspeth tried to put into nonmagical terms the things that they *had* learned, and Firesong added acidic rejoinders whenever someone questioned their progress. He was not a mage, and very little of what they said made sense to him. He could ask An'desha later, when he needed to write up a summation for Solaris.

Solaris. What was she doing, back home in Karse? Was she holding onto her leadership with the same firmness as before? *Surely Vkandis Sunlord will keep Karse safe, no matter what,* he told himself, and felt a twinge of guilt for such an unworthy thought. He was supposed to be thinking on a wider stage than just Karse; it was the welfare of the Alliance that was as important as Karse's welfare.

But Karse was where his interests lay, and it was Karse's interests he was representing. So was it so bad that he took comfort in the fact that Vkandis held His hand over His chosen land?

As a priest, he *must* believe that, anyway. To doubt was to doubt the word and the promises of Vkandis. . . .

Except that He has said in His Writ that we must rely on the intelligence and wit that He gave us, that He protects us only in extremis. What if there is a solution here and we

*simply fail to reach it because we do not try hard enough?
Would He still protect us then?*

He felt his face grow cold and pale.

The uncertainty of it all was terrifying.

Oh, glory—what was happening to him? Now was he beginning to doubt even his own God?

What could *he* do, anyway? He was no mage; he knew next to nothing about magic *or* mathematics. He could only place his trust in others, in the hands and minds of those who did understand all of this. Elspeth and Darkwind, the gryphons, Firesong and An'desha, the mages of Rethwellan recruited by Kerowyn, the fledgling Herald-Mages of Valdemar trained by all of the others, the Priest-Mages of Karse; these were the folk that needed the help and guidance of Vkandis in their endeavor—and any other deity who happened to be interested. Perhaps the best thing he could do now was to pray. At least he understood how to do *that.*

Right now, he was just very, very tired . . . and very homesick. *I would much rather be the secretary to* anyone, *even one of those rigid old sticks who disliked Ulrich and Solaris, than be the envoy myself. It's not that I don't want the responsibility—it's that I can't get the authority to take care of the responsibility.*

So today, rather than try to make anyone listen to him, he just took notes whenever he caught something he understood. *If I have a point I want raised, I'll write it down and give it to Elspeth or Darkwind later,* he decided. *That's still doing my duty by the Alliance as a whole, even if it isn't accomplishing anything for Karse.*

Right now, that was the only solution *he* could think of.

Three

An'desha dropped another pebble into the water-table, and watched the resulting waves break up and disperse on the model. The elegant concentric rings quickly turned into a chaos of wavelets and counterwavelets amid the barriers placed there, and he shook his head in despair. He'd been told about this, but he hadn't believed it until this moment. "This is too complicated even to see, much less measure and analyze," he said bitterly. "And this is only a *model*. The reality is a hundred times worse!"

Master Levy gave him a sidelong, sardonic glance of approval. "For an unlettered barbarian who believes in curses and spellcasting, you show a surprising grasp of logic," he said dryly. "And a remarkable understanding of the difficulties of measurement and analysis in a moving system."

An'desha was not about to be goaded. "For a hard-headed statue who only believes in what he can see, weigh, and measure, you show a surprisingly flexibility," he countered. "And besides, you know very well that I read, speak, and write more languages than you, so although I am a barbarian, I am hardly unlettered. Now, shall we dispense with the insulting small talk and get on with this?"

But Master Levy only sighed with frustration. "At the moment," he admitted, "small talk is all I have to offer. I am venting my frustration in sarcasm. You are correct, the reality *is* too complex to calculate. I haven't been able to derive any kind of formula, and if I cannot, I doubt that anyone else would be able to."

Unconscious or conscious arrogance that last might be; nevertheless, Master Levy was right.

"There must be a predictable mathematical progression in there somewhere," An'desha muttered, staring at the table and the last of the fading ripples. "The result is geometric, so there *must* be a way to derive the formula."

"I thought you mages were all certain that magic was entirely intuitive," Master Levy said with amusement. "I confess that I was hoping by bringing you here and showing you the demonstration you might be able to intuit the formula. As one of our youngsters pointed out, intuition *is* a valuable tool, since it merely consists of being able to put together facts so quickly that the progression from premise to conclusion is no longer obvious."

"Firesong is the only one of us with that particular affliction," An'desha replied absently. "The rest of us are rather fond of logic. Though it is beginning to look as if his way of doing things may be the only answer right now."

In truth, the reason he was here instead of at the *ekele* was that Firesong had not been able to "intuit" an answer either, and was rather short-tempered as a result. Things were already strained between them as it was, and on the whole, An'desha thought that his absence would be more valuable than his presence. Let Firesong rave at the plants in his frustration.

Ever since he and Karal had returned from their journey to the Iftel/Valdemar border, there had been stress in his relationship with Firesong. It was not, as he had first feared, that Firesong was jealous of Karal—or at least, he did not consider Karal to be a romantic rival. Which was just as well; it was rather difficult to prove such a nebulous negative as "Karal is my best friend, but I am not in the least attracted to him." If Firesong couldn't figure *that* out, he was less observant and less intelligent than An'desha had given him credit for.

It had taken An'desha this long to divine precisely what the problem really was between them, and it turned out to be something rather disconcerting. Something he knew *he* wasn't going to be able to remedy, in fact.

Firesong did not seem to know how to deal with the

"new" An'desha, an An'desha who was growing less dependent upon him with every passing day.

An'desha gazed down into the water-table as if the answer to his problem with Firesong lay there, as well as the answer to the question of what to do when the breakwater failed.

He doesn't seem to understand that just because he saved my life, and helped me when I was so confused that I didn't know how to cope with the smallest details, that doesn't make us automatically lifebonded. It doesn't even make us automatically best friends. I love him, and I owe him a great deal—but I do not owe him my total devotion for the rest of my life. No one "owes" that to anyone.

They had become lovers out of mutual attraction and An'desha's helpless dependence on someone, anyone, who might give him the support and security he desperately craved. And to his credit, Firesong had been very well aware that such dependence was unhealthy and infantile; he had done his best to wean An'desha away from that clutching dependence and to help him grow a real spine of his own.

But was that because he wanted me to be independent, or because I was strangling him? Hmm. Good question. Only Firesong knows the answer. Certainly being strangled is hardly comfortable, but he did wean me away as gently as possible, rather than simply shoving me away. But was that because he liked me dependent, but not too dependent? Another good question.

Now—well, the old proverb said, "Be careful what you ask for, because you might get it." Firesong had gotten an An'desha who knew who and what he was, and what he wanted to do with his life—and now Firesong was the one who was unhappy.

He wasn't exactly picking fights, but whenever An'desha said or did something Firesong didn't expect, he was visibly taken aback. Startled, even shocked, as if An'desha had turned into someone he didn't recognize. And when An'desha actually had a difference of opinion from him, Firesong would flash into a quiet and unobtrusive rage.

It never lasted more than a bare instant, and he never actually said or did anything except try to persuade An'desha that he was wrong—but that instant of rage was there. It was naked in his eyes and in the way he first flushed, then paled, then clenched his jaw hard and would not speak until the moment was over.

Firesong's solution, which An'desha had decided to emulate, was to avoid such situations by avoiding An'desha except at meals and at night.

At night, at least, they were still compatible, and it was a good tension reliever for both of them. But for how long would that last?

He shook himself out of his reverie; Master Levy was staring at him with curiosity, as if wondering what it was An'desha saw in the water-table. "Well, I'm not getting anything done here. Perhaps I ought to go take a walk and get some fresh air. Maybe I *will* intuit something that will help."

"I will go back to my angles and instruments, and see if I can't make something out of the result," Master Levy replied, but he sounded discouraged. "One of our problems is that the waves are coming from outside, yet our models rely upon waves generated from the center outward. We can extrapolate the results by formulas based on that, but it is still not an accurate enough representation."

On the whole, An'desha didn't blame him for being discouraged. What they needed was a new way of looking at this situation, a new approach. That was how they had come up with the breakwater, after all, a new approach—a mathematically-derived analysis of magical energies.

"Say . . . how about this," An'desha said quietly. "A hoop that can be dropped into the water model to create a circular wave from the outer edge inward?"

Master Levy examined his hands and reflexively cleaned under his fingernails for the twentieth time this conversation. "Mmm," he murmured finally. "That could help. I will put a student-artificer on the idea immediately. There are problems with the shortness of sampling time from the wave strike to edge reflection, but perhaps a large enough hoop could be made. . . ."

Master Levy went on in the same vein for a while. They could come up with ideas, small ones that added up, but they never felt like a master solution. Now they needed another source of inspiration. The trouble was, they had run out of new cultural influences to provide such a source of new thinking.

We need a god to help us out this time. Unfortunately, since it is not likely that we will all be wiped off the face of the world when the breakwater fails, I doubt that She is going to be inclined to help us.

He shrugged and picked up his quilted Shin'a'in riding coat, pulled it on, and buttoned it up to his chin. He left the Palace workroom in a state of absorbed introspection, but he was not thinking about the mage-storms as he walked through the dead and deserted Palace gardens.

Odd. Not that long ago I would have been worried sick if Firesong had begun avoiding me. I would have been certain he was getting tired of me and was looking for someone else to replace me. I would have been in a panic at the thought of being alone. Now—

Now it simply didn't bother him, in part because such avoidance also avoided confrontations between them.

And frankly, it wouldn't matter to me if he did find a new lover.

That surprising realization stopped him, right in the middle of the path. He repeated it to himself, and it felt logical—right.

It would not matter to me if Firesong found a new lover. In fact, it would be something of a relief. I would stop feeling obligated to please him for fear of hurtful response. A feeling like that has no place in a love affair.

Yet there was no one else *he* was even remotely attracted to! So what was prompting this sentiment?

Do I want to be—alone?

That felt right, too. Oh, he didn't want to be alone forever, but a third realization came to him, on the heels of the other two.

I'm starting to find things out about myself—not just all the things in the memories of Falconsbane-that-was, but things about me. I need time to think about them. And it has to be time alone.

Poor Firesong. *He must be sensing that I want to be alone, and he's thinking it means that I don't want* him *around.*

An'desha shook his head and started walking again, with his head down and his hands in his pockets. If only Firesong *would* find someone else, it would make things a great deal easier on everyone.

But the chances of that happening are not very good. There aren't a lot of she'chorne *around for him to choose from, and most of them are involved with each other. And the others—* He grimaced. *I'll be charitable and say that the others are understandably warped by unfortunate early experiences. But that doesn't make them pleasant or healthy to be involved with.*

She'chorne. When was the last time he'd heard, or even *thought* that word? *Back with the Clan, before Falconsbane—I hadn't been making any attempts to court any girls in the Clan, so Grandmother started asking if I would at least consider courting one of the* she'chorne *boys.* Such an alliance, though it obviously would not be possible to produce children of the blood, was still considered honorable. More than that, such couples could pursue the adoption of orphans from within the Clan. In fact, many Shin'a'in Clans encouraged such alliances so that there *would* be couples available to adopt parentless children. By Shin'a'in standards, a *she'chorne* couple, with no children of their own to support, always had the resources to support someone else, thus removing the burden from those with their own children to feed.

But that wasn't what I wanted either, and she started in on how I was as shiftless and rootless as my father. . . .

There wasn't much to examine in his relatively short "real" lifetime, but he'd been going over his memories, trying to find hints of what he was in what he had been. He'd also been examining the less-disgusting memories left to him by Falconsbane and all his previous incarnations, trying to find a common denominator.

There has to be more than one reason why Falconsbane grabbed me to settle into. By now, there must be a lot of Ma'ar's blood-children around, and at least a fair share of them should be mages. For that matter, given the way that Falconsbane and the rest used to ride out on little loot-and-rape expeditions just for amusement, there ought to be plenty of appropriate candidates out there. Somehow I have the feeling that there must be many common threads in my life and all of his . . . if only I can untangle them.

He'd already found one. Every single one of those previous lives had involved a person who, before Falconsbane moved in and took over, was someone who was despised or even abused by his natural family. Many of them had run away, seeking new lives elsewhere, actually seeking the implied power that came with being a mage so that they could return home and have revenge of one sort or another. That was why most of them had tried the fire-calling spell when they were alone; most of them had not yet found a teacher, yet had felt the stirrings of the power within them, and had decided to try it "just once."

I wonder if having a teacher would have prevented Falconsbane from moving in? I wonder if the presence of the teacher would have prevented him from even trying?

Possibly; Ma'ar, the original of all the incarnations, had been one of the craftiest wizards of all time. Surely he would have hedged in his search for a new body with all kinds of conditions.

But what of that common thread of abuse, neglect, and derision? What if being despised and ignored was also a prerequisite to possession? *When I ran away from the Clan, I wasn't sure what I was looking for—except a place to belong and a way to escape being forced into the life of a shaman. But I seem to remember that most, if not all of the others were actively looking for power when they ran. Some wanted real, bloody revenge, some just wanted to "show them all," with "them" being the people who had offered scorn and mockery.*

Now, wasn't *that* an interesting thought? Had that condition actually caused them to somehow welcome Falconsbane, at least somewhere deep inside?

Being possessed, giving up your own responsibility for the sake of revenge—that's beginning to make too much sense.

He stopped for a moment, and probed deeply into some of the earliest memories of possession. *Oh . . . this is interesting. The first time, Ma'ar didn't just rush in and take over,* he seduced! *He offered instant Adepthood, no tedious apprenticeship. My, my. It was only much, much later that he became impatient and careless, and just took over in a rush.*

That initial welcome would have been all he needed to get himself well established; in the time it took them to realize what it was they had welcomed, he'd be entrenched. By then, of course, it was too late; Falconsbane would not tolerate a second soul, a second personality in "his" new body. By the time any of them thought to rebel, Falconsbane eradicated them and reigned supreme.

But I didn't want him, and I didn't particularly want power. All I wanted was—people. Someone who wouldn't despise me, who would welcome me and give me a chance to prove myself. Was that the difference that made it possible for me to survive?

It might have been. It was just such a tiny wedge that had made the difference in the past.

There were other reasons for his survival; he had "run," hiding in his own mind, while Falconsbane settled in, rather than trying to resist the intruder. Once in hiding, he had made no effort to try and force out the Dark Adept.

A chill wind whipped through his hair, and he shoved his hands deeper into his pockets, hunching his shoulders against the cold. These gardens were good places to be alone, once bad weather had set in. Once the last of the wintering preparations had been made, not even the gardeners ventured out here.

It's odd, but a great deal of what Falconsbane and all his other "selves" did were the darker applications of things that could *have been very admirable. It's as if they couldn't create, they could only warp, twist, and mutilate.*

That was especially true in the way that Falconsbane had

manipulated people's minds and hearts, including that of his own daughter Nyara. Falconsbane was capable of inspiring true devotion from his servants, as well as devotion inspired only by fear. In fact, if An'desha went all the way back to the source of the memories, the Adept called Ma'ar, he found that Ma'ar seldom, if ever, needed to command by fear. He could, and did, manage to convince his followers that he was everything they wanted him to be, and that he truly cared for their welfare. If Ma'ar's memories were to be trusted, he had underlings who would gladly have flung themselves in front of an assassin's blade for him out of pure worship.

Compared with that, Falconsbane's sick and twisted love-hate-need relationship with his daughter Nyara was without sophistication, even crude.

I am glad that she and Skif were sent to be the envoys to the k'Leshya. Skif was growing restless with nothing to contribute, and she was not comfortable here. Neither was Need. I think she was afraid that one day Kerowyn would decide to make good on her threat to drop the sword down a well. He smiled to himself; there could not be two such supremely self-assured—not to say "arrogant"—females in the same physical location as Kerowyn and the sword called Need, without conflicts arising. It was just as well that Skif, Nyara, and Need were gone. The k'Leshya could use Skif's knowledge, and the sword knew magics even older than their own. And Nyara, of course, would be much more comfortable in a place where she was by no means the oddest looking person in the Vale.

What Falconsbane had done to her and with her just on an emotional basis was sick and demented by any normal standards. But just as intimate knowledge of the way that the body worked could be used to heal, as well as to kill and torture, could not Falconsbane's ability to manipulate minds and emotions be used for some other, benign purpose?

In some ways, wasn't that precisely what Ulrich and Karal had been doing to help *him?*

He chewed his lip thoughtfully. Did that make Falconsbane something like—like an evil priest?

Certainly on one level. A good priest is supposed to coun-

sel and guide his followers to their betterment, and Falcons-bane used similar tools of persuasion.

Bells at the Collegium rang, signaling the beginning of the dinner hour. That meant that both the Palace and Collegium libraries would be empty, and both libraries had comfortable reading areas with fireplaces—certainly much better places for continuing these introspections than the gardens, at this point! It wouldn't be long until dark, the gray light was fading into thick, gray-blue dusk, and the wind was getting colder with every passing moment. His nose and ears were getting numb, and the wind somehow managed to find every seam in his coat to blow through!

He turned his steps back toward the Palace, nodding at the guard at the garden door as he passed. One advantage of being who and what he was—he was instantly recognizable. Most guards let him by without a challenge, the way they let the Hawkbrothers and the gryphons pass.

The Palace library seemed the best choice; the reading area was smaller, and most of the people who used it were court functionaries. This was not a library filled with books of poetry, clever histories, and tales. The books here were dull chronicles for the most part, with a leavening of books on language, law, and custom. *Meaty and informative, but as hard to digest as a stone and about as entertaining.* It was tucked away between the room used for Valdemaran Council sessions and the office of the Seneschal, sharing a fireplace wall with the latter.

Only one or two lamps had been lit, but there was a bright fire going in the fireplace—and as An'desha had hoped, there was no one in the reading area. He chose a comfortably padded chair, draped his coat over the back, and sprawled sideways with one leg over an arm of the chair, staring into the fire.

So if Ma'ar and all his other "selves" were able to control and persuade people—would it be wrong to use that same power to help people? To get them to compromise with each other, for instance—would that be wrong? I wish I had some help with this . . . I have a feeling I'm getting out of my depth. The trouble was that he was too close to those memories; seeing such abilities and powers in action made it very tempting to assume that such things *could* be used for good purposes.

Someone once told me that even the deadliest of poisons could be used to heal—with expertise and great care, in the minutest of doses. How tiny a dose of "persuasion" was moral? He didn't know where the line should be drawn between "trying to help people," and "manipulating people."

Firesong would be no help at all, even though he was a Healing Adept. *His* powers were all concerned with the world of the material, not the world of the soul, heart, and spirit. He tended to get very impatient when An'desha strayed into the realms of what he considered to be "mystical." For all of his insistence on the intuitive nature of magic, he was bound up in the practical and had little use for mysticism.

I'd like to ask Karal, but he's already carrying so many burdens, I'm afraid to add one more to his load. It might be the one that breaks his back—or his spirit. Poor Karal! He was carrying far too much responsibility on those slim shoulders.

Perhaps that sweet lady, Talia? But—no, really, what he wanted wasn't *comfort*, it was a place to start figuring out ethical solutions.

This was the one place where his old nemesis, the shaman of his Clan, might have been useful. *The old man was as rigid as dried rawhide, but he was enough in tune with the Star-Eyed that he never gave anyone bad spiritual advice that I ever heard of. And he knew his ethics. . . .* The new Shin'a'in envoy was not a shaman; he was temporary, the brother of his Clan Chief, and An'desha really didn't like him any more than Karal did. If only Querna were still alive! He wouldn't have hesitated a moment in asking *her* help.

If only I had someone, anyone, to talk to! No, not "anyone." A shaman, a priest. But I don't know which priests here to trust except Karal; I'd rather talk to someone who comes from the same background as me. How ironic! I got myself into trouble by running away from the shaman, and now I would give anything to be able to talk to one.

The fire gave a sudden flare, and he jumped as a deep, purely mental chuckle washed warmth through his mind.

:You had only to ask, little brother,: said a mind-voice he had thought never to hear again, as the Avatar of the Star-Eyed that he knew as Tre'valen appeared in the fire before him. The last time he had seen the Avatar had been when he was in Hardorn, and Falconsbane had control of his body. Although he was told that the Avatars appeared in Valdemar when they transformed him and Nyara from their feline Changechild forms to something more human, that was one appearance *he* did not remember. Mercifully, perhaps; the transformation had not been without a great deal of physical pain. Flesh was torn loose from its Adept-shaped form and resculpted, even the hairs of his body were altered in one massive rush of magical power. A gift from the Star-Eyed for his bravery, but no changes were without pain.

As Tre'valen had often before—though *never* in Valdemar—the Avatar took the form of a hearth-bound vorcel-hawk that fanned and mantled its wings of fire amid the flames dancing in the fireplace. *:I am pleased that you have come this far, although the state of your heart is bringing you no peace at the moment. We have missed talking with you. I believe, little brother, that we can help you.:*

Firesong paced the floor of the sitting room of the *ekele,* looking out from time to time at the bare, wind-tossed branches of the trees outside the window. His high-cheekboned face bent with a frown. An'desha had gone off on his own—again. The young Shin'a'in was spending less and less time in the *ekele,* a complete reversal of the times when Firesong had been unable to get him to go beyond the doors of the indoor garden on the ground floor.

He's changed. He's still changing. Neither of those thoughts sat particularly well with him. He didn't particularly like the direction of those changes, and he definitely did not know how to cope with them.

It had been so pleasant when An'desha was uncertain of himself, when he looked only to Firesong for answers and reassurance in a strange and frightening world. It had given

Firesong such a delightful feeling to be *needed* so desperately. . . . No one had ever needed him like that before, although plenty of people had wanted him. That very dependence had been quite attractive.

On the down side, he had to admit it had occasionally been an annoying and even constrictive relationship, for he could not even joke and flirt with Darkwind without sending An'desha into hysterics.

But most of the time it had been very, very sweet.

His conscience said it had been more than just "sweet." *Admit it. It gave you a great deal of pleasure to have that kind of power over someone. An'desha would willingly have been your slave, if you'd asked it of him.* He winced a little; his conscience was altogether too accurate.

In those days it had been as if An'desha was barely afloat after a shipwreck and did not know how to swim, and absolutely depended on Firesong to get him to safety.

The room was exactly twelve long paces wide; ten, to avoid running into walls. *I was very content with that; with An'desha being passive, and putting all responsibility for his life into my hands.*

Well, not *all* responsibility. Even then, An'desha had shown flashes of stubborn will, even though the application of that will was hardly productive. Firesong's own conscience and memory reminded him of that, too.

Enough pacing! Firesong flung himself sullenly onto a couch and lay there with his hair and one leg trailing over the side, staring up at the ceiling. It was getting dark, but he did not bother to light any of the lamps, although he could have done so with a thought. His firebird looked at him curiously from his superior elevation on his perch, but when Firesong didn't show any interest in scratching him, the bondbird yawned and went back to preening himself. False sparks sparkled along the snow-white firebird's feathers whenever Aya roused all his feathers and shook them, and in repose, in this uncertain half-light, the quills of each feather glowed softly. Aya seemingly hovered in the air, his perch invisible in the near-dark, a glowing ghost of feathered light.

Firesong had lost patience with An'desha many times over

when the young man had refused to delve into the memories of past existences that Mornelithe Falconsbane had left behind. Even though it was obvious that crucial knowledge of the past lay there, he *still* had refused, out of the fear that such probing would somehow reawaken the dark Adept. This was one place where Firesong had failed him; it had been Master Ulrich and Karal that had convinced him that there was no danger of his becoming another Falconsbane, much to Firesong's hidden annoyance.

On the other hand, being no priest, I had no personal experience of possession, so I had no way to convince him that I knew what I was talking about. Perhaps that was when the separation started. It was certainly one more victory to Karal.

And there is the belief, as almost all people have, that keeping a memory of someone alive keeps that person *alive. So how could An'desha not believe that speaking of Falconsbane would keep the evil Adept's soul alive? Even when I reassured him repeatedly that I had shredded Mornelithe Falconsbane in my own spirit-talons? Yet another failure.*

Oh, but there were more. Firesong had also failed to convince An'desha to learn to *use* those magical powers he'd been born with, and the expertise in them that Falconsbane's tenure in his body had granted him. Now *that* had been not just annoying, but it was *damned* frightening. As long as An'desha had refused to use and practice those powers, they were dangerous—because where will failed, instinct might take over.

I could not convince him that ignoring his power was more dangerous than learning to control it. In many ways, Falconsbane had no control; he acted on impulse more often than he planned things. I tried to show him that such impulsive actions were second nature to him, and that unless he learned to control his power, it would control him.

It had been Karal who had devised a plan to show An'desha that he had the self-control to use his magic without abusing it—by provoking him to the point where, if he had *not* had self-control, he would have flattened the young priest.

I have to give him this much; that was sheer, unadulterated bravery on his part. I'm not certain that I would have trusted An'desha's will and ability to control himself in that situation, and I live with him. Or used to, anyway.

Not that Firesong hadn't tried other means of convincing An'desha, but the young man could not be convinced by his lover. The trouble was, Karal could convince him, because Karal's ploys had all worked.

Damn him.

Now An'desha, emboldened by his success and encouraged by Karal-damn-him, was looking for answers from someone other than Firesong. Suddenly he was no longer content with the guidance and advice he got from his lover. He was striking out in directions—often directions of a mystical bent—that Firesong didn't like and didn't want to take for himself.

It would be my luck that he'd find a priest to be his best friend. Priests make people so—deep.

Karal was not An'desha's lover; he wasn't An'desha's type in the first place, and in the second, as far as Firesong could tell—and his instincts there were seldom wrong where the extremes of sexual preference went—Karal was at the opposite end of the spectrum from *shay'a'chern.* Perhaps that actually gave him an advantage over Firesong; An'desha knew that he had no ancillary motives for his advice.

Once again, Firesong's conscience pointed out that Firesong almost *always* had ulterior motives behind anything he tried to get An'desha to think or do. Of course, he had An'desha's best interests at heart. They just happened to coincide with his own best interests.

I can convince myself of that quite prettily. I wonder if I could convince anyone else.

He ground his teeth in frustration and stared at a lamp hanging from the ceiling. At this point it was just a dark round shadow against the lighter ceiling. Soon he would have to light the lamps, if he didn't want to have to stumble around in the dark.

So what am I supposed to do now? Am I doomed to lose

him? Can't he see how I feel about him? It's not as if I haven't obviously been courting him. At least, I think I've been obviously *courting him.* It was a frustrating position to be in, since he'd never *had* to court anyone's attentions before; he'd always been on the other end of the courting, and others had always labored to catch and hold *his* attention.

Now, here he was, with the situation reversed. He was turning himself inside out trying to catch and hold An'desha's interest, and it wasn't working. *Now I know how it must have felt to Rainbird when I was oblivious to his overtures. The problem is, just what am I going to do about it? How am I going to get him back?*

He knew one thing that he was very good at that might work. Besides magic, of course. *I could certainly launch a seduction that would completely overwhelm him; I'd have him so swamped with sensuality that he wouldn't have the energy to even* think *about anything or anyone else.*

It would be a very successful seduction, too—for a while.

Unfortunately, I know precisely how long that particular tactic can work from personal experience, he thought glumly. *The "spell" of seduction only lasts as long as the seducer has energy. And the seducer is going to run out of energy before the seduced does.*

Besides, An'desha wasn't stupid, nor was his nature centered on sex or sensuality. The trouble, as far as Firesong's ambitions went, was that An'desha's mind was awake now and growing. It wasn't going to just "go to sleep" again, and a mind like An'desha's needed more than an overwhelming of the senses to occupy it for very long.

That led to another temptation entirely. Firesong was not—quite—a Mind-Healer, but he had many of the same skills, and one of his minor Gifts was that of Empathy. He knew enough that he could, if he chose, tamper with that too-awake mind and put it to sleep again, or paralyze it. *Oh, it would be* so *easy to take what I know and begin manipulating him. I know all of his weaknesses, all of his fears, everything that make him twitch, everything that makes him feel good about himself.* Yes, it would be so easy to twist An'desha around—

It was so tempting—but—

His stomach twisted, and he grimaced. *Oh, that's no answer either. It's wrong, and I know it. Father would have a cat, and Mother—I know what she'd have to say if she knew I'd even* thought *about doing something like that to another* person. He shuddered; he had faced monsters, mage-storms and Mornelithe Falconsbane, and none of them had frightened him as much as the prospect of facing his mother with a guilty conscience.

He grimaced again, this time at his own foolishness. *I don't care what anyone else thinks about me, but may the gods help me if Mother found* that *out.*

And besides his mother—oh, gods. *What if my dear ancestor Vanyel got wind of this?* He shuddered again; he definitely did *not* want to have to deal with that. Although, given the two of them, he'd rather be forced to deal with an angry ghost than his mother in a state of righteous wrath.

He sighed, and threw his arm over his eyes, feeling as if it wouldn't be such a bad thing to be a Falconsbane and not have to worry about angry mothers or guilty consciences.

That's why their way is easier, I suppose. Well, I've got a conscience and I'm stuck with it. He couldn't use his mind and his magic on An'desha to make him pliable again. Besides being wrong, it would be stupid. No matter what he did, if he played with An'desha's mind, what he would have when he had finished wouldn't really be "An'desha" anymore. So what would be the point to all the work? If he wanted someone to be his toy, he could pick someone at random, a stable-boy or page, anyone. That wouldn't be right either, and it *still* wouldn't be An'desha.

He swallowed with difficulty. *So where does all this leave me? The odd man out, with An'desha spending more and more time away from me. And I'll have to smile and pretend everything is fine.*

It looked as if he was going to have a great deal of uncomfortable time to fill as An'desha drifted farther and farther from him. But what else could he do? The single course that was open to him was confrontation, and *that* would only drive An'desha away faster.

He was not prone to depression, but now he tried to swallow a hard and uncomfortable lump of despair that seemed to have gotten lodged in his throat. *I thought I had finally found someone I could spend the rest of my life with, and once again it comes to nothing.* He felt so loaded down with melancholy he might never be able to rise again. No one understood. They looked at him, saw how handsome he was, how Gifted a mage he was, how intelligent he was, and thought that everything always fell into his hands. They didn't know, they couldn't guess, how hard it was for him to make and keep friends, much less lovers—never dreamed just how lonely he was. It was easy to find people who would fill his bed; impossible to find anyone who would fill his heart. Temporary lovers were easy to come by, but reliability was rarer fare.

I suppose the best thing I can do is to work, he thought dully. *If I keep* my *mind occupied, my heart generally leaves me alone.* That always worked in the past, and the gods knew that they had enough troubles now, trying to come up with the next solution after the breakwater.

I should go make myself available to Darkwind, Elspeth, and the Valdemaran artificers. That was what he *should* do, all right; it was the logical direction. But that was what An'desha was doing, which would only serve to put him in An'desha's company. An'desha might like the artificers, but they made Firesong think of bees or ants—logical, well-coordinated, but without souls. Their "magic" was a thing of gears and clockwork, regular and completely artificial.

Besides, Darkwind and Elspeth are much, much better than I am at this new approach to magic. It obviously doesn't feel artificial to them.

No. *No, I cannot learn to like these artificers. I cannot learn to think the way they do, or to admire the way they think.* Their odd, mechanical approach to what he still felt, deep down inside, was a process that was part instinct, part art, and part improvisation, robbed magic of all the beauty and the thrill he had found in it when he first began to make use of his Gift. Without beauty, what was the point anyway?

They've taken poetry and reduced it to a mathematical

formula, that's what they've done. But knowing the formula doesn't mean you can produce poetry; it only means you can produce well-crafted doggerel.

The more he thought about it, the more he rebelled, soul and heart. He had *tried* to work with them before, and in the end, neither he nor they had been comfortable.

They keep trying to find ways to measure things that should be felt, not measured. You can't take a ruler to a love affair, you can't hold up a gauge to weigh sorrow, and you shouldn't try to find a way to measure magic!

Melancholy had weighed him down a moment before; now irritation drove him to his feet again. He pushed himself up off the couch with a muttered curse, and flung his power around the room recklessly, lighting the wicks of every lamp within the walls with an ostentatious flare. Aya started, uttered an unmusical squawk of annoyance, and settled down on his perch with all of his feathers fluffed, glaring at his bondmate through a slitted blue eye.

Firesong ignored him, although he sensed Aya's own irritation in the bondbird's mental mutterings. Well, that was as much a reflection of his own unsettled emotional state as Aya's peevishness. When his emotional state was negative, so was the firebird's.

Maybe he'd better get out of Aya's way for a while, before their mutual irritation started to get out of hand.

A hot soak, perhaps. If nothing else, soaking in the hot pool in the garden below would unknot some of his tension-knotted muscles. If he *didn't* get them relaxed, he'd have a headache before morning.

Abruptly he turned and took the spiral staircase down to the ground floor of the *ekele.* Here, frosted glass lamps like little moons placed among the foliage displayed the wonders of a Hawkbrother Vale in miniature. Luxuriant plants spread their leaves in every part of the room, which had floor-to-ceiling windows comprising all four sides. Firesong had landscaped with rocks and plants until it was impossible to tell—particularly at night—that this was a little corner of Companion's Field in Valdemar, and not a private corner of a real Vale. Finally, after much forced growth, vines covered the uprights between the windows, the trees and bushes hid the glazing, and a canopy of leaves concealed the ceiling. As he had leisure, he added tiny spots to the ceiling that absorbed sunlight by day and emitted it at night, mimicking stars.

The centerpiece of the room was the soaking-pool, fed by a hot spring brought up from deep beneath Haven by Firesong's power—the heat source was partly natural, partly magical, and shielded as well as the Heartstone under the Palace. With all of the strange effects of the mage-storms about, the last thing Firesong wanted was to discover his spring gone either boiling-hot or cold as ice.

He stripped off his clothing as he walked, leaving a trail of discarded garments until he reached the side of the pool and dropped into it. It was too bad that there were no *hertasi* here; he would have to pick up after himself. But just at the moment, he didn't feel like being careful.

According to legend, it was Urtho, the Mage of Silence, who had first discovered the way to create these pools.

Hah. According to legend, Urtho is also responsible for first discovering the wheel, taming the horse, and cooking meat. Firesong sank up to his chin in the hot water, cynically reflecting on the many legends surrounding the last of the Great Mages. Obscure legends even claimed that Urtho had achieved much of his power by inventing ways to measure magic and to use it efficiently!

As if Urtho were some sort of Mage of Artifice! I don't think so. Urtho has become whatever the speaker wants him to be at the time.

That was the argument the gryphons had last used on him—that if Urtho had used ways to measure and ration magic, couldn't Firesong?

Of course, if anyone would know whether or not the claim was true, it would probably be the gryphons and the Kaled'a'in. They alone held actual records of the Mage-Wars and the time immediately preceding the Cataclysm. The people who had become the Shin'a'in and Tayledras had both escaped without any such things. Clan k'Leshya, the Clan that had welcomed outsiders, that had supported and cared for the gryphons, that had held both Urtho's trusted chief of wizardry and his chief *kestra'chern,* had been entrusted with the care of all of Urtho's records during the escape to safety.

Well, so what if he was *a superior Artificer Adept? Why should I change my ways of working—ways that have served me very well until now!—just to emulate someone dead millennia ago? For that matter, didn't* my *way of working take down his ancient enemy when he failed to do so?* He smiled into the steam, for the first time today feeling both smug and superior. *So, there's a great deal to be said for intuition and creativity! I'll wager none of these artificers could have figured a way to safely shut down k'Sheyna's rogue Heartstone either!*

Let Elspeth and Darkwind hare off after this "new thinking." Let even An'desha take to it with a speed that left Firesong gaping at him. Time would show which was the better way. *The ways of a so-called "golden" ancient time may not necessarily be better than the ways we have developed since. "Golden Ages" are often nothing more than fool's gold, or merest gilding over dross.*

He closed his eyes and leaned back against the sculpted stone of his seat. His shoulder and neck muscles were finally relaxing in the heat, and something else occurred to him. The one thing that *did* impress An'desha now was skill and competence. That was why Karal and the Master Artificers were currently high in his esteem. Karal had evidently proved his mettle at the border, and the Master Artificers had convinced the Shin'a'in that there was a cold beauty—and certainly there was logic—in their formulae and numbers.

But if Firesong could come up with an answer that superseded the breakwater, wouldn't *he* get An'desha's attention back?

Of course I would! He knows the ways that Falconsbane and all the rest worked, but he has never *had formal Tayledras training in magic, except for the little he's gotten from me so far! And if I can prove that my way is the better way, he'll be panting at my heels to learn from me again! I'll have his fullest attention and his admiration!*

Now *that* was an answer!

He'd seen the new water-table anyway, and it was obvious even to an idiot that the reflections within it were going to be too complicated to analyze. The artificers were setting themselves up for failure.

Maybe I shouldn't even try to work with that; it might be setting myself up for the same failure, to deal with a situation so complicated. Maybe I should just let the breakwater fail, then *put my own solution in place, between mage-storms.* Certainly the original problem had been much simpler to deal with, and the difference would only be a matter of degree. *More frequent, more powerful mage-storms, that's all. Did An'desha say something about Falconsbane-Ma'ar anticipating the original set of mage-storms and envisioning something to hold them back?*

When An'desha came back tonight, could he somehow coax his lover into talking about that? *That wouldn't make very good pillow talk, considering how he feels about Falconsbane. . . .*

In a strange way, Firesong actually admired Falconsbane—or rather, he admired the level of craftsmanship of which Falconsbane was capable in his rare moments of sanity.

Well, that wasn't precisely true; Firesong admired those abilities in Ma'ar, in which they had been the purest and the closest to sanity. Certainly *Ma'ar* had been able to create. He'd come up with his own forms of fighting-creatures, although he had sacrificed elegance for expediency and grace for brute power. The makaar hadn't been without intelligence, though; they couldn't have been stupid, or they wouldn't have survived a heartbeat in the air against the gryphons.

And as for Ma'ar's secret of immortality—in its way, that was the most elegant of all, although An'desha was hardly likely to agree with that assessment.

He does have the best right in the world to have an opinion on the subject, Firesong reflected sardonically. *But he's also not precisely unbiased on the subject.* Of all the people alive in the world at that very moment, there were only two who knew exactly how Ma'ar had lived long past his own death—and how every "incarnation" after that had managed to live long past the natural span without actually "dying" and being "reborn." There were drawbacks to that particular system, after all.

For one thing, it places your soul in the hands of the Powers Above, and if you've been naughty, you really don't want that to happen. For another, it seems that damn few people who undergo that particular process remember their previous lives. And last of all, so far as I know, you don't get a choice about who or what you return as.

Of course, if you were a good and virtuous person, none of these things would bother you. *However, Ma'ar was a very naughty boy, and he only got worse with each successive body he possessed. He* had *to remember who and what he was, otherwise he'd waste years relearning all he'd learned about magic. He had to have a choice about who he took over, or the body wouldn't have the ability to handle magic. And he certainly wanted no part of the Powers Above.*

That, at least, was Firesong's assessment. An'desha, of course, would know Falconsbane's full motivation, but Firesong doubted that An'desha would want to talk about it.

It was a clever—no, brilliant—scheme, though. And I'm in a position to recognize just how brilliant it was. Only he and An'desha knew how the scheme had worked; An'desha because he had seen it from the inside, and Firesong because he had destroyed the very foundation of the scheme.

Ma'ar-Falconsbane had avoided the hand of Fate by creating a stronghold for his spirit and personality in the Void, that place between Gates where neither the spirit nor the material could be told from one another. He had avoided *real* death by using the tremendous energy released by the violent death of his own bodies to catapult himself into that stronghold and seal himself inside until someone of his own direct bloodline matched a very rigid set of criteria and made his first attempt at the spell to create fire. *That* triggered the release of the spirit from the stronghold and flung it, with almost all of the original energy, into the new body.

An'desha said he couldn't find a single incarnation where

Falconsbane hadn't either suicided or been murdered. Feh. *The man must have been a masochist as well as a sadist.* Either death would release shattering amounts of energy, quite enough to accomplish the trick with power to spare.

Firesong was as intimately familiar with the process as An'desha because he was the one who had tracked Falconsbane's spirit to that stronghold, ravaging the stronghold then destroying Falconsbane, utterly and completely, shredding the Dark Adept's spirit to atoms and scattering them across the Void. Presumably the Powers Above *could* put the scattered spirit back together again—but if They did, it would be for Their purposes, and Falconsbane would likely see rebirth in a form that would horrify even him.

Say, as a helpless, impoverished cripple, unable to move without assistance, deaf and blind, utterly without magic or mind-magic, who spends every waking moment in pain. Or perhaps as a slug, a dung beetle, or a cloud of gnats.

That wasn't Firesong's business. What happened to what *had* been Falconsbane was of no concern to him, so long as the Dark Adept couldn't work the trick that had kept him turning up like a clipped coin, over and over, across the decades.

Still, the trick was a clever one, and that much Firesong could admire.

And in a way—if Falconsbane hadn't been what he was, it wasn't likely that Firesong would ever even have met An'desha.

For a moment he amused himself with the paths of might-have-been, trying to figure out what he and An'desha would have done—

Well, I might have met him, but he'd have been the age of my parents, and I never did care for older men. I keep forgetting that his apparent age and his chronological age are vastly different.

The Shin'a'in and Tayledras Goddess, in the persons of Her Avatars, had literally given An'desha back the body that Falconsbane had stolen away. They had returned his body to the state it had been when he had been possessed, at the age of seventeen or eighteen; perhaps a little younger, certainly no older.

By the same token, An'desha had spent so much of that time in hiding, in a kind of limbo within his own mind, that he didn't have the personal experience to match that chronological age. Emotionally, he was as young as he appeared.

Or he was, anyway.

Firesong licked salty sweat from his upper lip as he debated getting out of the hot pool. *Maybe a little longer. The longer I stay in here, the less likely it will be that my muscles will knot up again with tension as soon as I get out.*

He *should* be thinking—if he thought about Falconsbane at all—about those fugitive memories of Ma'ar's, and the "solution" that the Dark Adept had contrived to keep his own land safe from the mage-storms that were going to occur when Urtho died. That was where, if it was anywhere, the germ of their own solution would lie.

But his slippery thoughts kept coming back to that elegant little pattern of stronghold—possession—stronghold. It was just so very clever! And no one would have ever guessed what was going on if An'desha hadn't found a way to survive the possession.

I wonder what the other criteria were for possession, besides Adept-potential. I would think they would have to be solitary sorts, or his "new" personality would have given the signal that something was wrong.

If one could somehow assure that one returned in an ethical fashion, there wouldn't have been anything wrong with the entire scheme. *Yes, but just how would one displace another's spirit in an ethical fashion, hmm?*

Still, he kept coming back to that, as he climbed the stairs to the living area of the *ekele*. If only there was a way—

Well, infants were not ensouled, to the best of *his* knowledge, until the actual birth; it happened with the first breath. What if one arranged to slip in just before that critical moment?

It would mean a certain tedious time spent maturing, but that could be gotten around, I expect. At least, I could shorten that time, although it would certainly startle the

*parents. I can accelerate plant growth, so why not my own?
It would only be one more application of the same thing
Falconsbane used to change his own body.*

He combed his wet hair with his fingers as he walked,
pulling it forward over his shoulder. All his adult life he had
cherished a secret longing, born when he had learned about
his ancestor Vanyel and the love and lifebonding that had
lasted through time and across the ages with his beloved
Tylendel-Stefen. As foolishly romantic as it was, *he* had
longed to find someone, a lifebonded, a soul-mate. He
had really thought that person was An'desha.

Unfortunately, it didn't seem that An'desha shared that
conviction, and if there was one thing that Firesong was sure
of, it was that those who were lifebonded were *both* aware of
the bond to the point of pain if they were apart or at odds
with one another. They could not be lifebonded and be having the kind of personal problems they were now.

He searched through his wardrobe for something appropriate to his mood—black—and winced when his hand brushed
across one of An'desha's Shin'a'in tunics. *He's reverting
more and more to the Shin'a'in.* That in itself should have
told him this was no lifebond. Lifebonded couples tended to
dress *more* alike, even without thinking about it. Look at
Heralds Dirk and Talia—who always chose the same color
when they were off-duty. Or Sherrill and Keren, who dressed
like a pair of twins, even though Sherrill tended to prefer elegant lines and Keren to dress entirely in riding leathers
whenever possible! An'desha seemed to be choosing clothing
as opposite that of Firesong's elegant robes and tunics as possible, wearing the bright—not to say gaudy and clashing—
embroidered vests, and tunics and trews trimmed in the
bands of colorful wide braid that the Shin'a'in loved.

He sighed as he pulled a long, silken robe of unrelieved
black over his head. No, he was going to have to admit it.
This was no lifebond. And the bond he did have was, quite
frankly, falling apart.

Lifebonds were incredibly rare. The chances of ever finding
one's lifemate were remote, no matter how much one
looked.

He paused with his hand still on the wardrobe door as he was closing it when the inescapable thought occurred to him. True, the chances of finding one's lifemate were remote, *if* one only lived a single lifetime.

But what if you lived for several lifetimes?

What if you had a way to return, over and over, fully as yourself?

What if you managed to find that ethical way to return the way Falconsbane had? You could search as long as you needed to in order to find your lifebonded. And then?

Then, perhaps you could find a way to stay together forever. Vanyel and Stefen had.

And wasn't *that* a fascinating thought?

Four

Grand Duke Tremane looked out of the window in his office, gazing down through the bubbly pane of its poor-quality glass at the row after row of tents sheltering supplies down in the courtyard of his fortified manor. *Security. That's what lies down there, made tangible and visible.* The tents themselves were from the supplies he had appropriated; as soon as his clerks had found them in the records and his supply-sergeants had identified the crates they were in, he'd had them unpacked and set up to hold everything that could tolerate cold and didn't need to be under guard.

The courtyard was full of tents, with scarcely room to move between them. There were more tents lined up between the manor and the camp. Some of the supplies had already been distributed. Every man in his army now had triple bedding, triple clothing, double harsh-weather gear. They could *survive* a hideous winter now without barracks, although there would be sickness, frostbite, and other cold-related problems if they were forced to. That was more than they'd had before; if the worst predictions had come true, many would have died in the cold and snow.

He still couldn't believe that he had actually succeeded with his raid on the supply depot, and succeeded beyond his wildest dreams! All the men were current in their pay, including the bonuses he'd promised for odd or hazardous duty, and morale had taken an upswing, despite the fact that the drizzly weather hadn't broken for weeks. The extras that he had rationed out to them in the way of clothing and bedding hadn't hurt either; when he'd made a night inspection after lights-out, he'd seen the men were already making use of what he'd given out. Every tent contained a cocoon of blankets, with nothing visible of the man inside it but his nose, and the snores emerging from those cocoons had sounded very content.

The gold and silver entering the local economy wasn't hurting the morale of the townsfolk either, though he was glad he'd established a policy regarding double-pricing back when he'd first occupied this place. Any merchant found charging one price to a native and a higher price to a soldier—provided, of course, that the price difference *wasn't* due to the soldier being a poor hand at haggling—was brought up before his own fellow merchants and fined four times the difference in the price, half of which went to the Merchant's Guild, one quarter to the Imperial coffers, and one quarter to the fellow who was cheated. With all this new money flowing, his men could have been robbed blind without such a policy already in place.

Now his primary concern was to use his new stock of lumber to get warehouses up to shelter all the foodstuffs he'd looted. Everything else could stay under canvas, but the food needed real protection. That was keeping those of his men not robust enough to work on the walls quite busy. Even some of the clerks were taking a hand, since there wasn't as much need for them without all the Imperial paperwork to keep up with.

We have some space to breathe. That's the biggest factor. A great deal of the tension is gone.

The unspoken feeling of threat that was driving the work on the walls was still there, and certainly the men were thinking about the foul weather, looking at their tents, and wondering if a little canvas between them and a blizzard was going to be enough. Nevertheless, *now* no one was looking at his ration at mealtimes and wondering when those rations would be cut; no one was counting arrows, lead shot, or vials of oil for lamps and heating stoves. They all had been given a reprieve, and they all sensed it.

The mages were going about their new assignment—

finding a way to shield them from the effects of the mage-storms—with a renewed optimism about their own ability. The walls were going up faster than before.

And a small, select group of mages was working on a new project—to find the source of the storms.

He turned away from the window, but instead of going back to his desk and the welter of papers lying there, he took a seat in a comfortable chair before his fireplace. *I never felt the cold and damp so intensely before,* he thought, as he winced a little when he flexed stiff fingers in the warmth of the flames. *Is it age, I wonder, or is the weather affecting me that much?*

He gazed deeply into the flames and gave thought to the latest report from that smaller group of mages, a report that tended to confirm some of his own uneasy speculations. In it, they expressed severe doubt that Valdemar was the source of the mage-storms, and their evidence was compelling.

Valdemar's few mages have only begun working in groups, and are not, in our view, coordinated enough to have developed or produced these storms. If *anyone* knew about working group-magic, it was Sejanes. The old man had multiplied his own personal power far and above that of any single mage, simply by finding enough compatible minor mages to work with him, and by being careful that they never felt exploited, and so were not inclined to leave him. If Sejanes felt the Valdemarans were too new to group-magic to be effective at it, Tremane was going to accept that estimate without a qualm.

Valdemar has been feeling the same effects that we have, and it would be suicidally stupid to unleash a weapon that works the same damage to you as it does to the enemy. Well, he'd already figured that one out, so it hardly came as a surprise.

Valdemar has never unleashed uncontrolled area-effect magic, and their overt policy, at least, would preclude such a weapon. He couldn't exactly argue with that, either; he'd studied their past strategies, and there was nothing of the sort in any of them. In fact, right up through the war with Ancar they had plied purely defensive tactics.

It was hard to believe, but the Valdemarans were something Tremane had never expected to see in his lifetime: people who were exactly what they appeared to be, employing no deceptions and very little subterfuge.

Which means I misjudged them, and I sent in an assassin for no reason. Ah, well. He wasn't going to agonize over it. He had done what he thought he had to at the time, with his own best assessment of the situation. *Expediency. We are ruled by it. . . .* He had enough now to worry about with the welfare of his own men, and if a few Valdemarans and their allies had gotten in the way of his agent's weapons, well, that was the hazard of war.

At least, that was what he'd always been taught.

Never mind. But as for the mages, I might as well order them to stop chasing that particular hare and go after more promising quarry. If not Valdemar, then where *are these things coming from? And why now?*

The fire popped and hissed as the flames found a particularly knotty piece of wood. *Wood. My scholars have a good idea for shelters which requires a minimum of wood, and that is* good *news.*

These new barracks began with four walls of the same bricks he was building the defensive bulwarks with; heaped up against them, pounded earth, reaching to the rafters. There would be no windows and only two doors, one at either end. The roof frame and roof timbers would be of wood, but the roof itself would be thick thatch, of the kind that country cottages around here used. Each building would look rather like a haystack atop a low hillock. If snow started to build up on the roof to a dangerous weight, it would be easy to send men up to clean it off, but a certain amount of snow would insulate against cold winds. His builders liked the plan, for a fireplace in each of the outer walls that did not contain a door could easily heat the entire building efficiently.

We can start those as soon as the defensive walls are up. Thatch; that's straw, and there's certainly plenty of that. I can probably hire thatchers from the town. Brick he had in abundance, and plenty of earth. *If we have the time before snow starts to fall, I can build more of those structures with no fireplaces and only one door to use as warehouses for the foodstuffs, then take the wood from the warehouses we tossed up and reuse it elsewhere.*

Could these same buildings be used for army kitchens? He'd have to ask his people. Or better still, could he put a kitchen in each barracks, and use the heat from cooking to help heat the barracks?

And what are we going to do about bathhouses? His men were accustomed to keeping themselves healthy, and that meant clean. Perhaps he could find enough materials to build a few traditional bathhouses with steamrooms, and have the men use them in tightly-scheduled shifts. *But how are we going to heat them, and heat the water?*

And the latrines, the privies; how far along were the builders on those? His men who knew about such things had assured him that they would have adequate arrangements before the first hard freeze, arrangements that would not poison the local water supplies. Would they? Was there a progress report on his desk yet? He couldn't remember.

He almost got up to find out, but the warmth of the fire seduced him. If there was a report on his desk, it would still be there later, and if there wasn't, it wouldn't materialize.

Not like the old days, when one *might* have. *The old days—huh. The "old days" were less than six moons ago.* It seemed like a lifetime ago, and he was a different man then. He had already done things that Grand Duke Tremane would never have considered.

I have burned all my bridges.

The walls would be done in a few days. Then work could start on the barracks. He wanted to get everything done at once, and despite the number of men he had, there still weren't enough—and—

And we have gold. We have gold! Why can't I just hire some of the locals? Why shouldn't I? I've seen boys standing about, looking for work. Maybe there are only boys and old men, women, but not all the work will need strength. Oh, damn. We have gold, but I need to keep it in reserve if I can, to pay my own troops. Besides, how do I get those people to

*work for us? Not all that long ago, we were the enemy. How
do I manage to get the townspeople and my men to work together? How?*

His thoughts stopped as he realized that he was planning
for a long future. These new barracks weren't meant to
last for a season or a year; his builders had given him plans
for structures that would last for years. His sanitary men
were planning for decades of use.

Oh, a long future be damned. *Well, of course, they're giving me plans for good barracks. The winter is going to be
worse than anything we have ever seen. Tents or flimsy
structures made to last a season won't cope with the kind of
winter storms we're going to see. And one of the worst
things that could happen would be for our facilities to freeze
up; if we overbuild, that won't happen. Probably. Maybe.*

Better to concentrate on how he could hire some of the locals, how he might be able to keep the people of the town
and the men of the Imperial Army from going for each other's throats. If he could just find a way to get them to work
together—that was how the Empire had forged all the disparate people of its conquered lands into a whole in the first
place. Young men from all over the Empire were conscripted
into the ranks of the army, where they served out their
terms beside young men from places they might not even
have heard of before. By the time their terms were over, they
all returned to their homes unable to think of men from
places they didn't know as barbarians or foreigners, and capable of thinking in larger terms than just their own villages.

*I can't conscript the townsfolk, more's the pity. For one
thing, they wouldn't stand for it. For another, there's no one
worth conscripting. Ancar took every able-bodied man
away for his own army.*

"Sir!" One of the aides was at the open door, calling anxiously into the gloom. Of course, he couldn't see Tremane
from the door, hidden as he was in the oversized armchair.
"Commander, are you here?"

"Over here." Tremane stood up and turned to face the
door, and saw relief spread over the aide's features.

"Sir, there's a delegation here from the town, and they are

rather insistent. They say they must talk to you now." He made a gesture of helplessness. "They wouldn't leave a message or talk to anyone other than you."

Of course they wouldn't, they never have. The townsfolk didn't seem to grasp the concept of delegation of authority. They evidently thought that unless they spoke directly to Tremane, whatever it was they had to say would never reach him. "Send them in immediately." He moved back into his office and sat down behind his desk as the aide went off to fetch this delegation. Whatever they wanted, whether or not it was really important, he would make time for them. At all costs, he must stay on good terms with these people, but he must also make it clear—though with such subtlety that they themselves would not be aware he was doing so—that *he* was the real ruler here, that he *permitted* them their autonomy. Perhaps that was why they insisted on seeing him and him only; perhaps he had done his job too well.

Or perhaps, after years of terror under Ancar, they no longer believed in anything but the witness of their own ears and eyes.

Would it be complaints this time? It had been the last, though they were complaints from those living nearest the new walls about the noise and dust. He had made it very clear at the time that while such inconveniences would pass, he was not about to slow the progress of his walls by restricting the building to the daylight hours. Since the spider-creature had been brought in, interestingly enough, there had been no more complaints about noise. It was a pity that the town had no real walls of its own; people who had protective walls usually had a firm grasp on the *need* for protective walls.

The delegation was the usual three; the mayor of the city and his two chief Council members representing the Guilds and the farmfolk. The mayor, Sandar Giles, was a much younger man than Tremane was used to seeing in a position of authority, and was quite frail, with a clubbed foot, though his quick intelligence was immediately obvious when he spoke. Thin and dark, he looked like a schoolboy, although Tremane knew his real age was close to thirty. His eyes were the liveliest thing about him; large and expressive, they often betrayed him by revealing emotions he probably would rather have kept concealed.

Both the Chief Husbandman and the Chief Guildsman were old enough to be his grandsires, and the main difference between them was that the Chief Husbandman was weathered and wrinkled with years in the field, his face resembling a dried apple, while the Chief Guildsman wore his years more lightly. Both were gray-haired and bearded, both knotted and bent with the years, joints swollen and probably painful. Both had square jaws beneath the close-cropped beards, and cautious eyes that betrayed nothing.

All three took their seats, both of the Council members showing great deference to Sandar, seeing to it that he was seated comfortably before taking their own chairs in front of Tremane's desk. Tremane had always been more at ease receiving civilians in his office rather than in any kind of a throne room; the former implied a businesslike approach that he found made civilians more inclined to cooperate.

They all exchanged the usual greetings; Tremane sent for hot drinks, since he had learned that Sandar was quite susceptible to cold. As soon as the aide was out of the room again, he leaned forward across the wooden expanse of the desktop.

"Well, what is it that you need to see me about so urgently?" he asked, coming to the point quickly, something that would have been so unheard of back in the Empire that his visitors would have been shocked into utter speechlessness. "Not a complaint, I hope. Not only *can't* I do anything about building noise, I won't. We're racing the winter, and I hope by now your people know how badly *all* of us need those walls."

"Definitely not a complaint—or, rather not a complaint about you or your men," Sandar replied, with both thin hands cupped around the mug of *kala*, though it was still too hot to sip. "If I have a complaint about anything, it would be about the weather."

Tremane raised one eyebrow, and Sandar shrugged. "I hope you don't expect me or my mages to do anything about that," he replied, amused. "I wish we could, as heartily as you do. Not that we couldn't have in the past, but—"

"I know, I know, it's these confounded mage-storms!" growled the Chief Husbandman, Devid Stoen. "Hang it all, we used to have three good weather-wizards that could at least give us a few days of guaranteed clear weather for harvest, and did a fine job of telling us what was on the way. But that was before that damned puppy Ancar stole the throne and conscripted 'em all! For that matter, a pair of 'em trailed back to us just after your lot moved in and started building walls—but all they can do is tell us that they can't read the weather anymore, that because of the mage-storms, they can't do a thing!"

Tremane's other eyebrow rose to join its fellow; this was the first time he'd heard officially that there were any kind of Hardornen mages in the city. For that matter, it was the first time he'd heard the rumors his spies had reported confirmed. Were they admitting it just because those mages had proved to be powerless? Had they assumed he already knew? Or was it a slip of the tongue that Stoen was mentioning them now?

"If you can't do anything, and you know my mages can't either, then what is it about the weather that brings you here?" he asked carefully. No point in mentioning these weather-mages. If it was a slip, he'd rather they didn't realize he'd taken note of it.

"Well," Sandar said, after a pregnant pause, "you must have noticed that there is a decided scarcity of healthy, strong young men around about here." His expressive eyes were full of irony as he glanced down at his own frail body.

"Hmm. It's hard not to notice." He lowered his eyebrows. "I'd assumed that Ancar conscripted them, and—" He hesitated, not knowing how to phrase "used them as deployable decoys" politely.

"He used them up, most of them," Sandar said bluntly. "A few came trailing back with the mages, but most of them were slaughtered in his senseless war on Valdemar and Karse. That's how I became mayor; my father was barely young enough and definitely fit enough to be conscripted, and I had been his secretary from the time I was old enough to be useful. I knew everything he'd known, so I became mayor by default."

Tremane wasn't certain which aroused more pity in him; the old pain in Sandar's voice as he spoke so casually of the loss of his father, or the resignation and acceptance of the situation. *Don't become too involved with these people, Tremane. They aren't yours, they never will be. You have no responsibility toward them beyond the immediate, and only then in ways that will benefit your troops.*

"Virtually every healthy male between the ages of fifteen and forty was taken," Sandar continued. "And it wasn't just in the towns; he sent his butchers out to every farm, not once, but repeatedly. You might be able to save your sons once, twice, or even three times, but sooner or later Ancar's slavers would find them. That left us with old men, women, and children. In towns, that's not a situation that's impossible. At a task requiring skill rather than strength, old men and women are as good as any young man, and often better. At a task that requires strength, well, there were enough skilled crafts*people* in the town to come up with ways that someone with minimal strength can do the work of two or more powerful men. But out in the farms—" He shrugged.

Stoen took over. "The fact is, farms need strong people to run, and lots of 'em," he said, "And we don't have 'em. Things have been goin' downhill since Ancar took over, and that's a fact. Now we did all right this year at planting. We were lucky, we had lots of good weather, though you can't say that about other places in Hardorn. We did all right during the growing season, partly by not gettin' much sleep, partly because if you spread enough children out, they can do the work of a man. But now—it's harvest, we haven't *got* the good weather, and frankly, sir, we're in trouble. There's not a chance we're going to get more than half the crops in. We've tried, we've gotten some help from the city, but—" He spread his hands helplessly. "We can't really *pay* nobody, and people generally aren't bright enough to figure out that if they don't help out now, they're gonna be on short rations or *no* rations come spring."

"And I can't force anyone to work in the fields who doesn't want to," Sandar finished. "I can try to point out the consequences, but if they don't want to go, or say, 'let someone else do it,' I can't call up what old gaffers are left of the city constables and force people to go pull roots or gather wheat."

"Nor can I," said Master Goldsmith Bran Kerst. "Particularly not when there's money to be made selling to *your* men, sir. Can't ask someone to go pull roots in a cold, muddy field for nothing when he can be carting beer at a good wage here in town."

Rather than ask the obvious question, Tremane simply waited for them to get to the point.

Stoen sighed gustily. "The point is this, Commander. We only need help for a few days, a fortnight or two at most, but those days are critical, or the crops are going to rot in the fields. Could you see your way clear to sending some of your men to help with the harvest?"

Tremane pretended to consider it for a moment. "Let me ask you this, first. How many people in your Guilds are skilled or semiskilled builders? *We* have a problem, too. We need to get new barracks up and the walls finished before the weather gets too cold to build in." Before Kerst could say anything, he added, "They'll be paid a fair wage, of course— and work would go much more quickly with people who knew how to build than with those of my men who are fighters, not builders."

Kerst opened his mouth, then closed it again. Tremane waited for either him or Sandar to say something, then continued when they said nothing. "I'll be frank with you; I have enough supplies to last out the winter with no trouble. I don't need to purchase anything locally. Nevertheless, I am no fool, and I can foresee problems if *your* people don't have enough to support them. If your people are short of foodstuffs, there will be trouble here in my own camp before too long. Some of my men will steal Imperial stores and sell them illegally, some of *your* people will try to steal from our stores. I'll catch them, of course, and I'll be forced to punish everyone involved. I may have to order some hangings, depending on the amount of theft; I will certainly have to order some fairly harsh punishments to assure that I can keep order. This will mean—shall we just say—unpleasantness for garrison *and* town. I'd rather deal with the situation before it becomes a problem."

"How?" Stoen asked, leaning forward intently.

Tremane took a quick glance at his ledgers before answering. If the payment didn't have to be in hard cash. . . .

"My coffers are not bottomless, but I have a certain amount of property my people don't need at the moment," he said carefully. "If I can barter that property for services—or, say, sell the property to some of the Guilds for coin—we can muster the most efficient use of all the workers in the Imperial forces *and* in the town to get all of our projects done before the snow flies. Everyone who works will be paid a fair wage, according to the skill of the job." He gave each of the men a level look, and all three of them nodded as they met his eyes. "This will put some of my men—farm workers before they were recruited into the army—in the fields. That will be efficient for you; better to have one man who knows how to swing a scythe than five who don't. People from the town who are unskilled workers will either serve in the fields as common harvesters, or on the walls or barracks as haulers and other unskilled laborers. People from the town who are skilled builders will *definitely* be on the walls or the barracks. But for every man I send into the fields, I require someone to take his place here, and I will *not* send any builders of my own into the fields."

"Regardless, everyone who works will be paid?" Stoen asked.

He nodded. "I consider it an investment in peace," he replied frankly, as he mentally blessed the Hundred Little Gods for answering his prayers in such a timely manner. This was precisely what he needed, a way to mingle his men and Hardornens in a peaceful, productive pursuit where both sides benefited. He'd have paid double for this.

"I think this can work," Sandar said cautiously, then flashed an unexpected grin. "It is rather ironic, since *your* gold, paid into the taverns and the like, will ultimately pay for your supplies, which will in turn go back into the town in the form of wages."

"But I will have buildings and walls," he reminded them. "With any fortune at all, by exchanging unskilled workers for skilled, I will have them faster. I will even grant you this; for jobs requiring neither skill nor strength I will hire two boys—and by 'boys,' I mean children ten years old and younger—at a man's wage, and that is probably fairer than they would get anywhere else."

It was, as he knew very well, more than fair. Girls didn't normally work in the Empire, they went to school until they turned sixteen, then became servants or got married. Some few became mages, entertainers, or scholars, but seldom craftspeople. Boys who worked usually got whatever copper bits they could scrape up; if they were apprentices, they got room and board and stayed grateful for both if their masters were generous.

"I think we can agree to that," Sandar said quickly—as Tremane had thought he would. "Send a list of what you have to dispose of over to my office; we'll either barter the work of apprentices and journeymen for it or buy it outright, provided it isn't totally useless, like ornamental funeral urns or some such."

"Oh, I think I can guarantee it won't be anything of the sort," Tremane said agreeably. He was already making a mental list of things his men wouldn't need from the looted stores. Raw iron, tin, and copper bar-stock, for instance; *he* didn't have any smiths, but there had been crate after crate of the stuff in the storehouse. By now, this town must be running low on raw metals—wars disrupted trade, after all, and he hadn't seen any mines or smelters in operation around here. He had enough finished metal goods to last his men for years; he didn't need the raw material. He had more horse tack than anyone would ever need; he had cured leather by the stack, and he knew by the state of some harness he'd seen, mended with bits of rope or patched together with bits cut away from worn-out straps, that they'd welcome both tack and leather. Those were just the things he could think of immediately. No, there would be no trouble finding things these people would be very happy to see.

"In that case, we'll be getting on our way," Sandar replied, showing a bit more color in his thin face than he'd had when he came in—and a bit more hope, as well. "We'll have to send criers out all over town to round up the unskilled laborers, but Master Kerst will have an answer for you from the Guild of the Masons and Woodworkers shortly."

"Is there a—a Thatcher's Guild?" Tremane asked, wondering if he sounded like a fool for asking.

Stoen laughed. "No Guild, lad, but I'll have plenty of thatchers for you once the harvest's in. Never fear of that; most farmers know how to thatch a roof fair handily. You'll be wanting thatching straw, then?"

He nodded, relieved to have that out of his hands. "Yes, and a great deal of it, I suppose. These barracks are going to be barnlike buildings, and a thatched roof has been recommended."

"Just leave that to me," Stoen assured him. "Thank your gods, the one thing we've no lack of is thatching straw." He sighed. "Keeps well, and there've been fewer roofs to mend these days."

The men shook hands all around, and the delegation left, escorted by the aide. Tremane remained where he was, behind his desk with his nose buried in the account of the looted stores, going through the ledgers line by line, making up his list of barter goods. He found an amazing variety of absolutely useless items—useless to his men, that is. What in the name of all that was holy would they do with a hundred pairs of women's half boots? Or three crates of gilded copper bracelets? Or regulation Healer's tunics and trews in sizes too small for any man in the force? All of those could go; since his Healers wore the plainest of clothing without rank or regiment marks, even the tunics and trews could be redyed and used as common clothing. Tools—he had enough shovels to give every man two; he certainly didn't need that many. Small hatchets, hammer-ended, made for pounding tent stakes into the ground and cutting firewood—again, he had twice as many of those as he had men. Did he really need all those tents? He certainly didn't need six decorative dress-parade pavilions!

There were things he didn't need but was not inclined to put into the hands of former enemies—siege engine components and weapons, for instance. But why on earth had the Imperial supply depot been holding six trunks of costumes for veil-dancers? Or all the scenery, props, and costumes needed for a production of *The Nine-Days King?* Or an entire field mews for thirty hunting birds, complete with imping flat-drawered cabinets?

Though I do know why it had that "special tent and accoutrements for the Commander's recreation." Duke Clerance can't even field an army without his mistress, and she can't do without anything she's become accustomed to. That should certainly bring a pretty piece of coin. Best he didn't let on that it was meant for a courtesan, however. Let the ladies of the town that still had money argue over who obtained what.

There were oddments; insect veiling for swamp campaigns, white salve and suncoats for desert fighting, camp furniture for officers—a few of this, a dozen of that. Once he had his list, he gave it to his clerks to copy out in Hardornen and send to Sandar, then went about writing up the orders calling for volunteers for harvest work.

Those required very special care in phrasing. *No man receiving special pay for special skills will be accepted for harvest work.* As he'd told Sandar, he did not intend to lose a single skilled builder to pulling roots. He made it quite clear in his orders that he would not tolerate any "interference with or molestation or harassment of the women, married or unmarried, of the farms." He reiterated that Imperial Army rules regarding civilian women would hold and that there would be officers there to enforce them. He did this very deliberately; without coming out and saying so, he was telling the men that there would be attractive—or, at least, fresh-faced—young farm women working alongside them. They would know that there would be severe punishment for taking liberties with the civilians, but if a young woman and a young man decided to meet some time *after* the soldier was off-duty, and the soldier had proper leave to go off-grounds and conducted himself with respect for the lady's wishes. . . .

Farm labor might be hard work, but it was easier than building walls, and for those soldiers conscripted from farming families, it would be much more pleasant. And certainly the surroundings—especially surroundings including unattached young women—would be much more congenial.

I might get more volunteers than I can spare. I'd better make arrangements in advance for a rotation of duties so I avoid the appearance of favoritism.

As he sent off the orders and call for volunteers to be copied and posted, something else occurred to him. Romances, serious ones, were bound to come out of this. And, inevitably, marriages.

Oh, gods. I'd better find some local priests. I have to find out what the local marriage customs and laws are. I'll have to have the men briefed. Gods, and courting customs; I don't want to have cases where one party thinks it's a light flirtation and the other thinks it's a betrothal! Maybe I had better think about partitioning one of the barracks into cubicles for married quarters. Can we afford that? Or should I just tell married couples to make their own arrangements in town? But if I do that, how do I enforce discipline? This sort of thing had never occurred to him before; wives and sweethearts were always left behind when the Army marched off. When the men had been confined to the light women of the taverns, he hadn't had to worry about all that. A lady of negotiable virtue knew what the rules were, and so did her customer. But properly brought up girls of the town and the farms—that was something else altogether—

His hands and thoughts both stilled, as he realized what he was planning.

This is not an encampment anymore. It's a permanent post. I am planning for a long future here.

That was what had been nagging at the back of his mind despite his efforts to deny it. He *could* have chosen a flimsier structure for the barracks plans, something that would last a few years. Instinctively, he had picked the strongest, most durable structure his designers had offered.

This was no longer an armed camp, it was an armed holding. He was allocating the men to serve both camp and town.
He was planning for the mingling of both. He was planning
for a future that included married soldiers, children, families.

Less and less of what he had learned as a military leader
would apply, and more and more of what he had learned as
the manager of his own estate.

If they all survived the mage-storms and the winter.

He pulled his mind and his planning back to the present.
*One thing at a time. First, the walls, the barracks, and the
harvest. Then worry about what comes next.*

Sandar was evidently overjoyed at the list of barter goods;
late in the afternoon his messengers returned from town
with answers from the Mayor and Master Kerst. The note
from Sandar was good news, but the one from the Master
Guildsman was even better. Master Kerst had two stonema-
sons and their journeymen and apprentices, four brick-
masons and theirs, and a Master Builder and his. There were
also assorted plasterers, woodworkers, a furniture builder or
two, and others that Master Kerst felt might be useful. . . .

Might be useful? Tremane very nearly did a dance around
his desk, which would have either scandalized or terrified
his aides, depending on whether they thought he was drunk
or mad. He'd resigned himself to rough-finished walls in the
barracks and the crudest of appointments; the men would
certainly have seen worse in their time. Having skilled
craftsmen available meant there would be *real* walls, a floor
of something besides pounded earth, real bunks and mess tables for the men. And the answer from Sandar meant he was
going to have all this without touching the stores of coin
he'd taken from the Imperial coffers!

*I wonder if you'd thought about bathhouses or a substi-
tute for latrines?* Kerst's note continued. *We have men who
not only can advise you on both, but who have an idea or
two you might want to consider.*

Bathhouses *and* latrines? He scribbled off a note in semilit-
erate Hardornen to Kerst directly.

Instead of the quiet dinner he usually had, he sat down

that night with a tableful of men whose conversational topic was not usually considered appropriate over food.

By now, in order to deal with the locals efficiently, both his staff of chirurgeons and his builders had learned Hardornen, so the conversation was held in the local tongue. That was just as well. It was somehow easier to eat and listen to a conversation about latrines at the same time, if it was held in another language.

"—mix with wood ash and ground cob or chopped leaves, then you spread what you get out on drying racks," said one of the locals earnestly. "Depending on the weather, in a day or so you get something dry enough to bag, and that's what we've been selling to the farmers to put on their fields."

"You just need sewers and the treatment site, don't need sewage tanks, see?" finished his coworker. "Let the sand, gravel, and the rest of it purify the liquid, let it percolate through all the purifying layers, and you don't run the risk of poisoning our stream or our wells."

His own men nodded wisely. "We've been doing something like this in the cities and on the large estates, but you need magic," one of them said. "I've heard some people had a less sophisticated system on their estates because they didn't have a house mage. This will work."

"Well, it gets better," the first man said, grinning. "Bet you didn't know if you use the same system on cow dung, minus the wood ash and adding dried wood chips or sawdust, or ground woody plant waste, like heavy stalks, you can burn it."

"You have to compress it, make it into bricks, but it burns," the second confirmed. "Now, normally they'd take that cow dung and put it on their fields, but if you offered to trade them weight for weight for *your* dried sludge, they'll take it, and you'll have fuel you didn't have before. See, our stuff don't smell; it's dry and easier to handle than what comes off of a muck pile. They'd rather have ours. And we get fuel."

That got Tremane's interest. "Not for indoor fireplaces, surely—" he objected.

The two Hardornen sewage experts shook their heads.

"No, and not for cooking—unless you like your soup to have that particular flavor."

"But we don't need open fireplaces to heat the barracks!" one of his own men suddenly exclaimed. "In fact—Commander, that would be a wasteful use of burnables. I just thought of an old design used in some of the houses up north—look—"

Tremane had already supplied the table with old documents taken from the depot and plenty of pens; his man seized one of each and began sketching on the back of an old pay roster while the rest leaned over each others' shoulders, peering down with interest.

"Look, you have your—your *furnace* here, below the level of the floor, and fed from outside, with a tiny little iron door. Above it, you have a huge mass of brick riddled with tiny chimneys. This works like a kiln, you heat the brick, the brick heats the barracks." He sucked on the end of the pen for a moment. "Put the door to the barracks *here*, on the far end of the wall, fill up the rest of the end wall with the brick arrangement, and there you are. Two sides sheltered by the earth, two with brick furnaces. Or only one furnace, if you want a barracks kitchen with ovens and a cooking fireplace at the other end."

Tremane looked the drawing over; it looked and sounded feasible. Put the sleeping quarters near the furnace, the common rooms in the middle, the kitchen at the other end. "It'll still have to have some arrangement like a smoke hole," he pointed out, "or all the smoke from lanterns and candles will just build up in there."

"Yes, but you'll be using more of the heat from the furnace," his man pointed out. "And you can burn dung without smelling up the inside."

"I don't see anything to object to," the Chief Chirurgeon said judiciously. "Other than the fact that it will be darker than the eighth hell in there without windows, and I'm bound to warn you that will have an effect on the men's morale and health."

"Better dark than freezing," one of the others muttered, which only confirmed Tremane's own thought.

"Health you can deal with in their diet; sprouted beans and the rest of that stuff you chirurgeons are so fond of," he replied. "And as for morale—since they'll be on duty outside most of the daylight hours, I don't see a problem—but wait a moment, though," he added, as something odd occurred to him.

The chirurgeons hadn't listed a single complaint or difficulty since they made a permanent camp here. "*You* people aren't having any problems with the mage-storms affecting you. Isn't that laying-on-of-hands healing that you do a kind of magic?"

One of the lesser Healers choked behind his hands; the Chief Chirurgeon, a tall, thin, balding fellow with an attitude of aristocratic arrogance, favored him with a frosty smile. "Firstly, although the uninformed think of healing as a kind of magic, it is *not* the sort of magic that you mages are accustomed to using," he replied, in a lofty, superior tone of voice that made Tremane grit his teeth in response. "Mind you, I am a surgeon; my skills are in the excising of diseased flesh with the knife, in the stitching of damaged tissue with needle and gut-thread. However, I have made certain that I am educated even in those healing arts that I am not equipped to perform."

As you should have been, his tone seemed to imply. Tremane simply schooled his features into mild interest and nodded. He had learned long ago to keep his temper under more trying circumstances than this. Strangling the man would accomplish nothing.

Except to make me very happy. . . .

"So just how does this differ from the magic that I, as a mage, am familiar with?" he asked with exact politeness.

"In the first place, it is performed entirely with the mind," the Chief Chirurgeon lectured. "The only difference between a self-taught or untaught Healer and one who has gone through training is in the recognition of how to heal things besides obvious broken bones or wounds. The Healer's mind convinces the patient's body to restore itself to the perfect state it had before the injury or illness. That is why they cannot correct those who are born with deformities." He smiled smugly. "That is something only those with my skill can do."

"All right, but I still don't understand why you aren't encountering interference from the mage-storms," he persisted.

"*Because* the Healers don't work during a storm, when the disruptions in energy are the only things that could interfere with their talent," the Chief Chirurgeon replied, as if to an idiot. "Accelerated healing only takes place when the Healer is actively working. The rest of the time, the patient is simply doing what he would under ideal circumstances. Under ideal conditions, our bodies would always repair themselves and throw off disease; the Healer simply reminds the body of what it should be doing."

"Oh." He had some vague notion that, basically, the reason the Healers were unaffected was that they were essentially working very small, limited magics of extremely limited duration and at very close range, but he doubted that the Chief Chirurgeon would agree with his particular definition.

Evidently his subordinate didn't even care for his expression. "Healing just is *not* magic as you understand it," the man persisted. "There's an old term for healing and a number of other abilities all lumped together: mind-magic. No one these days ever bothers with most of the other abilities, except a few practitioners of some of the odder religions."

Mind-magic! Where have I heard that term used before! There's something very familiar about that term. "What *are* those other things that were lumped in with healing?" he asked, out of a feeling that the answer might be important.

"Oh," the chirurgeon waved dissmissively. "They're hardly important, things many educated people think are mostly delusional. Speaking mind-to-mind without the assistance of a teleson-spell; moving objects or even people with the power of the mind alone and no Portals involved; seeing and speaking with spirits of the dead; communicating directly with deities; seeing into the distance, the past, or the future without benefit of a mirror-spell; and imposing one's will upon another." He shrugged. "Most folk in the Empire are rather skeptical about those sorts of things. It is very easy to pretend to powers that are only in the mind, and thus very subjective."

He'd been speaking in Hardornen, though whether it was out of politeness for the company or simply because he'd forgotten to switch back to the Imperial tongue, Tremane couldn't have said for certain. The locals, who had been listening to his speech with some interest, laughed uproariously at that last statement. The chirurgeon glared at them in annoyance.

"I fail to see what was so amusing," he said acidly. "Perhaps you would care to enlighten me?"

"You people wouldn't be so skeptical if you'd ever met a Herald out of Valdemar," was the reply. "They don't use your 'real' magic over there, or they didn't until just lately. *Everything* they do is with mind-magic, and they think *yours* is poppycock and fakery."

Affronted, the chirurgeon turned his attention back to his own underlings; the Hardornen builders and Tremane's men got involved in a discussion of the best placements of "furnaces" and other devices to heat the barracks, and whether or not the walls really needed to be piled with earth. There seemed to be a brotherhood of builders, of stone and wood and metal, that transcended nationalities.

That left Tremane with an interesting tidbit to mull over. The Valdemarans did everything with mind-magic? That must have been where he'd first heard the term.

So Heralds must be the people born with these abilities; somehow they have a way of testing for them, I suppose. Then they get herded up the way the Karsites collect children with Mage-Talent, and sent off for training. Clever, to put them all in service to the Crown; the Empire could do with that policy regarding mages. And they aren't used to using real magic; it's new to them, so they don't rely on it. Fascinating.

No wonder they weren't having the kind of problems with the mage-storms that he was having! They simply didn't have things that would be disrupted by the storms!

There are plenty of folk in the Empire who would call that a barbaric way of life—but they can heat their homes and move their goods and we can't. . . . So who has the superior way of life now?

Heating homes . . . all very well to heat the barracks with cow dung, but what was he going to cook with? "Wood," he said aloud. "We have a problem; trees don't grow as quickly as wheat, and I don't intend to denude the countryside to keep my people warm if I can help it. Have any of you any suggestions?"

The Hardornens exchanged glances, and one of them finally spoke up. "Commander Tremane, you know as well as we do the state of things here. Half the people of Hardorn are gone. Whole villages are wiped out just because some lieutenant of Ancar got offended over something someone said, farms were abandoned when the last able-bodied person gave up or was carried off. We were going to suggest that once the harvest was over, your folk and ours go out together on foraging expeditions."

He considered this for a moment. "Do I take it that there is a reasonable chance that such expeditions will be left alone by the—the loyal Hardornen forces?"

The man snorted. "The loyal Hardornen forces aren't 'forces' at all. Most of them will be getting their harvests in, *if* they can. They're battling time and weather just as we are, and they won't have the extra men we will."

He nodded; that confirmed his own ideas. "How is the harvest looking?" he asked, thinking that this man just might be honest enough to tell him.

"That's another reason for foraging," the fellow told him frankly. "The harvest isn't bad, but some of us aren't sure it will hold the town over the winter. Sandar wants to send out foraging parties to some of the farms that have been abandoned and see what we might be able to get out of the fields, or even the barns and silos." He grinned. "There's sure to be stuff good enough for your thatching straw, if nothing else."

"You'd prefer to have some of my forces along, I take it." He made that a statement; another bizarre killer-beast had been taken today, after it had attacked one of the harvesting parties. This time no one was killed, and only a few men were hurt, but no one was going to forget that these things were still out beyond the nearly-completed walls. "So what do my people get out of this?"

"We find out just who's left—after Ancar, the Empire, and the mage-storms," the man said bluntly. "You get a census of who's around here, and where. You know who's got boys or men that might be tempted to make things difficult for your men in the name of Hardorn. Some of these farmers may have extra food to trade for. We find out what the storms have done to the land. If they're changing animals, what else are they leaving behind? And when we find abandoned farms, deserted villages, your people can move in and tear down the buildings. At the worst, you've got fuel. At the best, you've got fuel and building supplies. And—well, Sandar may be hoping for too much, but he thinks if we find any camps of the men from our side, we might be able to persuade 'em that you Imperials aren't the devils they think you are. Maybe we can get you a truce, if nothing else."

Tremane kept his face expressionless, his tone noncommittal. "I'll think about it," he said, and turned the subject back toward his barracks and the improvements the locals were suggesting.

But when everyone had cleared away, and he was back in his own room with another cozy fire going, he had to admit that the proposals didn't sound bad.

Provided, of course, that this wasn't just a way to lure him and his men out where the rebels could pick them off or ambush them.

Oddly enough, he didn't think it was. The idea of harvesting abandoned fields, rounding up and butchering half-feral livestock, and tearing down vacant buildings was a good one. With locals as guides, he would not have to send out sweep searches for such places, and run the risk of incurring the wrath of farmers who had *not* abandoned their holdings.

"I never thought I'd find myself in a position like this," he said aloud into the quiet night air.

His assignment had been to pacify Hardorn. He had never counted on his pacification force becoming the equivalent of the local government, yet that was precisely what was happening.

There would be no more battles; the worst he could expect would be skirmishes against men who were increasingly short of supplies and resources. In any other circumstances he would have laughed at the idea he could trust the people of Shonar to make and hold a truce with their fellow Hardornens. He would *never* have believed the half-promises made to him tonight.

But although nothing had been stated openly and baldly, it was very clear to him that these people no longer regarded him and his men as the enemy. Instead, they represented the one source of safety and order in an increasingly disordered country. They looked at their own men, ragtag bands of "freedom fighters" who were ill-armed and untrained; they looked at the strange monsters created in the wake of the mage-storms. They turned their eyes on the Imperial forces, well-armed, well-trained, and prepared to defend not only themselves, but the town of Shonar. It did not take a master scholar to figure the odds on which ones they would trust their safety to.

There would be no more reports to the Emperor; the agents still with Tremane would not take long to assess their own position here. Not that *his* ambitions regarding the Iron Throne were anywhere on his list of current priorities. No, he was past the point of thinking in terms of "acceptable losses." There was no loss that was acceptable now, and any deaths in his ranks would be avenged swiftly and with finality.

Now came the time for concentration on the minutiae that would save them all; the heroes of the winter would be the best managers, not the best generals.

He had pestered his clerks until his office was stuffed with papers, box after box of them, rank after rank of dossiers. He had the equivalent of the sheaf of papers that followed every Imperial citizen through his life for every man in his forces, three copies. One set of files was arranged, not by military rank or specialty, but by civilian specialty; what the man had done or been trained as before he joined the army. The second set was arranged more conventionally, in alphabetical order within each company. The third set was arranged by military specialty; all the scouts, all the infantry, all the cavalry, and so on.

Now, depending on what was needed, he could put his hands on the exact men with the precise skills that were required.

He did not believe that any other commander in the history of the Empire had ever done such a thing, not even when copying records had been a simple matter of a mage and a duplication-spell. Odd, considering what a bureaucracy the Empire was—but this was an innovation, and innovation was not encouraged in the Imperial Army.

For good or ill, he was in charge; Sandar's deference to his authority and the attitude of his Council made that clear. It was the position he had aimed for, but the implication that it had been granted him meant he was now, effectively, the liege lord of Shonar, with all the responsibilities of that office toward "his" civilians.

Five

Karal waited for Jarim to finish speaking, then got wearily to his cold, benumbed feet. *Why am I doing this? No one is going to pay any attention.* His face felt stiff and frozen as he addressed people that were not even looking at him—except for Firesong, Darkwind, and the Valdemaran Heralds, who at least pretended to listen.

I'm doing this because they're going to overlook the most significant statement in that spy report that Kerowyn read us, that's why. Jarim has already tried to bury it in rhetoric. "Herald Captain Kerowyn, I believe that you said in your report that the Imperial forces seem to be cooperating with and protecting the civilians of the Hardornen city of Shonar, and that the citizens of Shonar do not seem to be under any duress and are, in fact, cooperating with the Imperials. Did I misunderstand that report, or do I grasp the facts correctly?"

"That was the report from one of my operatives, yes," Kerowyn acknowledged. "Mind you, he got his information on Shonar only at secondhand. None of our operatives have penetrated that far personally."

"Nevertheless, the evidence is that the Imperials have been accepted as the authority for these people in and around Shonar. They are certainly acting in a protective manner." He swallowed and said the unthinkable. *This is it. They're going to think that I'm quite mad now. Or that I'm a coward.* "Given the appalling conditions in Hardorn, and given the fact that we know because of the reports from the Herald Captain's operatives that the mage-storms are causing more havoc on top of an already unstable and precarious situation, I believe we ought to leave the Imperial forces alone. Harassing them in any way would be counterproductive for the citizens of Hardorn." Well enough, he had said that before. But now he would go completely out on a limb. "My personal recommendation is that we at least *consider* opening negotiations with them so that we can give some aid to Hardorn without that aid being read as an attack."

Jarim predictably exploded; Talia interrupted his tirade before it began, as she stood up and repeated what Karal had said. "The envoy from Karse recommends that we at least discuss the possibility of opening negotiations with the Imperials," she said. "Doing so would give us an opportunity to render some aid to the people of Hardorn, and would certainly allow us to insert operatives in as far as Shonar. On purely humanitarian grounds, I second the envoy's suggestion and advise that we talk about this."

Although no one except Talia and Jarim had paid any attention to what Karal had said, when Talia repeated it, in practically the same words, the rest of the Grand Council suddenly took notice, and a real discussion erupted.

Jarim took no part in the talk but, instead, continued to glare at Karal from across the table. Karal just sank his head into his hand and listened to the argument and counterargument. *I've made my contribution; nothing else I say will matter until it all comes to a vote.*

None of this was new. Despite the early apology from the Shin'a'in envoy and the outward appearance of tolerance, Jarim's hostility had not abated and had become increasingly personal. Karal was not sure why. Perhaps someone had convinced him that the Karsites and Querna had not gotten along, although the reverse was actually true. He had admired the Shin'a'in Querna. Ulrich had considered her a friend on the personal level. If Jarim knew any of this, he did not seem to believe it.

Maybe he just resents the fact that An'desha, Darkwind, Talia, Elspeth, and the gryphons like me and they don't much care for him. Or maybe he's just a fanatic.

And despite the fact that Karal made it a point never to

speak up in the Grand Council sessions unless he had something of substance to contribute, no one ever paid any attention to what he said except Jarim, and Jarim paid attention only so he could immediately belittle it. In fact, Talia had taken to repeating what he said almost verbatim so that it would at least be brought up for serious consideration.

Was it just that he was so young? He'd tried everything save cosmetics and coloring his hair gray to make himself look older. He'd tried a dignified manner and cultivating a deep and booming voice; he'd tried wearing a stark black set of full formal Sun-priest robes. A more elaborate costume had been suggested to him, but he'd felt so ridiculous in it that he hadn't dared try it in public.

I felt like a walking shrine. Or an actor done up for a miracle-play.

He was grateful to Talia for her assistance, but this was no way for him to conduct his office. Before long, this kind of situation would affect not only how he was treated in this room, but how he was treated outside it. What little authority he had with his own people, the Karsites here in Valdemar, would soon be eroded by the fact that no one respected him in the Grand Council meetings.

He didn't know what else he could do. If an enemy, either of him personally or of Karse, had *wanted* to undermine his authority, they could not have organized anything more effective than what his own youth and perceived inexperience was doing.

Could it be Jarim's doing? I can't see how. The only reason anyone listens to him is because he shouts louder than I do.

His insides were nothing but one twisted, snarled knot, and had been that way for days. He had been living on herb tea and plain bread, for nothing else would stay in his stomach for long. *I'd be drinking myself to sleep, if I didn't know that the liquor would only come right back up after I drank it,* he thought glumly. He'd tried sending word of his difficulties back to Karse, but all he got in return were reassuring messages full of platitudes. It was as if Solaris or her advisers weren't even reading the pleas he'd been sending—or were ignoring the content as the vaporings of an inexperienced and homesick boy.

I am homesick, but only because I can't get anything done here. I'd happily go back to being a secretary, even under an unpleasant and unfriendly master.

If he couldn't even get his own people to listen to what he was saying, what hope did he have of convincing anyone here?

He needed authority, and not even his own countrymen were going to exert themselves to see that he got it.

I want to go home. I want to bury myself in books. I'm not important; I've done everything I needed to here. Anyone Solaris could assign here would be better than me.

He closed his eyes as his stomach cramped, grimacing and quickly covering it. *Karse would have been better off if Altra had protected Ulrich instead of me,* he thought, clenching his jaw to control his expression. *Before long, I will be doing my land great harm by remaining in this office, because disregard for me will become disregard for Karse.*

He had begged, pleaded for someone to be sent to relieve him, citing that very thing, but his pleas had been ignored. Why? He had no idea.

If it had not been for Florian, Natoli, and An'desha, he would have thrown himself into the river days ago. All three of them kept encouraging him—though the one creature who might have been able to help him was conspicuous by his absence. Altra had not put in a single appearance in all that time. Karal was beginning to wonder if he had somehow offended the Firecat. Or worse, offended Vkandis Sunlord.

Perhaps he has deserted me. Perhaps Vkandis no longer favors me. Perhaps He has abandoned me for the same reason that Jarim hates me—because I see no reason to waste time, resources, and lives in persecuting the Imperials. Aren't the mage-storms punishment enough? Must vengeance go on forever? Perhaps He thinks so.

That only depressed him further, and his stomach and throat knotted more tightly.

Why was he continuing in this farce? The only reason why

he didn't get up and walk out now was that he was just too tired. *Perhaps tomorrow I simply won't get out of bed. I'll cancel everything. I'll tell the servants I'm too ill to get up. The results of the day will be exactly the same. . . .*

But he knew he wouldn't do that. It wasn't in his nature. *I wish I really was ill; I wish I could break a leg or an arm or something, so I'd have an excuse not to get up. I wish I was really, seriously ill, perhaps with pneumonia, so they'd give me drugs to make me sleep, and I wouldn't have to think about any of this.*

What a fine pass he'd come to, when he would rather be seriously injured or sick than have to face his duty and his work!

He was supposed to join An'desha and Natoli and go to the Compass Rose as soon as the meeting was over, but he didn't have the heart for it now. *I can't face the others tonight. I'm no kind of company. I'll just crawl off to my room and see if I can't catch up on some of my correspondence. I can try one more letter to Solaris. . . .*

Maybe this was his punishment for not taking care of Ulrich as he had promised. Perhaps Solaris had decided that he should suffer for not keeping his promise. If so, it was certainly working.

Finally the debate wound down to a close, concluding, as he had hoped, that there was nothing to be gained by harassing the Imperials, and that the innocent civilians of Shonar could be harmed in the process. The group was split equally on the subject of opening negotiations, with himself, Talia, and Darkwind conspicuously on the side of negotiating and Jarim, Kerowyn, and Elspeth the leaders against. Finally, the session came to an end, and he was free to stand up with the others and trail out. He waited for everyone except the most minor of secretaries to precede him, hoping that no one would notice whether or not he had left the room; right now, he didn't want to talk to anyone, not even for idle small talk. His robes seemed to weigh down his shoulders like slabs of stone as he finally stood and collected his notes and his gear. He stowed them all in the leather pouch he had carried as Ulrich's secretary. His neck ached, and there were places beneath both shoulder blades that were so knotted it felt as if he was being stabbed there with a dull pick.

At that moment, he was perfectly well aware that he would have exchanged his lot in life for that of the lowest servant in Vkandis' temple. He'd gladly be a horseboy in the Temple stables. He'd cheerfully tend the Temple pigsty. He'd scrub the floors for the most ill-tempered priest in Karse. . . .

But it seemed that his misery had not yet reached its nadir, for Jarim was waiting for him just outside the door of the Council Chamber, and there were several other members of the Grand Council loitering conspicuously in the hallway. It was very clear to him at that moment that Jarim wanted a confrontation, and these jackals were waiting avidly for some entertainment.

The best way to avoid that is to avoid the confrontation. It takes two to argue, and I'm not going to give him the opportunity. He tried to ignore Jarim, keeping his eyes down and his face without expression as he attempted to ease past the Shin'a'in, but Jarim reached out and seized his arm before he could get out of the way.

"And where do you think you are going, traitor?" Jarim asked loudly, as he tried to pull loose without turning it into a physical fight. "Can't wait to get back to your kennel, dog, and howl to your Imperial masters? So eager to let them know the good news? And what bone will they toss to you for ensuring their safety? Land? Gold? Some of their magics, maybe? Not content with what your God can give you anymore? Is it so easy to betray your old master?" Jarim spat— not into his face, but at his feet. "Did you serve him only to get a chance to betray him, dog?"

Karal had expected an attack, but not this one—and not so vehemently. He froze, half paralyzed and quite unable to form anything coherent; he had no reply at all to Jarim's accusations. His head came up and he stared into Jarim's angry face, thunderstruck, and cold all over. He couldn't speak, he couldn't even think clearly. What demon possessed the man to make him so obsessed and so certain that Karal was a traitor, that Karal would have betrayed the one man in the world he had thought of as his second father?

Jarim snarled angrily at his silence; but when Karal didn't move, his grip loosened just enough that Karal was able to pull himself free. Karal's paralysis lifted, and he jerked his sleeve and arm out of Jarim's hand so violently that he staggered half a dozen paces down the hallway.

Then he stood there for a moment, chilled to the bone, staring back at Jarim and the Council members gathered beside him. Karal's mouth worked, but not his voice. Not even a whisper emerged—which might have been just as well, since whatever he might have said would have been incomprehensible babbling.

He backed up a pace instead, then another—then turned abruptly and fled, robes flying, back to his suite.

He knew that his silence in the face of Jarim's incredible accusation had only confirmed his guilt in the eyes of the onlookers. He was certain that by day's end, the rumor would spread everywhere that he had been working all along for the Empire; that he had survived the attack on Ulrich because he had been meant to by his Imperial masters. And he had no way, none whatsoever, to prove that the accusation was false.

Florian found him in the dead and deserted gardens, long past sunset. His suite had not been the refuge he had thought it, for the moment he reached its doors, it had occurred to him that Jarim knew where it was, and could very easily find him here. And if the Shin'a'in was as fanatical as he seemed to be, Jarim might well decide to deal with a traitor in Shin'a'in fashion; quickly and decisively, at the point of a hunting knife. Granted the murder of another envoy would cause him a certain amount of difficulty—unless he managed to convince everyone that he had proof of Karal's guilt. He just might manufacture that "proof," knowing that with Karal dead there would be no way to refute it.

So he had paused just long enough to snatch up his warmest cloak, a hat and long scarf, and a pair of mittens. Then he had fled to the gardens, in the hope of finding some peace there until Jarim's temper should cool. And in the somewhat desperate hope that something, anything, would occur to him to help him defend himself against his accuser. He found a secluded bench and sagged down on it, an anonymous form in a dark, hooded cloak, huddled in such a way as to discourage anyone thinking of approaching him.

It had been late afternoon when he went down; it was after dark when Florian found him, looming up out of the thick gloom as silently as a ghost. Karal saw Florian out of the corner of his eye, but he was so sunk in misery at that point that it didn't seem worthwhile to do anything about the Companion's presence. *:Karal?:* the Companion said hesitantly when Karal didn't even move to greet him. *:Karal, you're in trouble.:*

"Tell me something I don't already know," Karal replied bitterly without raising his head, speaking down at the ground between his feet.

:No, I mean real, serious trouble,: the Companion said, unhappily. *:Jarim has been going around the Court telling everyone—:*

"That I'm an Imperial agent. I know." Bile rose in the back of his throat, and he wondered if he was going to be sick right then and there.

:Worse than that, people believed him. Even Heralds. There were a great many people who couldn't believe that a foolish artist was the real agent at Court.: Florian shifted his weight, and a few pebbles rolled out from under his hooves as he scuffed them against the gravel. *:It is worse that Heralds believe him. Nothing I have said will convince them that you are not what Jarim says you are.:*

That surprised him in a dull way. "But—you're a Companion—"

:And you are not my Chosen. They won't believe even me since you aren't my Chosen. They believe that you have deceived me.: Florian sounded depressed, which certainly didn't help Karal's mood at all. *:I don't know what to do, Karal.:*

"Neither do I, except to saddle my horse and go home." *Or fling myself into the river, but that wouldn't accomplish very much either, although it would probably make Jarim very pleased with himself. Well, riding off would make him very pleased, too. I've certainly made a mess of this entire situation. I don't know how anyone could salvage it now.*

Florian couldn't seem to stop talking, although Karal would rather have been left alone with his own thoughts. *:I don't know who is on his side, precisely, nor how many there are. I only know for certain about the Heralds. . . . :*

"I suppose I might as well go back into the Palace and see how many people believe him," Karal said finally. "We might be pleasantly surprised, I suppose."

:You don't sound very optimistic.:

"Neither do you," Karal replied. "But before I saddle up and go home in utter disgrace, I might as well find out just how bad things are. I'd have to report just how much of a disaster I've created, no matter what."

He rose slowly and stiffly and wrapped his cloak closely about him, walking back to the beckoning lights of the Palace on leaden feet.

As he discovered the moment he entered the Palace, things were very bad indeed.

Conversations stopped the moment he entered the hallway; as he passed through one of the reception chambers, he was surrounded by an aura of silence. People would turn to stare at him, then deliberately turn their backs on him. Once he passed, though, conversations resumed, loud enough to make certain that he heard them.

"It's bad enough being a traitor, but being a coward as well. . . ."

"He must be some sort of mage, disguising himself. No one could be that vile and look that young."

"I'm surprised his own god hasn't struck him down dead before this."

Those were the personal comments; he was fairly certain he wasn't hearing the others—the speculations on how everything vile that was ever said about Karse must be true. How Solaris must have *known* he was a traitor—and had set that poor fellow Ulrich up as a sacrificial lamb to eliminate suspicion against Karse.

Servants pointedly ignored him as he passed, and once he

reached his suite, he found it precisely as he had left it. Which meant, of course, that no servant had set foot in here to clean it, and quite probably no servant would from this moment on. They would "forget," or leave the rooms until last, then "fall ill" just as they reached his door. If he had thought things were uncomfortable when he and Ulrich had arrived, well . . . the hostility now was more than double. All the old prejudices were springing back to life, with redoubled vigor for having been suppressed for so long.

He stood in the doorway for a moment, trying to make up his mind about what he should do. Should he start packing and leave this very moment? He thought he had just about enough money to get to the border, if he stayed in very modest inns. He would have to be circumspect when he talked, but his Valdemaran was fairly good now; he might be able to pass for a foreign priest from anywhere but Karse.

Maybe I could talk Florian into coming with me? I might be able to purloin some Herald's Whites from the Palace laundry and pass as a Herald until I got home—or better yet, it would be a lot easier to get hold of one of the gray uniforms the trainees wear. For once it wouldn't be so bad to look young.

Would Florian be willing to go along with the scheme?

He heard footsteps down the hall, and moved inside, quickly, closing the door behind him. Maybe he couldn't get Florian to help, but the idea of purloining a uniform gave him another notion. *I can get Natoli to find someone to loan me one of the unaffiliated students' blue uniforms. Then no one will bother me. I can just say I'm going home if anyone asks, and it won't be a lie.*

He started to turn toward his bedroom, planning to start packing immediately, but a knock on his door startled him into immobility.

Who could it be? He could think of any number of possibilities, and few of them made him *want* to answer the door.

The knock came again. "Karal?" said a soft female voice. "I know you're in there; I can sense you, and I know you aren't more than two steps from the door. It's Herald Talia, and you might as well open up."

Talia? She was one of the few people he had *not* thought of. He had to obey her, actually; in the hierarchy of Vkandis she was senior to him. He reversed his turn and let her in. She blinked at the darkness, for he had not had time to light more than the single candle beside the door.

"I see the shunning has begun already," she said dryly, and moved past him so he could close the door again. He nodded; both the Karsites and the Holderkin used the ritual of "shunning," where someone who had been cast out of the community was ignored and avoided from that moment on by all the faithful. It had driven sensitive people in Karse to suicide before this; presumably it had the same effect on Holderkin.

"I'm dealing with the Heralds on your behalf," she told him, taking the candle from the holder beside the door and moving with it to the other side of the room to light the lamps for him. "I am sorry that idiot Jarim started all this; it's going to take some time to untangle it and more time to undo all the damage from his foolish fanaticism."

Karal sagged down into a chair, depression overcoming him. "It's never going to be untangled," he said bluntly. "And I'm not sure it's worth the effort to try. Even if you manage to convince the Heralds, even if by some miracle you manage to convince everyone else, you'll *never* convince Jarim. It would be better for everyone if I just go home and let Solaris send another envoy in my place."

"Jarim would win," Talia replied. "Why should you let him?"

"Why shouldn't I?" he countered. "I wasn't particularly effective *before* he started all this, and you know that's true. Even if you convinced everyone that I'm the innocent victim of Jarim's prejudice, you'll never persuade them that I have a copper's worth of sense. I'm too young; I'm young enough to be the child of anyone sitting at that table, except maybe Elspeth, and I wouldn't bet on that. No one there trusts me. I'm too young to have any experience, too young to let my emotions take second place to my reason."

She didn't immediately reply as she went about the room lighting lamps and candles, and he closed his eyes for a moment. "Herald Talia—*Sun-priest*—we might as well both admit it. I am doing neither Karse nor the Alliance any good here. I might as well go home and let someone who is competent, experienced, and new take over."

She turned then, and looked at him with a solemn expression on her face, a single curl of reddish-brown hair falling over one eye. "Have you been recalled?" she asked, the candle clasped in both hands.

"Well, no," he admitted. "But—"

"Does Solaris speak for Vkandis, or not?" she persisted.

"Well, yes—but—"

"And don't you think after all this that if Vkandis perceived your presence here as detrimental to Karse you would have been recalled by now?" she continued mercilessly. "It's not as if Altra couldn't convey your recall papers from Solaris *immediately* if that was called for. Given the situation here, there is every reason to bring you back—unless there is a more compelling reason that Solaris and Vkandis are not ready to reveal to leave you here."

When he didn't reply, she fixed him with a sharp glare. "Well?" she prompted.

He gulped, and shrugged. "I suppose so, but—"

"No 'buts,' " she said, sternly, with more authority concentrated in her tiny figure than in a hundred generals he had seen. "As a Sun-priest, I can vouch for all of that, and so can you. There is a reason why Vkandis wants you here and no one else. We may not know what it is, but there is certainly a reason."

Then I wish He'd tell me what it is. "That's fine in theory," he replied, "but just at the moment it doesn't seem to me that anyone in Haven wants me here. How am I supposed to get anything done when most of the Grand Council thinks I'm working for the Imperials, and at least one envoy wants to murder me?"

She made a grimace of distaste and walked over to the door to replace the candle in its holder. "That, I must admit, I have no answer for," she said, with her back to him. "But I think you should at least absent yourself from the Palace for a few days, and stay away from meetings. Say that you're sick—or *I* will. I'll tell Selenay that you've been so overcome with shock at Jarim's accusations that you've collapsed." She turned back, and surveyed him with a critical eye. "From the look of you, I won't be telling that big of a lie. Much more stress and you're going to be the youngest man I know with a bleeding stomach. You're well on the way to it; you haven't been eating or sleeping well, have you?"

He stared at her. "No!" he blurted, "but how did you—"

"I *am* the one with the Gift of Empathy," she reminded him, "And I've been associating with Healers for most of my life. I think you ought to see if An'desha and Firesong can take you in again. I'll have the Healers send you over some medicines. Better yet, I'll send one of the Healers there in person."

He scowled, and she laughed.

"Oh, don't look at me like that," she said. "The teas and potions for stress and a rebelling stomach are probably some of the best things you'll have ever tasted in your life. They have to be; otherwise people who are under stress wouldn't drink them, and people with bad stomachs wouldn't be able to keep them down. Go pack," she concluded. "Pack enough for about a week, and I'll go find An'desha and see if there's room in that *ekele* for a third person."

She turned and started toward the door when another knock stopped her dead in her tracks.

"Karal?" came the quiet voice from the other side of the wooden door. "It's An'desha and Natoli. We're here to help you, if you want."

Talia opened the door so quickly that she left An'desha standing there with his hand still raised for another knock, Natoli fidgeting beside him.

"In," she ordered; both of them obeyed instantly, and she shut the door behind them.

Natoli spoke before either Talia or Karal could say anything, her words pouring out in a rush. "You didn't come to the Rose and we were both worried about you because you've been looking like death and we came back here to find out if you were all right and have you *heard* what they're saying about you? They're—"

"Saying that I'm an Imperial spy and that I'm responsible

for just about everything bad that's happened since I arrived, yes, I know," he interrupted, and sagged down in his chair again, one hand rubbing his stinging eyes. "Some people have probably even decided that I brought the mage-storms with me by now. Or that I was somehow to blame for Ancar being born."

"You're not far wrong. There're even some Heralds prating a lot of nonsense, and not even Father can talk any sense into them," Natoli said grimly, looking at Talia with a challenging expression, as if daring *her* to do something.

Karal was a little amazed at her audacity—a simple *student*, challenging the Queen's Own Herald? And not even a Heraldic student at that?

"I'm doing what I can, but it's going to take some time," Talia replied, and smiled thinly. "I'm beginning to understand what Herald Savil was supposed to have gone through over Vanyel when he was first Chosen. Like Vanyel after Tylendel died, Karal seems to be getting the blame for things that happened before he was born. It's going to be interesting."

Natoli gave an unladylike snort, while An'desha just looked bewildered.

"Meanwhile," Talia continued, turning to An'desha, "I'd like to get him out of the Palace for a while so that people can calm down, and I would like to see that he gets some rest before his stomach begins to bleed from all the strain he's going through. Can you and Firesong take him in again?"

"I was going to offer just that," An'desha replied. "Firesong's been off on some project of his own anyway, so he'll get lots of peace and quiet at our *ekele*. Are you going to claim he's collapsed with shock and stress?"

"That was the general idea," Talia told him. "And if I can get a Healer to confirm that, it will simply add to the story."

"Will you please stop talking about me as if I'm not here?" Karal asked plaintively, looking from one to the other.

An'desha patted his shoulder and looked down at him with speculation, as if there were a number of ideas going around inside his head and he was just weighing them all to determine which one might be the best. "Sorry, my friend," he apologized, then took a closer look at him. "You look like you've been dragged at the heels of a horse across the Dhorisha Plains," he said, with a frown. "Herald Talia, please have a real Healer attend us as soon as we get to the *ekele*, would you?"

Karal stared in surprise; that didn't sound like the diffident young Shin'a'in he knew. That sounded more like someone who took it as given that he was Talia's equal.

She nodded just as if she accepted his status, too, and slipped out the door before Karal had a chance to object. "You stay here with Natoli; I think I can manage to pack for you," the young Shin'a'in continued sternly. "Anything I forget, you can borrow from me. If *I* have anything to say about it, you won't need anything but a bedshirt for two or three days anyway."

As An'desha disappeared into his bedchamber before he could object to *that*, Karal looked at Natoli with a face full of woe.

"Don't I get *any* choice in any of this?" he asked.

He got no sympathy from her.

"No," she said flatly. "You don't. You've done your best, and you've gotten into a mess you can't do anything about. You're tired to death, you're sick with strain, and your judgment is not good right now. We're going to take over and let you rest, so you might as well relax and enjoy it."

Be careful what you ask for, he thought, as the memory of his earlier wishes flashed into his mind. *You might get it.*

An'desha and Natoli took Karal and his bag across Companion's Field, trailed anxiously by every Companion there. Florian led the parade, which under other circumstances might have been hilariously funny. A hard frost was forming; the stiff blades of grass crackled underfoot, and their breath hung in frosty clouds in the still, cold air. Behind them followed dozens more "clouds," the silent, white forms of the Companions. They weren't being herded; An'desha would have recognized that behavior. They were worried about

Karal, and although he was no Empath, their concern was strong enough it made itself palpable even to him.

The Healer was waiting for them just inside when they reached the *ekele,* her eyes closed as she breathed in the faint, sweet perfume of some of Firesong's night-blooming flowers. "Thank you for letting me come here. I know this is just a more sophisticated version of a forcing-house," she said to An'desha as they entered through Firesong's clever double door that kept cold drafts out. "But this place always seems the epitome of *magic* to me."

"You could build one of these yourself, with one of our steam boilers and pipes to send hot water through the room to heat it," Natoli told her matter-of-factly.

"You could *not* have plants this large and healthy in a matter of weeks without the magic, however," An'desha countered firmly, standing up for *his* discipline. "Here is your patient, lady Healer—" He pushed Karal to the front, as his friend seemed inclined to lag back, trying to avoid attention.

The Healer took Karal's wrist, put her free hand under his chin so that he could not look away from her eyes, and frowned as she stared into his face. "One would think you were a much older man—or a Herald—the way you have abused yourself. Come, child," she continued, although Karal was not a great deal younger than she. "I think you should be put straight to bed."

"I am very glad to hear you say that," An'desha told her, relieved. "Follow me, please."

Before long, Karal was indeed in bed, dosed with several potions from the Healer's bag, and blinking sleepily. An'desha had his instructions and a line of bottles of more of the same stuff with which to ensure that Karal remained in his bed and permitted his poor abused insides to heal. The Healer, who never had given her name, also left a list of what Karal was and was not permitted to eat.

"We can't do this for long," the Healer said warningly to both An'desha and Natoli. "These herbs in this row are powerful and dangerous, and they shouldn't be used for more than a week. However, I do not think that he will need to be forced to rest for more than a few days. After that, these other potions, these brews, and good, soothing foods should effect the rest of the cure."

"Provided we can keep Jarim from turning all our work into nothing," Natoli muttered. The Healer looked at her without comprehension.

"Never mind, she's just thinking out loud," An'desha told the Healer. "Thank you, we're very grateful."

"Well, *I'm* grateful that Herald Talia caught him before he had a real bleeding stomach," the Healer said cheerfully. "That's ten times harder to cure. Good night to you!"

After the young woman had gone off into the night, Natoli turned to An'desha with discontent written all over her intelligent face. "All my life I've heard about how the Healers can cure almost anything that's not congenital," she said. "I've heard how they can piece shattered bone together, how they can make wounds close before your very eyes!"

"So?" An'desha asked, heading back toward the stairs and the living area of the *ekele.*

"So why didn't she *do* something?" Natoli demanded as she followed. "All she did was look at him, put him to bed, make him drink a couple of messes of leaves, and that was it! He's been looking like grim death for days, and he doesn't look much better now, so why didn't she wave her hands around or whatever it is they do and make him well without all this resting and drinking teas?"

An'desha paused on the staircase and looked down at her, trying to think of an analogy for her. "Would you build one of your big steam engines just to convey a few pots of tea to the Grand Council Chamber all day?"

"No, of course not; that's what pages are for," she replied impatiently. "What does that have to do with Healing?"

"There is no point in this Healer using a great deal of energy—energy that comes from *within* her by the way—just to perform a task that her herbs and minerals will accomplish, particularly not when Karal's life is not in any danger." He raised an eyebrow and Natoli flushed; he figured he might as well not bother to point out that Talia could well have asked for an Herbalist-Healer rather than one who relied completely on her powers. "She is simply using her resources logically. You would scarcely thank her for exhausting herself over Karal if—oh, say later tonight the Rose were to burn down and she would be unable to help some of your friends who were burned, because she had no energy left. It's a matter of proper use of resources, my friend, and not any slight intended toward Karal." He looked back over Natoli's head, into the darkness beyond the garden windows, and smiled. "Of all of the many kinds of people who may have been deceived by Jarim's foolish accusations, you may rely on it that no Healer picked by Lady Talia will be one of them."

He looked back down at Natoli, who grimaced. "I suppose I'm jumping at shadows," she said reluctantly. "And I keep forgetting that Healers are supposed to work differently than you mages."

"Not quite; you are used to seeing the Masters and Adepts at work," An'desha interrupted, as he resumed his climb, with Natoli just behind him. "Journeymen and Apprentices—and what are called 'hedge-wizards' and 'earth-witches'—also rely entirely on their own reserves of energy, unless they are extremely sensitive to the currents of energy about them. Even then, they cannot use either the great ley-lines or the nodes where the lines meet. Only Masters can use the former, and Adepts can use both. But there are many, many mages who do their work very effectively with no more power than what lies within them."

Natoli shook her head in frustration; An'desha turned to face her again as she stepped up into the gathering room of the *ekele*. "It all obeys rules," he chided her. "It is all perfectly logical. Do not be the equivalent of a Firesong, who refuses to believe that the energies of magic cannot obey rules and logic. It is no more illogical to say that one must be born with the ability to become an Adept than it is to say that one must be born with the ability to become a sculptor or an artificer."

"That isn't logical either," Natoli replied with irritation. "All people should be born equal."

He laughed at her. "Now it is *you* who are being illogical, assuming that because the natural world does not follow what you perceive to be the regular pacings of the world of numbers, the natural world should be discarded!"

She didn't reply, but he heard her muttering under her breath, and it was probably not very complimentary. He didn't mind; in fact, he rather enjoyed teasing Natoli, who he felt was far too serious for her own good.

Not unlike myself, in some ways. He ignored the mutters and went back to the room that had once been "his," which had been Karal's temporary refuge once before.

Karal was still awake, but even to An'desha's inexperienced eyes he was fighting a losing battle against the potions the Healer had given him. "You should sleep," An'desha said, sitting down beside the Shin'a'in-style pallet that lay on the floor. Natoli knelt next to him.

"I 'spose I should." Karal yawned hugely, and blinked. "Funny. I *wanted* to get sick, 'cause then I could just—stay in bed—and—"

"Well, you *are* sick and you *will* stay in bed and do what you're told," Natoli said severely. "There is no point in trying to fight it."

He smiled, a smile of unexpected, childlike sweetness. "I won't," he replied. "Just wanted to say—thank you."

"You're welcome," An'desha told him, as Natoli patted his hand. "Now sleep."

To prevent any more attempts at conversation, he extinguished the lamp with a thought, and got up, leaving Karal and Natoli alone in the faint light coming from the lamp in the hall.

He went down to the garden again, leaving her to find her own way out. She and Karal had not had much privacy to be together for the past several weeks, and he thought it was about time that they had a chance for a word or two before Karal couldn't fight the drugs anymore.

I'll give them a better chance later, he promised himself.

As for him—he had some ideas that might be helpful, but he also needed some privacy to put them to the test. The primary one was that he should try something he had not attempted since Falconsbane leaped from his body as it lay dying.

He waited, watching the fountain, until Natoli descended the staircase again, wrapped in her cloak. She didn't notice him, and he didn't interrupt her introspection as she let herself out quietly. Then he let the falling water lull him until he was in that half-aware state in which it was easy to slip into a trance.

Then he sought the Moonpaths.

He was not certain he would be permitted to find them; after all, the Moonpaths were to be walked by shaman, Sword-Sworn and Goddess-Sworn, not for just anyone. The Avatars had taught him how to reach them so that he would have a safe place to meet them where he could talk with them while Falconsbane slept. But now he sent his spirit *out*, and *up*, in that familiar twisting of reality—

And he was there, standing on a path of silver sand, surrounded by a gray mist that glowed with its own pearly light.

I did it! He savored his elation; he was never certain when the Avatars would show themselves anymore, and it seemed best that if he *could* go to them, he should, rather than waiting for them to come to him. Their relationship with him had changed since he had come to Valdemar; when they answered his questions at all, it was obliquely. Rather than giving him answers or teaching him directly now, they gave him the briefest of guidance, leading him to find his own answers to his questions.

Then again, his questions were more difficult to answer, and the answers were of necessity more subjective than objective. In many ways, he was now determining what he wanted to make of himself and his life by the answers he uncovered.

I am learning what I am by determining what Falconsbane was in all of his lives, and determining why he did what he did and why he thought what he thought, then deliberately taking the opposite direction.

Well, that was grand philosophy, but at the moment he had need of some of those other answers, the simple ones. He hoped that the Avatars, particularly Tre'valen, could help him. After all, the real problem lay with Jarim, a Shin'a'in—and weren't they both the Avatars of the Star-Eyed? If Jarim got a visit from Tre-valen in all his glory, and was told in no uncertain terms that he was mistaken entirely about Karal, wouldn't that solve the entire problem right then and there?

That was his hope, anyway.

He sent his thoughts questing out into the mist, hunting for his teachers and guides; it was not possible to reckon the exact passage of time in that timeless place, but it was not too long before he was answered.

The mist above the path shimmered in a double column of light; then, with a shiver, solidified into two figures. One was male, the other female; the male of the two was clearly Shin'a'in, but the female was not. Her clothing and her hair, a long waterfall of silver, marked her as a Hawkbrother, Tayledras—or in Shin'a'in, Tale'edras—as were Firesong and Darkwind. Although they looked wholly human, there was a suggestion of great wings, wings of flame, in the air behind them. They, too, glowed with their own inner light, and their eyes, as they gazed smiling upon An'desha, had neither whites nor pupils. Instead, they were the dark of a night full of stars, and in the black depths shone tiny sparks of light.

When Shin'a'in called their Goddess of Four Aspects the Star-Eyed, this was what they meant, for She and all of Her spirit-servants and Avatars had eyes like this. It was a sure way to know them, and was impossible to counterfeit—so An'desha had been told.

"Well, little brother." Tre'valen crossed his arms in a curiously human gesture and looked upon his pupil with approval. "You have not forgotten your lessons."

"I would not have dared to come here, if I had not the need," An'desha said hastily. "I beg that you will indulge me—"

"Oh, we know, we know; you are altogether too diffident," said Dawnfire with a laugh. "So come, what is it that brings you here, seeking us?"

"It is my friend Karal," An'desha said. "The envoy of the Shin'a'in who replaced Querna is—is causing him great despair."

Quickly, for he had carefully rehearsed all that he wanted to say if he got the chance, he related troubles that Jarim had wrought since his arrival. Tre'valen and Dawnfire listened sympathetically, but when he had finished, their words were a disappointment.

"I am sorry, little brother, but there is nothing that we can do to help," Tre'valen said with finality. "I wish for your sake and for his that there was—but there is not. You and all the others involved in this sad situation will have to work your own way through this."

"Only if it is clear—clear to Her, that is—that we must act or the consequences will be catastrophic, will we be permitted to intrude," Dawnfire added, although her expression was sympathetic. "I am sorry."

An'desha sighed, but he did not bother to make any further pleas although their words disappointed him greatly. *I was brought up on all of the tales of the Star-Eyed and how She sends aid only when all other courses have been exhausted. I should not be upset at this.*

In fact, sometimes She did not aid at all—unless a price was paid in lives. That, too, was something he had known.

He should not have been so disappointed, but he was, and they saw it in his eyes. He thought of poor Karal, lying on that pallet, pale and too thin with trying and failing to do a job that was beyond his strength. He thought of smug Jarim, sneering at the halfbreed An'desha, radiating an unreasoning hatred whenever he looked at Karal. There was an awkward silence for a moment, then words burst from him. "She tries Karal past his endurance, and so does his own God!" he cried. "Is that fair?"

But Tre'valen only gazed at him steadily. "Fair?" the Avatar repeated. "You ask me if this is fair? And—you think that She and He are responsible for this?"

An'desha spread his hands mutely.

"Do you think that She is some sort of trainer of men, as one trains horses, heaping trial upon trial on a man to see if he shall fail, and how he bears up beneath the load?" Tre'valen asked. "Do you think that the Sunlord is a great clerk, with His ledger, noting what is fair and unfair and making a sheet of debts and credits?"

"It has been implied—" An'desha began.

"By men," Tre'valen said sternly. "By men, An'desha, who would take their own narrow views of the world and squeeze the gods into those views; who would put their words in the mouths of their gods. No. They are constrained, by Their own wills, to give *us* the freedom to make our own choices and live or die by them. We are Their fledglings, but when the time comes to leave the nest, They cannot fly for us. The world is what *we* make of it, for it was given to us—as your tent is what you make of it, for it was given to you. You may keep it neat and in repair, or you may let the poles break, the hides rot. That is the truth. It is a hard truth, but truth is often hard to bear."

An'desha flushed, feeling obscurely ashamed of his outburst.

"It is only when we have passed the bonds of this world that They may act—or when events have passed into realms where nothing men can do will mend them. Your events have come nowhere near that point." Tre'valen finally smiled at him warmly, and An'desha flushed again, feeling as if he had been taken gently to task for something that should have been obvious.

"There are many courses that *you* may yet take," Dawnfire suggested. "Think of all the friends that you and Karal have, those who will not be swayed by a hateful man's willful blindness. I can tell you that the Healer already spreads her tale of a poor young man tried past endurance, and there are as many sympathetic ears as unsympathetic. You might think on what ears you may find."

Well, that was true enough, and while Karal was recovering, Jarim would not have a target for his abuses.

Unless he takes me for a target—and then, I think, it is likely since he will not only have to contend with me, but with Firesong, and Firesong is a past master at making fools look as foolish as they truly are. The thought made him smile a little.

Still—it would not be easy for him to move among the people of the Valdemaran Court, defending Karal's honor and honesty. He still often felt gawky and out of place except during a crisis, when he was too busy to think or feel self-conscious.

But I am Shin'a'in. Jarim cannot deny my heritage. And I, beyond anyone here, can vouch for Karal. Did I not see him with his master, and the way the two acted with one another? Did he not bring me through my own darkness? Did he not place his life in jeopardy to protect not only his land, but those of all the Alliance? I can speak to all of this, these things that others seem to have conveniently forgotten.

"You have all the resources that you need to solve this trial without our intervention, little brother," Dawnfire said as he thought through all of this. "You need only to reason out where to look, where to reach, what to grasp, and how."

Tre'valen laughed. "And know who to ask, and guess what will result, and know how to cope with the results, and after that, the universe is easy to live with, hey?"

To his own surprise, An'desha laughed along with the Avatar, his earlier shame forgotten. He realized at that moment that he felt much more comfortable with the Avatars now than he ever had dreamed he would.

"We are your friends, An'desha," Dawnfire said, as if she was following his thoughts.

He nodded, feeling the same warmth he knew in Karal's company. They *were* his friends, as well as his guides and teachers—and could it be that the distance between them, that gulf between student and mentor, was narrowing more with every moment?

"Soon enough," Tre'valen said enigmatically.

Well, that might be. What was certain was that things were by no means desperate, though Karal had reached his own limit. Karal's own reticence and determination not to reveal his difficulties had actually worked against him. Most of his friends had probably not been aware of his plight; now they knew, and now was the time to organize them to *do* something about it.

The gryphons! They like Karal—and it would take a braver man than Jarim to cross them! I need to talk to them, let them know what's been going on—

"Now you are beginning to see your options," Tre'valen

encouraged. "And now, I think, you should go where you can do something about them."

"But return again, little brother," Dawnfire added, as he prepared to return to his body and the world he knew. "The Moonpaths are always open to your walking."

He gathered himself; flung himself *down*, and then *in*.

And only then, as he opened his eyes in the quiet of the garden, did he pause to think about the significance of that last remark.

The Moonpaths are always open to your walking. The Moonpaths—all Shin'a'in could walk them on the nights of the full moon, but for Dawnfire to say that they were *always* open to his walking meant that he now possessed a status, a power reserved for Sword-Sworn, Goddess-Sworn—

—and shaman.

An'desha looked in on Karal the next morning after Firesong had gone, to find him barely awake, drugged and sleepy and not really able to think well. He spoke in monosyllables, yawning between each phrase. That made him tractable, which so far as An'desha was concerned, was all to the good.

"Can't get up," Karal complained, and yawned. "Too tired."

"Then stay there; I'll get your breakfast," An'desha told his friend and left before Karal could object. He made certain that Karal ate—soft, mild foods that the Healer had prescribed—then saw to it that he drank all the potions the Healer had left. He left Karal alone with a book to make his own meal, and by the time he returned, Karal was asleep again, the book fallen from his hands onto his chest. An'desha smiled down at him and walked softly out.

Good. He should stay that way until this afternoon, and that leaves me free to prowl.

Rather than don his more colorful Shin'a'in garb, he ransacked his wardrobe to find a plain brown tunic and black trews, which he thought would blend nicely into the background. There wasn't a great deal he could do about his hair, but he thought that if he tied it back and kept to the sidelines, he should be, if not ignored, certainly less conspicuous.

He took an unaccustomed place at Morning Court, staying carefully on the edges of the crowd, near the curtains. He said nothing, but kept his ears open.

Karal was the major topic of the conversations he overheard; he had positioned himself as near to the Guild Masters as possible, mostly to see what people who could reasonably be thought to be uncommitted would say.

He strained his ears, eavesdropping shamelessly, the moment he heard Karal's name. ". . . the Karsite is not in his room," said the Master of the Goldsmith's Guild grimly. "The servants say he was not there last night. I fear that the Shin'a'in's accusations are too true."

"Your news is late and incomplete," replied a woman in the tabard of the Weaver's Guild crisply. "The Karsite is not in his room because he collapsed last night. The Healers have seen to him, and they say that he is ill with strain and grief." She looked at the Master Goldsmith in a way that made An'desha think there was a long history of rivalry between them.

"And this means that Envoy Jarim's accusations must then be false?" the Master Goldsmith retorted, with a broad gesture that nearly knocked the cap off of a young page next to him. "I think not! If I were an Imperial spy, I do not doubt I would be under great strain, and as for grief, we have only the Healer's word for that."

"And you doubt the Queen's Own, who says the same?" the woman snapped, crossing her arms over her thin chest. "One might well ask where *your* loyalties lie, if you choose not to believe what Herald Talia says!"

The Master Goldsmith smiled at her in a superior fashion. "I say only that it is strange that the boy survived when the master did not. I say it is strange that the boy was made envoy. It is strange that the mage-storms first appeared after his arrival, and it is strange that the boy preaches peace with the devils who are responsible for the death of his master." The Master Goldsmith was clearly not deterred by the vehemence of his fellow Master, and it seemed that Karal's plight represented a way for him to voice some agenda of his own.

There were plenty of people gathered around these two, courtiers and high-ranking tradesmen alike, all dressed in the fine costumes An'desha had come to expect for a Court ceremony of any kind. An'desha examined the faces of those within earshot of this conversation. All of them mirrored the same emotion; grim concern.

They think Karal's illness is nothing more than a corrob-oration of Jarim's accusations. An'desha knew that his face mirrored concern, too, but it was for a far different cause. He hoped there were enough people here who knew Karal too well to even suspect him of something so outrageous.

The two Guild Masters turned their verbal sparring match to another topic. He moved on, wondering what he should do about the situation, and circulated among the onlookers at Morning Court, still silent, still listening. Karal had his friends at Morning Court, and they were out in force—even Treyvan the gryphon made a rare appearance, and he was brief but adamant in his support.

But Jarim's adherents were far more vocal—and it was difficult to prove a negative. Karal's supporters had only their feelings and a few facts to support them; Jarim's had all the wild speculations they cared to concoct.

An'desha debated attending the Grand Council meeting, knowing that Jarim would do his best to turn it into an indictment of Karal. There had to be a way to keep him from having that official channel!

He debated it all through the Court, and finally decided to take full and unfair advantage of his position and approach Prince Daren himself.

He waited until Morning Court was over, extracted himself from the milling crowd, and presented himself at the door of the Queen's Chambers, requesting a private audience with the Prince-Consort.

He waited in the wood-paneled antechamber, watched carefully by both door guards, who clearly did not recognize him out of his normal costume. He found himself wondering if the Prince would even hear his request, or if some official, unfamiliar with his name and position and deceived by his modest costume, would simply intercept the message. *They'll probably ask me to come back later, or wait until the Grand Council meeting,* he told himself. *If it was Firesong who was asking—*

"Sir?" a page popped his head out of the door, startling not only him, but the two guards. "You're to come in immediately, An'desha, sir!"

As the guards stared at one another and at him, obviously wondering who he was that he rated this kind of reception, An'desha didn't wait for a second invitation. The page opened the door, and he slipped in past the boy and into the reception room of the Queen's Chamber.

Apparently he was not the only one who was wasting no time; rather than a servant, Prince Daren was standing right there in person waiting for him, one hand stretched out in welcome.

"An'desha!" he exclaimed, clasping An'desha's hand warmly as the Shin'a'in reached for the Prince's hand. "Talia warned us what was happening last night. How is Karal, truly? She wasn't certain just how he was responding." He gestured at one of the carved chairs that stood beside a small table in the middle of the room, and An'desha took it, although the Prince himself remained restlessly standing.

"Sick and asleep, Highness," An'desha answered gravely. "He will mend his body, and the Healers say soon, but it is up to us, I think, to mend this situation. If we cannot, he will collapse again from the strain."

Daren ran a hand through thick blond hair and sighed gustily. "I was afraid that he might be sicker than anyone had told us," the Prince said with relief. "He's—he's a good boy, but much too inclined to hide his hurts, I think. Listen, I intend to overturn every attempt by Jarim to make any accusations against Karal in the Grand Council meetings. If he won't come around, I'll exercise my prerogative as the Queen's proxy and dismiss the meetings altogether." He smiled grimly. "We can afford to do without these meetings for a week or two. The real work is being done by Kerowyn, the mages, and the artificers anyway. Frankly, we've been going through with them partly because we must keep the people appraised of our progress, and partly out of hope that something new might come out of them. I must admit that I would not mind an excuse to cancel these time-wasting exercises for a while."

Greatly daring, An'desha decided to ask a question that he had no right to ask. "Highness, have you heard from High Priest Solaris? I cannot believe that she does not know of all of this. She has had her ways of knowing things immediately before this."

Daren looked at him strangely. "I have," he said, slowly, "This very morning, a message from her lay among the correspondence on my desk, and it had not been there last night, nor did a page or a messenger bring it. And I believe that you should tell Karal what I have been sent. It was only two words long." He paused, and an odd, unreadable expression passed across his face. "It said, 'Karal remains,' and was signed by Solaris herself." He shook his head. "I am not certain what to make of it, but the meaning is plain enough."

An'desha nodded. "Karal is still her chosen representative. She could simply be keeping him in place, though, until this current crisis is over so that it does not look as if she is replacing him because of guilt."

"I hope so." Daren was too well-schooled to pace, but he shifted his weight uncomfortably from foot to foot. "We have done all we can to bolster his authority, but there is only so much we can do when he has to deal with people who have not known him from the moment he arrived here."

An'desha grimaced, and quickly changed the subject. He and the Prince discussed what they could do to try to redeem Karal's reputation, but both admitted that they were handicapped by Jarim's prejudice.

"I will see what I can do to have him recalled and replaced by a Sworn or a shaman," the Prince said finally. "But that will take time, time during which he is free to poison minds."

"And we must try to find an antidote to that poison."

An'desha hesitated, then shrugged. "I can think of nothing more to say or do at the moment."

"Nor I," the Prince admitted. "But thank you for coming to me. You have given me reasons to do things I had wanted to do in the first place. Jarim is not a bad person, but he is a miserable failure as an envoy. I suspect the Shin'a'in have not had much experience at selecting people to represent their interests off the Plains."

An'desha laughed as he rose to his feet and made his way toward the door. "*I* would make a better envoy than he, I'm afraid." At Daren's look of sudden interest and speculation, he added in warning, "They would never accept me unless I were to be made a shaman. I possess magic, and as such, I could never be said to represent them. No Shin'a'in can practice magics but the shaman, and there is an end to it."

"As one who practices magics and has endured more than a hundred warriors, you have an understanding that Jarim sorely lacks," Daren retorted dryly.

An'desha shook his head, thanked Daren for his time and patience, then took his leave, secure in the knowledge that the Prince-Consort would keep Jarim on a short leash.

He returned to the *ekele* to find that Karal was awake and sitting sleepily in the sun in the garden. Warm golden sunlight streamed through the eastward-facing windows, making a green-gold glory out of a scrap of lawn surrounded by flowering shrubs with aromatic leaves. Karal had made himself a soft place to sit with a rug purloined from among An'desha's things, a few cushions, and a blanket from the bed.

"What are you doing down here?" An'desha asked sternly, gazing down at him with both hands planted on his hips. "The Healer said you were to stay in bed!"

Karal looked sheepish, but he did not look away from An'desha's face. "I couldn't sleep anymore," he said. "I won't go anywhere else, and I'll drink everything except the sleeping potions, but I can't stand being so muzzy-brained." He looked pleadingly into An'desha's eyes. "I promise that I will take naps if I can, but I don't want to be forced into it. The drugs—" now he faltered, "—they're making me dream of—of the Iftel border."

An'desha shuddered; that was one experience he didn't particularly want to recall either, and he knew it had been worse for Karal. "All right. I must admit that I'd feel better knowing you weren't asleep and alone here. Herald Kerowyn has beaten enough self-defense into you that I think you can protect yourself if you're awake. Assuming anyone or anything could get past all the Companions out there." He paused for a moment. "Prince Daren asked me to tell you that he's heard from Solaris. It was a two-word message; 'Karal remains.' Maybe you can make more out of that than I can."

Karal only shook his head.

"I have a plan," An'desha continued, "but it's going to take a few days to put into motion. Meanwhile, your friends are out there defending you; you haven't been deserted. I think if I let them know that you're up to seeing visitors, you won't be alone here for long, either." At the sudden interest and veiled hope in Karal's face, he added, "I believe that Natoli in particular has plans to keep you company."

Karal's blush told him all he needed to know on that score. So, there *was* something brewing between them besides merest friendship.

Good. Very good. It's about time, for both of them. Natoli has been 'one of the boys' for too long, particularly since she isn't she'chorne any more than Karal is.

"And in the meantime, I have brought you books that have nothing to do with politics or wars or magic. Here." He dropped the three books he had taken from the library beside his friend. "You read them and think of nothing. I shall go off and attempt to exercise my Shin'a'in craft and guile."

Karal laughed at this, because of course the Shin'a'in were noted even as far north as Valdemar for being the least crafty and most direct people in the Alliance. "As straightforward as a Shin'a'in" was an old saying that An'desha had encountered more than once.

Perhaps that was because no one in the Alliance recognized how directness could be used as cleverly as guile . . .

nor did they realize how telling only part of the truth could be as deceptive as telling a full lie.

For three days, An'desha left the defense of Karal's honor in the hands of Karal's other friends and concentrated on Jarim himself. It had occurred to him that there might yet be a way to get to the man; he was not unlike the Chief Healer of Karal's old Clan. Tor'getha was not a bad man, but he was quick to leap to conclusions, and quick to look for enemies outside his own folk. Yet when he was presented with enough evidence, Tor'getha had been known to change his mind.

So the first thing was to establish that he really *was* what he claimed, and not simply some rootless vagabond pretending to Shin'a'in blood as a door to opportunities. Dressing conservatively, but unmistakably in the Shin'a'in style, An'desha hovered about the edges of any group that included Jarim. Karal's actual whereabouts were not known except to those few of his friends who could be trusted with the information, so Jarim was not aware that An'desha was playing host to the young Karsite. After three days of near-constant attention, Jarim had stopped frowning and sneering whenever he saw An'desha, and was watching him with a puzzled expression, as if he was wondering just what An'desha wanted.

An'desha let him wonder; his plan depended on Jarim approaching *him*, not the other way around. He felt very much like those who hunted falcons and hawks, who would bury themselves in sand or leaves with a live, fluttering pigeon in one hand, waiting for their quarry to come and take the bait. When the hawk descended, it would be a fight to keep him—though hopefully *this* particular quarry would not realize there was a struggle going on.

At last his patience was rewarded; the quarry came to investigate the bait. Jarim intercepted him on the third afternoon of Karal's absence, just as he was leaving the Palace, heading for the *ekele*.

Jarim was actually waiting for him at the door to the path through the gardens. "An'desha. I wish to speak with you."

He paused awkwardly, looking puzzled as he groped for words. Dust-motes drifted in a shaft of sunlight from the window above the door, lancing between them like a wall. "You claim Shin'a'in blood, yet you do not look Shin'a'in, for all that you ape our dress and customs and speak our tongue freely. I—" His mouth twitched as he tried to find diplomatic words and came up with no diplomatic way to say what he wanted. "I am the representative of the Shin'a'in here, and I would have no impostors claiming to be of the Clans."

An'desha smiled mildly. This was exactly what he wanted, to establish his credentials. "My father was Le'kala shena Jor'ethan," he replied steadily. "My mother was an Outlands woman, a weaver, dwelling at Kata'shin'a'in. My father, they say, had a need to wander, which took him often to the edge of the Plains, most often to Kata'shin'a'in, where he would see and mingle with the largest number of foreign folk." He licked his lips. "My mother died at my birth, and he brought me into the Clan to be raised there as a son of the Bear."

"Halfblooded, then—" Jarim began dismissively, clearly preparing to deny him true Clan status. An'desha interrupted him.

"I have more of the blood than most of Tale'sedrin," he replied boldly. "You cannot deny that. When did the Goddess create hair of gold and russet among the Clan, or eyes of green? Those are the legacy of Kethry shena Tale'sedrin, and if you would deny Tale'sedrin to be of the Blood, then you must answer to Kal'enel, for She decreed Kethryveris to be blood-sworn into the People."

Swallow that, old man. There is not a Shin'a'in on the Plains who would dare say Tale'sedrin was less than wholly of the People, yet the Clan-seed came from a man and a woman who never even heard of the People until they were full grown.

Caught without an answer, Jarim grimaced, his eyebrows drawing together into a frown. "When did the Goddess decree that the People might boast eyes as slitted as a plains-cat's?" he finally said. "Or hair bleached to silver by magic?"

Quickly, An'desha weighed all the possibilities and de-

cided on the boldest course. "Will you close your mind because of what your eyes see, as if you were an Outclansman
who believes only in what he has before his face?" he asked.
"Or will you hear my tale and learn what happened when
you were not there?"

Jarim reared back a little, his head coming up, his spine going stiff. He had not been challenged like this since he had
arrived here, and An'desha was well aware of this. But he
had phrased his challenge very carefully, appealing to blood
and clan, and the tradition that a Shin'a'in would *always*
hear out a fellow Clansman before he made a judgment.

Finally the envoy grimaced and jerked his head sideways. "Come to my rooms, then. I will hear you." He headed
toward a nearby staircase, and An'desha followed him
willingly.

Jarim's rooms were precisely as An'desha had thought they
might be; spare by Valdemaran standards, with most of the
furniture gone, but quite luxurious by the standards of one
who lived all of his life in a tent. At Jarim's gesture,
An'desha took a seat on a flat cushion on the floor, automatically dropping into the cross-legged position of anyone born
in the tents. Jarim's mouth twitched; obviously he had not
thought An'desha could even manage the seat on the cushion, much less the posture that marked a Shin'a'in the moment he sat.

*Interesting. I could almost believe that this man has not
bothered to learn a single thing about any of the people
here! Is that possible? Can he have been sent off so
ill-prepared?*

Perhaps that was why he had been so willing to jump to
conclusions about Karal and An'desha. If so—and if he would
listen with his mind open at least a little—this might be
easier than An'desha had thought.

"What do you know of me?" An'desha demanded.

Jarim paused, then shook his head, as if to say that there
was not much he could state truly. "That you claim
Shin'a'in blood, that you are paired with that too-pretty
Tale'edras sorcerer, that you have the white hair of a sorcerer

yourself. That allegedly you had a hand in building the protections which now keep the mage-storms at bay."

An'desha closed his eyes for a moment. *He knows nothing. We assumed too much. We thought that someone would have told him about all of us, and yet he has been working in complete ignorance, using whatever he happened to pick up in conversation and working it into the skewed and incomplete view of the situation he has built with poor information.* It seemed impossible, insane that anyone would have sent an envoy off so poorly briefed.

Then again, this was a *Shin'a'in* envoy. There were plenty of folk among the Clans who viewed anyone dwelling off the Plains with suspicion. He might not have felt it necessary to actually learn anything about the people with whom he was working. He might have decided that since his only duty was to represent the needs of the People, any such details were unnecessary.

But how to tell him what he needed to know in a way that would make him believe it? *He is less like the Healer and more like that stiff-spined old bear, Vor'kela, the shaman of my Clan.* Then he knew how to present his story—and Karal's—in the one way that such a close-minded individual would listen to.

He altered his position a trifle, taking the poised, yet relaxed seat of a shaman about to tell a traditional history; Jarim responded automatically to the posture without thinking, taking a counter-attitude of subservient reception.

And he didn't even realize he was doing it! The positioning of his own body would influence his mind; already An'desha had established who was to be the "teacher," and he had not yet spoken a word!

He began his own tale with the traditional opening words and cadence of such a history. And although they had been speaking in the tongue of Valdemar, he spoke now in the language of the Dhorisha Plains.

"Here is a tale; hear it with your heart, for it is as true as the Hand of the Star-Eyed and as sure."

Through half-slitted eyes, he saw Jarim start, his own eyes open with surprise that An'desha not only knew the words, but knew the cadence with which they were chanted. "In the time before the Sundering of the Clans, in the time when the Clans served a sorcerer called the Mage of Silence, in the time before the Plains existed and the Shin'a'in served to guard them, the great enemy of the Kal'enedral was Ma'ar, the Dark Adept."

Only a few of the traditional histories began with those words, but An'desha was about to add to them.

"When the Mage of Silence died, it is said that Ma'ar perished with him in the Great Cataclysm that formed the Plains. This is known and chanted among the Clans; what was not known until this very generation was that although Ma'ar's body died, his spirit did not—nor did it go to be weighed and judged. Ma'ar was a sorcerer of great power and greater evil, and he had discovered a way to cheat death." Jarim now was torn between fascination and impatience—fascination, because this literally was all new to him, and impatience because he could not see what this had to do with the present day. Nevertheless, long habit held him silent, for one did not interrupt a shaman in the midst of telling a tale, even if one did not see the point of it.

"He had found a way to hide his spirit, his soul-self, in a pocket of *this* world," An'desha continued, phrasing the truth in a way that Jarim would grasp. "There it would wait until a male child of his blood proved that it had the Gift of magic power by trying the spell that called down fire. At that moment, the door of Ma'ar's hiding place would open, and he would rush forth, possessing the child and obliterating its own soul. Then he would shape the body of the child to be that of a man of full years, and he would stride forth into the world in possession of all of his old, dark knowledge and powers."

Jarim forgot himself and tradition enough to interrupt. "But—this is the blackest of sins!" he cried, leaning forward to emphasize his words, his hands clenched on his knees. "This is the purest of evil!"

"And in these new shapes Ma'ar wrought more evil still," An'desha said calmly. "Taking care always to sire many children and broadcast them upon the land, so that there might always be another of his blood with the Gift for him to possess when he had worn out the body he had stolen. *We* knew him, often and often, for his hatred of the Mage of Silence extended to the People." He raised one eyebrow shrewdly, for in his memories was a particular "incarnation" that had made for much weeping among the tents of Jarim's own Clan in the long-ago. "Perhaps you know the name of Sar'terixa the Mad, whose evil caused the deaths of half of the young warriors of the Cat? That was Ma'ar, in the body he had stolen of a young mage of Kata'shin'a'in."

Jarim's lips thinned, and he nodded slowly.

"So; Ma'ar did this, and it was of great evil. The lives he stole were many, although there were times when a suitable child did not appear for generations. Then there was born to the Bear Clan a halfblood child, of a Shin'a'in father who called the boy An'desha."

Jarim's eyes narrowed, but he said nothing. This was encouraging, and An'desha continued. "Through the blood of his mother, An'desha had the gift for magic power, which is a thing forbidden among the Clans, but more than that, he was of the blood of Ma'ar's last incarnation, for the poor maiden was the child of rape although she knew it not. An'desha was a foolish boy, although he meant no harm to anyone; when he knew he had the gift of magic, he hid it as long as he dared. He feared the path of the shaman, but he feared more the loss of his gift, for in many ways he was less than ordinary, and this was all that set him apart. So he hid his gift until he could hide it no more, and then he ran away, intending to seek the Tale'edras and learn the use of his powers among the Kin-Cousins."

Jarim shook his head. "But why did he hide it and then run away?" the envoy asked in honest puzzlement. "Surely if he had gone to his leaders and told them he could not follow the path of the shaman nor give up the magic, they would have sent him there with a proper escort. It is no sin to seek the Kin-Cousins if one is unfortunate enough to bear that gift. I would send my own son to the Hawkbrothers if he wished it so badly."

Well, that was more than I expected out of him! There's some flexibility there after all!

"Thus speaks a man of generous heart whose Clan is as the flowers in springtime in their numbers," An'desha replied warmly. "Thus speaks a man whose Clan is generous, and lets the fledged bird fly where it will. But a man with only one son may not wish to see his blood leave the Plains and join that of the Tale'edras. And a Clan whose numbers are small has a fear to lose even one. An'desha would have had no choice; either he lose the power or become a shaman."

Jarim thought about that for a while. An'desha let him digest the blunt words. They did not go down well, but he finally nodded, and An'desha took that as a sign to continue.

I think it has finally occurred to him to admit that not all of the People are perfect.

"So An'desha foolishly fled, found himself alone and afraid in the Tale'edras forest, and in his fear and loneliness, tried to call fire to keep him company."

"And found himself possessed," Jarim filled in grimly.

"And found himself possessed." An'desha nodded. "But this time the case was different. An'desha did not fight, for he was not used to fighting. He fled, hiding himself deep in his own mind, and Ma'ar—who now called himself Mornelithe—*thought* he was destroyed."

Jarim settled back, wearing a look of speculation. "So An'desha lived on. Of Mornelithe called Falconsbane I know some, none of it good. It is said he shifted his form to that of a man-cat of powerful build." He quirked his eyebrow in silent inquiry, inviting An'desha to admit that this was where his odd eyes came from.

"He did, as you can see by this." He tapped the side of his head beside his left eye. "An'desha was a prisoner, for he dared never reveal his existence to Mornelithe." An'desha decided to cut some of this short. "Perhaps some day I will tell you some of what he endured and experienced. It is enough to say that it was more terrible than any human should ever endure. In the course of it all, Mornelithe Falconsbane became damaged, and also acquired as enemies the Clan of k'Sheyna, the Clans of Valdemar, and Firesong k'Treva. And it was at this point that the Kal'enedral took an interest."

"That I also remember," Jarim confirmed.

"It was soon thereafter, with Falconsbane's hold and sanity weakened and An'desha able to exist with a little more freedom, that messengers came to him." *Now, how far do I go with this? Better just describe them, and let him make his own conclusions.* "They were two, spirits, one called Dawnfire and one called Tre'valen."

"That is a Clan name." Jarim raised an eyebrow still higher.

An'desha only nodded. "They came in the form of vorcelhawks of fire, as well as in human form. They taught him to walk the Moonpaths, and their eyes were the black of a starry night." He did not wait for Jarim to comment, but moved on to the end of this part of the story. "They helped him to help the others in destroying Falconsbane *truly*, and for all time. Then—although *I* do not recall this—after all of them escaped to the safety of Valdemar, they appeared again. This time, to reward him, they transformed the strange body in which An'desha now dwelt alone back to the form that An'desha had borne those many years ago when Mornelithe stole it. They left only his eyes unchanged, to remind him and others what he had been, what he had endured, and the price he had paid. And now you have heard why it is that I appear the way I do. This tale I speak, that you may recall. This story I give, that you may learn."

Jarim sat in silence for a very long time. An'desha waited patiently: silence was a positive sign; it meant that Jarim was at least thinking. The fire in the hearth beside them burned brightly and quietly, not even a hiss or a crackle to break the quiet.

And, fortunately for An'desha, Jarim's thoughts had settled, not on the transformation, but on Those who had accomplished it. "They were Avatars," he said, slowly and reluctantly. "You have been touched by Her Avatars."

An'desha just shrugged. "I make no judgments, and you may determine the truth of what I have told you for yourself.

There are those who were present when I regained my true form who can describe what they saw to you. Among them are Darkwind and Firesong, whom I believe you trust."

"But if—if An'desha's body was host to the Falconsbane— he—you—are much older than you look."

"I believe," he said slowly, "that although They chose not to erase the memories, They elected to return to me all the years that had been stolen." *Do think about that, Jarim. Think about how one can* look *seventeen and actually hold the bitter experiences of twice that many years.*

"Now, we come to the next story, if you are ready to hear more."

Jarim made a wordless gesture which An'desha chose to interpret as agreement; his guarded expression held elements of awe, surprise, and speculation. An'desha rose to his feet, and Jarim automatically followed. "I should like to show you something, actually," he said. "Would you walk out with me for a space? Too much sitting is bad for the bones in this cold."

Jarim caught up his coat and An'desha's and passed the latter over. An'desha did not resume his story until they were outside, walking in the chill air under a pale but brilliant sky.

Once again, he told the tale traditionally as if "An'desha" was someone out of legend. "So An'desha was now in Valdemar, with his new friend Firesong. He had great power and did not know how to use it, feared to use it. He now felt things and was afraid of those feelings. Although his friend reassured him, An'desha knew that his friend had many reasons to want him to feel secure, and he mistrusted his friend's objectivity. Above all, he felt alone in this strange land, neither Shin'a'in nor Tale'edras, neither mage nor ordinary man. Further, terrible dreams foretold that there was a great danger coming to all the lands, yet he could not puzzle out what it was. He was as terrified as he had ever been, even when the Falconsbane ruled his body. Then he met a young man who was the apprentice of a priest come as envoy from *his* people." He decided not to name names; not yet. "Actually, it was Herald Talia who introduced them, knowing through her powers that both were lonely, both lost in the strange land, both in need of an ordinary friend. They came to be friends, and in his innocent wisdom, the young priest saw An'desha's terrible fears and knew the great danger that An'desha could pose if An'desha could not conquer his fears to grasp his powers."

They had reached the edge of a memorial garden, and An'desha paused long enough to take some of the greens—and in season, flowers—that were always left there for visitors to place upon graves. Holly for Ulrich, with the berries as bright as flame, and bunches of goldenoak leaves the color of butter, still on their branches.

"You see, possession is not a thing that is known among the Shin'a'in. An'desha feared that Falconsbane was not truly gone, or that he had so tainted An'desha's soul that nothing An'desha did would be pure or clean again, or that he had warped An'desha's spirit so that An'desha himself would follow in Falconsbane's evil footsteps." He glanced aside at Jarim, and saw the envoy nodding. "But such a thing *is* known among this young priest's people, for their history and magics are different, and he and his master gently taught An'desha what he needed to know, and led him by example out of the darkness of fear and into the light of understanding."

"And why did he not turn to his Avatars?" Jarim demanded. "Why did They not teach him? Would that not have been more fitting?"

"Perhaps because the Avatars saw that he had mortal teachers?" An'desha countered. "They did not come, and in his fear he thought that this was his fault; perhaps his fear kept Them away, or They felt that this lesson was better in the hands of mortals. Perhaps this was one of those times when She leaves mortals to choose their own paths, as She so often does. I do not make judgments upon what She directs Her servants to do."

Since this was precisely what any shaman of the Clans would have said, Jarim was again left without an answer.

"So, it was thanks to this brave young priest—who risked his life to show An'desha that he was not and would not be twisted into evil by having been touched by the hand of Falconsbane—that An'desha became a mage in truth, and wholly himself." Now they were at a particular small plot, one with four holders for greenery and a single bronze plaque that held Ulrich's name, rank, title, and the years of his birth and death in both Valdemaran and Karsite. An'desha added his handful of holly and autumn leaves to the other greenery there. Jarim looked puzzled, although he knew what this place was. The Shin'a'in burned their dead and scattered the ashes; the Karsites also burned their dead, but interred the ashes. Solaris had directed that Ulrich's be interred here, as a sign that the Alliance had been bound up the tighter by Ulrich's death.

"Now, here is what An'desha saw, when he observed that young priest and his master." An'desha described in great detail the fatherly relationship between Karal and Ulrich, the affection, trust, and honesty between the two. He also described in great detail all that the two of them had done for him. And he sent a silent prayer to the spirit of that brave Sun-priest to help him choose the right words.

I will not bring up Altra. I do not know that Jarim is open-minded enough to believe in an Avatar of any other deity but ours.

"It was during this time that the mage-storms began, and An'desha knew that *these* were the terrible dangers his premonitions and visions foretold. Then it was even more important that An'desha learn not to fear the dreadful memories he carried, for it was within those memories that keys to stopping the mage-storms lay."

"Of course," Jarim nodded. "That is obvious even to me. If Falconsbane was Ma'ar, and the mage-storms are echoing back from the Cataclysm, then within Ma'ar's mind might be the secret to stopping them."

"So. And just so." An'desha took a deep breath. "There was another complication; the presence of the Empire. It is thought that *they* believe that the storms were sent by the Alliance; at any rate, they told their agent in the Valdemaran Court to act, murdering by magic as many of the members of the Alliance that they could, in order to destroy it."

Jarim was not stupid, he glanced suddenly down at the plaque, read the name again, and looked up, his eyes wide. "This is the Karsite envoy!" he cried, "The one slain along with Querna!"

"And the young priest is Karal," An'desha said calmly. "And never in all my life have I seen such grief as Karal bore. It was my turn then to comfort him, and I truly think if he had not been burdened with the responsibilities of his office, if he had been left alone with his sorrow, he would have gone mad with it, and taken a knife and joined his master in death. He and his are much like our own shaman; they do not often show their feelings. To me he showed his grief, and it was terrible."

"But—" Jarim began.

"There was one thing that he *could* do to both avenge his beloved teacher and our own Querna, and to give himself an outlet for his sorrows. He made of himself the bait in a trap to catch the killer. He very nearly died in that trap." An'desha made certain that his expression was a grim one. "It was luck and the skill of a Herald trained by Herald Captain Kerowyn alone that saved him, and you may verify this yourself from those who were there, beginning with that redoubtable lady herself."

Jarim's expression was an interesting mix; so complicated that An'desha could not even begin to read it.

"As for the rest of the tale, I shall make this short as well. Although he is no mage, he apparently has some powers that permit him to channel magic. These were needed to create the defense against the mage-storms; further, the Iftel border would allow only *him* to cross into it in order to set that protection up, and so once again he risked his life and sanity to help provide the protection for us all." An'desha raised an eyebrow himself. "This, I can verify, for *I* was there, acting as the mage in the north and east with him. I can promise you that the experience was painful and maddening, and it was worse for him than for me."

He spread his hands. "So, now you have the end of the tales."

"But—" Jarim shook his head, as if he was trying to settle

all the contradictory things he had heard into an order that made sense. "With all of this—*why* is he urging peace with the very people that slew his master? If he is so brave, why is he speaking the words of a coward?"

"He is no coward," An'desha replied severely. "And as for his words—Jarim, he is a priest. He cannot speak *only* for himself, nor can he think *only* for himself. He must think and speak for the greater good. How often has She allowed things to happen that seemed ill, yet later proved to be the salvation of our People? Think of the First Sacrifice above the Plains! And I ask myself—which is the greater danger to the folk of the Alliance, the mage-storms, or an army which has dug itself in and cowers in its lair because it has lost touch with the Empire? The mage-storms, which increase in fury and frequency with every passing day, or fools who rely so on magic that they are desperate for a way to keep themselves warm this winter?"

Jarim shook his head again, but now his expression was easier to read. He was a greatly troubled man.

"Let me add one thing more," An'desha said. "Have you *ever* heard of a shaman being permitted to take Sword-Sworn black to avenge a wrong?"

Jarim's expression became blank as he searched his memory and finally shook his head. "Never in my knowledge," he admitted. "The oath of the shaman is too important for him to become Sword-Sworn for the sake of revenge."

"So why do you expect Karal to pursue revenge rather than the path of his priesthood?" An'desha countered. "Why do you expect him to seek a personal goal rather than that of his god?"

He gestured down at the small plaque. "This much I can tell you; if he chose to take such a path, I think that his own master would rise in spirit and scold him for it!"

And I hope you forgive me for putting words in your mouth, friend Ulrich.

Jarim pulled at his lip, and finally closed his eyes. "I must think about this," he muttered. "You have told me almost too much to take in."

"Well and well," An'desha replied. "Now, if you will forgive me, I shall return to the path I was taking when you asked to speak with me." He glanced about at the thin sun, the dead grasses waving in a chill breeze, and shivered. "I would prefer to put my feet on the path that leads me to my warm hearth and a welcoming fire."

"And I—" Jarim said, as An'desha turned and walked away, "I shall see what path I find."

There were no more outbursts from Jarim; in fact, the Shin'a'in envoy became amazingly quiet on the subject of Karal, much to the relief of An'desha and the rest of Karal's friends. An'desha did not hope *too* much, however; Jarim was thick-headed and stubborn, and not likely to admit that he was wrong without a great deal of coaxing and many facts refuting him.

There were promising signs. Jarim did take the time to speak to those people An'desha had directed him toward; Darkwind and Treyvan, Kerowyn and Talia, and even Elspeth. An'desha did not go to them afterward and ask what was discussed, however; it was none of his business. But he knew at least that these were some of Karal's staunchest allies, and they would have confirmed everything An'desha had said. He only hoped that they were convincing.

Kerowyn, at least, will give him the real facts about the assassination and about the uncovering of the assassin, he reflected when he learned that Jarim had requested an interview with *that* formidable woman. *She just might be able to give him other information as well. After all, if there is anyone in this Kingdom likely to know who the Imperial agents might be, it is Kerowyn! And I know she was absolutely beside herself for having overlooked that damned artist-assassin. By the time she got done with her checking and rechecking, I don't think another agent could get into the Court even disguised as a mouse!*

It was several more days before the Healers would permit Karal to resume his duties and his rooms at the Palace; on that day, the Prince convened the first Grand Council since Jarim's verbal assault and Karal's near-collapse. An'desha decided to attend this one since Jarim was no longer sneering down his nose at the "halfbreed." In fact, when he looked in An'desha's direction now, it was with mingled respect and a touch of fear. That was somewhat amusing, all things considered.

As if being singled out by Avatars made me any wiser! If anything, I suspect it only proves that I am a bit slower than others, and need the extra help!

He debated shepherding Karal into the Palace and finally decided to let the young priest handle the situation without a nursemaid hovering about him. He did lag a bit behind while Karal took his place, filing in with the others to the meeting—so he was the first person to see when Jarim intercepted Karal at the door, and took him off to the corner for a low-voiced, urgent colloquy.

He moved quickly to a position where he could hover in the background, and he wasn't the only one! Out of the corner of his eye, he noticed Talia moving unobtrusively into place at a similar position of potential rescue, and Darkwind doing the same. If Karal needed help in dealing with Jarim, there were going to be three people tripping over each other to see that he got it!

But Karal didn't seem particularly distressed; in fact, as Jarim talked, his expression changed from suspicion to surprise to open relief.

Had An'desha's plan worked?

Finally, Jarim said, in a voice fully loud enough for the entire room to hear, "I don't understand *how* you can feel that way, boy, but—well, according to the gods of both our people, that's more to my shame than yours." He shook his head and managed a grim half-smile. "I don't understand the gift of forgiveness and I never did, but there are those who do, and it seems you are among them. It's a good gift for a man of the gods to have, they tell me. Better than the opposite. I'm satisfied, and I apologize."

He slapped Karal on the back heartily, staggering him.

"Your apology is generous, and it is gratefully accepted, sir," Karal managed, also speaking loudly enough for the rest of the room to hear. "I never wanted any conflict between us. Our people need us to work together, not tear the Alliance asunder with misunderstandings."

"Good enough." Jarim glanced at the avid faces around the room and shrugged. "I'm sorry you were ill, I hope you're better, but we've wasted enough time waiting for you to recover. Let's get on with this."

With that, he strode to his seat, leaving Karal and the rest to take theirs. An'desha moved to the Tayledras delegation with a sigh; Firesong was not there, and he rather thought Darkwind could use another voice. He knew he was right when that worthy gave him a grateful smile as he took his seat.

Across the table, Karal was getting out his papers and pens, as usual, but his color was better and that look of strain was gone.

Good, An'desha thought with satisfaction. Karal would still have detractors, for there were and probably always would be people in Valdemar who would not trust *any* Karsite, but at least now he could work without fear of persecution. And maybe, just maybe, if Jarim started treating him with respect, the others on the Grand Council would, too.

Now, let's get down to the business we should be dealing with. The mage-storms aren't waiting for us to settle our internal quarrels. And settling grievances isn't doing a damned thing about stopping them.

Time is still against us, and we still do not have any answers.

Six

Firesong had found the most private place in the Palace, a place where no one ever intruded, and a place where his own magics were shielded from the outside by the most powerful shields available inside or outside of a Vale. He could disappear here for hours at a time, and he did.

It was not the place he would have thought of first as a very private spot, but no one seemed to want to spend any time in the chamber of Valdemar's Heartstone. Perhaps they found the sensation of all that power rather unnerving; the pressure of it was as palpable as hot sunlight on one's exposed flesh. Firesong liked it, but for someone sensitive, and one who was not used to being in the presence of so much power, it was probably very uncomfortable. He had been told that even those who had no Gift for mage-craft could feel the power in this room, and that in itself was impressive.

This was the most powerful Heartstone he had ever worked with; it represented the latent power of the Stone Vanyel had originally constructed and linked into the Web, and the power from k'Sheyna's Heartstone that Vanyel, now a spirit and able to work more freely with such energies, had cleverly purloined.

He opened the door—a door that was by no means obvious, even though everyone in the Palace knew it was here—and walked inside, allowing it to fall closed behind him. This chamber was identical to one directly above it that had been used for scrying for centuries. The room itself was tiny, with so many shields on it that even sound had difficulty penetrating the walls. A round stone table all but filled the available space, with four curved benches around it. A single oil lamp was suspended above the table, but it was not lit, for it was not needed. A single globe of crystal in the middle of the table itself glowed with enough light to illuminate the room perfectly. The fact that this light was merely a by-product of the power held in the Stone was astonishing. *I've never known a Heartstone to glow before. I wonder if it has anything to do with the fact that it is crystal? This is quite fascinating.*

That globe of stone was the tip of Valdemar's Heartstone; the globe was fused into the tabletop, which was fused in turn to the column that supported it, which was fused in *its* turn to the stone floor and the bedrock beneath it. If one chipped everything away, one would find a single column of fused, ultra-hard, heat-forged stone, topped by the crystal globe, extending downward into the earth until it touched the place where the rock flowed with molten heat. The end result would look rather like a charlatan's "magic wand."

Firesong felt completely comfortable and at home here, despite the fact that this room had no windows and was inclined to induce claustrophobia. He was one of two people who had been originally keyed into the Heartstone's powers, after all. Elspeth was the other, and they had both been given that particular "gift" because they were both descended from Herald Vanyel Ashkevron, who had created the Heartstone in the first place, and had taken the power of k'Sheyna's Stone to reactivate this one.

The chamber had dropped out of the minds of everyone in Valdemar during those years when, in order to strengthen the Valdemarans' reliance on the Heraldic Gifts of mind-magic, Vanyel's meddling had driven the memory and the belief in *real* magic clear out of their minds. The ward-spell he had set among the *vrondi* of this land to keep true mages at bay had served well enough to protect his land from the incursions of rogue magicians at the time. The sensation of being stared at by hundreds, thousands of unseen eyes the moment one cast a spell was enough to turn even the boldest half-mad.

But that was then. Now, everything was turned about; the protections at the border were down, and there were mages from four or five lands in Valdemar. Although magic had not taken a more important role than the Heraldic Gifts, Herald-Mages were certainly playing crucial roles.

But some of that *avoidance* of this chamber must still be in effect, for in all the times Firesong had come here, he had never found signs that anyone else had so much as touched the half-hidden door. Perhaps Elspeth came here now and again, but he doubted it. She didn't need to come here to feel the power of the Stone. It was in her blood more deeply even than in his, and it sang in his veins, hummed in the back of his head. He was too used to power for it to intoxicate him.

Perhaps the power-song frightened others. That was certainly fine with Firesong, for it gave him a place to work and to think without any danger of being interrupted.

Ever since An'desha had begun drifting away, he had been searching his memory for details about Falconsbane's spirit-sanctuary and the journey he himself had taken through the Void to find it. He had many questions about the whole procedure, and rather than ask An'desha about any of it, he thought he'd rather see if he couldn't deduce some answers himself.

When he was reasonably certain that he remembered where to go and what to look for, he launched his spirit out into the Void in search of the spot where the sanctuary had been.

He hadn't really expected to find anything but a few clues at best. After all, very few magical creations ever survived the deaths of their creators, much less the creator's total dissolution. Then there was the Void itself to contend with; changeless, yet ever-changing, how could anything so foreign to it remain after it had been ripped open?

Yet when he sank himself into a mage-trance and projected himself to the general area that he thought he remembered, not only was the sanctuary still there and open, it was intact except for the damage he himself had done to it! Even that was mending, as if the sanctuary were alive and had the power to heal.

He was able to examine it in detail and at his leisure. One of the oddest things that he noticed was that it was substantially unaffected by the mage-storms echoing through the Void. There was a bit of surface turbulence, but the fabric of the sanctuary was unaltered.

He considered that as he took his seat on one of the stone benches in the room of the Heartstone. *The sanctuary is so oddly solid; rather like the fabric of the land beneath a series of great thunderstorms. Even if the storms cause floods or landslides, beneath the movement of a little topsoil, the shape of the land and the contour of it remains the same.*

With the ease of what had become habit, he settled himself on his bench, linked his own power in with that of the Heartstone, and leaped out into the Void, leaving his body behind.

The "track" of his passage was well-worn by now; he actually left a trail of residual power that linked his body to the sanctuary. Through the swirling, multicolored energy patterns, sparkled with tiny fireflies of power and now turbulent and roiled by the passage of so many mage-storms, the trail remained steady and unchanging, though faint. Then he came to the open mouth of the sanctuary, disguised in the swirl of energies by a swirl of chameleon colors on its surface.

He settled "himself" in the comfortable womb of the sanctuary, and the very existence of that link set off a train of other thoughts, other observations. As he gazed out into the wild chaos of the Void with all of its tumbling energies, he noted two "links" back to his physical body. One was the tenuous path he had made, the traces of all of his journeys, a sparkling golden trail of faint sparks of power, a dusting of silver-gilt leading back to the Heartstone. The other was the stronger, brighter, ropelike silver link of power that tied him to his own physical self.

He'd made note of that before. But suddenly, what he noticed was that the path and the link were both comprised of energies that were completely homogeneous. That made sense, of course, for both were *his* energies; even the power he drew from the Heartstone had to become his before he could use it.

But the energies the sanctuary had been built from were *not* homogeneous. Here they were, layer upon layer, warp and weft of a hundred, a thousand different threads of power. Some of them he recognized as having the taint of Ma'ar about them, the dried-blood dark-red and muddied energies of death and blood-magic. But others were quite clear and clean, pure, though thin. How had *they* come here? They had nothing to do with Ma'ar or any of his incarnations.

Finally, he found the clue, as he found every one of those pure, clear strands of power tagged at the very ends with the muddied colors of Ma'ar. And then the entire secret of the sanctuary's construction and the life it now had of its own unfolded before him.

The link between a living creature and a place like this one, similar to the link between his spirit and his physical body, could be artificially created or inflicted upon another. And when such unwitting victims died, a great deal of their power would go along that link to wherever the link led. And for that matter, a stronger link could be forged between a mage's physical body and this sanctuary and stretched as tightly as a harpstring. Even if the moment of death were instantaneous, making it impossible for Ma'ar to do what Falconsbane had done and make the conscious flight along the link into the sanctuary, the release of the tension at the end linked to the living physical body would literally snap the spirit into its sanctuary, whether or not the mage himself was even aware of what was happening to him.

So here was the answer to all of the questions. By investing the power of many, many followers in this place, the willing and unwilling, the witting and unwitting, Ma'ar had created a sanctuary that would outlast everything. By creating more links to underlings throughout the ages, Ma'ar had strengthened his creation so that it actually attained the permanent quality of a node. By putting in place the strong, tight link between himself and his sanctuary, Ma'ar ensured that he would *always* come "home" to it at the moment of his death.

While the result was appalling, the concept was intriguing. *Oh, this is fascinating.* Everyone knew, of course, that it was possible for an unscrupulous, immoral mage to make use of the power of someone's life-force by wresting it away in a violent death. Violent death was what often created a link to the physical world, in fact, as the power released, combined with the dying person's wish to live, forged a bond holding the spirit to the earth past the end of his life. That was how ghosts were created; that was probably how the spirits of Vanyel, Yfandes, and Stefen had been able to join with the great Forest in the north of Valdemar. Vanyel had done consciously, and under control, what others had done by sheerest accident and panic.

Now, there was no doubt that killing someone to take the power of their life-force was wrong, evil. But what if you simply forged that link to drain it off when they died naturally? Why would that be bad? The original owner wouldn't *need* that power, and it would only dissipate back into the energy-web that all life created. That would be why so many of the power strands woven into this sanctuary were so clear and clean; this power hadn't been stolen, reft away by violence. It had simply been taken up when the original "owner" no longer needed it.

No, there would be nothing immoral about that, no more than inheriting a house or a book from someone.

Hmm. This requires a great deal of thought. Granted, it does take power to create these links, but the outcome . . . when your donors did die, the power would go to whatever receptacle you had created for it, where you could tap it at will. It wouldn't even need to be invested in an object like this sanctuary.

Falconsbane could very easily have used the power in this sanctuary to keep himself aware of the world, even to keep track of those of his bloodline, picking and choosing among his "candidates" until he found one about to make that crucial step, opening himself to invasion by opening himself to magic.

All the pieces of the puzzle had fallen into place, leaving Firesong with a most intriguing whole.

The view from here is enchanting indeed. Enough for one day. It certainly answers the first part of my question—how I create the same kind of sanctuary that Falconsbane did. Now he was left with the other half—how did one find a new body without stealing one?

He followed his link back to his own body, and opened his very physical eyes on the tiny stone-walled room, the stone table, and the glowing crystal.

It wasn't cold in here, or he would have gotten a great deal stiffer than he was. He stretched, getting his blood moving again. An'desha had said this morning that he would gladly take Firesong's place on the Grand Council; Firesong was not certain what had prompted that offer, although he was mildly grateful for the gesture.

Today, too, they were finally rid of Karal again—he'd gone back to the Palace and his official suite.

Today Karal was supposed to take up his duties again. And An'desha wants to be at the Grand Council meeting. Coincidence? I think not.

He frowned and rubbed the side of his nose with his finger in irritation. Karal and An'desha were entirely *too* solicitous of each other. And could Karal actually be the one responsible for An'desha's increasing independence? The Karsite had all manner of odd notions in his head; could he be imparting them to An'desha? After all, An'desha was perfectly tractable until he began spending so much time with Karal.

Well, if Karal keeps aggravating that Shin'a'in, he's going to find himself with more trouble than he can handle. It wouldn't surprise me too much if the man decided to declare blood-feud, which would certainly solve all of my difficulties with him.

A gloating, gleeful thought occurred to him. Karal's career as an envoy—as well as his life—seemed destined to be very short, given the number of times he'd been attacked and the number of enemies he'd collected. Perhaps he could persuade Karal to be a part of his own experiment with capturing the power of another's life-force. And then—perhaps he could play with the situation a bit—

No, that's probably not a good idea, he decided immedi-

ately. *And I don't want to link a Karsite Priest into anything
of mine; the Goddess only knows what Vkandis would do
about* that. *Nor do I really want to manipulate the situation
to get Karal into difficulties, even though an accident to
Karal would make certain that An'desha was in great need
of comforting, and pliant with grief.*

He stretched again, grimacing at the numb state of his
rump. *Stone benches. How very typical of this place! Elegance without comfort. . . .*

He had come to realize that he was very discontented here.
He hated the feeling of eyes on him every time he ventured
out of the *ekele,* and so perversely went out of his way to be
outrageous. Not that he hadn't been the center of attention
back in the Vales, but the attention he attracted here was not
the unalloyed admiration and indulgence he got back home.
Here he was stared at because he was alien, flamboyant by
the standards of these curiously dull people. When he gave
vent to some strong opinion, people looked at him as if he
had committed some breach of etiquette; often as not, when
he inquired after something that *should* have been common-
place, they gave him looks that said clearly they thought he
was out of his mind.

*I miss the Vales, damn it all. I miss decent food that I
don't have to prepare for myself. I miss my* hertasi *servants.
There is no reason why I should be forced to pick up and
clean after myself; there is no reason why I should have to
devote a single moment to anything other than mage-craft!
I am a mage—why should I do the work of a menial?* Oh, he
could have servants coming in, but he didn't want snoops
from the Palace making free with his private areas.

He missed the way he didn't even have to *ask* for something he wanted at home; *hertasi* would anticipate what he
wanted without his asking. He missed the varied tempera-
tures of all of the springs in a Vale; here he was confined to
one spring of hot water and one of cold. Most of all he
missed the gentle, cultivated warmth of the Vales, the un-
varying climate, the presence of flowers and fruit everywhere, at every season. His own *ekele* was a poor substitute

for a Vale. It was too small, and there was no way one could pretend one was alone in a wilderness.

And I am mortally weary of the prudishness of these Valdemarans. One cannot even soak in a pool without some sort of modesty covering.

He was tired of their limited diet, tired of their limited understanding, their limits upon everything except their curiosity.

I have very simple tastes. I am not asking a great deal. Just some of the amenities of civilization, including civilized behavior.

As for the reason he was here, there were no answers and far too many limitations there as well. The mage-storms were too strong, too chaotic in their effects, to respond to the magics *he* knew, yet he could not bear to admit that they defeated him. If he had all the Adept-level mages of all the Vales at his disposal, he *might* be able to concoct a shield, but that was by no means a certainty. The storms themselves came and passed so quickly he could not study them properly, and even if he could, he simply didn't have the resources he needed.

He wanted, longed to go home, but to do so now would be to admit he had been defeated, leaving the field to those artificers An'desha was so enamored of.

Nothing in his life was satisfactory at the moment. He could not find success or contentment in his environment, his personal and emotional life, or his work. And no one cared, wrapped up as they were in themselves.

It was all so bitterly ironic! *He* had been the one they had all turned to when they needed problems solved, but when he wanted a little attention, a little consideration, they all found other things to do.

It would have been very pleasurable to find something or someone on which to vent some of his frustration.

He rested his chin on his hand and stared into the crystal globe of the tip of the Heartstone. *Frankly, it seems to me that this land and its people owe me a great deal. If it had not been for me, Falconsbane would be secure in his sanctuary even now, waiting to find another body to seize. If it had not been for me, the mission might not even have gotten as far as the capital of Hardorn. Certainly neither Elspeth nor Darkwind would have survived their encounter with Ancar, much less made it back home to Valdemar.*

So why weren't the leaders of Valdemar falling all over themselves to make certain that he was content here? Why weren't the people begging to be permitted to thank him? Why did they all treat him as if what he had done was his duty and no more? He didn't *owe* these barbarians anything! He wasn't one of their foolish Heralds, who practically stood in line for the chance to fling themselves in front of some danger!

I don't have to be here. I could go right back to the Vales at any time. I'm the most powerful Adept they have, and even if I haven't figured out a solution to the mage-storms yet, I have the best chance of doing so. I could have gone right back home as soon as everyone was safe in Valdemar after we got rid of Ancar and Falconsbane. I could leave this very instant. I wouldn't even have to go home; I could go to k'Leshya Vale instead.

With An'desha obviously *not* the lifebonded mate he had hoped for, with everyone here trying to prove they didn't really need him, maybe he *should* go.

Once I'm gone, let's see just how independent An'desha really is!

But if he left, he wouldn't have the satisfaction of seeing An'desha learn that he was not as self-sufficient as he thought.

But there might be a better idea.

I'll stay. Too much is unfinished. And perhaps I can find a way to engineer something that will prove to An'desha just how much he and everyone else still needs me. And then I'll get what I deserve!

As usual, the Grand Council chamber was too cold. Nevertheless, Karal remained in his seat after the adjournment of the Grand Council, ostensibly writing down more notes, but in reality just delaying his departure so that he could cool his temper and swallow some of his sour disappointment. Everyone else was getting out as soon as they could so that they could warm their frozen feet and noses, and he didn't blame them. It was going to be a dreadful winter.

"I'm sorry, boy," Jarim said in an undertone, leaning over and patting Karal on the arm in a decidedly paternal manner as he rose. "I wish there was something I could do to help you."

Karal managed to smile weakly at his odd and new-found ally. Jarim seemed determined to make up for his hostility by displaying a fatherly interest in the young Karsite. To his credit, not only had he dropped all of his opposition and outrageous charges after that public apology, *he* no longer treated Karal as if he were still a mere secretary. They now sat side-by-side at the Council table, the only two who took their own notes rather than leaving it up to a secretary. Of course, in both their cases that was a matter of necessity; there were no secretaries conversant enough with the written forms of Shin'a'in and Karsite to listen in Valdemaran and write in either tongue simultaneously.

"I wish you could, too, sir," he sighed. "Unfortunately, there is nothing that I can do about my youth." There was the core problem, all right. *It* hadn't gone away, and he was still trying to convince his superiors of that.

Jarim shook his head, the small braids in front of each ear swaying with the motion. "Perhaps it is only that among my people, men your age are found leading border-scouts, and as the fathers of families. These soft and civilized sorts see your lack of years and assume, because *their* sons have no more sense than a green and untamed colt, you must be equally foolish, to their thinking." He scratched his temple with a callused finger. "They also may be confusing the evidence of their eyes and the evidence of their ears."

Karal shrugged; Jarim had summed up the entire problem most succinctly and with a surprising amount of insight. It could be, now that Karal and others were taking the time to brief him on the background of all of his fellow Councilors, that he would make a better envoy than anyone had guessed.

The Shin'a'in envoy patted his arm again, and took himself out of the room, possibly sensitive to Karal's unspoken distress.

Though he might just be anxious to get back to his own hearth-fire. He might be a toughened Shin'a'in, accustomed to spending the winter in a tent, but that doesn't mean he doesn't feel the cold as sharply as any of the rest of us.

The latest twist in the situation was that the other envoys had settled into a pattern of asking Karal for confirmation from his superiors in Karse for every single suggestion, statement, or decision. They had to see his authorization for every agreement or even statements of fact. Jarim alone was treating him as an equal, but in a way that was doing him more harm than good, given the Shin'a'in envoy's flamboyant and volatile temperament. At the moment, the only hope he had of changing anyone's opinion of him was to impress them with his diligence. He was not particularly sanguine about his chances of success.

When everyone else, including the secretaries, had cleared out, he finally packed up his own papers and left. He headed for his rooms, which once again were a sanctuary of peace, if only a fleeting peace.

The wave of warmth met him like a welcome. He closed the door carefully behind himself, and went directly to the waiting kettle on the hob. He poured hot water—now kept ready for him at all hours by orders of the Healers—over the handful of herbs in one of the mugs waiting on the mantelpiece. He had an entire series of those mugs lined up, refreshed every day by one of the servants. At least, thanks to the stomach-calming potions the Healers had prescribed for him, he was still able to eat, although he had given up his favorite sausage rolls and other spicy or fatty foods, none of which agreed with him anymore. At this rate, he would be reduced to living on turnips and cress.

Is it just me, is it only that they simply cannot accept me as their equal? he wondered as the tea steeped. *Or is it an actual and calculated affront? Can it be that now that the immediate crisis is over, many of those people on the Grand Council are trying to alienate Karse?*

He could not dismiss the possibility, and he was not feeling steady enough to judge whether it was a silly, childish fear or a real concern. He wished he had the ability to read thoughts that some of the Heralds boasted. He wished he had the ability to read *intent.*

:*I wish that I did not have to make this particular request,:* said a familiar, but long-absent, voice in his mind, speaking in a tone of considerable reluctance.

Karal spun around, hardly able to believe his "ears" and hardly daring to hope—but there was Altra standing behind him in a pool of sunlight, ears slightly flattened and tail twitching. There was a message-tube at his feet, but at the moment, that hardly seemed important.

The Firecat looked no different than he had the last time Karal had seen him; to all outward appearance, a blue-eyed, cream-coated feline with orange tabby markings on paws, ears, facial mask and tail, and thick, soft fur. Of course, there *was* one thing that marked him as out of the ordinary; his size. He easily stood with the top of his head even with Karal's hip.

"Altra!" Karal exclaimed joyfully, relieved beyond words at the Firecat's appearance and all that it implied. *Vkandis is not displeased with me! I have not been heretical or blasphemous! I have been doing what He wants here—I have not been abandoned to my punishment—*

Altra flattened his ears further, looking decidedly apologetic. :*I am sorry, Karal. We have tried to be patient, and it is not your fault, but it does not seem that you are being granted the respect that you are due here. No one in Karse wanted to undermine your position or your authority, but things are getting out of hand. Would you feel terribly betrayed if Solaris took control of the situation here?:*

Karal could not help himself; his jaw went slack with surprise for a moment. At last—at *last!*—the plummeting situation was going to be taken out of his hands and put into the hands of someone old enough to deal with it properly!

"Not only would I *not* feel betrayed, not only would I *not* be disappointed, I would be overjoyed," he replied, trying not to laugh aloud with relieved gratitude. "I thought I have made that perfectly clear in my dispatches! I am here to serve the interests of Karse and Solaris, not to indulge myself in fantasies of prestige!" He finally gave way to his feelings and laughed giddily. "I cannot even tell you how happy it will make me to be able to go back to being a simple secretary again!"

I might actually have something of a real life again!

This was the last thing he was going to admit to Altra or anyone else, but this message could not have come at a better time. His enforced idleness had given him a great deal more time with Natoli than he had ever enjoyed before, and things were developing in ways he found both pleasant and a bit unnerving. He would much have preferred to be able to capitalize on that—except that once he had resumed his duties, he had gone back to the same dull round of not having enough time to spend on anything *but* duty. It had been frustrating, to say the least.

But I'm not telling Altra that! Oh, no!

The Firecat's ears came up, and his tail stopped twitching. :*You know I promised you that I wouldn't rummage around in your private thoughts, and I haven't. So I really didn't know how you would feel about being relieved of your authority.*:

"Relieved is the correct word," Karal told him, taking his mug to the table and sitting down with the sensation that a vast weight had been taken from his shoulders. "Who is coming here as envoy? And how soon?"

:*Ah—that's the thing I was told to prepare you for,*: Altra replied nervously, :*But I'm not certain that I can prepare you for it. The—person—is only coming up here to reestablish your credentials in such a way that no one will be able to treat you like a nonentity without creating a diplomatic incident. And the—person—is Solaris.*:

He was very glad he was sitting down; doubly glad that he had not been drinking his tea, or he would have choked. "Solaris?" he repeated, dazed. "*Solaris?*"

:*She wants to make a state visit.*:

"Can she do that? Is she secure enough at home?" Solaris' rule was by no means rock steady; there had been several times in the past when only the intervention of events—or Vkandis—had kept her on the Sun Throne.

:Oh, she's secure.: Was that a hint of a chuckle in Altra's tone? *:Believe me in that. Karse is closer to the Dhorisha Plains than Valdemar, although it's farther away from Lake Evendim—and before the breakwater went up, things were very . . . interesting. There is not a man, woman, or child in Karse that does not know how this Alliance has saved them.:*

"Oh." *Now* he took a gulp of tea, as much to steady his nerves as his stomach. That was important information, but it was not something he had truly wanted to hear. Some small part of him had hoped that because Karse was so far from Evendim it might have been spared some of the worst effects of the storms. Evidently its proximity to the Plains caused nearly as many problems. He couldn't remember the model; couldn't remember how many intersections of the two series of waves happened over Karse; it was the intersection points that were the places where real damage took place—

Altra went on, ignoring Karal's furrowed brow. *:She thinks now that it is time she actually met Selenay in person—and equally time that Selenay met her.:*

"I have to admit that I find it difficult to disagree with that," Karal told him candidly. "I think it would prevent misunderstandings when things get tense again if each of them knew how her counterpart thinks." He frowned. "But I'm still not certain about this. Even if she feels secure enough to come *here*, can Karse afford to be without her? Things can happen without notice, without warning. What if a crisis arose and she wasn't there to deal with it?"

Altra looked a bit sheepish, an odd expression on a feline face. *:As to that, she's arranging things so that even most of the Sun-priests are not going to be aware that she is gone.:*

"Hansa isn't going to 'jump' with her, is he?" Karal felt his own stomach lurch at the idea. "I don't think that's a very good idea!"

Altra had the audacity to chuckle at him, irritating the young Sun-priest, although he refused to show his irritation.

:No, Hansa and I are going to establish a Gate between us, so that Solaris can come and go without depleting her own powers.:

Oh? This was the first he'd ever heard of that particular talent! Karal allowed an eyebrow to rise. "Well, isn't *that* convenient," he drawled.

Altra sniffed derisively. *:If you had troubled to continue reading in those books that Ulrich left you, instead of bothering yourself with making letter-perfect copies of your notes to send to Karse, you would have seen that Firecats have created Gates between them in the past, when there have been two or more of them about. It is just an extension of "Jumping," after all, and you could logically have deduced that. It is not—:* he added smugly, *:—an ability shared by the Companions.:*

Karal rolled his eyes at that last, but let it pass without further comment.

:And I must point out to you that we could not have put you and your mentor in place this way, because I was not here, and I could not have come here without you. I am linked to you and to no one else.:

Another interesting bit of information. Altra was certainly being generous with it today! Was he making up for his prolonged absence by dropping his secretive stance?

:We had always intended to use a Gate in an emergency to remove you—or—or Ulrich, if we had to.: At the mere mention of Ulrich, Karal felt his throat knot and his eyes sting. *:Unfortunately, it takes more time to establish a Gate than we had when—:* Altra faltered for a moment, then went on. *:Just remember that is always an option for you, if there is an untenable situation.:*

"I will," Karal promised solemnly, after he managed to clear his throat and rub the suspicion of tears from his eyes. "Now, am I to be the one to make the request for this visit official?"

:Precisely.: Altra tapped the tube with one paw, and it rolled over to Karal until it ran into his foot. He bent down to retrieve it.

:That is an official document from Solaris to Selenay, re-

questing her permission for a Visit of State.: Altra looked pensive. *:I hope she is as sensible as we believe, but this is bound to come as something of a shock.:*

Well, that was something of an understatement. The leader of a land that until very recently was Valdemar's deadliest enemy was now asking to come to the heart of Valdemar? "Then the sooner I get the shock over with, the better," Karal replied, drinking the last of his tea—more grateful for its stomach-easing properties than ever—and standing up. "I think I had best get on the way with this now, before something else happens."

He looked down long enough to put his mug securely on the table; when he looked up again, Altra was gone.

The Queen's Chambers were less impressive than Karal had expected. The furniture was in keeping with her station and extremely comfortable, but hardly constructed of priceless material. It showed slight signs of wear, the wood of the desk and chairs showed a few scratches no amount of polishing would remove. Karal waited, standing in front of that desk in respectful silence with his hands folded in front of him, while the Queen of Valdemar read through Solaris' letter for the third time. Her look of absolute incredulity had not diminished since the first reading.

Talia, however, did not seem particularly surprised. *Then again,* Karal reflected, *she knows Solaris, perhaps better than many of us in Karse.*

Finally, Selenay put the document down and looked up into Karal's face. For all the stress she had been through in her life, Selenay looked remarkably young. Karal could easily imagine that in her place, he'd have aged about fifty years in the past ten. "I have to admit, Ambassador Karal, this comes as something of a surprise," she said carefully. "I think I would be safe to say that it is altogether unprecedented."

"Not entirely, Your Highness," Karal said carefully. "The Crown Prince of Rethwellan has been here on at least two occasions; the Prince-Lord Martial Daren also, arriving at the head of an army."

To her credit, Selenay did not point out that Valdemar and

Rethwellan had *never* been at odds, much less at war for generations. "But the King of Rethwellan has never been here," she pointed out instead. "I honestly cannot say that I can think of a single monarch who has made a state visit to Haven. In the past, when monarchs have conferred, they met at the border. This—this shows a great deal of trust on Solaris' part."

"And on yours, Highness," he felt constrained to tell her. "You have only my word and hers that she will not bring an armed force through this Gate."

But both Selenay and Talia smiled, and it was Talia who spoke. "The queen gave her greatest trust when she sent me into Karse with an escort of two," Talia said gently. "And logically speaking, it would take a great deal of time to bring an army through a Gate, one man at a time. I am sure we could do something about disrupting the Gate long before she could bring enough people in to threaten us."

"As for this," Selenay tapped the letter with her finger, "you know, of course, that I cannot possibly give you a yes or no answer immediately?"

"You must first consult your Council, if not the Grand Council," Karal agreed. "And I am certain you will have many questions, both of a personal nature and involving logistics, that you must put to Solaris." He spread his hands wide. "I am at your disposal."

"And Altra, too, I presume." Selenay's mouth quirked in a quick smile. "Although the idea of a cat being at anyone's disposal is rather at odds with the species."

Karal chuckled; he couldn't help it, since she was far too accurate. "Altra is also at your disposal to convey messages directly to Solaris so that you can have your answers immediately. If you would prefer, he and I can wait just outside your Council Chamber; you can have your pages bring me questions and Altra can take whatever communications you wish to have sent to Solaris, bringing back the answers. We are willing to remain on duty however long this takes to get settled."

"You may regret that offer." She wrote out something quickly; an order for an emergency Council session, he guessed. Talia took it outside to a page, and Selenay herself stood up. "I think we should hold the meeting here, in the interests of security," she said, and nodded at a door just to the side of the office. "You can remain there since you have offered. I will send a page to you every so often to make certain you don't perish of hunger or thirst. Is there anything I can send one for now?"

"Hot water and the row of mugs on my mantlepiece," he replied quickly. "It is medicine I am supposed to be drinking. Or else send to the Healers for more of it." His stomach gave a lurch, as if to remind him that it would be a bad idea to forget that medication.

Selenay gave a glance of inquiry at Talia who nodded. Satisfied, she returned her gaze to Karal.

"If you would go in there, I shall see your medicines are brought," she promised, as Talia rose and walked over to the door, opening it for him with an ironic bow and a little flourish. "If you would please take your place?"

He bowed to her with no irony whatsoever, and followed her gesture to the door Talia was holding open. The Queen's Own closed the door behind him, and he found himself in quite a cozy little room, equipped with a piece of furniture that could serve as both a bed and a couch and was supplied with a blanket neatly folded at the foot of it. There was a single table, and one wall was a floor-to-ceiling bookcase full of books. A tiny fireplace kept the room comfortably warm; at the moment the light from the single window was more than adequate, but there were candles on the table for after darkness fell.

A page's waiting room, or else the Queen's reading room, he recognized, and relaxed. If the meeting went on for very long—

:Not bad. You can sleep in here if they decide to debate things for hours.: Altra faded into view; predictably, he appeared sitting on the couch. *:They probably will—and you can certainly use the rest.:*

"You don't mind my promising your services as a messenger?" That had been the one thing he'd been nervous about.

:I expected it. I'll be pleased and surprised if they can

agree on this in a day. It may take several.: Altra curled up
on the couch leaving ample space for Karal. Karal took the
implied invitation and sat beside him. *:Karal, I am very
happy to be with you again. Believe me, it was not my
choice that I was away for so long. I was needed elsewhere,
but if there had been an emergency, I would have come to
you at once.:*

Impulsively, he hugged the Firecat who purred just like
any ordinary feline and rubbed his face against Karal's. "I
can't even begin to say how happy I am to see you. I've
missed you, Altra, I've missed you for *yourself,* and not just
for what you are."

:I'll bet you didn't miss the cat fur up your nose.: Altra
batted him playfully, which practically left him speechless.
He'd never seen the Firecat in quite so light a mood!

*:I don't need to scold you into sense or spine anymore.
You're doing quite nicely on your own, leaving me free to be
your friend as well as your adviser.:*

Karal blushed with embarrassment and pleasure, and was
left utterly speechless. But that was perfectly all right, since
Altra was quite willing to fill in the silence.

*:You might as well pick out a good book and get comfort-
able. There will be a page along shortly with your medicine
and something to eat for both of us.:* Altra curled up on the
foot of the sofa, the end of his tail twitching ever so slightly.
*:I believe that the fish is for me. Meanwhile, enjoy your
leisure.:*

Karal smiled, scratched Altra's ears, and followed that very
sound advice.

In the end it took two days of solid negotiations before an
agreement was reached, two days broken only by an adjournment to sleep. Selenay or Talia often looked in on Karal during the process to make certain he was all right, and to keep
him briefed on what was going on with the Council. This
was a meeting of *only* the officials of Valdemar, as Karal had
anticipated. What he had not anticipated, although he was
very grateful for it, was the attitude of Valdemar's Councilors. They were all cautiously in favor of the visit when it

was first proposed to them. What they felt needed clarification was precisely how this visit was to take place.

In the end, there were precautions asked for and conference on both sides. Only Karal, Altra, and Florian would be present at the Valdemar Gate-terminus as Solaris stepped through; that was her demand, and it was a wise one, since she would be particularly vulnerable to attack at that moment. All others, including the Herald-Mages on guard against trickery, would remain at a distance.

At the edge of Companion's Field, to be precise. The few standing remains of the Temple in the middle of the Field included the arch of the doorway. That doorframe had been used as a Gate-terminus many, many times in the past, when there had been mages and Herald-Mages able to create such things. Such use tended to attune the terminus to the forces of Gate-energy, and make each subsequent Gate construction a little easier, a little more stable. An'desha had said that he thought that this very tendency of stone to attune itself might be part of the basis for the long-lost ability to create the permanent Gates of the past.

One day, An'desha swore he intended to go all the way back to his past as Ma'ar, and try to fathom out more of those secrets. Ma'ar had never known how to make permanent Gates; that mastery had been reserved for Urtho, the Mage of Silence. But Ma'ar knew many of the secrets, and An'desha hoped that by consulting with modern mages and the mages of k'Leshya he might be able to rediscover the long-lost method of building permanent Gates.

That was on the end of a long list of other priorities, however. And given what they were all going through because of the mage-storms, Karal doubted that any of the Allies would ever be willing to rely entirely—or even regularly—on permanent Gates for transportation. Physical transportation was far more reliable, and less likely to be affected by anything short of utter catastrophe.

Karal knew why it had only taken two days to come to this agreement. The Valdemarans (although they would never admit this) were willing to trust to the Companions as an informal front line and expected Florian to warn them if anything or anyone besides Solaris herself came through the Gate. And, no doubt, the Valdemarans knew he knew, and he knew they knew he knew, and so they were all very comfortable together, for that which could not be admitted could still be tacitly acknowledged.

It took another two days to make the necessary arrangements, and somehow it was all accomplished without anyone but the Council members and those who were immediately involved finding out. That in itself was a minor miracle.

At least, it had been accomplished without anyone likely to make a public nuisance of himself finding out. Without a doubt, people with other agendas than public ones had learned of her arrival. That was why, if the Valdemarans had not insisted on the Gate being in Companion's Field, Solaris would have insisted on it being either there or in the heart of the Palace. The Companions would work equally well to guard Solaris as to guard against her.

The weather even cooperated; it was clear and sunny, though very cold, as Karal waited beside the tumbled stones of the old Temple. There had been a thick, hard frost last night; where the stones were still in shadow, they were covered with a heavy coating of white. The ruin stood in the heart of a thickly wooded grove; *the* Grove, the Valdemarans called it, and for all that it stood in the center of Haven, in the middle of the Palace grounds, there was an air of great age and mystery about it. The ruined stones were piled around the foot of a bell-tower still in relatively good repair; the only other place where there were still two stones on top of each other was the stone arch.

:*Well, here we are*,: Florian said as his breath puffed out into the still morning air. :*Everything is as ready as it is ever likely to be*.:

"Except me," Karal replied. He was dressed in every bit of Sun-priest regalia he or Ulrich had ever owned, and it felt as if he now labored under twice his normal weight. He couldn't imagine how any of the high-ranking Sun-priests managed to wear these things day after day.

"Why did you volunteer for this anyway?" he continued,

as Altra daintily picked his way through the stones and examined the ground to find a place fit for his regal rump.

:*It occurred to me,*: the Companion said, with grim humor,
:*that anyone from Valdemar who might consider putting an
arrow through Solaris would think twice about doing so
with a Companion in the way. And I intend to be in the
way at all times.*:

"Ah." Karal inserted a finger in his collar and pulled on it
to ease it a bit. "Well, that's certainly logical. I can't imagine
anyone in Valdemar having the temerity to shoot anywhere
near one of you lot."

:*Thank you.*: Florian had been groomed to within an inch
of his life this morning, and although he was not wearing a
saddle, he did have the full formal barding and belled halter that Companions normally wore for special occasions.
His mane and tail were braided in multiple strands with
blue and silver ribbons, and each braid ended in a silver bell.
:*May I say that I hope your rigout is not as uncomfortable
as mine?*:

"Oh, it is; probably more so." Karal smiled. "If it was any
heavier or stiffer, I wouldn't be able to walk."

:*And they say that rank is not a burden!*: Florian tossed
his braided mane to the wild chiming of tiny bells, and
whickered his amusement. :*I could wish I was a Firecat; at
least they don't have to put up with being beaded and
braided.*:

The Firecat looked back over his shoulder. :*No, but when
I am done, you will be glad you only need to bear beads and
bells. Building a Gate is not like Jumping—well, you'll see.
This is, in my opinion, a small price to pay for the great
good that will come out of it.*:

With that, Altra examined the ground further, and something occurred to Karal. Altra was going to expend a great
deal of energy—and concentration. He wasn't going to be
able to concentrate if he was shivering. He needed to be off
the cold ground, but none of them had thought to bring anything for Altra to sit on.

Wait a moment—Florian was not wearing a saddle, but he
was carrying an ornamental blanket.

As he turned to ask Florian if he could borrow the blanket, Florian reached around and pulled the silver-embroidered blue blanket from his back with his teeth, clearly with the same idea in mind.

:*Here. There's something appropriate about Altra sitting on a Valdemaran blanket to bring Solaris here from Karse, isn't there?*:

Altra pivoted to face them again as Karal took the blanket from Florian. His blue eyes went from Karal to Florian and back again. :*Thank you*,: he said simply. :*This is why the Alliance will work.*:

:*At least it is why we three make a good team, pulling as one in the same harness*,: Florian said with amusement.

Altra snorted, indicating a place for Karal to lay the blanket with a tap of his paw. :*Trust a horse to say we work in harness. I would have said we were running the same prey.*:

:*So you would*,: Florian replied agreeably, watching Altra settle himself on the blanket. :*And you may have my share of the mice we take.*:

:*And you, my share of the corn they were eating. Gentlemen, are we prepared? Hansa is ready on his side.*:

It was a rhetorical question, and they all knew it. Karal gave his tunic a last tug, while Florian positioned himself very carefully beside him. They both turned their attention to the stone arch.

Every muscle on Altra's body was tense; not even his tail twitched. The stones of the arch began to glow, faintly at first, but the brightness increased with every passing heartbeat. Then, between one moment and the next, there was blackness inside the arch instead of the view of the stones and weeds on the other side.

A few tendrils of energy licked across the blackness; slowed lightning was all Karal could think of. Every hair on Altra's body stood on end, puffing him up to twice his normal size. More tendrils appeared, and still more—

Then, just as suddenly as the blackness had appeared, it vanished. But the view through the archway was not that of the ruins; it was of a wall of books and a wooden floor—and

Solaris, with Hansa sitting beside her, the precise mirror-image of Altra.

The scene held for only a single moment, not even as long as it took to cough. Solaris wasted no time at all in acting, stepping through the stone archway with all the casual aplomb of one walking from one room to the other—

Except, of course, that she was stepping across a distance so vast it had taken Karal weeks to cross it. And that she, too, was in her full formal robes as the Son of the Sun, the Voice of Vkandis, the ruler of all Karse.

She glittered with gold; her robes were sewn with plates of it rather than simply being embroidered with gold bullion and braid. Her jewels of office were twice the size of Karal's. She was as covered with gold and sun-gems as the statue of Vkandis Himself. Karal wondered how she could move.

But move she did, from Karse to Valdemar and away from the Gate quickly, so that Altra and Hansa could break the connection and close it down. The instant she was clear, that was precisely what they did; the Gate went black, then vanished completely, leaving only the view of the ruins in the picturesque archway.

Altra sagged, and Solaris bent quickly to support him for a moment until he regained his strength. "Thank you, Altra," Karal heard her say very quietly. "That was well and smoothly done."

If Altra made any answer, he made it only to her, for Karal "heard" nothing. When the Firecat seemed better, Solaris straightened and turned her attention to those waiting to welcome her.

Karal quailed beneath that direct gaze, as hard to meet as the full glare of the sun at noonday on the Summer Solstice. He shivered and tried to drop his eyes, entirely overwhelmed and not just by the fact that he was in the presence of his ruler. He now had what he had *never* wanted, the full and undivided attention of the Son of the Sun. But more than that, he stood before Solaris with a heavy knowledge in his heart that he had failed her; he had broken his promise to her by failing to keep Ulrich safe.

He trembled, and her gaze softened; for a moment he saw

the woman beneath the High Priest. Her mask dropped altogether at that moment, she took several swift steps forward, and before he could bow to her, she caught his shoulders in her hands, then embraced him.

"I need not be the Sun's Son just yet," she whispered into his ear as he forgot to breathe. "And Karal—I know. I know what you feel. You did the best you could, and if you can be said to have failed at all, it is because I gave you tasks suited for a score of seasoned mages and priests, not for one young man alone. The trouble is, I did not have those seasoned mages and priests to send here. I had only you, and hope, and you have repaid that hope by accomplishing more than anyone had a right to expect."

He felt caught in the silence and could not reply.

"Twice now, I have unthinkingly given you a task too great for you, and I am sorry. Can you forgive me?" She released him so that he could look into her anxious eyes. He nodded dumbly, and her eyes brightened with a suspicion of tears. "Oh, Karal," she breathed, "I miss him too!"

That was too much for him; with a spasm of heart and throat, he lost all of his control and broke down, weeping. But she was doing the same, and the two of them wept together in silence.

She regained control of herself first, though she did not push him away. Instead, she held him while he wept himself out, while the pain of loss ebbed, and released him only when *he* made a tentative move to free himself.

"Here," she said, handing him a handkerchief which she produced out of the capacious sleeves of her robes. "I had the feeling this would happen, and I came prepared." She managed a wan smile, for a moment more, no longer the Son of the Sun, but just a harried and weary woman. "The one thing these robes are good for is being prepared. I could hide a donkey, a week's provisions, and a small tent in these sleeves."

That made him laugh, as she must have known it would. He composed himself as she carefully removed the last damage from her tears and resumed her dignity. Karal blotted his own face, glad that the cold air would quickly restore him

and that the redness of his eyes would be attributed to staring into the bright sun for too long. When he was ready, he
nodded to her, and with Florian at her left and himself at her
right, and a much-subdued and slightly shaky Altra bringing
up the rear, they moved out of the Grove and toward the
waiting delegation.

Selenay waited there, clearly visible among the rest in her
white and gold, as impressive in her simplicity as Solaris was
in her ornate robes. Beside her stood her Companion, as
beaded and belled as Florian, but wearing full formal tack,
including a saddle; behind her stood Talia and Prince Daren
and their Companions, likewise bedecked, and the rest of the
welcoming delegation behind them. Those who were not
Heralds had dressed in sun colors as a tribute to Solaris; they
made a bright and welcoming patch of warm color against
the dead, gray-brown grass and barren branches.

It was an interesting moment; the first face-to-face
meeting of two strong-willed, strong-minded women, both
the rulers in their own lands, and each of them once the
greatest enemy of the other. Karal felt the pressure of their
gazes as Solaris approached with that graceful, gliding step
he could never emulate. Neither of them had an iota of attention for anyone else.

Finally Solaris stopped, no more than a pace or two from
her counterpart, both of them eyeing each other for a breathless moment of assessment.

Breathless, indeed; once again, Karal forgot to breathe.
Would they hate each other? When they were so far distant
from one another, personal feelings had meant nothing, but
now that they were within touching distance, it was imper-
ative that they at least be able to tolerate each other! What
if they were instant enemies?

His heart pounded painfully in his ears as he waited for
one or the other of them to speak—or *something!*

Finally, though, it was Selenay who broke the impasse, and
she did it with a smile.

"Talia told me that we were much alike, Holiness," she
said, as Solaris answered that smile with a wary one of her
own. "I suspect that she was being tactful."

"Very tactful, Majesty," Solaris replied, in that peculiar, carrying voice that never seemed to rise above conversational level, yet could reach clearly to the back of the Temple, "But I would expect that level of tact, knowing Our Priestess."

Cleverly phrased; Karel marveled at how clever—in the same breath, by saying "I" first, she had given Selenay notice that they were equals and she was claiming no special precedence for herself, even as Selenay had not. But by referring to Talia as "Our" Priestess, she reminded Selenay that unlike the Valdemaran ruler, Solaris spoke with more voices than her own. Talia was a Priestess to Vkandis as well as Solaris, and where Solaris was, so, too, was her God.

"I suspect," Solaris continued, reinforcing that status of equals with another 'I', "that what she truly meant and would not say is that we are *too* much alike."

She raised a long, thin, elegant eyebrow at Talia, for the first time taking her attention from the Valdemaran Queen. Talia had donned Karsite Sun-priest robes—but they were in white and silver, rather than black and gold, in token of her dual duties as Priest and Herald. Another nicely balanced gesture.

Talia blushed, as Selenay chuckled very softly, and relaxed the tiniest bit. Karal relaxed a great deal more than that; finally letting out the breath he had been holding. *They like each other! Oh, thank you, Vkandis!* Solaris was *never* that frank except with people she liked and trusted. She would never lie, but she was a past master at partial truth and dissimulation. She had to be, after all; she could not have gotten as far as she had if she was not.

Then again, although he could not speak from personal experience, Selenay was probably just as clever.

Solaris moved forward the remaining few paces and held out her hand. Selenay took it immediately, clasping it heartily.

"Now, Holiness," the Queen of Valdemar said, turning adroitly so that she now stood side-by-side with the Son of the Sun, "if I may begin the introductions. Talia you know— and this is my husband and consort, Prince Daren. . . ."

Karal took a discreet step to the rear, placing himself in a modest position behind his ruler; at last laying all the intolerable burden of authority on the proper shoulders to bear it.

Seven

Dear gods, it's a frozen wasteland out there. Commander Tremane—who no longer thought of himself as a Grand Duke, nor in any other context than as the commander of his men—gazed out at the now-empty courtyard of his stronghold. It was buried beneath snow that reached to the knee, and the weather-wizard from the town said that more was coming. Even though the old wreck couldn't *change* the weather anymore, he could still predict it, and he thought he could teach one or two of Tremane's mages the trick. *Snow. I haven't had to deal with this much snow since the years I spent on my estate.* In the Imperial capital, of course, all snow was neatly steered away from the city itself, except for a dusting that looked ornamental and could easily be swept from the streets.

Winter had arrived, bypassing most of fall altogether. But with the help of his men, the locals had gotten their crops in, the foraging parties had brought in bales of hay, baskets of wheat and root crops, pecks of nuts and fruits, and even some livestock that had not gone altogether feral. The armed parties had brought back some of the livestock that *had* gone feral, in the form of carcasses now hanging frozen in a locked warehouse in the city. Ownership of those carcasses was not a matter of dispute; Tremane owned them, traded one-for-one for Tremane's half of the living animals collected. The fresh meat would be a welcome change from the preserved and salted meat in the Imperial warehouses—having it so far from camp, while it increased the chances of pilferage, ensured that the cooks would do as he had ordered, and plan meals that alternated fresh meat with preserved. He didn't want the fresh meat used up all at once, leaving only preserved. The men would complain, and rightfully, if meal after meal was nothing but the salty stews and other dishes that were all that could be made with preserved meat. It was a little thing, but in winter, and under the conditions that the men were now living in, little things could amount to great problems of morale.

It could be worse. Snow is not the worst thing that could happen to us. He was happy enough with snow, actually, because two days ago what had come down out of the sky was an ice-storm. Snow was infinitely preferable to ice that made walking between buildings into an ordeal. There were two men down with broken legs, five with broken arms, and a half dozen with broken collarbones, according to the roster.

Such injuries were not the calamity they would have been a few weeks ago, when he had needed every able-bodied person. The walls were completed; so were the new barracks. The builders had arrived at a clever and elegant solution to the heating problem—or, rather, one that made the best use of limited fuel and equally limited time for building. It was a variation on the idea of a furnace that one of his own men had concocted.

The barracks were still being finished inside, but that could be done while the men were living in them. As long as there was room to put down bedrolls, that was what mattered. They were similar in design to the plan of the earth-sheltered buildings he had looked at earlier, but instead of making the entirety of one wall into a chimney, these plans arranged for the warm air to run under the floor to the opposite wall, and there were additional chimneys built into the support posts. Directly above the furnace were brick ovens for baking and depressions shaped exactly like the huge army kettles for heating water and making soups and stews.

That meant there were *no* windows, so all light came from candles and lanterns. What the barracks lacked in light, they made up for in warmth. Tremane reflected that if a vote had been taken, the men would probably have voted against windows in favor of heat in any case.

Of course, since they had not been consulted, the men called the new barracks "the holes," or "the caves," and although they were not happy about living in such dank and poorly-lighted places, a fair majority of them admitted that the barracks were far, far preferable to not having solid shelter.

They had still been in their tents when the first ice-storm hit. They had been a great deal less happy about that, as fully half the tents had collapsed beneath the weight of the ice that had built up on them. It was amazing how quickly the last bit of building went up after that.

There was a faint but persistent smoky animal odor about the places, caused by the dung bricks and peat blocks they were burning instead of wood in the furnaces. It wasn't too unpleasant, though the men complained about that too, claiming it got into the bread and the soup. He had given orders that strong herbs be added to both to cover the scent and taste.

There were plenty of complaints; the rumor mill was positively acidic these days, but the complaints and rumors were all of the sort that appeared when people had an excess of time and energy, and none were the kind that presaged mutiny. In fact, in a strange way they were a sign of health; the natural result when men who were used to activity were confined in comfortable but boring surroundings.

I will have to find creative ways for them to use up all the energy. Wood gathering parties—hunting parties, too. But that won't take very many. Snow maneuvers? Or perhaps something in the town? But what? I don't want to have them take over the duties of the local constables this soon; that could only cause resentment.

Tremane had made certain that the men were given leave to go into town on a regular basis; there was no point in cooping them up in barracks when a mug of beer and an hour with a pliant girl would make them cheerful again. The townsfolk were getting along reasonably well with the men and vice versa; the only incidents had been caused by drunk-

enness, either on the part of the soldier or more rarely of one
of the townsfolk, and all had been resolved. As might be expected, the man who was drunk was usually to blame, and
punishment was meted out by the appropriate authority. Between them, Tremane and the Shonar Council had established a list of infractions and punishments, based on the
Imperial Code, that was applied to townsman and Imperial
soldier impartially.

On the whole, Tremane's world was in relatively good
shape, as long as he kept his gaze within the walls of Shonar.

Outside, however—

From somewhere beyond the walls, out in the snowy
gloom, came a high, thin wail. *One of them.* That cry had
not come from the throat of a wolf, a lynx, or a feral dog; it
had come from . . . something else. He heard them howling
and wailing at night from dusk to dawn, and the sentries on
the walls reported shadows by dusk and glowing eyes in the
dark, gazing up at them and then vanishing. Whatever they
were, they were smarter than the spider-creature, for they
had not been caught—but he pitied the farmers who had declined the hospitality of the town for the winter. It must be
terrible to hear those creatures crying beneath the windows,
and know that only one thin wall of wood separated you and
your family from them. Did they snuffle at the cracks under
the doors, and sniff at the barred shutters? Did they scratch
at the walls or gnaw on the doorposts? He hoped that long
before the beasts became a danger, those farmers would
change their minds and pack up what they could, and head
for the high brick walls of Shonar, driving their stock before
them. Thus far, whatever they were, the walls were keeping
them out—but every mage-storm brought more and poten-
tially worse creatures to roam the snow-covered landscape.
And the winter had just begun. . . .

Turn your eyes within your walls, Tremane.

The roofs of his barracks, like the roofs of most of the
buildings in town, were thick thatch, and pitched steeply
enough that a buildup of ice merely broke free and slid down
the straw rather than collapsing the roof. That had been necessity rather than wisdom, but it was fortuitous; the same

storm that had collapsed half of the tents had collapsed the roof of one building in town that had been covered with plates of slate rather than bundles of thatch. Yes, with thatch there was a danger of fire, and that was a consideration. By design, though, there would be no chance of a soot fire in Tremane's barracks, for all soot built up in the roof of the furnace itself, and could be poked loose when the furnace was stoked.

Tremane's roof here was slate—but laid over stone rather than wood. This manor had been designed to last for centuries, which was no bad thing at the moment. Some of the rooms were perishingly cold, but very few of the officers or mages spent much time in their tiny closet-sized rooms. If the room was cold, one could always warm up in the Great Hall before retiring, send a servant in with a bedwarmer first, and then bury oneself in blankets with a hot brick for comfort at bedtime. There was no lack of servants now; plenty of folk were happy to serve in Tremane's manor. *Imperial coin spends better than their own now. Ours is of fair weight, and theirs has often been shaved and clipped.*

But there were few places, other than his suite here, that were truly warm. In that much, he envied his men their "caves." Many of the floors on the first story of the manor were of stone and no treat to stand on; even through thick bootsoles, cold numbed the feet. Someone had recalled the old country trick of covering the floors with a thick layer of rushes mixed with herbs to keep them sweet, and he'd ordered the floors of those rooms with no carpet so buried, which had helped with cold drafts coming up the legs of one's trews. The men on housekeeping detail and the newly-hired servants had appreciated the move, since it meant they no longer had to sweep and wash the floors on a daily basis. The only exception was in the room he was using as the manor mess hall; there he would allow no rushes, and the daily sweeping and scrubbing went on as it had in the summer.

Outside the bubbly glass of the window, snow fell in fat flakes the size of coins. You couldn't even make out the clouds when you looked up, for the sky was a solid sheet of gray-white. *Clouds? You can't even see the sun!*

His nose itched, and he sneezed convulsively as his foot crushed a sprig of a pungent herb carried up from the lower floors. He let it lie there; the stuff was everywhere anyway, and just as well. The only product of the mage-storms to pass inside the walls was not a huge, vicious monster, but a tiny, vicious monster, and a prolific one at that. It had probably begun life as a flea; it was about the same size and general shape as a flea, but it was venomous. Not enough to poison a man, but certainly unpleasant; its bite left painful boils that had to be lanced and drained immediately or they went rotten. One of the locals had found a common herb that kept them away, so now every clothes chest, every bed, and every storage closet smelled of the stuff. Sprigs of it were in the rushes, and crushed on the bare floors. Both town and barracks were coping with the plague, but there were many poor people who couldn't afford the herb and were suffering from the bites of the thing. He'd heard that the poor were carting off the discarded rushes and searching through Imperial rubbish piles for the dried-out bits of the herb. He'd left orders not to stop them. He hated to think of children covered with bites from the things. . . .

At least the cold weather would probably kill what specimens were outside, and as for those inside—bored men were hunting the things down and keeping tallies of the kills. It might be prolific, but it couldn't last long under those conditions, unless it lingered in the slums.

So there is my life; reduced from candidacy for Emperor to a war against monsters and fleas.

Well, better monsters and fleas than other things he could name.

He had a full war sentry out on the walls; men posted every few paces with pitch torches burning between them at night. The watches were for four marks, but if it got as cold as Tremane feared it might, he intended to reduce the watches to two marks. It would be pretty pointless to make all this effort at building tight, warm barracks only to afflict the men standing sentry watch with frostbite.

Those that were not standing watch he'd assigned to finishing their own barracks. The floors were rough wood and needed to be finished and polished so they could be kept clean. There were still the partitions to put up, the bunks and storage lockers to build, walls to plaster, furniture to put together. And when they finished all that, he'd think of something else for them to do. Maybe build attic space beneath the thatch; lowering the ceiling would conserve still more heat.

And still no contact from the Emperor, not that he had expected any. Oh, it was *possible* that one of his agents could have made it back to the capital to report the looting of the warehouse, and it was possible that the Emperor would then have gotten together a score of powerful mages to open a Portal and fetch Tremane home to justice. It was even possible that Charliss would have sent a physical message with a physical, overland courier or with a troop of heavily armed men and mages. Whether or not he did so would depend on how badly the Empire was suffering the forces of the mage-storms—if indeed the Empire was suffering them at all.

But as the days had stretched into weeks, the possibility of Imperial recontact diminished rapidly. Now, with the onset of winter, there was no way that even a physical courier would be able to reach them. It would take something the size of the army he already had to do so, for travel across the winter landscape would be impossible under these conditions unless one had an army.

So now Tremane stared down at the wintry isolation beyond his windows that was an uncomfortable mirror for the state of his own spirits.

Well, I certainly have my empire now. A small one, but all mine. I doubt that anyone is likely to dispute me for it until spring.

"Commander, sir?" One of his many aides was at the door; he turned to face the boy, composing his own expression into one calculated to bring confidence.

"Yes, Nevis?" he replied, keeping his tone even.

"Sir, there is a rather—odd group of men here to see you." The boy was clearly puzzled. "Frankly, sir, I don't know what to make of them. They're none of them from the same units or even the same disciplines, but they say they wish to see you for the same reason and that they must speak with you personally."

"And they won't tell you what it is?" He pursed his lips at the aide's nod. "Well, perhaps you'd better show them in. It might be we have another nasty little insect to contend with, one that bites people in . . . places they'd rather not discuss."

The boy flushed, which amused Tremane; how *had* that youngster managed to climb through the ranks and still be able to blush at the idea of a flea that bit a man's privates? "I'll bring them up, sir," he said hastily, and took his leave.

Blue dusk outside the window gave little light for a meeting, and one thing they had in abundance was candles. There must have been hundreds of sealed caskets of candles, and hundreds more of the cruder tallow dips. Tremane set about lighting them himself before the delegation arrived. He'd set the last one alight and was trimming the wick when Nevis brought in the men.

They were a very mixed bag, some dozen or so of them. One mage, one of his high-ranking generals—which was probably why Nevis hadn't dared send them away without consulting Tremane—two sergeants, two leftenants, and an assortment of scouts and troopers.

That's odd. The one and only thing these men have in common is that they were all someone's agent, and I doubt any of them know that the others are agents—

He sat down behind his desk and contemplated the sober-faced group before him while Nevis closed the door. "Well," he said finally, "I hope this is not the prelude to a mutiny."

General Bram laughed. "Hardly, Commander. In fact, that's the point, and I'll be brief. I've no doubt you already knew this, but we're all spies—some of us reported to your rivals; I reported to the Emperor. We've decided to come admit it and fling ourselves upon your mercy. You're too good a leader to throw us away; our request is that you retain us in our current positions."

Tremane was very glad that he was sitting down; agents were not normally that blunt and open. *Not normally? This*

*is unprecedented! A mass defection to my side? I don't
think that's ever happened in the history of the Empire!*
"I—ah—take it you all knew each other?" he said, hoping he
did not sound as dazed as he felt.

"Of course," said the mage—a minor fellow, Tremane
didn't even remember his name, but he had just recently
been graduated from Apprentice. "Just as you knew who we
were." He shrugged. "That's the whole game-within-the-
game, now, isn't it? We all knew each other, though until we
all got together this afternoon, none of us knew who the
masters of the other fellows were."

"Were," Tremane repeated carefully. "Not 'are'."

"Were," General Bram said firmly. "What's the point in
beating around the bush, hoping to flush a bird that scuttled
away hours ago? We haven't had any more contact than you
have, and what's the point of serving a man you haven't
heard from since the beginning of a crisis? About half the lot
that stayed on the other side when you organized that raid
on the storehouse were agents, too, and if our masters were
ever going to contact us again, it would have been a week or
so after the raid." He shrugged. "There's no point in pretending otherwise; we've been abandoned out here, and we
all know it."

"Bram called us all together to talk it over, but we'd all
been thinking the same thing," the mage said, scratching his
unruly hair. "They're there, and you're here; you could have
had the Portal opened just for you and an escort big enough
to get you to your estate. You stuck with us. By our way of
thinking, that makes you a better master than the ones back
home."

"The gods know you're more dependable," said one of the
scouts in a disgusted voice. "Anyway, we came to show you
who all the agents in your ranks were just in case you'd
missed any of us, and let you know we're coming over to you
so you can stop worrying about sabotage from inside. That'd
be like poking a hole in the bottom of the boat you're riding
in anyway."

"I see." He took a moment to settle himself, for of all the
unlikely events he'd endured in the last several months, this

was the least likely of all. It was utterly unprecedented; agents simply did *not* go over to the man they were sent to spy on, much less come over *en masse!*

"Fact is, Tremane, you're the most popular commander I've ever seen," Bram said, with wonder and a tinge of envy. "There isn't a man out there, for all the complaints, who doesn't know you could have left us high and dry, doesn't know everything you've done since we bivouacked here has been aimed at keeping 'em all alive and healthy. It wasn't just the way you kept up their pay; after the way you went around digging the men out of collapsed tents and making sure none of 'em was hurt or frostbit, there isn't one of 'em that wouldn't serve you for nothing. I'll stake my reputation on that."

I'm a popular commander? he thought, with another twinge of bemusement. Again, it was nothing he had expected, although it was something he had hoped would happen. He hadn't a clue what made a "popular" commander, and he wasn't certain anyone did. Commanders who had not only kept up pay, but paid bonuses, had not been popular; successful commanders had not been popular. Even commanders who had made attempts to curry favor with the troops had not been popular. *I'm working them hard and I intend to go on doing so to keep them busy. I've asked them to perform tasks wildly outside their duty. I might have been keeping up with their pay, but it's no secret that the pay chests are going to run dry some time in late spring or early summer. I try to be fair and impartial when I'm administering justice, but there is no guarantee that I will always be right. I simply haven't done a thing that should make me so overwhelmingly popular that even Bram should notice.*

But if Bram and the other agents had made note of the fact that he was "popular," there was no doubt it must be true, and he was not about to inquire too closely into the lineage of this particular gift horse.

I can only hope that I continue to enjoy that popularity. The winter is young. And it's going to be the hardest winter these men have ever seen.

"Gentlemen," he said finally. "I accept both your allegiance and your request to remain in your current positions. I only ask that you in your turn continue gathering intelligence—or rather, let us call it, simple information— and report back to me directly." He fixed Bram with a stern gaze, picking the General as the ringleader of the group. "I don't want to hear about the men's private lives. I don't want to hear about simple grumblings. You are all experienced enough to know when the men are just venting frustration. I want to know about *real* difficulties, complaints that need attention, things I can *do* something about. Or serious situations I might not be able to do anything about directly, but which I must be aware of."

With thought, or even direct appeal to the men, I might even be able to cope with those. The Hundred Little Gods know that no one in the Imperial Army has tried direct appeal to the men in generations.

"Oh?" Bram replied, putting a volume of meaning into the single word.

"I have no choice," he said heavily. "I am being frank with you all, because you are all intelligent men. *We* have no choice. I believe I am the only man in this benighted place with the experience, with the *fitness* to lead here. You must think the same, or you would not be here. If I am to be the leader, I must have all the information I can get, and I must not ignore unpleasant information because I don't like it. I rely on you to bring me that unpleasant information because I am not sure my own people will, every time."

That was a bit of a lie, but a tiny lie of that nature might well cement them further to his cause. And the truth was, these men who had been used to looking for weaknesses in his leadership on behalf of another master were more likely to see such weaknesses than his own agents. They'd have had practice, after all.

General Bram nodded, very solemnly. "We can do that. Are you at all interested in any of us taking a more active role, if we see something a word or two can set right?" He smiled rather grimly. "The Hundred Little Gods themselves know we are used to looking for situations where a word or two can set them wrong."

"Yes," he replied decisively. "You aren't stupid; you know not to expose yourselves. I'll make this bargain of trust with you. You can trust me to do the best I can for every man in our forces; I will trust you to do the best you can to keep me in power." Again, he fixed Bram with that gimlet stare. "This is not a situation where the men can be permitted to rule by popular vote, for there will be things I must do that will not be popular. *My* hand must remain on the reins, mine and no other, or there will be disaster." He smiled slightly. "There is a saying that it is not wise to change drivers in the middle of a charge. I am the driver of the war chariot in this charge, and you had all better stick with me or be thrown beneath the wheels while you're grabbing at the reins."

Bram, who had led no few charges in his time, nodded. "I can agree with all of that—and I believe that I can speak for all of us in agreeing with your conditions." He looked down at his feet for a moment, then looked up again, with a peculiar expression on his face. "You are the best leader we could hope for in this situation, Tremane. You've got civilian experience we old war dogs lack; and where you get your foresight, I'll be damned if I know. And you've got two other things that can't be calculated; you've got luck, and you've got heart. We won't be rid of a leader with that combination."

Tremane closed his eyes for a moment. Of all the many things that had happened here, this was of a piece with the rest. Luck, was it? Well, he was not about to spit on luck, and he would capitalize on every piece of luck he got, but he was not going to count on it either. Perhaps that was the essence of luck.

He opened his eyes. "Gentlemen, thank you. Never forget that we must all work together to save our people here. Remember that *our* people now include these Hardornens of Shonar, although they may not yet realize that fact—and never forget that in the future, to continue to preserve all our lives, we may have to look for friends in strange places."

The General saluted slowly in answer to this, and without

another word, led the delegation of former spies out and back to their posts.

After the snow cleared off, they had steady cold but sparkling and beautiful weather for two days. The weather was *so* cloudless that Tremane began to wonder if the Hardornen weather-wizard was losing his talent at weather prediction to the mage-storms. The old man kept insisting that there was more bad snow on the way, and a great deal of it, but where was it?

If they couldn't rely on the weather-wizard for predictions, it would make preparations a great deal more difficult.

The third day dawned just as clear and beautiful as the first two, and Tremane was just about resigned to the fact that the old man was slipping. Restlessness made him eager to stretch his legs in the afternoon, after a long day of dealing with the paperwork needed to keep up with the state of the supplies in the warehouses, and he decided to go in an unusual direction. Rather than taking his walk down, to make another informal inspection, he would go up, to the walkway at the top of his tower. The weather was good, the air still, the sun bright enough that even up there, exposed, he shouldn't get too chilled until he'd walked out his restlessness. The tower was the highest spot in all of Shonar; he should get a good view of the surrounding countryside outside the walls from there. He might even spot one of the furtively lurking monsters.

It was a long walk, but worth it; he left his escort at the foot of the last stair, for he intended to savor the rare experience of being outdoors and yet completely alone.

I have not been alone except in my own rooms since I accepted this post. I have not stood alone beneath an open sky since my last hunt on my own land.

The stairs came right up onto the roof; there was a small slant-roofed affair covering the last few of them, rather than a trapdoor one had to push open. He approved of the arrangement; if there'd been enough heavy snow, he wouldn't have been able to budge a trap door.

He opened the door at the top to emerge into brilliant sunlight that made his eyes water even as it lifted his heart. What was it about sunlight that made a man feel so much better? He was glad now that he'd ordered a general standing-down for all the men during the past two days; he'd heard they were doing absurd, lighthearted things, acting like schoolboys, making snow forts and having snow fights— creating snow sculptures. *I wonder if I ought to give out prizes for the best snow sculpture? Should I order a winter festival? That wouldn't be a bad notion! It would give the men something to occupy them that had nothing to do with duty!* He resolved to find out what sort of festival these people celebrated; he could make it a joint effort of garrison and town, foster some friendly competitions between the two.

Skating races, sled races—an archery contest—could we somehow adapt stickball to snow or ice?

Someone had been up here already, clearing away the snow. The brilliant sun had evaporated what had been left behind, leaving bare stone beneath his sheepskin boots. He moved forward to the edge of the parapet and looked down.

Below him were part of the manor, a few of the barracks, and beyond them, the walls. His men stood at their regulation intervals along it; not at all like statues, for he had made sure his orders included that they move about to keep themselves warm, and that each man be permitted to chat with the ones next to him provided they kept their regulation distance and didn't bunch up. Some of them were stamping their feet to warm them, others leaned on the edge of the wall, talking, and one was even making snowballs and lobbing them off into the distance, while the ones stationed at either side of him watched. They were probably wagering on how far he was throwing them. There was no sign at all from here of the night-monsters, although prints had been reported in the snow and the mages were trying to work out what kind of creature could make such prints. Tremane wished them luck; judging by the spider-creature, there was no telling what odd beasts might suffer changes into something unrecognizable.

I would rather not imagine a vole, which must eat its own

*weight in prey three times a day, transmuted to something
the size of a cart horse.*

He made a quarter-turn, and now looked out at Shonar, all
of which lay beneath the level of this tower. It was not a big
town by the standards of the Empire, and from here it was
easy to see the signs of decline; abandoned houses where the
thatch had disappeared or rotted, warehouses and workshops
where walls had fallen in or been broken down. There were
a lot of them; more than he had guessed, and certainly more
than the Town Council would want to admit. If Ancar had
not been killed, he would have driven his land into oblivion
in a few more years, by taking the able-bodied and leaving
behind those unable to keep towns, farms, and businesses
going.

He was mad. There is no doubt of it. Irrational anger
stirred briefly in Tremane's heart, but it faded quickly, for
what, after all, was the point? Ancar was dead, dead as last
year's grass. What was important was this; there were empty
and abandoned structures in the town that could be taken
over and put to good use. *That* was what he would do when
the men were finished with their barracks; he'd send them
into town and begin repairing and refurbishing the houses,
warehouses, and workshops. Those would become Imperial
property—and he would have his quarters for married couples, his workshops for men wanting to retire into a
profession.

Satisfied with that idea, he made another quarter-turn to
look out over more of his barracks and empty land beyond
the walls.

The men down below him were drilling in an area cleared
of snow; the ones on the walls doing much the same things
as the men on the other side. The one difference was that
two of them were having a snowball-hurling contest with
improvised slings. *Now there's an idea for a festival compe-
tition. Target-throwing snowballs with bare hands and with
slings. There certainly won't be any dispute about where
they hit!*

But as he raised his eyes past the level of the walls and out over the landscape beyond, he was puzzled, sorely puzzled. There were no mountains in that direction, so what was that long, dark line on the horizon? A forest of exceptionally tall trees? But it was so far away!

A moment later, a wind sprang up out of nowhere, and the long, dark line moved nearer—and he knew what it was.

Huge clouds, black and heavy with snow, were hurtling toward him on the wind that blew into his face. The old weather-wizard had been right!

Before he could call out anything to the sentries on that side, they had already reacted to the rising wind by leaving off their games and conversations and peering toward the horizon. It took them longer to see what he had because of his higher vantage, but as the clouds raced into their field of vision, they reacted.

"Is that a storm?"

"Looks like one to me!"

Shouts up and down the line quickly confirmed what Tremane knew, and one of the men with an alarm-horn at his belt lifted it to his lips and began to blow.

Three long, steady tones and a pause, repeated for as long as the man had breath, that was the agreed-upon signal for a heavy storm approaching. It might seem alarmist to signal the approach of a storm, but Tremane was taking no chances. He'd heard of dreadful snowstorms in the far north where men could get lost and freeze to death not a dozen ells from their own doorstep. If there were men outside the walls, hunting or gathering wood, he wanted them alerted and homeward bound before a storm hit.

Other men with alarm-horns all across the walls took up the call, amplifying it and sending it out over the snow-covered fields and into the woods.

The men drilling stopped what they were doing at a barked order; a moment later, the officer in charge divided them into one group for each barracks, and marched them off to the piles of dung bricks, peat bricks, and wood to stockpile fuel beside each barracks furnace. Below him, Tremane saw men going off purposefully in small groups, presumably sent on other errands by their officers. He didn't even *have* to send men into town to fetch back the ones on leave of absence—they were coming in through the gates by threes and fours, secure that although their excursions had been cut short the time would be made up later.

It was all running like a smoothly-oiled clockwork, and he marveled at it. *It wasn't just my foresight; they understand why the orders are there, and they're cooperating. If a bad storm is on the way, I want our men here so that their officers can account for all of them and we can send out search parties for the missing.*

Well, *he* had better get back to his desk so his officers knew where *he* was! The clouds had already filled up half the sky to the north, and now even the men below the walls could see them. They weren't getting any lighter the nearer they got, either, and the wind was picking up. There was a damp bite to the wind, something that was almost, though not quite, a scent.

Was that lightning? He paused for a moment and stared in fascination. It was! It was lightning! He'd *heard* of lightning in a heavy snowstorm, but this was the first time he'd ever seen it!

As if to remind him that he was lingering too long, a growl of thunder reached his ears.

He turned and pulled open the door to the roof, hurrying back down to the escort of guards waiting.

"Bad storm coming," he said to them.

"We heard the alarm, Commander," the leader told him. "Is there anything you want to assign us to?"

He thought for a moment. "Just to be on the safe side, once you leave me at my office, go down to the chirurgeons and see what they'd want in the way of a snow-rescue kit and put one together for them. I don't believe there's anyone of ours likely to get caught out there, but you never know, and that's one thing I forgot to look into."

The leader of his guards saluted, and once the escort left him at the door to his office, they hurried off to follow his orders.

He walked back to his desk and sat down, but restlessness was on him and it was hard to just sit there and wait while the windows darkened and the alarm call rang out, muffled by stone and glass. The one thing he could *not* do in a case like this, however, was to run off and see what was going on. If there was an emergency, he needed to be where people expected to find him.

Search parties . . . if I need to send out search parties, how can I keep them together, and prevent their getting lost? How can you set a trail in a blinding snowstorm?

As long as they weren't searching a forest, the men could go roped together like a climbing party. That would prevent them from getting separated. But what about a trail back to safety?

If it's still daylight . . . sticks? Red-painted sticks? It was too late to go painting sticks—*No, wait, we still have all the sticks from surveying the walls and a lot of chalk line.* He made a note to get both out of storage. *You might see lanterns through thick snow.* Another note. *Bells. You might hear bells. Weren't there ankle and wrist bells with those dancers' costumes that no one in town wanted to trade for?* He noted down the bells as well. The chirurgeons would know best what a half-frozen victim would need; he'd leave that part of the kit up to them.

I wish there was a better way of getting around in snow besides walking. Well, there wasn't and that was that. *But if they're looking for someone who's half-buried in snow, perhaps they ought to have walking sticks to probe the snow for a body. Blunt spear shafts would do, and they might make walking easier. Wait, I'd better insist on every two men staying very close together, one to probe and one to guard, the Hundred Little Gods only know what's out there and a storm will give those howling things lots of cover for an attack.*

He tried to think of anything else that rescue parties might need and failed to come up with anything else. Putting his notes into a coherent form, he called in one of his aides and sent the young man down to ferret out all the disparate rescue objects and lay them out on the floor of the manor armory.

By now it was too dark to see without a light; it might as well have been dusk rather than just after noon—except for the weirdling flashes of lightning, a strange and disconcerting greenish color, that illuminated the office in fitful bursts. He lit a twist of paper at the fire and went around his office, lighting all his candles and lanterns himself. He waited until he had finished his rounds to look out the window, and when he did, he was astonished.

He couldn't see a thing beyond the thick curtain of snow, and the snow itself slanted obliquely. The wind driving that snow howled around the chimney of his fireplace, and vibrated the glass of the window. No wonder he couldn't hear thunder now; the wind was drowning it out. The lightning strikes were not visible as bolts; instead everything lit up in unsettling green-white for a moment.

Now I know what they mean by a "howling blizzard." And I'm glad we designed the barracks around those furnaces, rather than fireplaces. It'll be harder for the wind to steal the heat from the fires. That was always a problem with a true fireplace; in a high wind most of the heat went right up the chimney. He couldn't afford that to happen in his barracks. They'd use up most of their fuel in no time.

One by one, his officers brought their reports, and he lost a little of his tension. Everyone was accounted for; the hunting and wood-gathering parties had returned before the blizzard hit, in fact they had returned even before the alarm went up. All the barracks were provisioned for a long storm; ropes had been strung between the buildings, barracks, and manor so that no one would get lost.

"You can get lost out there, sir," one of the last of the officers said, as he brushed at snow that had been driven into the fabric of his uniform coat. "Make no mistake about it. You can't see an ell past your feet once you're out of shelter. I've never seen the like."

"Well, there'll be plenty of fresh water at least," Tremane remarked, initialing the report. "Just melt the snow."

The officer nodded, then paused for a moment. "Sir, you did know most of the men in my barracks are from the Horned Hunters, didn't you?"

Since the Imperial Army made an effort to integrate all of the recruits into a single culture rather than cater to individual cultures, Tremane didn't know a thing about it until that moment. "Actually, no—wait, *they* ought to be used to this sort of weather, shouldn't they?"

He had an obscure notion that the Horned Hunters were a nomadic tribe from land so far to the north in the Empire that they never saw summer. "Don't they herd deer and travel by sled?"

"You're thinking of the Reindeer People, sir. My lot are a sect, not a tribe. Shamanistic, animal spirits, that sort of thing." The officer coughed and looked a little embarrassed. "They sent me with a request, since we're all going to be confined to barracks for a while. They want permission to turn a corner of the barracks into a sweat house permanently. *I* don't see anything wrong with it, but I told them I had to have your permission."

"I believe this comes under the heading of Article Forty-Two—'the Empire shall not restrict the right of a man to worship—' and so on." Tremane smiled slightly. "I don't see the harm so long as they understand there won't be any ritual fasting without special permission, and if they want to undergo any prolonged dream quests, they'll have to apply for and use their leave days to do it."

The officer sighed and looked relieved. "That was the one thing I was worried about, sir, and using leave-days takes care of the problem. Very well, sir, I'll tell them. I doubt they'll have any trouble with it."

"I certainly don't have any difficulty with it," Tremane told him. "And if we get multiday storms like this all winter . . . well, I might even make concessions on the leave-days. If you're cooped up in the barracks, you might as well send your spirit out for a little stroll, hmm?"

The officer laughed. "May I tell them that, too, Commander? I think it would appeal to their sense of humor."

He shrugged. "I don't see why you shouldn't. If they know I'll let them have their proper rites, it'll probably keep them more content."

The officer saluted and headed back down to return to his men. Tremane toyed with a pen and wished he had an outlet for pent-up energies for all of his men that would match the Horned Hunters' dream quests. If this storm went on for too long, there'd be fights as the men got on one another's nerves. While many commanders did not like having the odder, shamanistic cults going on among the men, Tremane had never minded; provided you made an effort to understand what they wanted and see that they got it, they were generally easier to please than the "civilized" men.

There was something to be said for diversity, though it sometimes did complicate matters.

Once all of his officers had reported in, he relaxed. Now, no matter what came up, he knew where all the men were. He tried to think of ways they could fill in long days of being snowbound once the insides of the barracks were finished.

Well, now I wonder. The Emperor's Guard has their Guard Hall all hung with captured banners and painted with murals of great battles of the past, and those were all done by the men themselves. So—what about seeing if we can't dig up a few men with some artistic talent, then let each barracks decide how the inside of their place should be painted? The lad with the talent can rough things in, and the rest of the boys can color it. We've paint enough for a thousand barracks. That would encourage division pride, camaraderie—

Should he let the Horned Hunters do their barracks with religious symbols? *Yes, but only in the sweat lodge area.* That would work. And if there was another cult that wanted to do up a small shrine, he'd let them build that, too. *Better standardize a size, or they might get greedy and take over half a barracks.*

"Sir!" His aide Nevis interrupted his train of thought. "Men from Shonar with an emergency, sir!" The young man didn't wait for permission to bring them up—which was quite correct in an emergency—he had the group with him. Tremane didn't recognize any of these people, but their expressions told him they were frantic. He recognized their type, though; farmers. Rough hands, weather-beaten faces, heavy clothing perfectly suited to working long hours in harsh winter weather—they were as alike as brothers. That, and their expression, told him everything he needed to know.

And they came to me instead of to Sandar Giles or Chief Husbandman Stoen.

"You've got people lost in this, outside the walls, right?" he said before they could even open their mouths to explain themselves. "People you sent out with herds? Children?"

The one in front, delegated to be the spokesman most likely, dropped his mouth wide open in surprise. Clearly, that was a correct guess. Tremane seized his arm and led him over to the map table, clearing the surface with an impatient brush of his arm, seizing one particular map from the map stand. Nevis scrambled to pick up the discarded maps while he released the man and spread out the map of the countryside around the town his men had finished just before the first snow, anchoring it with candlesticks so it wouldn't roll up. He glanced at the man, who still hadn't spoken, and who still looked stunned.

"Shake yourself awake, man!" he snapped. "What else could have brought you here? Now show me where these people were *supposed* to be; the sooner we get out there, the better the chance of finding them before the damned boggles do!"

That seemed to bring the man around, although it took him more than a moment to orient himself to the map. Evidently, he'd not seen a map before with symbols on it instead of rough sketches of landmarks.

When he finally did open his mouth, his accent and vocabulary betrayed him as the rough farmer Tremane had assumed he was. "We didn' send 'em out too fur, sor," he said apologetically, "Kep' 'em within sight uv walls. We niver thought lettin' 'em take sheep out tedday would—"

"Of course not, you wouldn't have sent them out into danger, I understand, now just show me where they were," Tremane interrupted. "You can apologize later. Show me where they last were. Frankly, man, as fast as this storm blew up, they could have been within sight of my men on the walls and be lost now. You can't have known that would happen."

The farmer stared at the map, his companions peering over his shoulder, and poked a finger hesitantly at the white surface. "Here—there's three chillern with sheep. Here—Tobe's eldest with cows. Here—the rest uv the sheep with Racky Loder—"

"That's five children, in three parties." Tremane signaled Nevis. "Go to the barracks; explain what's happened. Call for volunteers to meet me in the armory, then go get kits from the chirurgeons. I'll lead the party going out the farthest." That would be the group going after the sheep with the lone boy in charge. He turned to the nervous farmers, who were twisting their woolen hats in their hands. "I'll want you to go with us; the children might be frightened of strangers and run away from us; they won't run from you."

Without waiting for one of his aides to help him, he dashed into his bedroom and rummaged through his clothing chests to layer on two heavy tunics and pull woolen leggings on over his trews and boots. Then he caught up his heaviest cloak and the belt from his armor stand that held his short sword and long dagger, and belted it on *over* the cloak, holding the fabric against his body. A pair of heavy gauntlets reaching to his elbows completed his preparations, which were accomplished in mere moments.

Despite the bulky clothing, he took the stairs down to the bottom floor two at a time, leaving his visitors to clamber along behind him. He waited for them at the bottom of the staircase, then led the way to the manor armory.

Despite his own expectations, he and the farmers were not to wait long for his volunteers. Men began to straggle in before he had a chance to grow impatient, and soon the armory was full to overflowing with snow-covered volunteers. It soon became obvious that he was going to get far more volunteers than he had thought.

By now Nevis was back with his three rescue kits from the chirurgeons, and with two of the chirurgeons themselves. "Nevis, stay here and send any stragglers to the Great Hall," he called. "The rest of you—we need more room, let's go."

He did not lead them; there were too many men between him and the door. He simply went along with the crowd, and only when they had reached the frigidly-cold Great Hall did he push to the front. Someone brought in lanterns; he took one and climbed up to stand on the table. "Right; we have five lost children. Hopefully the three that were together have stayed together. You, you, and you—" he pointed to three of the farmers. "You go after the three children with the sheep. You and you, go for the boy with the cattle, and you come with me after the last boy. Now, *you* go to that corner, *you* over there, and *you* stand by the table. Men, divide yourselves into three parties and position yourselves with these farmers."

He watched them separate and distribute themselves with a critical eye. He redistributed the result a trifle, adding more men to his group, which would be going farthest out. "Right. Weapons—boar-spears, long daggers and short swords. Bows are useless out there. One man is responsible for taking stakes and surveying cord and marking your trail out. When you get to the general area your children are lost in, he stays there with someone to guard, blowing a horn at regular intervals."

They hadn't had time to practice moving while roped together; wiser to use some other way to keep track of each other.

"The rest of you spread out in a line, but make sure you're always in sight of the lantern of the man next to you. If you find anything—kick up a sheep or a cow, for instance, yell for the others. The rest of you—when someone finds something, we all gather on that spot."

That should work. He continued. "Watch out for boggles;

keep your weapons out. This would be prime hunting time for them. When you find the children, yell again; we'll gather, retrace our steps, and follow the horn back to the stake man. If you get lost, try first to retrace your steps, and remember to listen for the horn. You lot going after the three children, take the west gate, you going for the boy with the cattle take the north. Got that?"

There was no dissent, and the men looked determined, but not grim. "All right, then. Let's move."

He led his group out of the manor and into the driving snow, each man carrying a weatherproof lantern. Snow pounded at his face, and the wind tore at his clothing; it wasn't quite sunset, but you still couldn't see more than a few paces away; the lantern light reflected from the snow in a globe of chaotic, swirling whiteness. Now he wished devoutly for magic lights that would neither blow out nor be extinguished if they were dropped in the snow. He wished for a mage-rope that would hold the men together without interfering with their movements. He wished—

To hell with wishes. We make do with what we have. Wishes are no good anymore.

The wind and snow came at them from the side, and he was glad he'd belted his sword on over his cloak; he'd never have been able to hold the fabric closed. He led the entire troop across the practice grounds, and past the hastily-erected warehouses that held the supplies so vital to them. Many of these warehouses were nothing more than tents with reinforced sides and roofs, just enough to keep the snow off; these structures loomed darkly out of the undifferentiated blue-gray of the rest of the world. The walls were first visible as a line of spots of yellow light above a black mass— the lanterns of the men on guard along the top. The men guarding the gate looked startled to see them, but the officer in charge had a good head on his shoulders when he heard where they were going.

"I'll have my men build a beacon fire above the gate!" he shouted over the howling wind. "If we shelter it on three sides it should stay lit. And if you get lost out there anyway, have your man blow the storm signal, and I'll have mine answer it."

Well, the beacon might be invisible at fifty paces and the horn inaudible, but it was another slim help and worth doing. He nodded his agreement, the stake man tied off the end of the survey string to the gate, and out they went.

Every step had to be fought for; despite his swathings of clothing he was still freezing before they had even reached the point where they were to spread out. He and the rest of the men had swathed their faces in scarves, but every exposed bit of skin stung and burned under the pinpricks of driving snow. He frankly didn't know how the old man leading them knew where he was going, although frequent checks of his own north-needle showed him that the old boy was keeping a straight heading. He'd pulled the hood of his cloak tightly around his head, but his nose and ears were numb in no time. Now he was glad he'd had the foresight to order the men out in pairs, one with his weapon ready and one with a lantern; if there were monsters out here tonight, you'd never know until they were on top of you.

The snow had been about calf-high before the storm began; it was thigh-high now, and drifting with the wind. There'd be drifts up to the rooftops in some places by morning.

His feet were frozen and aching with cold; his legs burned with the exertion of pushing through all that snow. Convinced that the old man knew where he was going, Tremane finally handed the lantern over to him and took out his sword; the old farmer handled his boar-spear like a pitchfork, and probably hadn't the least idea how to use it.

Is it his boy we're looking for, or perhaps a relative? There was no doubt of the single-minded determination he'd seen on the man's weathered and leathery face. Now, of course, he couldn't see much of anything!

Finally, after an eternity, the man stopped. "Here's the edge of the Grand Common!" he shouted over the wind. "The boy should be somewhere out there—" He waved vaguely in an east-to-west semicircle.

Tremane waited for the rest of the search-party to catch up and gather around. "Stake man, horn man, stay here!" he shouted. "The rest of you, spread out in pairs—and remember what I said about keeping each others' lanterns in sight! I'll take farthest left flank, the rest of you fill in."

He led the old man off to the left, determined to hold down the farthest position so that he could be certain of one flank, at least. He positioned the pairs of men on his side himself, then marched off into the dark with the old man still at his side until the last lantern was a fuzzy circle of light through the curtain of snow. He turned and moved north again, slowly, and the lantern at his right kept pace with him.

He had the uncanny feeling that they were completely alone out here; that the world had ended, and the lantern to his right was nothing more than a phantom to torture him. *When did the last mage-storm hit? Gods, if one comes in while we're out here—* He'd be helpless, as helpless as a babe. Anyone with mage-power, mage-senses, was completely flattened by the storms. He tried to calculate the times in his head. *I should be all right. It shouldn't come in until tomorrow or tomorrow night.* But if he was wrong, if it came in and sent him reeling into that maelstrom of hallucination and disorientation *now*, while he was out here—

Then hopefully the old man would know enough to call for help, or drag him over to the next pair.

If I ever want to punish a man worse than simply executing him, I'll send him off in a blizzard like this one. Impossible to tell how long they'd been out here; impossible to tell where they were! There was just the burning of his legs, the burning ache in his side, the knotted shoulders, and the cold, the cold, the everlasting cold and dark and the tiny space of light around their lantern. . . .

Then the snow in front of him exploded upward, in his face! It boiled skyward as something hiding beneath it lurched for him.

All discomfort forgotten, he shrieked and floundered back, sword ready, fumbling for his long dagger, his heart pounding.

"*Baaaaaaa!*" the snow-monster bawled. "*Baaaaaaa!*"

Tremane tripped over something hidden beneath the snow and fell over on his rump as terror turned to relief. He coughed twice, and the coughing turned into helpless laughter as the old man helped him back up to his feet. And now the snow all around him was moving, as more of the flock became aware of the presence of humans, humans who must surely represent safety to them in all of this mess. "Swing that lantern and call!" he ordered the old man. "We've found the flock, the boy has to be in here somewhere."

The farmer obeyed him with a will, bellowing like one of his own ewes, and soon more lights came up through the snow as the rest of the men got the message and gathered to this new spot. By now the sheep were pressed up against Tremane like so many friendly puppies, and except for the fact that they kept stepping on his feet, he was rather glad to have them there; their woolly bodies were warming his legs. More sheep came floundering up out of the snowy dark. Once again the men divided up and this time used Tremane as their center point for the search, and it wasn't long before the boy Racky was found, safe and warm, lying down between two of the biggest ewes Tremane had ever seen, with the sheepdog lying atop him.

While the old man greeted his nephew—for that was who this boy was—and the men congratulated one another with much backslapping and laughter, Tremane caught his breath and took careful note of the faces of those he could actually see. What he read there made him smile with satisfaction.

They're mine. By the Hundred Little Gods, Bram was right.

Now, if he could just keep them.

"All right, men—back to town!" he shouted over the howling wind. "I'll order hot spice-wine for all, and throw a joint on to roast!"

With a cheer, the men formed a long line, with the best tracker in front, the one most likely to read the falling traces of their passage in the snow. Tremane, the old man, the boy and the flock brought up the rear. He hadn't thought the sheep would be able to keep up, but they plowed valiantly along, spurred on by the sheepdog. And perhaps urgent thoughts of a warm byre and sweet hay, and shelter from the wind and snow moved through those woolly heads as well. They shoved right along beside the last of the men, their bleating barely audible over the wind.

The last traces of their path were obliterated by the wind, but at that point, by listening carefully, some of those with the best hearing made out the sounds of the horn calling out. By spreading out again, they quickly found the men left beside the end of the string-and-stake markers. At that point it was an easy task to make their way back to the gate, and the beacon fire over it was a welcome sight indeed.

Tremane sent the old man and his charges off to the town without waiting to hear his thanks; for one thing, he wanted those sheep out of his garrison, and for another, he wanted to know how the other two parties had fared. With a word to the quartermaster to break out some barrels of wine and mulling spices, bring in a joint of beef for each building, and send them all along to the barracks, he paused only long enough to leave his snow-caked cloak in the hands of an orderly. He ran up the stairs to his office, leaving lumps of melting snow from his boots in his wake.

Nevis was waiting for him, with a smile on his face. "The other two parties are back, Commander," he reported. "There was some injury due to frostbite, and one man hurt by a boggle, but it was a minor wound. All the children and the better part of the livestock were recovered."

The last of his energy flowed away like the melting snow, and he collapsed into a chair. "We have had *more* than our share of good luck," he said heavily. Nevis nodded vigorously.

"Have you any orders, sir?" the young man asked.

He started to say no, then changed his mind. "Yes, I do," he told the aide with a smile. "First—you and the other aides see that the men get that hot spiced wine I ordered. Second, see to it that the volunteers get spiced brandy instead of mere wine; you have sufficient authority to order it, so do so. Third—" he got up and began walking toward his bedroom, shedding wet garments as he walked. "—pick up this mess, and see that I am *not* disturbed. I intend to hibernate. Is that clear?"

"Yes, Commander—" Nevis began.

And if he said any more, it didn't matter. The closing door cut it off.

Eight

Firesong stood at one of the windows of his *ekele* garden, feeling the chill coming off the "glass," frowning out at the snow-bedecked landscape beyond. The first snowfall of the season in Valdemar was usually nothing more than a light frosting of white; this snow had fallen for hours, and covered the ground to an uncomfortable depth. Firesong had not troubled to leave the *ekele* since he'd last returned to it to warm his bones. *Snow. I hate snow,* he thought rebelliously, arms crossed over his chest. *It isn't worth crossing all that muck to get to the Palace, not for anything short of a terrible emergency.* An'desha wasn't in the *ekele;* he hadn't been "home" last night or the night before. Much as Firesong would have enjoyed indulging himself in a jealous fit, he knew he couldn't legitimately permit himself one. The same snow that kept him here had discouraged a weary An'desha from coming back. Firesong knew where both Karal and An'desha had been for the past two days. Karal was dancing attendance on Solaris, and when she Gated back to Karse, he was busy with Natoli, with whom he was spending most of his free time. An'desha had been working with the artificers the entire time. On nights when he worked late into the morning, he had taken to staying at the Palace—sleeping chastely enough, taking a bed in the pages' and squires' dormitory. Had Firesong cared to, he could have used a touch of magic and the still water in a basin to see exactly that, as he had the first time An'desha spent a night at the Palace.

He couldn't even be angry at An'desha anymore; the

Shin'a'in was hardly to blame for the fact that they were drifting apart. An'desha's changing interests alone dictated that. He shifted restlessly from one foot to the other and his heavy silk clothing shifted softly against his skin. *He's gone mystical, and I never could handle mystics. And yet, at the same time, he keeps trying to make magic into a craft rather than an art—something controlled by formula rather than intuition.* Both of those positions were in diametric opposition to Firesong's own beliefs; An'desha could not have chosen anything more contrary if he'd planned to.

Firesong gritted his teeth until his jaw ached. *Logically* he couldn't be angry at An'desha for failing to fulfill Firesong's dream ... but emotion does not respond to logic. Part of him wanted to let An'desha go with a sad blessing, but most of him wanted An'desha to be just as miserable as Firesong was.

So An'desha didn't need or want an emotional bond? That was fine for *him*, but what about Firesong? *I am not growing younger, and my opportunities become fewer with every passing year.* Shay'a'chern *number no more than one in ten; how can I hope to find a permanent partner when all like me are already paired up? Why must I go through my life like a white crow, cast out by the flock?* Hadn't he earned his rewards by now? Didn't he *deserve* them?

All right, so he wouldn't have An'desha. He was resigned to that; he wouldn't go around beating empty bushes, hoping to flush birds from them. He needed more time, youth, more years of life! *Then,* perhaps he might find his soul match, given decades to search rather than mere years.

And he knew how to do it, too.

But it was wrong. That was what Ma'ar had done, though for different reasons. Ma'ar had wanted power, and there was not time enough in one life to accumulate all the knowledge and power that Ma'ar craved.

I only want—love. Is that purpose enough to make us different?

Not unless he could find a way to get those years of life without cheating anyone else of his. There *must* be a way to work the trick without hurting anyone!

His frustration grew as he stood there, once again racking his brain, trying to find a way to make the trick viable. It was so *easy*, that was the worst part! Ma'ar and all his successive incarnations had done all of the hard work, all the really *dark* work. Now the Sanctuary was in place and self-sustaining; he had only to power it a bit further and link himself to it, and then he would have all the leisure he needed for his searches.

And even if I was old when I finally found him, I could link him there as well, and then find new bodies for us both. . . .

Was that so wrong? Was it possible to use something built with blood and not be tainted himself? What dark paths were these thoughts leading him down?

But they kept intruding on everything he did. Solutions a bit less shadowed than the ones Ma'ar had used whispered to him. *Would it be wrong to take the body from someone who does not deserve to live? A murderer, perhaps? A blood-path mage such as one of Ma'ar's or Falconsbane's underlings?*

There was the small matter of needing a physical bond, however—Ma'ar had used the bond of blood-relationship. Could another bond serve as well? Could he inflict that bond on someone?

Aya stirred behind him and uttered a tense trill. Aya did not approve of the path his thoughts were tending—or at least, the bondbird did not approve of the little he understood. That irritated him further. Bad enough to be troubled by his own conscience, must he put up with Aya's as well?

And what does a bird know? he thought impatiently, dismissing Aya's discomfort. Was he going to have to follow the dictates of the wayward mind of a bird? He had a flash of regret for not having chosen a raptor over the flashier firebird; Vree was certainly amoral enough, and not much inclined to consider anything in the way of a conscience when plump prey or a gryphon's crest-feathers were in sight!

As if to compound his troubles, *now* An'desha came trudging cheerfully into view, up to his knees in snow, looking far too happy to fit in with Firesong's black mood. And it was too late to go up into the *ekele* to avoid him; the Shin'a'in saw him standing in the window and waved to him.

Damn, damn, damn. His black mood soured further. He did not want to be good company for anyone, least of all An'desha, but he'd better make a try at it. He put on a mask of a pleasant expression, and waited for An'desha to enter the protected area between the two doors. There was a further wait for An'desha to shake off the snow encrusting his legs inside the first of the doors, then enter the *ekele* itself.

"You'll never believe what's here!" An'desha called, as Firesong opened the second door. "The city's in an absolute uproar—there hasn't been such a carnival procession since—well, since *you* arrived! Anybody with a free moment at the Palace and the Collegia is gawking like any country cousin!"

"I can't imagine what you could be talking about, or what it is that's come," Firesong replied, curiosity piqued in spite of himself. "Well, what is it? A captured monster? Solaris parading through the city with a portable Temple of Vkandis?"

"Neither." An'desha pulled off his quilted Shin'a'in jacket with a shower of droplets from the melted snow, and grinned. "A floating barge from k'Leshya. They've been Gating their way across country with help from the gryphons, which is why we didn't know they were coming; the gryphon-mages were taking it in turn to fly ahead, scout a remote location, and come back to build a Gate to the next spot. That let them get within striking distance of Haven without raising a fuss. Once they got there, they came overland by road the rest of the way. They were just waiting to see if the breakwater would hold before they chanced a Gate."

A barge? From k'Leshya? "Who? And why?" he blurted without thinking. "And why now?"

"To answer the last question first, *now* is because they had to. Among other things they brought someone who calls herself a *trondi'irn*; apparently she's a sort of gryphon-keeper, and she's come to make sure our four stay in good health. About a quarter of the barge is full of her stuff, or rather, the stuff for the gryphons." An'desha looked quite smugly pleased with Firesong's surprise. "There's also one of *my* people, a Sworn-Shaman like Querna, but a man. He's supposed to be here to advise Jarim, rather than replacing him, and I must admit Jarim seemed kind of relieved to see him."

Firesong got the feeling that Jarim wasn't the only person relieved to see this shaman. Another point of difference, of rift, between them?

But An'desha didn't notice his silence. "Then there's an expanded delegation from k'Leshya, about a dozen, counting the *trondi'irn*, and three more gryphons, and they've brought a lot of things Darkwind's been fussing over—" He interrupted his own description with a shrug. "I'm starving and I missed breakfast and lunch at the Collegia. Well, why don't you go see for yourself?"

"I believe I shall." Surprise gave way to a consuming curiosity. "Would you mind if I offered them the hospitality of the *ekele*? I can't imagine any of them would feel all that comfortable in the Palace."

An'desha flushed faintly. "Actually, I wanted to talk with you about that. Would *you* mind if I—moved temporarily into the Palace? I seem to be spending all my time there, and I've been offered a room in the Palace if I want it. That would—ah—leave you more room for the people from k'Leshya."

For one moment, Firesong throttled down rage. *Deserting me already? How dare he—after everything I did for him!*

But he hid it carefully. Getting angry at An'desha would only drive him further away. Instead, he tried assuming a mask of indifference. "If that's what you really want, it's fine with me."

"I would think it will just be until we find another solution for when the breakwater goes." An'desha looked at him pleadingly, and Firesong now felt a surge of satisfaction.

So—since I agreed so easily, now he's worried? Good. Maybe I can make him jealous for a change!

He shrugged, deepening his pose of indifference. "Whatever you want. I'm going to go see if I know any of these folk, and tender my invitation."

He felt his mask slipping and turned away. Then, so that An'desha did not see any of the conflicting emotions on his

face, he ran up the stairs to fetch his own cloak and boots—
which fortunately were not in the bedroom. He heard
An'desha following slowly and waited until the Shin'a'in
was rummaging around in the bedroom, packing up, before
he went back down to the garden again. Aya joined him with
a trill of satisfaction, flying to take a secure perch on his
shoulder as he went out the doors.

He pushed through the snow with his restless thoughts
flitting from one subject to another. For one thing, he hadn't
given any thought to the gryphons' health; he'd just taken it
for granted that they *were* healthy. They always recovered
quickly from injuries, and never seemed to be ill.

But the youngsters were about to fledge; this fall they'd
been making short glides from the tops of fences and wood-
piles. *Well, not quite glides. More like controlled plummets.*
They still were only about half the size of their parents, so
they probably had one major growth spurt coming. If they
doubled their size in a year or so, from all Firesong knew of
other creatures, he was certain that would put a tremendous
strain on their bodies. There would be special nutritional demands to keep up with such a growth spurt. Perhaps that
was why the *trondi'irn* was here. . . .

Or perhaps it was because of Treyvan and Hydona themselves. There might be some traces of minerals or other
things they needed that they couldn't find for themselves.
They are *a created race, after all. The Mage of Silence made
them up, and I don't care how much of a genius he was, he
couldn't possibly make every detail perfect.* Humans had
been around for a great deal longer than gryphons, and look
how imperfect they were!

*Even our bondbirds get strange ailments; that's why we
each have to be an expert in the treatment of each particular type of bird.* He hated to think of all the strange things
that might go wrong for a gryphon.

As he broke through the trees, it was clear that there was
something causing a great stir at the regular Palace stables.
There was quite a crowd there, and something bulky and
dark in the middle of them. The floating barge?

Probably. Firesong recalled very clearly how he had coveted one of those wonderful creations; coveted it as he seldom coveted any material object. Like many other creations, only k'Leshya had retained the knowledge that made them possible after the Cataclysm, largely because only k'Leshya had custody of as much of the Mage of Silence's library as had been saved. Based on the kind of covered barge that transported goods and trading families up and down the rivers of the time, the floating barges did just that—float. They generally hovered about an arm's length above the ground, but could go as high as the treetops or as low as the width of a single finger. It was possible to use magic to move them forward, but normally they were drawn by teams of horses, mules, or oxen—beasts being far "cheaper" to use than a mage. The biggest advantage was that they could carry literally as much as you could stuff into and strap onto them, for they were "without weight" and could be drawn by beasts with scarcely more effort than if they were moving unencumbered. Since they did not have wheels, they could go where there were no roads. Firesong could easily picture being able to load everything he owned into one of these barges, and traveling the world. . . .

He hurried his pace, and saw the package-laden top of the barge rising above the crowd around it. An'desha must have come to fetch him as soon as the delegation arrived; it didn't look as if anyone had even unpacked as yet.

He joined the crowd of curiosity seekers; as soon as those nearest him saw he was there, they parted for him, enabling him to work his way in to the center. There seemed to be a lot more baggage than even a delegation of a dozen could account for—what had they brought with them?

The newcomers were instantly obvious from their costume; a blending of Shin'a'in and Tayledras style, but with a curiously antique feeling and exotic cut to it, and in colors as vivid as the flowers of a Vale. The gryphons were already in attendance, all four of them, paying close attention to three *new* gryphons and a young woman in brilliant orange and scarlet garments billowing out to the elbows and knees, where they were then confined by wrapped bands of black-and-orange embroidered straps. Beside her was a man in vivid blue and white, whose long black hair and back seemed oddly familiar.

Treyvan raised his head and spotted Firesong. "Heigho!" he said. "And herrre at lassst is that old frrriend of yourrrsss, Sssilverrrfox!"

Silverfox? Firesong froze in mid-step, as the *kestra'chern* Silverfox turned to greet him with a cheerful face lighting up with pleasure. *Why didn't An'desha tell me Silverfox was here?*

For a moment he was angry all over again, but reason prevailed. *How could he have known I even knew Silverfox? That was long, long before we met each other, and I don't recall ever mentioning the k'Leshya except in passing.*

His temper cooled again quickly, and he was able to greet Silverfox with unalloyed cheer—which was just as well, because the quality of the embrace that the *kestra'chern* gave him was very promising indeed.

"What brings *you* here, of all people?" Firesong asked as they separated. "I should have thought you would have preferred to stay in the Vale and not plunge yourself headlong into *this* inhospitable clime!"

"As to that, it's no worse than the weather outside the Vale," Silverfox replied easily. "And as to what brought me—we traditionally send members from each of the Disciplines when we put together a delegation." He nodded at Treyvan and Hydona. "The first to make an approach are always from the Silver Gryphons, of course. The Silvers are—well, I suppose you'd call them our version of Heralds. Peacekeepers, law enforcers, and so forth, but they also include our scouts. Usually they aren't actual gryphons, unless we're sending them *quite* far away. That was why Treyvan and Hydona were first selected to find the Vales, and then volunteered to come to Valdemar."

"But why a *kestra'chern?*" Firesong repeated.

Silverfox laughed. "Because the *kestra'chern* are one of the Disciplines, pretty bird!" He indicated his fellow k'Leshya with a long finger as he told off the "Disciplines." "Artisans, Administrators, Scholars, Silvers, Husbandry, Mages, and *Kestra'chern.* Actually, there are two of us *kestra'chern;*

trondi'irn come under the Discipline of *Kestra'chern*. And we never send the last Discipline—that's Shaman—out with a delegation. There's no need for that, and besides," he added with a grin, "we brought Lo'isha shena Pretara'sedrin with us, so there's rather a superfluity of priestly types."

As if responding to his name, a Shin'a'in garbed from head to toe in a dark, midnight-blue turned and flashed a pearly smile in their direction, before returning to his conversation with Jarim.

A cold burst of air reminded Firesong just how ridiculous it was for them all to be standing around in the snow. "Look, I can't imagine why we're all freezing out here when we could be warm. I came to offer you the hospitality of my home. I *think* you'll all fit in; there's at least a few amenities of civilization—"

"Oh, Whitebird will want to stay with the gryphons, so that will be one less—and Artisans, Administrators, and Mages will want to set up a proper embassy suite in the Palace. I suspect you're only likely to get me, Husbandry, and the Scholar," Silverfox said cheerfully. "That's only four. And we store easily. If you've got a hot pool for soaking, the rest will probably come use it. Summerhawk of Husbandry is a marvelous cook, so they'll probably come to eat as well, but I suspect otherwise they'll want to be where the business is." He smiled apologetically. "I'm afraid they are all very earnest and intent on their duty. They're planning on spending every waking moment with your mages and artificers, developing the next set of protections from the mage-storms."

Firesong was secretly relieved that the k'Leshya mages would probably not be taking him up on his offer. He doubted any of them would think highly of his excursions to investigate Falconsbane's Sanctuary, much less that he was considering using it. . . . He'd been able to conceal his activities so far from the other mages at Haven, largely because he was better than most of them. *I don't know that I can hide what I'm doing from mages with unfamiliar skills. Gods only know what k'Leshya has still in the way of magics we've lost. And as for what they might have developed, I can't even begin to guess.*

"We need to unpack—and I think you ought to stay for that much of it, my friend," the *kestra'chern* continued. "We brought some things along I suspect you've been missing. Our *hertasi* made you up some new clothing for one—you came here rather lightly packed, and I doubt these folk, pleasant as they are, have any notion of fabric or design!"

Firesong shuddered, recalling some of the things he'd been presented with by well-meaning tailors of Haven. *No* sense of style, and as for the limited palette of colors, the less said, the better! They wanted to dress him as a molting peahen.

"Introduce me to everyone so I can make my offer and they can decline or accept it on their own, would you?" he said, rather than commenting on the deficiencies of Valdemaran costume. "That way we can take the luggage and all straight to the *ekele* and you can get settled in properly."

"Luggage and *presents,* my dear friend," Silverfox said slyly. "I oversaw that part of the packing myself."

Firesong laughed. "Should I be greedy or polite? Being polite, I should pretend I don't have any great urgency to see what you've brought, but being greedy, that is the only reason why I would willingly stand here in snow up to my elbows while you sort yourselves out!"

Already his heart felt lighter for Silverfox's presence. And as he helped unload the barge and sort packages and bundles, something else occurred to him.

Here, presented on a platter as it were, was the perfect way to make An'desha anxious and jealous, if it could be done at all. He had one last chance to win the Shin'a'in back.

Silverfox reclined indolently in the hot pool several days later, after having given Firesong a profoundly satisfying demonstration of at least one of a *kestra'chern*'s sets of skills. "I fear we have annoyed one set of your artificers with our arrival," he said lazily.

"Oh?" Firesong was feeling too pleased to be annoyed at the mention of the artificers. "How is that? From all I hear, your mages are getting along splendidly with them. It's a bit awkward cramming Treyvan and Hydona into the room so that there are enough translators, but so far as I've heard that's the only thing like a problem."

"Oh, it is the ones who are messing about with boilers and steam," Silverfox chuckled. "I must admit I fail to see the attraction; the only places *I* care to have steam are in the kitchen, in the steam-house, and rising above the waters of a soaking-pool."

Firesong laughed. "Oh, I understand what the trouble is. That girl Natoli and her friends were helping the steam fanatics when you arrived, but now they are crawling all over your floating barge, day or night. And when they are not examining the barge, they are trying to take apart some of the other useful things you brought with you. In the meantime, they have deserted the steam proponents to learn what mechanical wonders you have devised."

"That is why we brought artisans, dear friend," Silverfox retorted, with a half-smile. "So that the rest of us do not have to attempt to explain what *we* do not understand. So far as *I* know or care, it is *all* magic!" He laughed. "I told one of them that it is all run by magic smoke. When the smoke escapes, the object ceases to function!"

Firesong had to laugh at that, too—since most of the mechanical contrivances of the artificers normally emitted great quantities of smoke when *they* stopped working, exploded or burned to the ground, especially the ones powered by steam boilers.

"Your friend An'desha has been making himself invaluable to them, so they tell me," Silverfox added.

Firesong's thoughts darkened at the mention of An'desha's name, and he controlled his expression to avoid giving himself away. He had been paying Silverfox his exclusive attentions in the hope that if anything would bring An'desha back it would be jealousy, but to his dismay, An'desha actually seemed pleased and relieved to see him so often in the *kestra'chern*'s company. His last attempt to fix An'desha's wandering attention had certainly not turned out the way he had thought it would. In fact, another kink in his plans had developed, for when An'desha was not translating for the k'Leshya, he was most often in the company of the Sworn-

Shaman, which certainly put paid to any hopes of weaning him away from his growing mysticism!

Yesterday he'd decided to bury the remains of the relationship before they began to stink, although he was not at all happy about the end of it. That really only left him back in the same position he'd been in when the k'Leshya delegation arrived. Either he resign himself to a life predominately alone, or—

Or I find a way to extend that life and even my odds of finding my lifebonded.

Just as his thoughts took that grimmer turn, however, Silverfox stretched languidly, striking an unconsciously provocative pose that distracted him. Steam veiled Silverfox's head and torso, giving him an air of mystery. "You've been rather quiet and subdued for the past several days," the *kestra'chern* observed. "If I didn't know you better, I'd say you were brooding over something, but you keep saying it's only the weather. Is the weather here really depressing you that much?"

"Oh it isn't the weather, really—at least it isn't the primary problem," Firesong found himself admitting. "I do confess that I hate leaving all that snow where I have to look at it every moment, though. Back in our Vale you'd never know it was winter unless you went outside the protected area, and I generally managed to avoid that in bad weather."

"Hmm." Silverfox stretched again, arching his back and closing his eyes for a moment. "Still. There's something rather pleasant about being in *here*, where it's warm and comfortable, and being able to look out there and know that if you don't want to subject yourself to miserable weather, you don't have to. Don't you think?"

Firesong shrugged uncomfortably. "I said it wasn't the primary problem."

"So what *is* depressing you?" Somehow Silverfox had managed in all his stretching to work around behind Firesong, and began massaging his tense shoulders with strong, skillful fingers. "Perhaps I can help."

"What depresses anyone?" he countered with irritation. "I'm *shay'a'chern*, alone, surrounded by people who have paired off comfortably—Elspeth and Darkwind, Treyvan and Hydona, Karal and Natoli, Selenay and Daren, Kerowyn and Eldan—and gods save us, Talia and Dirk, who are mature parents and *quite* old enough not to be mooning over each other like a pair of romantic teenagers! Everywhere I look, I'm surrounded by hopeless romantics!"

"And here you are, a bird with a perfectly charming nest and no one to share it with." Silverfox managed to make that sound sympathetic without being syrupy. "I understand; that's enough to depress anyone."

"The lifebonded couples are the worst," Firesong continued acidly. "There seem to be more of *those* here than is decent by anyone's standards."

"Perhaps it has something to do with the fact that all the Heralds congregate here," Silverfox observed casually. "It would be rather like concentrating all the *shay'a'chern* in Valdemar and the Vales in an institution that was something like the Collegium. It makes such meetings of matching souls much more likely."

If only I could *do that. . . .* But if he could extend his years, that would have the same effect. "Still. It's indecent, and it's irritating."

"I can see where it would be, although I find it rather charming. And at the same time, I rather feel sorry for them." In spite of Firesong's resistance to being soothed, Silverfox's ministrations were having an effect. But that last statement was positively bizarre.

"Why on earth would you feel sorry for them?" he asked in surprise. "I thought everyone was looking for a lifebonded mate! Isn't that the point?"

"I'm not looking for a lifebond," Silverfox said firmly. "I would much, much rather have someone who loved me out of pure attraction or simple affection than have someone who *couldn't help* loving me. So far as *I* can see, the difference between being in love and being lifebonded is rather like the difference between doing something because you want to and doing it because someone came along and put a geas on you to compel you to do it. You might have wanted to do it anyway, but the notion of being compelled to it makes me very uncomfortable." He uttered a dry chuckle. "No—not uncomfortable; it makes me very rebellious. Quite frankly, if I met my lifebonded, I would try to fight the compulsion just because it *was* a compulsion. And I would insist that something more than a compulsion held us together."

"I can't see that." Firesong shook his head. "Lifebonded mates are so devoted to one another, so bound up with each other, it seems the perfect way of life to me. Being lifebonded means there are no misunderstandings, no jealousies, no incompatibilities; none of the things that cause so many problems in ordinary relationships—"

But Silverfox was chuckling in earnest now, as if he had said something very amusing. "Who told you there were no misunderstandings, no incompatibilities? Did you read it somewhere? Do you know any lifebonded couples intimately enough to say that with authority? *Believe* me, I've had lifebonded couples as clients in the past, and they have their share of both those things. The only difference between them and ordinary couples is that if *they* don't resolve problems quickly, they're going to suffer far more agony of spirit than you or I would."

"That sounds like an advantage to me," Firesong retorted stubbornly.

"Huh." Silverfox did not seem to have a response to that statement. "You seem very sure of that."

"I am." Firesong was not going to back down on this one. "And I can't see where 'agony of spirit' is any worse than the fires of jealousy. I'd say a person would be better off if he was forced to reconcile differences; I think it's better for two people to be impelled to fix things between them than for one to suffer heartache while the other goes off blithely about his business without a care in the world. That would make life a great deal more even-handed," he finished grimly.

"Now *that* was certainly stated with conviction," the *kestra'chern* observed. "I might almost suspect you've found yourself suffering the slung shot of jealousy a time or two."

"Enough," Firesong replied cautiously. "Enough to know it's probably one of the most poisonous of emotions, and that it encourages obsession. How is being so obsessed with someone that you can't get your mind on your work any better than being forced to be compatible?"

Silverfox moved his ministrations to below Firesong's shoulder blades. "You have a point. Certainly for some people it would make getting one's work done much easier. Obsession is a fairly ugly condition, and as you said, it is poisonous. It tends to warp one's outlook."

"And it is one that is hard to cure." Firesong winced as Silverfox's fingers encountered a particularly knotted muscle.

"So that is what is depressing you? Loneliness, jealousy, and obsession?" Silverfox sighed. "That is a combination sufficient to depress anyone, even at the height of summer and with all going well. Given the current situation, I marvel you are getting anything accomplished. I am not certain I would."

When did I admit that I was obsessed? Firesong caught himself, keeping himself from saying anything further. Silverfox was the most persuasive person that Firesong had ever encountered, not excluding Herald Talia. This was not the first time that the *kestra'chern* had managed to maneuver him into admitting something he had not intended to.

And despite the fact that he was anything but a nuisance, Silverfox had been doing a remarkable job of somehow being present whenever Firesong contemplated a little trip over to the Palace and the Heartstone for another visit to Falconsbane's Sanctuary. If Silverfox had been anything other than what he was, Firesong would have been dying to get rid of him by now, and he would have considered the *kestra'chern* to be a prime nuisance.

As it was, every time the *kestra'chern* turned up so very inconveniently, he managed to change the encounter into something pleasant, enjoyable. His timing was amazing; too coincidental to be an accident, but how did he *know?* How could he know? And he never made anything so obvious as an outright interception; he was just there when Firesong's thoughts turned grim, striking a casually provocative pose, or flirting cheerfully with him.

This was not the first time that he'd gotten Firesong to

confess things to him, but this was the first time he'd coaxed the conversation into the dangerous grounds of emotional obsession, jealousy, and anger. This was *very* dangerous ground, in fact, since it might lead to other deductions.

Firesong restrained growing anger—not at Silverfox, but at the impossible, intolerable situation.

"It doesn't matter; there's nothing I can do about the situation, so I might as well just endure it with proper Tayledras stoicism," he lied, trying to steer things off that precarious ground and hide his own feelings.

"Ah, but it does matter," Silverfox countered. "You are a mage, and as such, your control is dependent on your emotional state. As a Healer-with-knives should not practice when his hands are unsteady, a mage should not practice when his nerves are unsteady. You know that well enough to teach it!"

Firesong's muscles knotted again under Silverfox's hands, betraying his temper to the *kestra'chern*. "I do know that, and my nerves are steady enough," he replied, "I know what I'm doing. And to tell the truth, at the moment my skills are not needed anyway."

"Oh, my friend," Silverfox sighed, releasing him. "Your body tells me a different story." He slid around to his former position, and his expression was dead sober. "The chiefest language of the *kestra'chern* is that of emotion; his chiefest skill is in the matters of the heart rather than of the mind or spirit; we leave the former to the Scholar and the latter to the Priest. *That* is what we do, but there comes a point when we cannot do our work without cooperation."

Instead of getting off that dangerous ground, they were now firmly atop it. Firesong feigned incomprehension and stifled alarm. "Why would you need my cooperation for anything more than you already have?"

But Silverfox frowned. "You already know the answer to that question. I do not know all, by any means, but I do know a few things. You are lonely and profoundly unhappy here, you live in a bower built for two but you are alone in it, you tense with anger when Karal and the artificers are mentioned, you tense with pain when An'desha's name comes up. Your heart is in turmoil, your body reflects that, and your mind must of necessity reflect both your heart and body. Even an apprentice in my art could put those facts in their proper order."

"What, is that all you have deduced?" Firesong retorted, more sharply than he had intended.

Silverfox looked directly into his eyes with unveiled candor. "There is more, but those are the things *I* can do something about, and only if you will talk about them."

"Oh, you can, can you?" Firesong hoisted himself up out of the pool abruptly, wrapping himself in an enveloping robe so that his body would not betray his thoughts any further.

Silverfox heeded his example, and followed *him* when he headed for the stairs to the *ekele*. "Yes, I can, and it is not a boast. That is my particular avocation, and I am as skilled in it as you are skilled in your avocation of mage. I have been studying and practicing my art for as long as you have."

Firesong remained silent for the time it took to climb the stairs, but turned angrily to face the *kestra'chern* when they both reached the top. "I suppose you can do something about the way that An'desha has turned away from me, then? And you can silence that interfering sprout, Karal, so that An'desha gets no more stupid ideas, no more obsession with mysticism? Things between us were perfectly adequate until *he* came along! If there is anyone to blame here, it is Karal! An'desha depended on me, not on some idiot priest from a land that considers the Star-Eyed's people to be barbaric eaters of raw meat!"

Too late, he realized that his mouth had run away with him again; he flushed, turned away, and flung himself sullenly onto the couch. He stared out the window rather than looking at Silverfox. It should be easier to keep a tight rein on his mouth if he wasn't staring into the *kestra'chern*'s eyes.

If only it were possible to keep a tight rein on his emotions.

Outside the window an interlacing of stark, leafless branches against the snow reminded him of clutching talons.

A soft *shush* of fabric told him that Silverfox had taken a seat nearby, but not on the couch itself. "An'desha is not your lifebonded mate, and you knew that the moment he began to turn away from you. You also must know that nothing you could have said or done, nothing that was said to him, could ever make him into something he was not," the *kestra'chern* pointed out with cool logic. "And as for the way he no longer depends on you, is that as a result of meddling by Karal, or as a result of things you yourself did? You are a Healing Adept, Firesong—your own heart surely told you that such clutching dependence as you have described to me already was not healthy. You yourself must have set in motion the course that eventually led him away from your side; you could not betray your own avocation. Heal he must, even if it leads him away from you."

Firesong flushed again, and before he could stop himself, he had turned to face Silverfox once more, his anger smoldering within him and threatening to burst out. "But Karal's interference ruined everything! Where he led An'desha was *not* the direction I intended to take things!" he stormed. His voice rose, and his throat tightened as he clenched both his fists with barely restrained rage. "Damn him! He has *no* idea of my forbearance—a hundred times I could easily have *killed* him to get him out of our lives!" His rage rose into a killing thing. "I still could!" he shouted. "I wish I had!"

Across the room, Aya shrieked, and simultaneously, a vase shattered.

Silverfox did not even wince, but the crash of splintering glass dampened Firesong's anger as effectively as a bucketful of cold water splashed into his face. He stared at the heap of glass shards on the table with his jaw clenched.

What am I doing? I haven't let my temper rule my power since I was an apprentice mage! What's wrong with me? Where did my control disappear to?

"Firesong, if it had not been Karal, it would have been someone else," Silverfox said calmly into the heavy silence. "Given that he is half Shin'a'in, it would probably have been Querna. I cannot picture a Shin'a'in Goddess-Sworn leaving him in the unsettled state you have described to me yesterday. He was and is going to grow and mature, and short of damaging his mind, there is nothing you could have done to change that."

I admitted I want to murder Karal, and he says nothing. Doesn't he care?

"What would you have felt if it *had* been Querna rather than Karal?" Silverfox persisted. "Would that have made it any easier for you, as he grew away from you? Would you have been less angry than you are now?"

Of course he cares; he just realizes I still have that *much control left that I wouldn't murder Karal out of hand.*

Would I?

"No," he said slowly. "No. If he had turned to Querna, that would probably have made things worse. Karal is not precisely the figure of authority that Querna was; a Goddess-Sworn would certainly have turned him to mysticism much more quickly than Karal did."

Only now did Silverfox rise and take a place on the couch beside Firesong, although the *kestra'chern* made no move to touch him. "As you have said yourself, if it had been Querna who helped him answer his questions, we both know you would have lost him sooner," the *kestra'chern* said quietly. "As it was, since in some ways both An'desha and Karal were groping for the truth through the same fog of uncertainty, you held him to you longer. You cannot keep a chick in the shell, my friend, no matter how hard you may try."

Firesong had no answer for that, but Silverfox didn't appear to expect one. *Fine, so I couldn't hold him back—but why did he have to grow away from me?*

"There are many ways in which his spirit was scarred that you and I will never and can never understand, thanks to the Gods," Silverfox continued, his blue eyes thoughtful. "I have talked to him since I arrived here, since I became aware of your troubles."

He has? I didn't know that—

Silverfox paused and smiled slightly. "I knew at once that I was not the one to help him in his personal quest, but I did learn some things. I think, perhaps, that he will never be able to have a strong emotional bond to any one person—not because he is not capable of one, but for other reasons. He has seen how emotions can be a weapon in the hands of someone as unscrupulous as Falconsbane, and I think he will avoid emotional attachments for fear of using them himself in that way." The *kestra'chern* closed his eyes for a moment. "For him, the best and surest path may be that of the spirit and intellect rather than the heart. I could wish for your sake that this was not the case, but that is my reading of him."

Bitterness welled up in him, as much at the logic of Silverfox's words as at the conclusion. It matched what he himself had observed, all too closely. *It is true, but I am not going to rejoice over this!*

"But where does that leave me?" he asked, allowing his bitterness to well over into his words. "I spent all of my time here caring for An'desha when I might have been cultivating other possibilities. Now he has found other interests, and the possibilities I might have had when I first arrived are closed to me. Should I return to the Vales, I would find that all those of my inclination have paired off. So what am I to do? Where am I to look? He has had our time together *and* he has all that he now wants! Am I to have nothing for all my work and care but a few memories?"

Silverfox pursed his lips, then grimaced. "Well, I must admit that you have me there. You have given of yourself and your abilities here when you could easily have gone back to your own Vale or to k'Leshya. You have benefited a land and a people that are not even your own. Now, in fairness, I must point out that there are many who find your life and your position enviable, but that does not help how you feel now." He sighed. "I do not have a solution for you, or even much comfort to offer. Being exclusively *shay'a'chern* as you are limits you, and we both know it."

"And I am no pederast, to go looking for companions in the nursery because all those of my own years are paired," Firesong said sourly.

Only now did Silverfox offer to touch him, and only to place one hand on his knee. "Firesong, my pretty bird, I like you very much. What comfort, physical and otherwise, that you feel you could accept from me I gladly offer—and that is

as a friend, not as *kestra'chern*. I know that it does not
help—"

"But it also does not hurt." He managed to smile thinly. "I
will have to find a solution for myself."

I think it is best if I leave it at that.

The sitting room of Karal's suite was warmer and quieter
than the common room of the Compass Rose, and you didn't
have to wade through snow to get to it. A cheerful fire
burned on the hearth, and a kettle of hot tea and one of hot
water hung on hooks where they would stay warm. Karal
stood behind Natoli as she scribbled numbers and watched
intently; he didn't understand anything he saw, but that
didn't matter. Behind him, An'desha lounged on the couch,
pretending to read a book. Karal knew that he wasn't actually reading, because he hadn't turned a page since he
sat down.

"Damn and *blast!*" Natoli exclaimed, suddenly standing
up and tossing the papers of scribbled calculations over her
head in disgust. "Every time I make a calculation, it comes
out differently!"

"Have a cup of tea," Karal advised, before the last of the
pages had hit the floor. He took a hot pad to seize the nearest
kettle, pouring a fresh mug full and dosing it liberally with
cream and honey. He brought it over to her and handed it to
her with a smile he hoped looked encouraging. "I know you
wanted to try for yourself, but that's the same conclusion all
the others, even the Masters like Master Levy have come to.
Sun strike me, but they can't even agree on when the breakwater will finally erode to the point where it doesn't protect
us anymore! They say it's all too complicated for any human
to calculate."

She grimaced as she took the hot mug from him. "All
right, Florian was watching me calculate through your eyes,
and through him all the rest of the Companions that have
any interest in mathematics were also watching. So what
does *he* have to say?"

:Tell her what I told you the third time she went through

the calculations,: Florian advised. *:That answer hasn't changed.:*

"He says that as far as the Companions can tell, the solution will have to involve Hardorn because we'll have to put something in place beyond the existing breakwater. Some of them believe that we need to make a different kind of breakwater and some think we'll have to do something new, but as the storms strengthen, we will have to move the protections outward. Others just have the feeling, too vague to be a ForeSeeing, that Hardorn will be involved in finding the next solution." That was a surprising conclusion, coming from Companions, but it was a welcome one, as far as he was concerned.

And Natoli went a step further. "We might as well *talk* about what we've all been hinting at for the past week. Hardorn and the Imperials. We need them, and we all know it, so let's start trying to figure out a way to get them without getting anyone in trouble or murdered."

:The Son of the Sun isn't going to like this, Karal.: Altra switched his tail nervously and got up from his spot on the couch to pace over to Karal.

"What about you?" Karal asked him, looking down into his intensely blue eyes.

:In the abstract, I don't object. I do not much like making allies of people who personally attacked my own charges, but in the interest of the greater good, it is probably going to be necessary. Solaris, however, will dislike such expediency.:

Yes, well, Solaris' reaction was going to extend rather beyond "dislike." But from the look on An'desha's face, the news was fairly welcome to him.

"So, what about you?" he asked his friend.

An'desha sat up. "They have snow up to the eaves, monsters rioting through blizzards, they're starving and freezing over there. Even Kerowyn isn't urging any kind of confrontation with the Imperials," he said obliquely. "You heard her this afternoon: 'Let General Winter take care of them.' And even Jarim agreed with her. *She* thinks that 'General Winter' is going to kill them, I bet. The trouble is, a lot of innocents are going to die, too."

"So, you're saying—?" Karal prompted.

An'desha spread his hands wide. "Haven't the people of Hardorn and the Imperials—even the guilty ones—been punished enough?"

Karal sat down at the desk that Natoli had abandoned and cupped his chin in both hands. "I know what you're saying, and I know what Florian is saying, but I've got another problem here. I want to know what the Imperials are going to do if they're desperate and feel they have nothing to lose? More assassinations? By Vkandis' Crown, what *better* time could they strike but when Solaris is here for a meeting? How can we keep that from happening and at the same time keep them from using an opportunity to talk to us as one to strike at us?"

"By bringing them within our protections of course," Natoli said firmly, sitting down beside An'desha in the spot that Altra had abandoned. "If they're protected from the mage-storms, that should make them less desperate. What's more, I think we need to work with *their* mages as well as with the ones from k'Leshya. The Masters all think we need an entirely new set of observations anyway, and a new set of outlooks on magic could be what we're missing. It worked the last time."

"All very well and good," Karal pointed out, "but to get Imperial cooperation, we have to *find* someone with sense about the whole situation—someone who will think rather than react when we approach him. In point of fact, it will have to be someone high enough up in their ranks that we have a chance of negotiating with their leaders. So *who* do we find and *how* do we find him? I can't exactly send in a messenger with a flag of truce!" He snorted at the very idea. "I can't exactly send anyone anywhere! I don't have any authority to do anything of the kind!"

:Perhaps just as a point of beginning we could scry and try to find someone of sense?: Florian suggested diffidently.

"Florian says we should scry to see if we can find anyone who might listen to us. How we're supposed to do that with no target and over such a huge distance, I have no notion," Karal relayed, trying not to sound as if he thought the idea was completely lunatic. "Qualifications of 'authority and good sense' seem a bit vague to hang a scrying spell on."

"Well," An'desha said slowly. "As for the distance part, there's a perfectly good way to boost the power of a scrying-spell, and that's to use the Valdemar Heartstone. I'd have to ask for permission, but if I'm careful who I ask, I think I can get it. I *am* an Adept, if rather unpracticed. I think I can manage a simple scrying spell."

:*Tell him to ask Talia to ask Elspeth and he will get permission,:* Florian said with authority. :*Rolan and Gwena both agree.:*

Karal relayed that information. "Are you going to use the kind of spell that makes a picture anyone can see and sounds anyone can hear?" he asked hopefully. He'd always wanted to see a scrying, but Master Ulrich had never used that kind of spell.

"It's the only one I know," An'desha replied ruefully. "It takes a lot more energy than the kind that works like Far-Sight, but I don't have a choice since I don't know that one."

"I'd prefer it even if you did have a choice," Natoli replied, tucking her hair back behind her ear. "With others watching, you have extra sets of eyes and ears to catch what you might miss."

An'desha smiled. "True. Right, well, that's how we'll have the power."

:*As for a target, why don't you use the Imperial arms?:* Altra said, unexpectedly. :*You're not likely to find that anywhere except in the quarters of someone with authority, either on the wall or on documents—we already know from Kerowyn's spies that they've taken the arms off their uniforms.:*

"Using the Imperial arms as a target—that's what Altra suggests. Can you do that?" he asked An'desha. "Then we can just observe people to see if they fit what we need."

An'desha looked blank for a moment. "Well, I don't know why I couldn't. Given that, we can decide how we speak with our chosen contact once we actually have him."

:*I'll find Talia for you.:* Florian "vanished" from Karal's thoughts for a moment. Karal discovered how agreeable it was to be able to use the varied abilities of Companions; normally they would have had to go in search of Talia, but through her Companion Rolan, they were able to "ask" her to come to them in Karal's suite. They couldn't convey anything in detail, however, since Talia, unlike most Heralds, did *not* have Mindspeech. Rolan could only "send" an image of them and convey a sense of need.

When she finally arrived on Karal's doorstep, she wore an expression of faint annoyance overlaid with curiosity. "I hope this is more important than what I was doing," she said without preamble as Karal let her in.

"I think so, Sun's Ray," he said, calling her by her priestly title. She raised an eyebrow at that, but permitted herself to be coaxed into accepting a chair and a mug of tea. "Natoli will explain what we're up to, and I hope we haven't overstepped our authority."

Ulrich used to say that it is easier to apologize than get permission. I hope he was right.

Natoli did explain, not only their conclusions but the reasoning leading up to them. Talia listened patiently, nodding from time to time, until Natoli was finished.

"You've come perilously close to overstepping your authority," Talia told him, "but you succeeded in staying *just* on the right side. I'll ask Elspeth, and honestly—I think she'll agree with you. She's become more pragmatic since the mission into Hardorn after Ancar and Hulda than I gave her credit for being."

"I think it was traveling through Hardorn, seeing how the people were suffering *then*, and knowing that it must be worse now," An'desha suggested. "She might not be in line for the throne anymore, but you can't remove the sense of responsibility that you trained into her."

Talia smiled faintly. "One hopes. Well, let's see what can be done—and I have a suggestion for a place where you can do your scrying. Directly above the Heartstone chamber is a room that mirrors it exactly, right down to having a crystal sphere in the center of a table. You could use that, and it's shielded to a fare-thee-well. We've used it for FarSeeing in the past." She put her mug down on a side table and stood up. "I'm beginning to think that the Queen ought to recognize you lot as a working entity; I'll have a word with her about that as well. You're all adults, you're all responsible, and you're all coming up with ideas, if not actual solutions. We ought to grant you enough authority that you can test out some of your ideas without constantly coming to one of us."

That last had Karal staring at her with an open mouth for a moment.

"Don't get too excited," she said, with a slight hint of a smile. "It won't be a great deal of authority. But you have a fair amount on your own, you know. You and An'desha are aliens on our soil, and do not necessarily have to answer to any authority in Valdemar for your actions so long as you don't break any major laws." She put the mug down decisively. "Now, if I'm going to catch Elspeth alone, I have to go now. I'll send you word through Rolan and Florian."

She walked to the door, and Karal opened it for her again, but just before she left, she turned and looked at him with a peculiar, penetrating stare. "You are something of a puzzle, young priest," she said at last. "You are the only person I have ever encountered that has a Companion speaking with him who was not also Chosen. I wish I knew why."

"So do I, Sun's Ray," he said fervently. "I would sleep better at night if I did."

Inside the scrying room, it was as silent as a cave. Even noises from outside were muffled to the point of vanishment. An'desha settled into his seat, now softened with a down cushion, brought by the ever-practical Natoli who could not see any reason why the four of them needed to get numb behinds from the hard benches when there were plenty of cushions kicking around in the Palace storerooms. The others took their places at equal distances around the table—in Altra's case, *on* the table, licking his back fur—and waited expectantly for him to begin the spell.

Their initial few attempts had ended in nothing more exciting than warehouses and a few barracks, for the Imperials might have taken their embroidered arms from the tunics of their uniforms, but they still had their battle banners displayed prominently in their barracks and the Imperial mark burned into the sides of crates. One or two had even begun murals including the arms on the walls as well. The trouble with this spell was that once it was set on a target, you couldn't move the point-of-view more than a foot or two from the target without starting over, and he couldn't do that more than two or three times a day. The spell might take most of its energy from the Heartstone, but it still required his personal power to control it.

"You know—I've got an idea. You might try the arms in the form of a seal," Natoli said after some thought. "That might at least get you a place where we can see a clerk in the headquarters. Then you can shift your target to him and set the spell again; sooner or later he's bound to go to someone in authority."

An'desha made a gesture of helplessness. "That sounds like as good an idea as any; we certainly haven't made any other progress."

"We wouldn't say that," Karal objected, speaking for both himself and Altra. "You found Shonar and the Imperial Army—and you didn't catch on to something over in the Empire itself. That's not bad for not having a specific target."

An'desha smiled faintly, and flexed his hands to warm up the muscles before he placed them palm-down on the table in front of him. He stared at a point a little above the crystal ball in the center of the table, and reached for the weighty power seething below him, embodied in the Heartstone of Valdemar.

There was no way of describing just how it felt to him, to seize this incredible energy, a force both ordered and chaotic, and with a rudimentary consciousness of its own. Were other Heartstones like this one? If so, no wonder Falconsbane had wanted to learn the secrets of constructing them! Nodes were powerful, even deadly, but this Heartstone was a hundred times more powerful than any node he had ever encountered. Linking himself in with it was similar to walking the Moonpaths, in that he found himself "somewhere else"; this "somewhere," however, was a crystalline structure thrumming with ordered power. Once there, he was possessed of the strength to do just about anything he chose, if only his control could hold up.

That was the real key, control, and it was what required so much of his own strength. *If I were riding an unbroken warsteed that happened to like me, and had decided to permit me to sit on her back, it might be like this. There is a sense that at any moment I might be thrown and trampled. "Ordered" does not mean "tame."*

Once he had the reins of power in his hands, he dropped his gaze into the crystal itself, setting the patterns and sigils written only in the invisible fire of magic to burn about it. He knew the moment it was all complete; the ring of power fused into an unbroken whole, and the "setting" sat empty, waiting for the target object.

This was the only purely mental part of the spell; he concentrated on the Imperial arms in the form of a wax impression, a seal such as he had often seen on other documents of importance. *This is what you want,* he silently told the spell as he set that image within it. *Go and find it, and bring us the picture of where it is.*

Distance meant very little to this spell if it had the power it needed to reach as far as it had to. He felt the spell straining to be off, a restive hound with the quarry in view, pulling at the leash.

He let it go, and immediately sensed power flowing from the Heartstone, through him, and into the set-spell. Oh, it was sweet. Now all he had to do was control the flow of power so that it was even, and sit back and watch the crystal with the others.

A red blur formed in the heart of the crystal, transparent, but three-dimensional. It could have been a reflection of something on the table, or something one of them was wearing; except that they all saw it, for they all leaned forward at the same time.

The haze of red solidified, the blurring focused, and the indistinct image became a clear, sharp picture, a blob of red sealing wax, centered by the now all-too-familiar arms of the Eastern Empire. The image showed him nothing more, because that was all that the spell had been set for; it did not even show the document the seal was on.

That was just *fine*, for now that he had his target, he could widen the parameters of the spell.

He seized more power from the Heartstone and wove it into new patterns, ones that told the spell to broaden its "gaze" and to open its "ears." Round about the crystal he set the new patterns, weaving them in and out of the old ones, until once again the energies fused into a whole.

The image changed; the blob of red wax grew smaller, down to a mere pinpoint, as it seemed to recede into the middle distance. It became a dot of red on a sheet of yellow-brown parchment; the document lay on a desk, on top of a stack of similar documents. Behind the desk sat a man in a sober and severely cut tunic and trews of that no-nonsense styling that says "military," both of which had the familiar look of the Imperial uniform. The desk itself was the only piece of furniture in a very small room, lit by a single lantern suspended from a chain above the desk. The top of the desk was littered with papers, inkwells, and all the paraphernalia of a clerk.

"Yes," Karal hissed under his breath. An'desha did not bother with self-congratulations; this part of the spell manipulation was too delicate. He rotated his viewpoint, slowly, taking it down and around until at last his "eyes" were in the middle of the desktop, staring up at the clerk working so diligently there.

There was no sound but the scratching of the clerk's pen and the hiss of his breathing—and, occasionally, a sniff as he took a moment to rub his nose with the back of his hand. An'desha stared intently into his surprisingly young face, a very earnest face, and one showing a fierce concentration on the work at hand. It was not a particularly memorable face for all that it was young; the clerk was very much of a "type." His brown hair was cut short, and from the precision of the style, An'desha guessed it was probably a regulation haircut. His brown eyes were neither very large nor very small, neither deepset nor bulging, neither far apart nor set too near the bridge of the nose. His forehead was not too broad or too narrow. His cheekbones were neither prominent nor flat nor buried in fat. His nose was neither hawklike nor pugged, neither thin nor spread, absolutely average in length and shape. His mouth was neither thin nor generous, his chin neither square nor pointed, rounded nor prominent. It would have been very difficult to pick him out in a crowd, but he *did* have one tiny scar crossing his left eyebrow and another marring the otherwise average chin. An'desha concentrated fiercely on those two flaws, branding the man's face in his mind.

Once he was sure he had the clerk as firmly in his mind as possible, he broke the spell, shattering the brittle energies with a single burst of power. He sagged down on the table for a moment as the shattered remains dissipated; feeling his own strength melting away with it.

Natoli and Karal were both ready for that moment; instantly they were each at his elbows, Natoli with a cup of something sweet and hot, Karal with cheese and bread. The moment of weakness did not last long. He had the Heartstone to draw on, after all, and he was soon sitting up again and restoring his physical strength while his magical energies slowly rose to near the level they had been when he began.

"Looks to me as if we got an Imperial clerk, one with enough status to handle important documents," Karal said, as An'desha drank the restorative brew and nibbled on the cheese.

"I hope so," An'desha said, doubt now creeping into his mind. "I don't know about that office, though. Would someone with any status be shoved away into that cramped little closet?"

But Karal only laughed. "Oh, certainly," he said, with the surety of one who has been a clerk himself. "First of all, this man wasn't wearing a heavy cloak or even a particularly heavy tunic—that means wherever he is it's warm. We know that Shonar didn't have a Great Lord, so the manor that the Imperials took over isn't going to be huge—and the Commander has consolidated all of his officers there. As many of them as can will be in the manor, not the barracks. His mages are probably in there, too. That's a lot of people to be crowded into one smallish manor house; any clerk that has his own office, and a warm office at that, *must* be of a fairly high rank."

An'desha nodded; that made good sense. "Well, I'm ready to try for him again if you are," he said. "If I can, I'm going to put a magical 'link' on him, so that it won't be as difficult to get him in the future."

Natoli nodded but also sighed. "We're likely to be doing a lot of watching before he goes in to see whatever official he reports to."

He shrugged. "There's no escaping that. I'd rather be watching him than watching the men in the barracks play dice and scrub floors."

Natoli laughed at that, since she had been the first to complain about watching the floor scrubbers and gamers. "I don't even know who to bet on!" she had protested. "That would at least make it a little more interesting!"

Once again, An'desha set the spell, this time with the face of his chosen clerk as the target. Once again the power settled into the familiar patterns, the energies drained through him, and an image formed in the heart of the crystal.

This time, he changed the point-of-view to one just above the clerk's shoulder, so that they were looking down at what the man was doing. "Another lesson in Imperial script?" Karal asked dryly.

An'desha didn't bother to answer, since Karal was the one who had suggested they use these opportunities for just that. They'd all learned what they could from one of Kerowyn's agents, and now from their various vantage points they were polishing and adding to what they'd learned. Predictably, Karal was the best at picking up the language; Natoli and An'desha were about even in their lower level of proficiency.

It was harder to concentrate on the spell and read than it was to do so and listen. An'desha soon gave up. "What's it say?" he asked Karal.

The Karsite licked his lips and narrowed his eyes as he peered into the crystal. "Something about snow—oh, it's a report about the last blizzard they got. I wish I knew what their measures meant, I'd have some idea how deep it is. Deep enough that he's writing orders to the barracks commanders to build arches out of snow blocks and turn the paths between the buildings into tunnels so the men don't have to keep digging themselves out."

An'desha whistled. "Sounds pretty grim."

"Huh." Karal was already on to something else. "Well, if Kerowyn is still counting on 'General Winter' to starve them out, she's in trouble. The supplies are holding up very well; they even have a warehouse full of frozen meat. Oh—I've got the name of the man in charge of the whole army, it's 'Grand Duke Tremane.' That's a name we've heard a time or two."

Indeed it was, and usually it was with something complimentary attached to it. The men of the Imperial Army had both a competent and a popular commander, and that wasn't always the case.

"Let's not tell Kerowyn unless we find out we can't make any headway with our idea, shall we?" Natoli suggested delicately. "I don't want her to try something that might make the Imperials nervous. I'd rather they weren't nervous as long as Solaris keeps attending Grand Council meetings."

An'desha nodded vigorously, and so did Karal. "Solaris keeps trying to get me accepted as her *trusted* representative, but I'm still too young for most of the Council members to think of as a real envoy. And as long as they are thinking that way, she's either going to have to find someone to replace me or keep showing up here herself." He sighed. "I'm tempted to think that she likes getting away. Maybe she does; she doesn't get out of the High Temple grounds anymore, so maybe this is a nice change of scene for her."

They watched the man write out several more copies of the same set of orders, until Karal and Natoli were cross-eyed with boredom and An'desha felt his control slipping with fatigue. Finally, he let the image dissolve and broke the spell.

"That's all for now," he said. "We'll have to try again tomorrow."

The next day, with their scrying session sandwiched in between other duties, was just as boring and disappointing as the first in many ways. But on the other hand, they soon learned that the orders being copied were actually straight from the hand of Duke Tremane himself—and in An'desha's opinion, they showed a remarkable amount of that sense they were all looking for in a contact. Dared he hope that *Duke Tremane* would prove to be the man they needed?

Finally, very late on the third day of their vigilant watching, the clerk was summoned out of his tiny office. They followed his image through hallways and up staircases, until he was stopped by a pair of well-armed guards outside a door. An'desha held his breath; the clerk identified himself and the guards let him pass. There didn't seem to be any kind of checks for someone spying by the means that they were using!

At long last they were about to see the Enemy himself, the author of so many of their troubles, Grand Duke Tremane—

That's him? *That's the enemy?*

"That can't be Tremane," Natoli said in an astonished voice that reflected her disbelief. "No. That's some other clerk."

But their target saluted the unprepossessing man behind the desk as "Commander Tremane, sir," and there was no doubt. No matter how much like one of his own clerks the man looked, he *was* Grand Duke Tremane.

"How can that be him?" Karal wondered aloud. "I expected a monster like Falconsbane, or some rock-faced hulk in armor. This man looks like—like—"

"Like a petty bureaucrat," Natoli supplied. "Like the man who makes out requisitions, the man who sees to it that you never have exactly what you need, or who demands to know how you could go through a dozen pens in a month."

"Exactly!" Karal replied. "How could anyone who looks like *that* have done what he did?"

"That's precisely why he could have," An'desha said slowly. "Because to a clerk, people who are not immediately around him are nothing but numbers. They aren't *people,* and it doesn't matter if you just ordered their deaths, because you don't know them and you never will—all you are interested in is that a certain result is achieved. The most evil people in the world might be such clerks, because everything is just another number to the ones who don't consider the implications of what they are doing, who concentrate only on making the numbers add up the right way." He shivered as old, old memories drifted through his mind. "Dying soldiers don't matter—they're 'acceptable losses.' Burned crops don't matter—they're 'denying resources to the enemy.' People starving and homeless don't matter—they're 'non-taxpayers.' All that does matter is getting the numbers to come out your way, no matter what it takes."

Both Karal and Natoli glanced at him with odd expressions of interest. "How did you figure that out?" Karal asked warily.

"Ma'ar," he replied shortly. "Ma'ar thought like that—as an apprentice he was also his mage-master's petty clerk and he learned to think like that. Worse, he learned how to make other people think that way, how to reduce the enemy to a faceless, dispassionate number." He shook his head, and shook the memories away at the same time. "Well, that's how Tremane *could* order terrible things on a regular basis—but that doesn't mean he has. He can't have slipped as far into that way of thinking as Ma'ar or he wouldn't be as popular with his men. At least, I hope I'm right in that—give me some time to study him so I can switch the spell."

While the clerk was absolutely average, Tremane was not. He was not *handsome* by any means, and certainly was not An'desha's idea of the way a leader should look, but it was possible to remember his face very clearly without having to strain to find tiny flaws or other marks of identification.

Just as their clerk was dismissed, An'desha felt he had Tremane's face adequately in mind, and broke the spell.

The moment he did, exhaustion overcame him so suddenly that he actually blacked out for a moment, and came to just in time to catch himself falling face-first into the table.

He would have done exactly that if Altra hadn't made a leap across the crystal ball and inserted his body between An'desha's face and the marble table. He got a mouthful of fur, but not the crack to the head he would have if it hadn't been for Altra.

"*Browf!*" the Firecat grunted as An'desha's face hit the cat's side. Karal was beside him a moment later, pulling him up and then forcing his head down between his knees. Once he was in that position, his dizziness began to clear. Eventually he was able to sit up again.

"Th–thank you, Altra," he said as the Firecat stared at him with real concern. "I nearly knocked myself out!"

:You're welcome,: the Firecat replied in his mind, and followed the words with a swipe of a rough, wet tongue across his nose. *:I hate having to clean up blood, and you'd have split your forehead wide open if you'd hit the table.:*

He took the inevitable mug of tea from Natoli and sat there sipping it while he assessed his own condition and tried to make up his mind about what he should do next.

"I want to do another, while I still have Tremane fresh in my mind," he said after a moment.

Natoli frowned. "Is that wise?" she asked sternly.

"No," he admitted, "but it's necessary. And the two of you can catch me if I pass out again. I want Tremane; I want him before he has a chance to slip out of my mind. Once I've put a link on him, it won't be too hard to get him again."

Karal studied his face. "You think Tremane might be our man, don't you?"

He hesitated a moment before answering. "I think if he isn't our man, he'll take us to someone who is," he replied, after that pause to think. "I'm torn. I'd like to believe that he is for a great many reasons, and that's why I don't want to trust my judgment alone on this. It would be so much easier if we were able to work with the man on the top, for one thing. But I have the feeling that if I don't establish a link to him now, we might lose him."

"All right," Karal said, after a long pause of his own. "You're an adult; you have the right to decide what you're going to do for yourself. You certainly know what you're letting yourself in for if you exhaust yourself."

"Mostly one demon of a headache," An'desha told him candidly. "What I'm doing just isn't that dangerous."

In that, he was stretching the truth—or rather, not telling the whole truth. *It isn't that dangerous providing that Tremane doesn't have magical protections against little scrying attempts like mine.* That was the one thing that worried him. It was possible that his faint was due to brushing up against such protections. Actually touching them—

He didn't know. It wouldn't be fatal, not after the batterings such shields would have taken during the mage-storms. But it probably wouldn't be pleasant.

On the other hand, he had learned to trust his intuition about magic—knowing very well that in his case, "intuition" was really the result of an unconscious analysis of many lifetimes of accumulated memories, few of them directly available without an effort.

His "intuition" said that he'd better establish that link quickly. *Maybe it doesn't have anything to do with Tremane—maybe it's because of the mage-storms. The links seem to hold up well as the storms pass through, but the ability to scry past the breakwater might not hold up immediately after a storm if I don't also have a link.*

The paths that magic took were seriously disrupted after a mage-storm and it took time to reestablish them. Perhaps because he was Shin'a'in, the reason seemed clear enough to him. One of the effects of the storm was to "wash" everything away ahead of its cresting power, exactly like a wave of floodwater washed away things in its path. And, like on the floodplain, when the water receded, the roads and markers that had been there before the flood were gone. You had to build them all back up again.

At least, it made sense that way to him. He'd tried to explain it to Master Levy, but the artificer had only shaken his head. "If I could 'see' your magic, I could tell you if your analogy works past the surface into manipulation," he said frankly. "But I can't, and I can't test it, so I'll take your word for it. If I work out a way to test the analogy, I'll let you know. Who knows? It might give us another clue to solving our predicament."

Our predicament. It all sounds so ordinary when he calls it by that term.

He steadied himself, and when he placed his hands on the table, they were quite still, not trembling at all. "I think I must do this," he said quietly. "I know that I can with such friends standing by to help me."

Again, he established the spell, then the target; Tremane's face and upper torso appeared in the crystal, but he had someone with him other than the clerk. An'desha quickly widened his view. It was a middle-aged, ordinary woman, dressed roughly, but not poorly; she looked like a farmer's wife. There were no women with the Imperial Army, and this woman did not have the look of a camp follower about her.

The woman in question was absolutely hysterical, wringing her hands as tears poured down her face. She spoke so fast that An'desha, with his limited command of Hardornen, could not make out what was the matter.

Nor, it seemed, could Tremane. After several embarrassed and abortive attempts to calm her, he finally walked over to the door and called something An'desha did not catch.

A moment later an old man shuffled in, a man dressed in several layers of rich woolen robes. ". . . see if you can't get her to calm down enough to explain where she thinks the children might have gone, will you, Sejanes?" Tremane said in an undertone as they passed into the area of the spell's influence. "I can't make head or tail of what she's babbling, and nothing I do makes her anything other than hysterical."

The old man chuckled. "Boy," he said, in the Imperial tongue, "you never could manage a woman. Leave her to me."

Indeed, in a few moments, the old man did have her calmed down, in spite of the fact that his Hardornen was extremely limited and horrendously accented. He patted her shoulder and made soothing noises, and extracted information in usable bits between her bouts of sobbing.

Evidently she *was* a farmer, as An'desha had guessed. After the fright of seeing one of the mage-born monsters on the prowl, she had brought her family to the town to spend the winter. Restless at being more confined than they were used to, her children had taken it into their heads to make off somewhere outside the walls of Shonar. She *thought* they might have tried to go home, to their farm; several of them had left toys or wild animals that had been made into pets that either had been left behind in the packing or were considered to be too much of a nuisance to deal with in town. But she didn't know, because they had somehow slipped out without anyone noticing. She begged "Lord Tremane" to send men out to find them before the "boggles" did.

"Lord Tremane" sighed. "Take her off and feed her, Sejanes. I know how the brats probably got out; I'd bet they left with the children tending the flocks or herds. The guards wouldn't notice a few more children with the animals than usual. Tell her we'll see to it; I'll take a party out to question the herding children, and we should have our hands on her wandering brats before dark."

The old man took the weeping woman off, and to An'desha's surprise, Tremane went to the next room and began pulling on heavier clothing, boots, and weapons. "Come on, boys!" he shouted out as he struggled to fit boots over two pairs of heavy socks. "Get me more volunteers, we've got some lost children again! I'll meet them in the armory, as usual."

"And thanks be to the Hundred Little Gods," he muttered as he stamped to get the boots comfortable. "At least this time it's not during the height of a blizzard."

"Unbelievable," Karal breathed, as the Commander of all the Imperial Forces, Grand Duke Tremane, trotted down the stairs to the armory to *personally* organize a rescue party. And not just any rescue party, but one chasing after a handful of lost Hardornen peasant children. "Solaris wouldn't do this. I don't even think Kerowyn would."

"Maybe he just appreciates the excuse to get outside," Natoli said cynically, as Tremane led his group down snow-walled and -roofed tunnels. It was light enough in there; light came right through the thick snow, illuminating the interior in a blue twilight. Still, it could get very claustrophobic.

But just at that moment, Tremane's little troop got outside the walls of Shonar, and into the hard, diamond-bright sunlight, and confronted the brutal, snow-covered wilderness beyond. The only tracks were those made by the herds he had mentioned, tracks cut through snow up to the waist of a grown man with drifts going higher than his head. Moving dots off in the distance might represent the herds he had mentioned, browsing on the ends of branches and whatever greenery they could get at under the shelter of the trees. The men themselves adjusted scarves wrapped around their faces to stave off frostbite before they trekked across the snow after their leader.

"Firesong should see this," An'desha remarked. "He thinks *our* weather is bad; this is brutal!"

Before he forgot, and while the man's concentration was elsewhere, An'desha reached out tentatively and laid his "link" very carefully on the Grand Duke himself.

He was jolted back in his seat by the reaction of Tremane's shields. Energy backlashed painfully through him for a fraction of a heartbeat, setting every nerve screaming.

In the next moment, it was over, though Natoli and Karal were at his elbows supporting him anxiously. His head throbbed in time with his pulse, and he knew he was going to have that appalling headache he had mentioned, but otherwise he was untouched.

"I'm all right," he assured them, checking the crystal to see that the spell had not been broken.

It hadn't; what was more, Tremane did not appear to have noticed his meddling. The link was in place, and he would be able to scry the Grand Duke no matter what havoc the next mage-storm wrought among the Planes.

"Do we need to see anything more?" he asked them. Natoli shrugged, and Karal shook his head. He broke the spell and let his weight sag into their hands.

That was all—and it was certainly enough—for one day. He let them assist him back to his room and make a fuss over him; they were rather charming about it, actually. If his head hadn't hurt so much, he would actually have enjoyed it.

The next two days proved equally enlightening. The Hardornen townsfolk appeared to have adopted Tremane as their new liege lord, and were perfectly happy with the situation. And as for Tremane himself, the man was taking equal care with the town as he was with his own men. He sat in on meetings of the town Council, his own Army Healers were serving the townsfolk, and townspeople were working to help finish the interiors of Tremane's barracks. Things were not working with absolute smoothness—there were conflicts to be resolved all the time—but Shonar was not rejecting the Imperials, and Tremane was not riding roughshod over Shonar.

Even Florian remarked through Karal that Grand Duke Tremane had all the earmarks of an excellent commander in anyone's forces.

There was no doubt in An'desha's mind that the man they needed to communicate with was none other than the leader himself. He was sensible, he seemed sensitive to the needs, not only of his own people but of these who had adopted him as their leader. He was a man inclined to reason and reasonableness.

There was only one small problem.

By watching and listening they had learned one thing further from the man's own lips. He, and no other, had been the one who had ordered the assassinations that had killed Karal's beloved Master, the Karsite Sun-priest Ulrich.

Nine

Firesong burned with incoherent outrage. *Someone* was meddling with the power of his Heartstone! Granted, it wasn't much power being drained off, but still, no one had asked *him* for permission to tap into it directly, and he might need that power for his experiments!

He hadn't been able to get past Silverfox to visit the Heartstone chamber in days, but that didn't matter as far as keeping track of what was going on with the Stone itself. He could tell what was happening to the Stone even at a considerable distance, and he caught the unmistakable traces of meddling although he could not identify the meddler. It wasn't Elspeth or Darkwind; he knew the signatures of their power. It wasn't the gryphons either, although he hadn't thought either of them were keyed to it. There were no other Valdemaran mages powerful enough to tap into the Heartstone directly. Initially, he suspected the new mages from k'Leshya, but one by one he eliminated them as he ascertained that they had not been linked into the Stone yet either.

Finally, this very afternoon as he was waiting for Elspeth and Darkwind to arrive for a consultation in the hot spring, he realized who it was—who it *must* be. The obvious answer had been right in front of him, and yet it was not really obvious at all.

An'desha. It had to be An'desha.

He was an Adept, and it would not have been at all diffi-cult for him to persuade Elspeth or Darkwind to give him access to the power of the Valdemar Stone. He had been helping the artificers *and* Karal with the practice and theory of magic. One or the other had probably come up with some idea that required so much power that only that of the Heartstone would do.

And, of course, none of them deigned to ask *him* about it!

Of course not. Why should they? I'm only the most experienced Adept here! An'desha may think he has experience, but all of it is tainted, slanted Falconsbane's way. What's more, he has no experience in any form of working with a Heartstone. But naturally, Karal has convinced him that he doesn't need me anymore. He thinks he has everything he needs to go sailing off on his own, I'm sure. He wasn't ready to work alone, and he wouldn't be ready for years! There is no way he could possibly be ready to work alone, especially not with Heartstone power! But Karal has probably told him the opposite—made him believe he doesn't need any help just when he needs it the most.

He paced back and forth angrily, forgetting that he was expecting visitors, as Aya fluttered and chirped in distress on his corner perch. The firebird began to send out false sparks with every flutter of his wings, trails of brilliant motes of light that cascaded from the bird's feathers like dust. Firesong ignored those signs of growing tension in favor of his own anger.

Rage seethed unchecked inside him. *Karal! That's who's to blame for this! By the gods, I should do something about him, the interfering fool boy! The Alliance doesn't need him anymore, not with Solaris coming here. An'desha certainly doesn't need his brand of advice!* Karal was the cause of all his problems—Karal was dangerous! He was meddling in things he couldn't even begin to understand, and he was encouraging An'desha to do the same. How long before he coaxed An'desha to try something more dangerous than just tapping into Heartstone power? How long before he encouraged An'desha to try to *change* it? Wasn't that how the k'Sheyna Heartstone had gone rogue in the first place? Pure primal rage colored everything scarlet, and his pulse sounded in his ears like the beat of a drummer gone mad. *I ought to get rid of him—I have to get rid of him, before he ruins everything!*

A high-pitched sound of ripping punctuated his murderous thoughts, and a decorative drape tore away from the wall. It shimmered with the side effects of the power he was projecting, falling slowly into progressively smaller shreds.

I should be doing that to Karal, that indolent, wet-eared whelp in diapers. . . .

Firesong ground his teeth, letting the anger grow into a fury, not even concerned about the damage it was doing to his *ekele.* Let it happen! It didn't matter. The sound of splitting wood was reassuring—that was what breaking bones sounded like, and right now, wishing bodily mayhem on *everyone* who hadn't appreciated him enough felt *very* good.

The wooden legs of the serving table split lengthwise, in halves and thirds, twisting the surface this way and that before finally pitching sideways in collapse. The mugs and plates that slid off shattered before reaching the floor.

It is far and away past time I woke up!

At that moment, Aya gave an ear-shattering shriek of absolute terror, and a corner of the *ekele* burst into flame.

Firesong whirled, howling with anger at Aya's idiocy. The firebird leaped from his perch and fled into the corner to cower in fear under the last almost-intact table. Firesong snarled, deep in his throat, and willed the flames to *go out—go out now!* The fire only surged brighter when he directed his rage-edged power toward it. It engulfed the tattered wall hangings in a bright yellow sheet, producing an even thicker gout of smoke. He attempted to fling a blanket on the flames to smother them, and succeeded only in burning both his hands in the process. The pain only made his anger worse. He couldn't even think clearly.

Finally he clenched his burned fists and screamed at the fire.

"*I said stop!*"

The smoke belching out from the fire froze, and then receded back into the fire, flattening against it, smothering it, leaving the walls coated in the black of charred tinder. Finally, all that was left was a sweat-soaked, shaking Firesong, splinters of destroyed furniture, the haze of smoke, and a terror-filled firebird.

Firesong took a deep breath through his tight jaw, and his gaze darted around until he found Aya. He opened his scorched fists and lunged at Aya. The firebird fled.

He chased Aya around the room as the firebird hid under broken furniture, screaming in fear of Firesong. "You *damned* bird!" Firesong shrieked. "You *miserable* bird! How dare you!" His words degenerated into incoherent growls. Still shouting with anger that had built beyond his ability to control it, he cornered the firebird and prepared to strike Aya where he cowered, every feather shivering.

"Don't!"

The shout from the stairs made him pause—and that moment was all it took for Elspeth and Darkwind to bracket him.

"Firesong, that is your *bondbird*," the Tayledras scout said angrily. "*Your. Bond. Bird.* Are you out of your mind? Don't you realize that *you* are to blame? All *he* did was reflect what was wrong with you!"

"Get out!" Firesong spat. "This is *my* home and *my* bird, and I'll—"

"This isn't a home, it's a funeral pyre, Firesong. Strike Aya down, and you'll follow him," Darkwind warned, tapping a rhythm pattern with one foot that Elspeth quickly picked up—a pattern Firesong recognized vaguely from the containment spell they had all worked to confine the power of the rogue Heartstone of k'Sheyna. "I'm not bluffing, Firesong. We can counter anything you can throw at us, and we'll drive it right back into your teeth. It won't be pretty."

For another long moment, he stood there with his hand upraised, like an executioner ready to drop the ax, staring into Darkwind's implacable eyes. Those blue eyes bored into his coldly, promising that the words were not a bluff. His friends were prepared to cut him down.

Prepared to cut me down. . . .

Firesong's burned hand shook and then unclenched as the impact of what was happening sunk in.

Then the anger drained out of him as suddenly as if they

had lanced a suppurating boil. He dropped his hand and stared at it, appalled.

"Oh, gods—" he whispered in disbelief. "Darkwind—what did I do? What was I going to do?"

What kind of a monster did I turn into? What was I thinking? The Heartstone isn't mine, *An'desha has every right to follow his own path, and—Karal is as innocent as Aya! Aya. What is wrong with me? Aya, my bird, my bondbird. . . .*

Sudden and profound grief took the place of rage, flooding in to fill the void the loss of anger had left behind. His knees gave out and he dropped to the floor, sobbing. Darkwind and Elspeth held their positions, watching steadily. If they continued tapping that rhythm, Firesong could not hear it over his own crying.

Aya, my bird, my bondbird, Aya . . . you didn't mean to, you were scared, I scared you, and I was going to. . . .

Aya raised up from his cowering, just a little, and false sparks showered off him in bursts. The firebird stepped forward hesitantly, and slipped into Firesong's arms to cuddle against him, crooning softly. Firesong apologized to his oldest and dearest friend through his tears, rocking forward and back, losing all track of time.

What did I do . . . what have I done. . . ?

All the world was hazy from the tears and the smoke, out of focus, out of mind. There was a slow-moving blur on his right, large and graceful, with a sweep of long black hair. Someone dropped down beside him, but it was not Darkwind nor Elspeth. He squeezed his eyes shut, feeling them sting even worse, and looked up to find himself gazing into the compassionate and understanding eyes of—Silverfox?

It *was* Silverfox, whose eyes showed a soul more intricate than all the magic that Firesong claimed to understand and control. Firesong stared through streaks of soot-stained white hair, his arms full of trembling firebird.

"What have I done?" he cried to the *kestra'chern*. "What's happened to me? I've turned into . . . a . . . monster!" He sobbed, stricken with equal parts grief and guilt. "How could I have let myself get this way?"

Silverfox reached out a smooth, long-fingered hand, and swept the damp strands of hair from Firesong's face.

"That's what I hope to show you, my friend," Silverfox said quietly. "Your hands are burned by more than just fire. Now you are willing to see it all, and undo some of the harm you have done to yourself. Now you are ready. But it was a very near thing, and you must never forget it."

The *kestra'chern* stood up and offered his hand. Still burdened by the firebird and shaken by all that had just happened, Firesong took it. Darkwind and Elspeth stepped aside, their expressions sympathetic, and let them pass.

Silverfox led him into his own room, and sat him down on the bed. The *kestra'chern* sat beside him, though he made no move to touch him.

"Now rest a while, and listen to me carefully," Silverfox told him. "I will try to explain some of what has happened, but it may be complex. Be patient and open, and I will explain it all. Do you remember how the mage-storms affected you before they were stopped?"

He nodded, as Aya tucked his soft-feathered head beneath his chin.

"They affect every mage, but they do more to you than you were aware, you or anyone else. You are a Healing Adept; you are attuned to the way that magic affects the land around you, but not only are you *sensitive* to it, magic that affects the land *will* cause changes in you." He paused to see if Firesong understood, and continued at his nod of surprise. "That is why I am here; we found evidence in the records from the days of Skandranon that the same thing happened to one or two other mages of his era during the unsettled time after the Cataclysm, and it took them *years* to discover what had unbalanced previously rational people. The Vales have all been warned. I came here, in part, to see if any of you had been affected, because the changes are subtle and not particularly obvious. That is only part of what happened to you; you are ill, Firesong, but it is an illness that few Healers would sense unless they knew what to look for. There are subtle changes physically in your brain rather than your mind. They have made you quick to anger, slow to reason. They are things that make you see enemies and conspiracies where there are none."

Firesong croaked, "So," and then swallowed twice to steady his voice. "So . . . my own body and brain are no better off than the land."

Silverfox nodded and interlaced his fingers. "Thus and so. But there are other things; patterns of thought you have established that are your own doing, though these changes made them worse."

Firesong licked lips gone dry, and stroked Aya's backfeathers. "Looking to blame anyone but myself?" he said tentatively. "Searching for a scapegoat to be the author of all my problems?"

"Obsessing on finding a lifebond, as if a lifebond meant the end to every problem in life?" Silverfox added dryly.

Firesong hung his head, thanking his Goddess silently for the fact that Silverfox had not ever learned of his plan to extend his life so that he could *find* a lifebond. *I will tear the Sanctuary down and scatter the pieces tomorrow,* he pledged Her. *I will destroy it as I should have done in the first place.*

Could it be that some of the taint of Falconsbane had lingered in that bloodstained place he had created? Could that also have been the origin of some of his madness?

If it was the origin, I still gave in to it, cultivated it, and cherished it. I, and no other. No one held me down and drove those thoughts into my head like so many spikes.

"I have been an idiot," he told the *kestra'chern* remorsefully. "Oh, Silverfox. No amount of ability or talent can make up for acting like a tyrannical madman."

Silverfox smiled warmly, reassuringly. With question and answer, riddle and verse, encouragement and reproach, the *kestra'chern* led him gently to bare his soul to the bones. And a few hours later, Firesong knew—just a little—how An'desha had felt, in *his* arms, not so very long ago.

Karal struggled with his demon, after finally asking Natoli to give him a little time to himself to think.

Tremane is the only optimal choice to approach. We can't let the people of and in Hardorn continue to suffer—and we

*need them. Tremane is an honorable man by his own
standards.*

But Tremane had also personally ordered the cold-blooded
murder of not only Ulrich but several other important folk of
Valdemar and the Alliance. The only reason those other attempts had not succeeded was purest good fortune. But he
still had the blood of two perfectly innocent people on his
hands, both of them servants of their respective deities,
which could by some lights make it twice as heinous.

Karal was having a difficult time reconciling the Tremane
who had ordered those deaths with the one who went out
into dangerous conditions to rescue children.

*On the one hand, I want to open negotiations with him.
On the other, I want to make him suffer as much as I have.
Then I want to kill him slowly and painfully, the way
Ulrich died.*

If the latter reaction was wrong, it was only human. Karal
tried to think of the greater good, but he could not get his
thoughts past that anger. Just as much to the point, he could
not see how they could *trust* someone who would write someone else's life off as casually as erasing a name from a ledger.

*If I just knew why—if I just knew that he hadn't done it
in cold blood, in indifference, the way An'desha described—*

—if I just knew he had regretted *it, even a little!*

If I just knew why he did it—

He paced until he thought he was going to wear a hole in
the carpet, and still got no further than that. It was already
full dark, and the darkness outside was no less impenetrable
than the darkness surrounding his heart.

*I can't agree to open negotiations with someone I can't
trust! That's pretty basic to the proposition of negotiations,
isn't it!*

Only one man knew why Tremane had issued his orders,
done what he had done, and that was Tremane.

I have to know. I have to talk to him. Somehow.

"I have to talk to Tremane," he said aloud. Altra raised his
head from his paws and stared at him as if he had sprouted
fur and fangs.

:You must be joking,: the Firecat said flatly.

•

Karal shook his head. "I have to find a way to talk to him myself, Altra, before the others do. I have to know *why*. And I need to know if he'd do it again. What's the point in trying to deal with someone we can't trust?"

:*I could give you a number of answers, but I don't think you're in the mood to hear them.*:

"You've got to find a way to help me talk to him, Altra, please!" Karal dropped down to his knees beside the Firecat, looking pleadingly into those blue eyes. "You're a mage."

:*Not precisely in the way you mean.*:

Karal ignored that. "Can't you do a scrying and make it work both ways?" he begged. "Can't you give me Mind-speech, or find some other way that I can talk to Tremane?"

:*I think this is a very, very bad idea, Karal.*:

"I have to do this, Altra," he said warningly. "The other two won't follow through with the plan if I don't agree with it, that was the bargain. And I won't agree until I've had a chance to talk to Tremane myself, face-to-face if necessary!"

Altra looked at him measuringly. :*I do believe that you would pack a bag and walk across two countries if you had to, in order to speak with this man.*:

Karal nodded. "I won't have to, though. I'll bet Florian would help me rather than let me get into trouble. I'll bet Firesong would help me just to get rid of me!"

:*Unfortunately, I'm sure you're correct.*: The Firecat sighed heavily. :*Very well. Since you're so insistent, I'll help you. But I can't create a scrying spell for you. What I can do is to take you there myself.*:

Karal felt sick. "Jumping?" he faltered.

:*It's the only way.*: Altra cocked his head to one side and narrowed his eyes. :*It's either that, or give up the idea. At least if I Jump you into Tremane's study, I can Jump you out again instantly if things go wrong. I can also hold him and keep him from doing anything for a limited period of time, which should make it possible for you to ask your questions of him without his raising an alarm. And don't forget that I also know the Tell-Me-True Spell, so the answers you get will be the ones you say you want to hear.*:

"Jumping." His last experience with Jumping had been a

dreadful one, and he had pledged that it would be the *last* time he let Altra Jump him anywhere. For one moment, Karal contemplated giving up—

No. I have to know. I can't make a decision unless I know!

"All right," he said, and was rewarded by Altra's ears flattening in dismay. "Now. Tonight. Before I change my mind."

:*I'd prefer that,*: the Firecat said sourly.

"I know you would," he retorted. "That's why I want it to be now."

Tremane rubbed his aching eyes and glanced at what was left of his candle. It had been a long day, and a longer night, but he and the Mayor's Council were working on consolidating Imperial Law and Hardornen Law into a single codex that both Town and Barracks would be living by. He wanted to be sure *they* understood all the nuances of Imperial Law; the laws of Hardorn didn't seem to be as specific, which was no great surprise. *Simpler society, simpler laws.*

Nevertheless, the Imperial forces had brought a more complex society with them, and in some ways the people of Shonar were going to have to learn how to cope.

And in some ways, we are. A hundred compromises every fortnight.

He wondered what time it was; well past midnight, certainly. He'd dismissed all of his orderlies, aides, and clerks several hours ago. Just because their master chose to short himself on sleep to work like a maniac, that didn't mean *they* should. It was good to work like this, deep into the night, in the quiet of a building in which most people were asleep. Outside, the only men awake were the ones on the walls. The city of Shonar slept, too—there would be no more emergencies tonight, and he could work without interruption, secure in the knowledge that he was completely alone in his offices.

But suddenly, he was no longer alone.

His skin shivered; the hair on the back of his neck stood up in an atavistic reaction to the power flaring up in this room.

Power! But it isn't time for a mage-storm!

He looked up from his papers in startlement, just as a boy in an outlandish set of elaborate black robes appeared in front of his desk, his arms burdened with a huge orange-and-white cat that to his shocked eyes looked to be the size of a small calf.

He tried to reach for the dagger on the top of his desk; tried to shout to alert the guards patrolling outside his quarters. With a chill of panicked terror, he found he could do neither.

The cat glared at him with widened blue eyes, eyes whose pupils reflected greenly at him, as he struggled against the invisible bonds imprisoning him. Its eyes narrowed in satisfaction as he gave up the unequal contest, and it began to purr audibly.

It's the cat! *That* cat *is doing this!* He stared at it in astounded disbelief, and yet at the same time he was absolutely certain his conclusion was the right one. The *cat* held him pinned in his place! What was going on here?

The boy cleared his throat self-consciously. "I am here to be asking you some queries, sir," the boy said, clearly enough; although the words in the Imperial tongue were thick with the inflections of several accents warring with one another. Tremane switched his gaze from the cat to the boy—and saw that the "boy" was not as young as he'd thought. This was a young man about the same age as most of his aides, although his slight build and childlike face left the impression that he was much younger than his years. "You will not be permitted to speak above a whisper, and only in answer to the question I ask." He looked a bit green, and his eyes were not quite focusing, as if he was a bit ill.

Questions! He wants to ask me questions! He transports himself here by magic and holds me prisoner in my own office to ask me questions! Am I mad, or is he! Who is he! What is he!

"This, my first question is. When you loosed forth the man in the Valdemar Court whom you had sent to murder folk by stealth, the man who was the art-maker, did you send him forth with instructions exact? Had you made a choice of who he was to kill?" The young man stared at him as if he would, if he could, bore a hole in Tremane's head with his eyes and extract the answers directly.

The paralysis eased a little, and Tremane found that he *could* speak. "I haven't the slightest idea what you're talking about," he tried to say, but his mouth would not speak what he intended to say! His lips moved, but he could not push himself to speak the untruth he thought. When his voice finally worked, the patterns it made were not the ones he had set it to! At first he stammered, and then he relaxed into speaking the truthful things he had tried to veil moments before.

"Not precisely," he heard himself whispering, to his own horror. "Not precisely, no. I ordered that people of a certain rank or station be eliminated. I really have no idea of the identities of people over there; my agents are simply not that good. Actually, at this point, they might as well not exist at all, since they can't get through to me with their information. I ordered that envoys and allies be removed; people vital to the continuance of the Alliance. I also ordered that the Queen be eliminated, but I frankly did not think *that* would succeed, as she is too well guarded."

He listened to himself, appalled. How was the young man *doing* this to him? His heart froze with fear—not because of the magic itself, but because of the implications. If this boy could do this, now, what would he be able to do later? Or was it the cat who was doing it?

The boy stared at him with eyes full of anguish. *"Why?"* he asked, his voice tight with emotion. "Why did you order such a thing?"

I have to speak the truth. It might as well be truth of my phrasing and choice—the whole truth instead of parts. There is something more to this boy than—than an assassin, or an agent sent to capture me. Something personal; this boy would be a poor choice to send to interrogate an enemy commander, powers or not! His lack of composure betrays his extreme agitation and emotion. There is something larger here than one might first think. And with this compulsion to speak only what is true. . . .

"I was certain at the time that the mage-storms that have

been laying waste to the land originated in Valdemar," he told the boy. "They left me and my men cut off from the Empire, with weapons and protections we depend on for our lives utterly disrupted. Our supply lines were cut, our communications nonexistent, our organization fragmented. My men were in a panic, my mages helpless, and we were strung out along a line we could not possibly defend. If an opposing force had come against us, they could have slaughtered us. I was absolutely certain that these storms were a new weapon of the Alliance, made possible only because the mages of the Alliance were all working together. Disrupting the Alliance was the only way I could see to stop the storms."

The boy continued to stare at him in anguish, and although he no longer felt the compulsion to say anything more, that anguish urged him to continue.

"These are not men I had chosen, nor is this a command I would have picked if I myself had a choice," he said. "But the moment I accepted this command, these men became my personal responsibility. I *must* see to their safety, even before I see to my own. They must be fed before I eat, sheltered before I sleep, and although they are soldiers and expect to face battle and death, it is my job to see that their lives are not thrown away—if possible, to see that victories are with a minimum of bloodshed. At the time, I saw disaster overtaking us, and I had to do something before it caught us. If these storms had indeed come from Valdemar, they were a terror-weapon, and one tailored to strike particularly at *us*, because so much of what the Empire depends on in turn depends on magic. I thought, at the time, my action was justified if it saved my men. This was not something they could meet in combat or face over the edge of their shields."

. Did this boy understand? At least he was listening, and Tremane was still able to speak.

"This is something I did not know when I first commanded men—when I was your age, in fact. Command is more than issuing orders, it is knowing what those orders might mean to the lives of your men and knowing that *you* and you alone are the one responsible for the outcome." These were the things he had never discussed with anyone else; in the spy-haunted milieu of the Empire, he would not have dared. "The men look to me to get them through each encounter; no man enters the army assuming he will die! They put their trust in me; I have to be worthy of that trust. To a good commander, no lives lost are 'acceptable.' "

The boy's gaze flickered, as if something he had said had touched a responsive nerve.

He gestured at the windows, as a cold blast shook them. "Look what these storms have wrought! Tell me I was wrong to fear for the lives of my men! I think that if it had not been for the walls we built here and the organization we gave them, the people of Shonar would be fighting monsters in the streets by night, and starving by day!"

The boy's eyes flickered toward the windows and back.

"As for what I ordered—my own mages have since told me that Valdemar did not send out the storms. I was wrong, I didn't wait for verification of my assumption, and as a result—I ordered something that was completely unjustified." He felt himself flushing hotly, and wondered at his own reaction. "If Valdemar had sent the storms, I am not certain now that what I did would have been justified either. Sending one weapon of terror in response to another is not a moral answer—but as a commander I don't often deal in moral answers, I deal in expediencies. I'm not used to moral answers, or moral questions. That is a failing of life in the Empire." He paused and added a final statement. "That is not meant to stand as an excuse, but as a reason. It is difficult to think in terms that one is not habituated to, and the center of life in the Empire is expediency."

True enough as far as it goes. There is no point in going into detail about Imperial life. Could anyone from Valdemar—I assume he must be from Valdemar—ever understand the Empire?

He had hardly admitted any of that even to himself, and he was surprised that he had poured it all out to a total stranger.

But this—young man—with the look of a priest has appeared in my office, with a cat in his arms that paralyzes me with a look. A single thrown knife, and I would be dead, and with my life goes the organization of my troops. Per-

haps that is why I am explaining all of this. Perhaps it needed to be said so that I could acknowledge it to myself, too.

The cat's eyes were on his, gazing at him with such intensity he almost expected the beast to speak. The young man's face bore a thoughtful expression; the pain was still there, but it was secondary to the sense of introspection.

Finally, the young man nodded and put the cat down for a moment. Once his hands were free, he drew something from his sleeve about the size of a dagger. He placed it on the desk.

It was a message-tube.

He picked up the cat again, and stepped back a pace as Tremane stared at the tube, perplexed. But the young man's next words solved his perplexity.

"If you wish to open a dialogue with Valdemar and the Alliance," he said quietly, "place your opening message in this. It will go where it needs to. I can assure you that the Queen and the Son of the Sun will see it, once it has been judged safe."

That peculiar shivering came over Tremane again; his eyes suddenly refused to focus. And when he could see again, the boy and the cat were gone.

He shook his head violently; he could move again perfectly well. Had it all been a hallucination brought on by too much work and too little rest? Had he fallen asleep over his papers and dreamed the whole incident?

But when he looked down at his desktop, the message-tube was still there.

It was real. It happened. Someone from Valdemar magicked himself into my office, without the use of a Portal, and interrogated me.

Not only that, but he must have "passed" his verbal examination, for here was the way to end at least one of the conflicts facing him and his men.

Truce with the Alliance. Perhaps even membership in the Alliance?

Certainly the Allies were not suffering as Hardorn was. They had not originated the mage-storms, but they had a defense against them, a defense that the Imperial forces did not have.

Should I? It could be a trap. Dare I risk it?

A howling buffet of wind shook the stone walls of his office; snow actually drifted down to the floor from the triply-shuttered and glazed windows. And midwinter was not even here yet—

—and the mage-storms were getting worse. It was only a matter of time before they changed something or someone *inside* the walls of Shonar. It could have already happened, perhaps they just hadn't discovered it yet. What would he do if that happened? He didn't know; he hadn't been able to plan for it, though his new agents in the ranks told him that the men themselves had come up with an answer. If it was an animal, it would die, no questions asked. If it was one of their comrades, and he retained his mind, they would find a way to make him useful. If it was one of their comrades and he attacked them, they would cut him down like any of the other boggles.

I must risk it. There is too much at stake.

He picked up the message-tube and placed it carefully in a desk drawer; then he stood up and blew out his candle. There was also too much at stake to risk writing a document that important when he was half drunk with fatigue.

Tomorrow he would close himself in his office and send word that he was not to be disturbed unless it was an emergency. This might be the most important letter he would ever write in his life.

:*I didn't think you'd be so sick,*: Altra said apologetically from the foot of Karal's bed, where he lay curled up around Karal's feet, keeping them warm. :*I wouldn't have brought you home so fast if I'd thought you were going to react this badly.*:

"It's all right," Karal replied faintly, as he lay back against his pillows. "Once there's nothing in my stomach things seem to settle down a bit more. The tea is helping. This is a nasty way to get a rest, though."

Altra had not even allowed him a single breath between

Jumps, and his nausea had become a single overwhelming force that took over mind and body. The moment he reached his suite he had been forced to the bathroom, where he had clutched at the convenience and retched until he thought he was going to throw up his toenails. When he could stand without retching, he had dragged himself to the bellpull and summoned a "servant." As before, the "servants" who tended to his needs, especially at night, were actually Heraldic students. That was why he tried so seldom to bother them—but this time he had no other choice. He couldn't have gotten any farther than the chair he collapsed into if he'd been prodded with a hot poker.

The young man who had appeared had been seriously alarmed at his appearance, and had gotten Karal into bed before summoning a Healer.

"Stomach cold," the Healer had decreed—although Karal could tell she was profoundly puzzled by his lack of other symptoms. She had left him with several packets of herbal tea and instructions to drink as much of it as he could; the young man had made some up immediately and left it at Karal's bedside. He made up a snowpack to ease Karal's headache, and had also left a stern admonition to pull the bell to call him if he felt *any* worsening of his condition, or if he needed so much as a dry cracker.

"I'll be all right in a day or so, and meanwhile this gives me an excuse to be alone and think," he told the Firecat.

:*If you were anyone else, I'd be surprised you want to do anything except lie there.*: Altra curled up around his feet a little tighter, and his icy feet finally began to warm up. It felt very good, and the snowpack the young man had made for his head was finally doing something about the throbbing in his temples.

"Well, that's the curse of being what you and Ulrich made me. I can't stop thinking even when I'm miserable." In fact, he was torn in so many directions that it was going to take some time to sort them all out.

I want to hate Tremane. His need to hate the man warred with the reality of the man himself, making him want to scream in frustration. It would have been so simple if the

Grand Duke had been a liar, a fraud, a man who did generous things because it would put people into his debt. Unfortunately for simple solutions, Tremane was none of those things. Altra knew the Karsite equivalent of the Valdemaran "Truth Spell," and he had held it on Tremane once his first spell successfully controlled the Grand Duke's body. Tremane could not have spoken anything other than the truth as long as Altra held that spell active.

Which made things that much more difficult for Karal.

The problem was, he understood Tremane and Tremane's motives. It was just as he had said to An'desha; he was cursed with being able to see all sides to an argument, and the validity of each and every side.

I would not have done what he did, but I have never been in the position he was. And I was not brought up to power, nor in the Empire. It is my reflex to take the moral path, and it is his to take the path of expediency.

The worst of it was that, given what Tremane had honestly thought was true and faced with Tremane's situation, he could not in all candor say that he would not have made the same choice—and issued the same orders. By Tremane's background, what he had done *was* probably incredibly moral, as well as expedient—eliminating a handful of people, to possibly prevent the deaths of many hundreds of his own men *and* of the citizens of Hardorn.

It is easy enough to justify yourself by saying that something is in self-defense, or is called for because someone else did something heinous. He could not say that he would not have given in to that temptation.

He might never lose his dislike of Tremane's attitudes, and he might never be able to forgive him, but he understood the man, and so he could not hate him for being what he was—which was the product of a world full of more duplicity and deceit than anything Karal had ever known. How could Tremane have expected anything else *but* an opponent who would cheerfully sacrifice innocents to take out an enemy? He probably met opponents like that every day in the Emperor's Court!

It was hardly fair.

I know. Life's not fair. He sighed. *And I'm putting off stating a decision I've already made.* "You took my message to An'desha?"

:As soon as you wrote it. He'll scry as often as he can, and check the tube for a message. Just as you asked. If there's anything there, he'll send for you and you can send me to fetch the tube,: Altra told him, blinking his eyes lazily. *:Don't expect an immediate answer, though. It's probably going to take a few days before he makes up his mind, but we both know he's going to do it. He can't afford to pass up this chance.:*

A few days. Altra was probably right, but these few days were going to seem like an awfully long time.

:Excuse me,: Altra said suddenly. *:I should be going.:*

The Firecat stood up, and vanished, the weight of his body lifting magically from Karal's feet and leaving behind only an impression in the blankets.

Now what on earth could have caused that?

"Altra? Altra?" Karal called in confusion. "What—"

Someone tapped on the outer door in the next room, and opened it. Light footsteps neared the door of his bedroom.

Natoli stood in the frame of the open door, one arm loaded with books, and the other holding the doorpost.

"Hello," she said. "I thought you might be lonely. I figured I could keep you company as long as you're sick. Just don't pass it on to me, all right?"

He smiled. "I promise I won't," he said, knowing that was a promise he *could* keep. "I couldn't tell the Healer, but it's only Jumping Sickness. Nothing you can catch."

"Oh, good," she said, smiling, and sat down beside him. "That's just what I wanted to hear."

Those few days are going to pass awfully quickly.

Karal and An'desha were pretending to look over some papers before the Grand Council meeting, but that was only the excuse so that the two of them could have a word before they upset everything with the little burden Altra was going to deliver.

"You're sure it's all right, the message is safe?" Karal asked

An'desha in an urgent whisper. "I mean—look, there's Selenay *and* Solaris sitting together. One trap could eliminate them both!"

"I checked it, Altra checked it, and you checked it," An'desha replied. "Really, Karal, given the propensity for nasty surprises that Ma'ar and his successive incarnations had, and all the information on them they left in my memory, you *can* trust me to find a mage-trap in a piece of paper! And anyway, Altra says that a mage-storm hit the Imperials again just before he went to get the tube. He doubts anything as delicate as a complicated trap would have survived."

"All right," Karal sighed, fiddling with his pens. "I'm just nervous."

An'desha gave him an oblique look. "You should be. I have to go sit down or it's going to look odd—we all agreed that it shouldn't look as if *we* had anything to do with this when it happens. I'll see you later."

An'desha hurried to his own seat as the latecomers for the Grand Council meeting arrived. When Tremane had finally put something in the message-tube, Altra had gone to get it, but he had not given it to them immediately. He asked them to think first about how it was to be presented.

Karal had wondered about that phrasing, until it dawned on him that if Solaris had any idea that he had gone behind her back to open negotiations with Tremane, she would probably see to it that the overture never got any further than that first message. She would also flay him alive, but that was incidental to the bigger scheme of things.

For that matter, Selenay might feel the same as Solaris about being circumvented.

The only person who knew they were going to be investigating the Imperials was Talia, and she had no notion that they intended to make contact. For all that the three of them were trusted, it was only to a point, and that point did *not* include haring off and sending messages to the enemy inviting him to come and play nicely.

That was when they all agreed that it would look as if *Altra* was the instigator. After they checked the message for any kind of trap, Altra would take it and present it himself to the Queen and the Son of the Sun at a Grand Council meeting, as if it had been *his* idea to contact Tremane. Solaris would no more question the reasoning and motives of a Firecat than Selenay would question a Companion. And she could hardly take a messenger of Vkandis to task for stepping outside his limits!

This was to be Solaris' last meeting for some time. She had at least managed to establish to the other members of the Council that she trusted Karal, and that Karal would never act or speak contrary to her will—and if other people on the Council had a problem with her will, that was another story altogether, and would be dealt with by negotiation. Although many of them obviously still felt that he was too young for his job, the same people felt confident that since he *was* so young, he would hardly dare to say or do anything contrary to orders.

So in theory, this would be the last time for several weeks or even months that Solaris sat in the seat beside Selenay. In theory. He had the feeling that once Altra showed up, the plans would change abruptly.

The members of the Grand Council took their seats, the Council session opened, and everything seemed routine, right down to the fact that his hands and feet were numb with cold. Things proceeded at the usual orderly pace, up until the moment that Selenay asked if there was any new business.

Which was, of course, the very moment that Altra showed up.

He simply appeared, dropped the message-tube between Solaris and Selenay, and vanished again.

Selenay was the one who picked it up and opened it, but both of them leaned over the paper rolled up inside. Karal knew what it said by heart.

To Queen Selenay, High Priest Solaris, and the members of the Alliance. Grand Duke Tremane, leader of the former Imperial Divisions of the Hardorn Pacification Force, acting Lord of Shonar, and Commander of the combined Hardorn and Imperial Armies, greets you. Tremane wishes to inform you that his relation with the Emperor and the Empire has been irrevocably severed. It is in the interest of both of our parties to negotiate a truce, preparatory to further negotiations, extending to, but not limited to, solidifying an alliance among all our peoples. To this end, he solicits an answer from you regarding such a truce, and such negotiations.

It was signed and sealed with the Grand Duke's personal seal, not the Imperial Seal, a nicety that Altra seemed to find amusing.

It was written in Hardornen and it didn't take long to read, although it was repeated in Karsite, the Imperial tongue, and Valdemaran. Tremane must have scoured the town to find someone who knew Karsite—perhaps a trader, or a priest. That was another nice touch, even if the grammar was atrocious.

Solaris and Selenay read it with their mouths clamped into tight, thin lines. Selenay passed it to Daren without a word; the Prince-Consort read it aloud.

And just as Karal had figured, all of hell itself broke loose when he finished.

Men and women leaped to their feet, each of them demanding the right to be heard *immediately.* Initially, as always with this Grand Council, there was a great deal of shouting and carrying on, mostly on the part of people who had very little to say. Solaris was ominously quiet, which made Karal very nervous. She sat beside Selenay in a pose so motionless she could have been a statue. He knew that pose; she only took it when she was being her most formal, taking on the full persona of the Son of the Sun, the Falcon of Light, Defender of the Faithful.

He kept quite silent, although Jarim more than made up for his silence until the moment when Lo'isha, the Sworn-Shaman, simply put one hand quietly on his sleeve and stared at him. Then he sat down abruptly and didn't speak for the rest of the meeting.

Solaris finally softened a little, but she kept casting suspicious glances at him all during the rest of the meeting, which made Karal even more nervous than before. He could deal with the Son of the Sun; he wasn't certain he could handle an angry Solaris who was concentrating on *personal* outrage.

Karal took notes diligently, avoiding Solaris' gaze whenever possible. The meeting finally ended when Selenay stood up and announced, "This is too important to decide on the spur of the moment. I'd like to dismiss this meeting so that we all have the opportunity to think over the positive and negative aspects of this proposal. We'll reconvene tomorrow; be prepared to present your analysis in an orderly fashion." With that, she gestured to Daren, and the two of them left the meeting, which meant that whatever else happened, it was no longer official.

That certainly put an abrupt end to the confusion. Karal gathered up his things quickly and made his escape while most of the other Council members were still arguing among themselves. But he noted that Solaris was also leaving by the same door as Selenay, and he only hoped that she was going to spend a great deal of time talking with her Valdemaran counterpart. With luck, he could be out of the Palace and down at the Compass Rose before she remembered her suspicions and sent someone to look for him.

But today his luck was out. Solaris was waiting for him in his suite, sitting on his couch as formally as if it was her throne.

"Shut the door, Karal," she ordered, as he stood in the doorframe in shock. Numbly, he did as she ordered, and turned to face her. His joints felt like carved granite, as he stood, unable to relax under her gaze.

"You were behind this, or at least you were aware of what Altra was doing, and don't bother to deny it," she said stiffly, as he stood with his back to the door and his knees shaking. His stomach quaked. "Altra is *your* Firecat, and he would not have attempted anything so audacious if you were not aware of it. Somehow you persuaded him this was a good idea. You and two of these foreigners have been closeted doing some form of unspecified scrying, according to Selenay. I do not require a spell to show me the truth or to put obvious facts together into a whole."

He swallowed, and nodded, admitting everything with that

single gesture. His throat was too tight to get any words out, anyway.

She stood up, crossing her arms and narrowing her eyes as she strode toward him, anger in her every step. This was what he had feared most—Solaris, angry in herself. "This man ordered the murder of Priest Ulrich—*your* mentor, *my* friend, and a Black-robe of Vkandis! How could you even contemplate consorting with him? What possible reasons could you have for approaching him?"

After two tries, he at least got out an answer. "Because—we had to, Radiance," he said weakly. "Because there was no choice."

With that, she unleashed all of her formidable intellect and equally formidable anger on him in an interrogation that was as thorough as it was merciless. Karal answered her as best he could, but the next two marks left him weak, sweating, and shaking before it was all over. Solaris could be absolutely brutal when she wanted to be, and all without ever raising a hand or her voice. Her cross-examination was relentless and thorough, and during it she dissected his personality and left every personal weakness he knew of and some he had never suspected lying exposed. She prowled around him like a hunting cat, she moved to within a hair of his face to hiss directly into his eyes, and stood off at a distance as if she didn't want to get near him. She left his spirit flayed, and convinced him a dozen times over that she was about to demote him to least-senior cleaner of the Temple latrines—*if* he was lucky and she was feeling generous.

Nevertheless he managed to remain adamant and unshakable in his conviction that, repugnant as it was, they could not afford to allow Tremane to remain an enemy.

Finally, she sat down again, although she did not permit him to do so. Ten heartbeats later, she spoke.

"Let me see if I understand all your reasoning, such as it is," she said coldly. "First, you believe that the folk of Hardorn and even the men under this Tremane's command have been suffering for far too long. Second, the best indications are that the new boundaries of whatever solution we come up with when the breakwater fails must include the eastern border of Hardorn. Third, there is some thought that if we had access to the mages trained in the Empire we might be able to find that solution sooner. And fourth—" she leveled a stare at him that was as opaque as steel. "Fourth. You have come to the conclusion that Tremane can be trusted."

"He was under Altra's Tell-Me-True all the while he answered my questions. He has protected the people of Shonar, even though he didn't have to," Karal reminded her as he shivered and did not bother to try to hide the fact. "More than that, he has done things for their benefit personally, things that could not possibly be of profit to him. He has kept every pledge he made them, and every pledge he made his own men."

"Hmm." Her expression did not change.

"I would add a fifth, but it is quite subjective," he said, feeling sweat run down the back of his neck. "I believe he— regrets his actions."

"Regrets." Her mouth tightened, and she stood up again. "There are some things I must do, but as of this moment, *your* authority is in abeyance. You will remain here in these rooms until I give you leave to go elsewhere, and *where* that will be is going to depend on what I learn in the next few marks."

She swept past him; he held open the door for her, and she swept out, leaving him shaking with anxiety and reaction in her wake.

After he closed the door behind her, he went straight to his bed and lay down on it, his body as exhausted as if he had just run around the city walls, and his bones gone all to water. No need to tell him to stay here, for he couldn't have left his room if it had been on fire.

He didn't know what she was going to do next, but every possibility left him shaking with fear. Not for himself, but for her, and for everything the Alliance had done here.

Tremane watched his windows shake as another blast of icy wind hit them, a wind laden with so much blowing snow that there was no view outside. The cat had appeared as soon as he put down the message-tube; it had materialized on his desk, placed a paw on the tube, and vanished again, taking the tube with it.

They were in the middle of another blizzard. He had waited until another blizzard struck and had been active for some time before actually putting his carefully-worded overture into the tube; he wanted to be sure that he would have a time when he would be able to stay in his office for several hours, waiting for a reply. There had been no emergencies, and now the folk of the Town and Barracks were safely buttoned up in their lodgings, passing the time until the storm blew itself out. No one would need him until that happened. He could wait for as much as two days for an answer to his overture, if nothing went wrong.

Which was precisely what he was doing now; waiting. He fully expected the cat to show up alone, but with a written reply, a tentative suggestion that his overture was being considered. It was also possible that the cat would show up with the boy, though that was less likely. Negotiations took time, and many exchanges of paper, before anything concrete came of them.

He did *not* expect the answer he got—a cat all right, but with the cat was a woman, garbed in elaborate robes of gold and white, robes that he recognized from the descriptions passed to him by his spies. And now he cursed his stupidity for not recognizing a less-elaborate, masculine version of the same robes on the boy.

This was High Priest (*not* Priestess) Solaris, the Son of the Sun, the secular and sacred leader of all the people of Karse. And from her expression, she was perfectly prepared to whip that ritual dagger she was carrying out of her belt and slit his throat on the spot.

He, of course, could not move. Once again, the cat held him paralyzed.

Her eyes glared at him with a fire of rage that gave even him, a battle-hardened veteran, pause. Her face was as white as the snow outside, but her hands were steady. "You give me one good reason may, why killing you I should not be, as murdering my friend you did," she snarled, in heavily-accented Hardornen.

Not bad, considering that she probably hasn't studied it much.

His mind raced. What should he tell her? What *could* he tell her? What would she believe?

Nothing, probably.

No, there was no reason to defend himself or his actions. Coming up with excuses would not save him.

He would have drawn himself up in his chair if he had been free to. Instead, he gazed directly into her eyes. Once again, he would probably be forced to speak the truth, so why not simply do so to begin with?

"I cannot," he told her with bald honesty. "By the laws of your land and of my own, my life is certainly forfeit to you. I committed murder, if only by secondhand. I cannot justify a decision that has proved to be so very wrong, and so ill-conceived."

Her eyes narrowed a trifle, as if she had expected duplicity, or at least an attempt at it. Had she *not* put that magic on his lips that forced him to speak truthfully?

"By the same token, my best information at the time was that the mage-storms were a weapon of terror sent by your Alliance," he continued. "I sent my own weapon of terror to disrupt your Alliance. I proved by that assumption, I suppose, that my moral standards are lower than yours, since I could even *think* that you might send terror-weapons that strike at armies and civilians alike. I further proved the same thing since *I* retaliated with a weapon of terror. The Empire is a bad enemy to have, lady, and we have made worse enemies over the centuries. We are prepared to see just about any atrocity, and to meet it with the same."

Her frown deepened, but her eyes widened a little.

"But I put this to you, Son of the Sun—as a leader, I would venture to say that you have been in similar situations. Whether you would have responded in the same way, only you can say."

That hit home; he saw it in her eyes, in the way she winced slightly. But her anger had not lessened.

"For the first time in this, my life," she said through clenched teeth, "I considering am my ban upon the demons revoking, and up the demon-mages bringing to those terrible spirits turning loose upon your troops. *That* is what you have me brought to!"

He thought very carefully before speaking. "By all repute, Solaris, you are too just to levy upon the innocent a retribution due only to their leader."

Her chin rose. "So. You offer to me your life?"

He only raised one eyebrow—that much movement, at least, was permitted him. "The people of this place depend on my leadership, as do my men. Without me, Shonar and the barracks will be in chaos, for there is no single man that they will all agree on as leader. Likeliest, it would be one of my generals who triumphed; a general who would not know as much about you, and who would still consider your Alliance to be his mortal enemy. *You* are too good a leader to slay a *former* enemy who might be replaced with someone who will still be your enemy." He tried a touch of boldness. "I am not your enemy. Solaris. I told the truth in my missive. We have lost touch with the Empire, and the Empire has abandoned us. My duty to my men dictates that I see to their safety and there is no safety in continuing an aggression on behalf of someone who has left us here to rot." He managed a slight shrug. "The real enemy we both face is the force that sends these mage-storms. Isn't it better to face that enemy together?"

Her eyes narrowed to slits in speculation, although her jaw was still clenched tightly in anger.

"You have not attained and held the rank of Son of the Sun without learning the lesson of expediency, Radiance," he finished. *I believe this is the place to stop—while my luck is still holding. One more word might turn her the other way.*

"No," she hissed. "I have not."

She stepped back, and he felt relief sweep over him. She was not going to kill him—which meant that she *was* possibly going to support his bid for a truce and an alliance of his own.

Much as she might hate it, she knew that it would bring the greater good.

She suddenly waved her hand, then gestured with a clenched fist, and he felt the poor, sad remains of his shielding against magics collapse and disintegrate. What the storms had battered, her magic finished—and he felt dread clench at his guts.

"But I do curse you," she said, with a grim smile. "I curse you, with something the touch of which you have already felt. Your help we need, but know you I do not, and trust you I do not. In the Name of Vkandis Sunlord, and with the power He has granted me as His Son, upon you I lay that you will never to me lie, nor to anyone else tell an untruth, whoever questions you. *Never.*"

Chill spread through his body. *She could not have imagined a more terrible curse for a son of the Empire,* he thought numbly. *I can never, ever go home again. . . .* Not that he could have anyway, given what he had already done.

"Feel the curse—or the freedom—of truth," she finished, her smile widening, her eyes glowing fiercely, "And then will we see what measure of man you are truly."

She swept up the cat in her arms, and vanished.

With her disappearance, the paralysis vanished also, and he sagged in his chair, gone boneless with relief and reaction.

He let out his breath, and laid his head down on his arms on the top of his desk, nearer to tears than he had been in all of his adult life. In all of his checkered career, he had never had quite so close an escape, not even on the battlefield— and in all of his life, he had never gotten out of such a situation by doing as he had, telling the truth.

Now I will have no choice, he thought, that chill passing over him again. *But—perhaps she overestimated her power. I should test this.*

"I am Grand Duke Tremane," he said aloud raising his head from his arms, "And I am a mage of average powers, forty-five years of age."

He cursed, silently. He had *meant* to say, "A mage of astounding powers, and sixteen years of age." He had *thought* right up until the words emerged from his mouth, that this was what he was going to say.

The curse was working, and it worked even without having anyone to hear him but himself.

The curse of truth, he thought, propping his head up on one hand as a headache started. *How my enemies would laugh!*

But she was right. Now even *he* would find out just what a measure of a man he was. He only hoped he would be able to live with what he learned.

Ten

I am still envoy, I still have all my limbs, my skin has not been flayed from me, and Vkandis help me, but I am actually holding up under this pressure.

Solaris had finally gone, and the wonder of it was that no one but Karal had ever learned about that torturous interview in his suite. She left him and his authority intact and never mentioned to anyone else that the opening of negotiations with Tremane had been anyone's idea but the Firecat's. There was even a peculiar sort of respect in the way she looked at him now. Respect for standing up to her? Perhaps that was it. Perhaps it was respect for the fact that he stood behind his convictions, that he had not let personal feelings interfere with what was important for the greater good.

He did not know for certain just what it was she had done after she left him. He didn't really want to ask. Whatever it was, she had gone on to Selaney and convened a small meeting of the envoys and heads of state—that is, a meeting of herself, Selenay, Prince Daren for Rethwellan, Jarim and the Sworn-Shaman for the Shin'a'in, Treyvan for the k'Leshya and Darkwind for the Tayledras. With that smaller, much more manageable group, a basic reply to Tremane was worked out and sent, not via Altra, but via Hansa.

I don't think she's ever going to forgive Altra.

Karal had no idea what had made Solaris change her mind, but whatever it was, it pleased her enough that she tacitly forgave him for what he had done.

And, eventually, it was Hansa who Jumped back to Haven

with Tremane's chosen representative—Karal was just as glad that they would no longer be treating with Tremane personally. He did not think that he would ever be able to face the man without wanting to perform some very painful and undiplomatic experiment upon his body involving knives and large stones.

Karal had given up expecting anything, after learning that the leader of the Imperial Army looked like a clerk, so he wasn't particularly surprised when the man Tremane chose to represent him was a mage so old and decrepit it looked as if he might break up and blow apart in a high wind. But although the mage Sejanes was old, there was nothing whatsoever the matter with his mind. He was as sharp as anyone Karal had ever met. He already spoke Hardornen well enough to please some of the Hardornen exiles living at the Valdemaran Court, and he began picking up Valdemaran *and* Tayledras with a speed that left Karal gasping.

Finally, though, the old boy confessed that it was the result of a spell, one used successfully in the Empire for centuries. "If we hadn't had it already, we would have been forced to concoct it," he said, eyes twinkling. "Or our clerks' time would be taken up with learning languages and not with their real duties."

"And what duties are those, sir?" Darkwind had asked.

"Why, running the Empire, of course," the old fellow countered. "Everyone knows it's the clerks that run the government and the rest of it is all just for show. At any rate, I'm glad I'm in a place where I can cast it again, without having to recast it every few days."

Surprisingly, the old man had completely won over Solaris, perhaps because he reminded her of Ulrich. He had spent several marks closeted alone with her when he first arrived, and when they emerged again, Solaris demonstrated a considerably softened attitude toward the Imperials—and a positively friendly one toward Sejanes himself.

Well, what they had said or done was also none of Karal's business, much as it might eat at his curiosity. If she or Sejanes ever thought he needed to know, they would tell him. Otherwise, there were many things in the world he would never know the answer to, and this was just one more.

Much to Firesong's chagrin, the Imperial mages were *all* taught an analytical, logical approach to magic. Faced with overwhelming odds against the superiority of "instinct," the Tayledras Adept gave in, and subjected himself and his techniques to a similar analysis. It was just as well, considering that the information Sejanes brought with him indicated a failure of the breakwater just past Midwinter. Firesong volunteered to calculate the exact time, by intuition only, as a last effort to prove the validity of art over mathematics, but he finally acquiesced and helped with the more scientific method. Work on a solution proceeded at a feverish pace. All around them, the capital was preparing for Midwinter Festival with dogged determination, but there would be no time for festivals for the mages and artificers hunting for that elusive solution.

In the anxious concentration on what magic might do to save Valdemar and her allies from the same fate known of in Hardorn, the other projects the artificers and their students had been working on suffered the neglect of the masters.

There were some projects that should never have gone without supervision. It was a week before Midwinter that the artificer's experimental boiler on the Palace grounds exploded.

The Palace rocked to its foundations, and everyone in the Grand Council Chamber looked up in startlement. Like the worst clap of thunder anyone had ever heard, increased a thousandfold, it vibrated the Palace and everything in it. As it shook the building, it shook everyone who heard it with sudden, atavistic fear. Of everyone in the chamber, only Karal had an inkling of what the cause was.

"The boiler!" he cried, and sprang from his chair in a scattering of pens and papers, heading for the door. He tripped over the legs of his fallen chair, caught himself by flailing his arms wildly as he staggered across the floor, and continued his run. He burst out of the door to the chamber, startling the guards no end, and tore down the hall in the direction of the Collegia.

One of the student artificers had been working on the boiler-engine project before all the turmoil about the break-water failure began. Natoli and Master Isak had been helping him with it until the breakwater project occupied their attention; and ever since she stopped helping him, Natoli had been feeling guilty about neglecting him. He had no aptitude for the breakwater project and had been working on the boiler alone and unaided for some time. His idea was to heat the Collegia with the waste hot water from his boiler, while using the steam-piston contrivances attached to it to drive a water pump bringing water up from wells, and to do other mechanical work needed at the complex. Chopping wood, for instance; he had a design for a steam-drive wood splitter that would save servants endless time. His innovations included plans for an ingenious mechanism to supply wood and water to the boiler itself on a constant basis. That was the tricky part, and the one Natoli had agreed to help him with.

This was one of the largest steam-boilers anyone had ever built, almost the size of a man, and it was inherently dangerous. Boilers had exploded before this. He remembered the talk from the Compass Rose. If the boiler overheated, or boiled dry—if it had boiled dry and they weren't aware of the fact, and they'd then added water to it—

He burst out of the Palace doors into the daylit gardens, and floundered across the snow-covered grounds, oblivious to the cold. Other people ahead of him surged out of the Collegia buildings, heading in the same direction.

The boiler was at some distance from the Collegia, and had been set up inside its own little brick "false-tower" so as not to be a blight on the landscape. Those brick walls would have contained the explosion—

And if anyone was still inside the building, they'd have been caught between the explosion and the brick walls!

This was like a nightmare, where he ran as hard as he could, until his side and lungs burned and he couldn't even catch his breath, and he still made no progress in the knee-deep snow. By the time he reached the scene, plenty of other people had already arrived, and the injured had been taken away. All that was left to see were the remains of the boiler and the tower. The wooden door- and window-frames had been blown out of the walls in a shower of glass and splinters, and the brick walls themselves were cracked and bowed ominously outward. Some folk were throwing buckets of snow into the interior of the tower, presumably to put out a fire and cool the remains of the boiler, and every bucketful that went in produced a billow of steam and an ominous hissing.

Karal spotted one of the Masters; the one concerned with mechanics and clockwork, Master Isak. The old man was just standing in the snow, his square, lined face blank, his coat on inside-out. "What happened?" he cried, grabbing Master Isak's sleeve. "Was anyone hurt? Who was here?"

Isak wiped his forehead, his shock of white hair and side-whiskers standing out like an angry cat's fur. "The boiler itself didn't rupture," he said vaguely. "It was the offset pipe—just blew, tore the boiler out of its footing and drove it into the far wall in an instant. There were four students here, and they were all hurt, but only Justen was hurt badly. Poor boy! Poor boy! He tried to get the safety valve opened wide to let the pressure off, but it wasn't enough—he ran for the door, but—he was still inside the building when it went, the rest were already at the door and the explosion blew them into the snow. Horrible . . . just horrible."

"Was Natoli here?" Karal demanded, shouting and shaking the poor man's arm. "Was she?"

"They took her with the rest to Healer's," Isak mumbled, staring blankly at the blood-spattered remains of the door and wringing his hands with anxiety. "The Healers have them all. I don't know anything else. They just left—"

Karal dropped Isak's arm and sprinted—or tried to—in the direction of the Healer's Collegium. Running through the heavy snow was like trying to run in loose hay; it was impossible to make any progress. And by the time he got there, they had taken Natoli off to a little room by herself and wouldn't let him or anyone else near her.

"She just has a concussion, some bruises, and a broken wrist and ankle" they told him. "But we don't know for certain, and we can't let anyone in to upset her right now. She's upset enough as it is."

Why, he soon found out—Justen, the boy she'd been helping, had lost both legs to the knee, and was badly scalded elsewhere. Only the fact that he had been blown out into the snow through the door saved him from worse burns. His clothing had been saturated with boiling water, but the snow had cooled it quickly enough that the burns where his clothing had nominally protected him were superficial, though painful.

"At least it wasn't his hands or his eyes," one of the Healers said grimly, wiping his bloodstained sleeve against his sweating brow. "As an artificer, he can get along without legs, but not without hands or sight. And considering that he was in the same room as the boiler, he could have been killed."

That was the general consensus; it could have been a lot worse. That was no comfort to Karal. *It is bad enough!* He loitered about the quiet halls, trying desperately to find someone to question, but everyone in the Collegium who was concerned with the four injured students was busy, and none of them had any time to talk to him. Anyone else he asked would only say apologetically that he knew as much as they did.

Finally, he gave up and headed for the chambers set up in the Palace where the artificers were working with the mages. Maybe someone there would know something.

No one did; there was a general air of gloom pervading the place. Some, like Master Levy and An'desha, were working grimly at the water-table or at other tasks; their set expressions and the tight lines of their mouths told him that they were trying to distract themselves with work. Others were making no pretense at work; they simply sat with hanging heads and nakedly anxious expressions, looking up with wide and hopeful or fearful eyes whenever someone came to the door.

He joined the pair at the water-table; they were trying

some new trick of An'desha's that involved dropping a ring into the table rather than a single stone, and seeing how the waves reflected inward toward the center of the ring. Since the waves of the mage-storms were "echoing back" to their original center, this seemed to be the best way to simulate the effect.

They did this, over and over again, making minute changes and repeating the experiment mindlessly, then making notes in ledger after ledger. More and more people came to the room, as if aware that any news from the Healers would come here first.

Karal sat on a bench and watched the ring drop, over and over. Elspeth and Darkwind sat next to him and Elspeth put one hand gently on his shoulder; he hadn't seen them come in, but he wasn't surprised that they were here.

The walls of that tower were bowed outward, and the boiler was nothing more than metal scraps, he thought, feeling an invisible hand squeezing his heart. *How could she be all right? Pieces of metal must have been shot through the air like lances! Were they just telling me that to make me feel better?*

If only he knew! If only someone would come with word!

A box full of the round pebbles they used in the water-table lay on the bench beside him, and he began picking up handfuls and dropping them back into the box, one at a time. Darkwind began wrapping the shaft of a feather with fine silver wire, and Elspeth began methodically sharpening one of her knives. The stropping sound blended with the *tick tick* of pebbles dropping into the box, forming a peculiar and hypnotic pattern.

:Karal!:

Karal's hand closed hard on the pebbles; Altra materialized with lightning suddenness right in front of them.

Elspeth dropped her dagger.

:Karal, I've just been to Natoli—she's fine. Or rather, she's no worse than the Healers told you. Concussion, cracked collarbone, bruises, broken wrist, but only a badly sprained ankle.:

Karal babbled all this to the rest of the room, as quickly as

Altra relayed it to him mentally. As he spoke, the atmosphere in the room changed dramatically.

:*Justen* will *live, and in fact he's already making rather narcotic-induced plans for artificial legs or a wheeled chair. His burns are painful, but they have new dressings and new narcotics from the k'Leshya that will make a big difference. Ferd's concussed and his wrists are both broken, but they'll heal fine, David broke three ribs and his arm. That's it. That's* all. *They're going to be all right!*:

Cheers rang out across the room, although Karal's mind was only on Natoli. He let out a whoop, and threw his handful of pebbles into the air. An'desha yelped and dropped the hoop he was holding onto to cover his head with his hands as pebbles showered down around him.

The hoop and one of the stones hit the water simultaneously, the stone falling in the middle of the area enclosed by the hoop. An'desha ignored it, vaulting across benches to join Karal in a back-slapping indulgence of relief.

But Master Levy ignored *them,* leaning over to peer intently at the water-table.

When they finally stopped acting like a pair of demented idiots, he beckoned imperiously to An'desha. "Get over here, would you? Something interesting happened this time."

Heads turned all over the room at that, and a sudden silence fell, for Master Levy never used the term "interesting" unless something of cosmic portent had occurred or been calculated. An'desha trotted back to his place beside Master Levy and picked the hoop up out of the water.

Master Levy picked up a stone.

He gave the signal to An'desha to drop the hoop, and at the same time dropped the stone into the exact center of the area defined by the hoop.

"There," he said, as An'desha leaned over the table. "Where the two sets of waves meet—you see?"

"They're canceling each other," An'desha breathed. "The water isn't exactly smooth, but it's just a minor disturbance. It jitters . . . it breaks up."

Darkwind rose to his feet with alacrity, Elspeth following. "Do that again!" he ordered. "I want to see this."

Others quickly gathered around the table, including those who had only come here on the chance that there was word about the injured students. The experiment was repeated, over and over again, with the stone being dropped simultaneously with the hoop, a heartbeat after the hoop was dropped, and a heartbeat before. In all cases, the waves in the water caused by the hoop were at least partially canceled by the waves from the dropped stone.

And the trick worked best when the stone was dropped in the exact center of the area defined by the hoop.

"This is it," Master Levy breathed, his eyes lighting.

"But how are we going to set up an opposing force, in the proper modulation, that will cancel the mage-storm waves?"

Karal came back to hear Master Levy ask one of his typically brutally precise questions. He would rather have been at Natoli's side, but the Healers still weren't letting anyone in with the students. Now he was back, half a candlemark later, and the discussions were still going strong.

"More magic, like a Final Strike," Darkwind replied promptly. "The storms were caused by magic. We can set up a canceling force by magic, something that releases an immense amount of energy all at once. We've canceled magic before—we do that all the time to blunt effects, in containment spells—those are just spells that exactly counter the force coming out of someone or something." Now his face lit up as well. "That's our answer, for now at least! We can't replicate something that will exactly duplicate the force of the original Cataclysm, but I bet we can come close enough to buy us some more time! Or at least—"

"But—" Master Levy began.

Darkwind waved at him, and he closed his mouth on whatever he was going to say. "Or at least clip the top off those waves. I don't know how, but I know that there has to be a way. We've got mages from four different disciplines here, and if among all of us we can't find an answer, I'll eat my boots without sauce!"

"I hope you have a taste for leather," Master Levy muttered, but only Karal heard him.

"I'll reconvene the mages in the Grand Council chamber," Elspeth said, and ran off before anyone could stop her—not that they wanted to. Darkwind looked at An'desha, who shrugged.

"We might as well," he opined. "It isn't even dark yet. We have the whole night to argue."

The group, when it finally assembled, included not only the mages of the Tayledras, Sejanes, the k'Leshya mages, and the White Winds mages who were still teaching at the Collegium, it also included Karal, Altra, Lo'isha the Sworn-Shaman of the Shin'a'in, and one of the Karsite Mage-Priests who had fought Ancar, the same one who had saved Natoli's father's life. They had to use the Grand Council chamber as there was no other room large enough to hold not one, but four gryphons. Master Levy had the water-table emptied, brought to the chamber, and refilled so that he could demonstrate their discovery.

All of those present leaned over the table with extreme interest; Master Levy and An'desha demonstrated their experiment many times over so that everyone got a chance to see what was going on in detail.

"Now," the Master Artificer said, when everyone had looked his fill, "I am out of my depth. I leave it to you to determine if this model is accurate to the situation, and if so, what can be done about it."

"For a beginning, my people back in Shonar have been measuring the strength, duration, and timing of the storm-waves," Sejanes said briskly. "We have all of those that occurred right up until the moment I departed, but in the interests of complete accuracy, we should get the most recent. If my lord cat over there will take a message—"

Altra bowed his head gracefully.

"—I can get them to send the most recent of their records, and we can work out just how large an event we'll have to create for the canceling effect." Sejanes scribbled a brief message, and Altra paced across the table to take it from him. The Firecat vanished; by now the mages were so used to the way he came and went that they paid no attention.

"We do have a major problem," Master Levy pointed out.

"We have, not one, but two event-centers, and one is absolutely inaccessible unless you happen to be a fish."

"That's true," said one of the human k'Leshya mages, "but the real problems are occurring where the waves intersect. Those are the places where weather disruptions are forming, where monsters are created, and where there is transportation of land. We might find that if we only have to deal with one set of waves, the effect on magic would be temporary and can be shielded against for a time if we can just cancel out the Dhorisha waves."

Master Levy shrugged and spread his hands. "I make no pretense that I understand magic; I only observe and deduce what I can."

Sejanes cackled and slapped him on the back. The old man was stronger than he looked; Master Levy actually staggered for a moment. "Hiding arrogance behind false modesty, boy? Don't bother; we all know we're in elite company, and you're included in that. Now, the question is, just what is our pebble going to be?"

"The generating force is going to have to be powerful," Darkwind said soberly. "Very powerful. I need to point out, friends, that I do not think it is going to be possible to generate anything powerful enough to counter that final wave—the echo of the Cataclysm itself. Not without creating another Dhorisha, another Evendim. And I don't think any of us want to do that."

"So far as that goes, I don't particularly want a massive explosion in the heart of my homeland," Lo'isha put in. "We rather like the Plains the way they are, and I'm not certain we can persuade the Star-Eyed to put it back if we ruin it a second time, however lofty our motives."

"No—now wait a moment," Sejanes interrupted. "The problem is that the original Cataclysm was the result of two events, both intended to do the maximum in physical damage. Remember? *Physical* damage. Your Mage of Silence wanted to destroy his enemy's entire force, *and* destroy his own Tower so that if the enemy somehow survived, he wouldn't be able to find anything to use. But if *all* we want to do is to send out a counter in the energy-plane of magic, is there any reason why we can't just do that, channel all of the released energy into the energy-planes? Frankly, tearing up huge tracts of land is rather wasteful of power we could focus elsewhere!"

Darkwind opened his mouth as if he were going to say something, then got a thoughtful look on his face and shut it again. One of the new gryphons, a burly hawk-type, clacked his beak thoughtfully. "If we concssentrrrated the powerrr in that plane, we could do morrre with lesss enerrrgy than the Cataclyssssm itssself requirrred."

"Or more specifically, on the 'edge' between planes where the waves brush against our world, and cause the physical damage," Elspeth chimed in. The gryphon nodded firmly.

"Which brings us around to the question again, and that is *how!* We need a focused burst," Sejanes said, "and not a sustained release. Most of us are not used to thinking in those terms; the only focused bursts of energy *I'm* used to creating are lightning strikes and similar unpleasantness. Or Final Strikes, but the mage who does one isn't going to survive the experience, and I'd like to survive."

Lo'isha looked very, very thoughtful and stood up, clearing his throat and getting everyone's attention. All activity slowed and stopped, and attention went to the Shin'a'in.

"For the sake of clarity, I am going to impart something that some of you may already know," he said. "This was once a closely-guarded secret among my people, but there is a time when secrets need to be revealed. After the Cataclysm, all of the people formerly known as the Kaled'a'in—"

"Except for Clan k'Leshya—" interrupted a k'Leshya mage.

"Yes, except for k'Leshya—gathered at the edge of the crater that had once been their homeland—which was also the place where Urtho's Tower had stood. They divided over how magic was to be dealt with in the future, and became the two cousin-peoples, the Shin'a'in and the Tayledras. To the Hawkbrothers, who chose to follow the ways of the mage still, the Star-Eyed Goddess gave the task of cleansing the lands warped by the magics of the Cataclysm. To the Shin'a'in, who chose to ever after *avoid* the use of all magics save those of the Shaman, she gave another task." He paused, closing his eyes for a moment. "In exchange for this, she restored our home, and since we were vowed to use no magic, we did not experience the effects of the mage-storms of the time. The task we were given was to guard the Plains from all outsiders. This much is common knowledge. What is *not* common knowledge is the reason for the task. In the center of the Plains, at a site known only to the Sworn of the four faces of the Goddess, lie the remains of Urtho's Tower. Buried beneath the surface are the weapons Urtho did not and would not use. They are very powerful. And they are still alive and ready for use, according to our traditions. At least one of these should be the very thing that we need."

The Shin'a'in drew his dagger and laid it flat on the table. "It is time to end the Guardianship."

Jaws were dropping all around the table, Karal's not the least.

"Here is the one problem that I foresee—and given that we have our Kaled'a'in brothers and sisters of k'Leshya with us, this may be less of a problem than I had thought," the Sworn One continued. "Once we unearth the weapons' vault, which should still be intact, we will have to search through what is there to find a suitable weapon. And we will have to determine how to make it work, or how to adapt it to our need." He smiled slightly. "Needless to say, Urtho did not leave an inventory nor a book of instructions with them."

Karal realized he had stopped breathing with surprise, and forced himself to take a deep lungful of air.

Treyvan shook his feathers, and nibbled a talon. "I rrrecall a litany, much like the Tayledrrrasss litany of 'frrriendly beasssstss,' that we magesss of k'Lessshya arrre all rrrequirred to learrrn."

"The 'Garland of Death,' of course," supplied one of the humans. "That *could* be an inventory and set of descriptions! But I always thought it was just a memory-exercise with a particularly morbid name—"

"And ssso it isss," Treyvan agreed. "But like ssso many thingsss in ourrr teaching, it hasss morrre than one purrrpossse, I think."

"Another problem—" said a voice from the door. Firesong strode in, with Silverfox beside him. "I beg your pardon for being late, but I was checking some calculations of my own. Ladies and gentlemen, we knew we were chasing a deadline, but I now know the exact moment of that deadline. How are we to get to the Dhorisha Plains before the breakwater collapses? We have only until a fortnight after Midwinter Day to reach the Plains—in the winter, across two countries. Then we must travel to the center of the Plains, and sort through the contents of this Vault. Just how are we to manage that?"

Silence. Then, into the silence, Elspeth spoke.

"There is a permanent Gate near k'Leshya Vale on the rim of the crater," she said. "There must be—Falconsbane vanished from there, and how else—"

"*Yes!*" An'desha shouted excitedly. "There is, I remember! I know right where it is! But how are we going to reach there from here?"

"Piffle. A trifle," said Sejanes.

Now all eyes turned to him, as he smiled broadly and presented his knowledge to them as a wise old grandfather presenting candy to a room full of children.

"We of the Empire are the Masters of Portals—you call them Gates. We can find them at great distances, we can key into strange Portals, and we can build Portals that are permanent structures. But most of all, we know how to construct them using energies outside of ourselves, or the joined energies of several mages." His smile broadened, and he spread his hands wide. "I can teach even the apprentices among you how to join together with a single Adept to construct such a Portal, and given that another permanent Portal will anchor the other end, we should be able to make it self-sustaining for a limited time. Will *that* serve as our means to your ruined Tower?"

After all the tumultuous months of bickering, near-blood-feud, fear, derision, and anger, they held more than just nebulous hope in their hands. Inventive minds, people of different cultures and backgrounds, had come together and despite the friction between them, had held on to reason. It all sounded too easy, to hear it spoken in series—and yet, the pieces had all been there. Once the need was identified, they slipped into formation like well-trained soldiers. Karal was dazed at how nearly they had escaped disaster—

We could still have a disaster, he cautioned himself. *Don't count the larks until they are safely fledged.*

But. But! If he had not overcome his repugnance and started in motion the negotiations with Tremane—if k'Leshya had waited to send their delegation—if the Sworn-Shaman had decided to leave things in the hands of Jarim—if Elspeth and An'desha had not recalled how Falconsbane had made a miraculous escape from the Shin'a'in Sword-Sworn—

Yet everything had been *there,* and who was to say that if they had not put this solution together there would not have been another one? *Altra and Hansa could Jump people in pairs. Or maybe more than pairs—Altra Jumped me, An'desha, and Florian at the same time. We might have been able to work out something with Final Strikes, only less drastic. We could have shielded the Heartstones with everything we have, waited until the breakwater failed, endured a single round of the storms, and* then *gone to the Plains.*

No, this was not the only solution, and any of the pieces that had fallen neatly into place could have been replaced by another piece—but just at the moment, it looked as if it was the best solution.

What was important was that everyone who *possessed* a piece to contribute, *had.*

Once a start at a solution had been identified, people began volunteering—or declining to volunteer—for the expedition. The usual restless souls volunteered—Firesong, Treyvan and Hydona (who would have flown through fire for a chance to visit Urtho's Tower, or the remains of it), An'desha. There were some surprises—Elspeth and Darkwind declined, planning instead to hold the shielding on the Valdemar Heartstone, and Silverfox volunteered, saying that they had better have someone along with rudimentary Healer knowledge. *Florian* volunteered ("To stand for Valdemar"). The Shin'a'in

Sworn Shaman Lo'isha was going, of course, it was his homeland. The White Winds mages declared themselves out of their depth. Altra was going.

But last of all, Karal was going though he was no mage; An'desha and Altra had both insisted on it, although he could not imagine why they needed *him*. :Contingency,: Altra had said cryptically.

He only hoped this "contingency" would not involve a situation similar to the one on the Iftel border. Acting as a channel for whatever power that held sway behind those magical barriers—whatever it was that a channel *did*—had ranked right up with all of the worst personal experiences in his life. He really didn't want to repeat it.

An'desha said that he just wanted Karal as a buffer between himself and Firesong. *That* was a role easier to handle.

He wanted to stay with Natoli, and his sense of duty warred with his wishes. If Altra wanted him to go, there must be a reason connected with his duties as a Priest. But Natoli needed him, too.

It was finally Natoli herself who solved his dilemma for him.

He went to visit her in her room at Healer's Collegium, and described all the preparations being made for the journey to the remains of the Tower. She listened with interest, as she nursed her bandaged and splinted wrist close to her body.

"I wish I could go," she said wistfully. "Even though I probably wouldn't actually see anything happening. Just think of how old that Tower is! Think of what you could learn from inscriptions there if there are any! And what if there are books preserved in there somehow—why, who knows what new tracks they would send us off on!" She sighed, and looked ruefully at the bandages still covering her injuries. "But I can't, and that's that. You're going to be traveling fast to get across the bowl of the Plains in time, and you can't have anyone along who would slow you down."

"What do you mean by, '*you're* going to be traveling fast'?" he asked. "No one's ordered *me* to go."

"No one's ordered you, but I thought you told me that

An'desha and Altra both wanted you to go," she replied with surprise.

"They can *want* as much as they please," he said stubbornly. "I'm making up my own mind on this one. I've had my fill of other people making it up for me."

She frowned. "Are you going with the mages to the Plains or not?" she demanded. "If you don't want to because *you* don't want to, that's one thing, but you'd better not be wavering on this because of me!"

He was taken aback by the stern tone of her voice, and the hint of anger in her eyes. "Why not?" he asked.

"Because I won't have it, that's why!" she exclaimed. "If Altra wants you to go, doesn't that mean it's your duty to go? I won't have you neglecting your duty just because you want to keep me company! I don't expect or want that kind of behavior out of you, and you'd *better* not expect or want it out of me!"

Her vehemence left him speechless for a moment, and she filled in the silence.

"My *job* is to uncover new facts, find new ways of doing things, and sometimes that's dangerous," she continued, calming her tone of voice somewhat. "Well, look what happened with the boiler. I could have been killed!"

"I know—" he said numbly.

"So?" she gazed at him demandingly. "Would you ask me to choose between you and my work?"

If I did, I'd lose her, he realized. *She has a right to her work, her life. I don't have a right to ask her to give up any of that.*

"No," he replied quietly.

"And I don't and won't ask the same of you," she replied, as her fingers brushed restlessly back and forth along the bandages on her arm. "It's not fair and it's not right. This thing the mages are doing—it's dangerous, isn't it?"

He shivered. "More than dangerous. The Shin'a'in know where the Tower is, of course, and they've been working to uncover the entrance to the Vault since we decided what to do—but once we get in there, we'll be sorting through weapons that are very old, probably unstable, and not all of them are magical in nature. The mechanical weapons may be *very* unstable, the others think. Then when we find what we're looking for, we aren't sure what, exactly, we're going to be dealing with."

He heard himself saying "we" before he thought about it, and knew she'd noticed the phrasing when she smiled.

"So you're going." She made it a statement.

He sighed. "If Altra wants me along *and* he's being cryptic, it's because there's something he thinks I might have to do, and it's something he knows I probably wouldn't do if I had any choice." He grimaced. "I'm sure if I *don't* go, they'll find a way around any problems they encounter, but I'm also sure that it will be easier if I do go. In a case like this—the next best solution might not be good enough."

She reached for his hand with her uninjured one. "You know how you'd feel if this failed because you weren't there."

"If this fails, we're going to be in worse trouble than Hardorn is now," he corrected and shivered. "Think what would happen if the shielding all failed on the Heartstone here."

She blanched, as well she should.

"But we may be worrying at nothing," he went on, "And I may prove to be no more useful than an extra pair of hands to brew tea. If Altra *knew* I was needed, he wouldn't be giving me a choice. He said I should go as a 'contingency' measure. We've had everyone with *any* kind of ForeSight trying to probe in the direction of this situation, and none of them can tell us anything. They say that the images are all too confused, and that there is no clear path to the future once they get past the fact that we *do* find the Vault and we *do* find the weapons there." As he squeezed her hand, he allowed himself a moment of annoyance. "Now tell me this— what good does it do to be a Priest or to be able to talk with Avatars if neither your God nor the representatives of your Goddess are going to give you any clues?"

Natoli chewed her lip thoughtfully for a moment. "I've been listening to you and An'desha talking about Vkandis and the Star-Eyed, and I wonder if this isn't another one of those cases where there are many choices, and since none of the choices are a Second Cataclysm, They aren't going to help. I mean—they watch while people kill people and let people die all the time, and only take a hand in things once in a while, when it will make a big difference down the road. The rest of the time, people have to do what they feel they should, and accept the results. It's that 'free will' thing again."

He groaned. "I could do with a little more guidance and a little less free will!"

"I couldn't." Once again, she surprised him. "I want to make my own decisions, and if they're the wrong ones, then I'll learn from them. I want to be an *adult,* not a child. I don't want to be led along the safe path! The safe path is never new, and the safe path never teaches you anything others don't already know!"

Had she always been like this, or had the enforced idleness given her time to think about these things? He was astonished at the clarity and fearlessness of her outlook. "A lot of people wouldn't agree with you," he replied, answering her as seriously as she had spoken. "A great many people would rather have the safe path, and be taken care of. They'd rather have all their answers assured, neatly packaged, with 'the end' put on the last page."

"Then they can look for that neat package, but it's a false one, and they're only fooling themselves." Her eyes were shining, and her color heightened with excitement. "There *is* no end to questioning, except decay. And I'm not ready to sit and rot, and neither are you."

"You're right, I'm not." He leaned over then, and dared a kiss; her lips were warm and soft, and she didn't pull away. "And you're right; I should go. I'll be lonely without you, but I'll go."

Natoli squeezed his hand and whispered, "Be brave, Karal, and be careful. Come back to me."

Sejanes led a group of mixed Herald-Mages and White Winds mages who would be establishing the Gate under his direction and control; as Altra and Hansa had, they were using the old ruin in Companion's Field. "They're going to be worthless when we're done," he'd warned Selenay. "And they're going to be weak as newborn kittens for at least a day." Accordingly, she had sent along a contingent of servants with litters to carry them off when they collapsed. Sejanes had approved.

Now the expedition force stood in knee-deep snow beneath an overcast sky while Sejanes reiterated the plan. "We'll hold the Portal open long enough for you all to get through," he said, squinting into the bright snow glare. "That's all this lot will be good for. We'll reopen it in a fortnight, and you'd better be up on that rim when we do."

"You'll reopen it if you can," muttered one of the k'Leshya mages. "If they don't succeed, you'll have more than the Portal to worry about."

Sejanes ignored that—or perhaps he simply didn't hear it. "If you aren't there, we'll reopen it one more time a fortnight later, then send word to call up search parties down there." He paused and favored the k'Leshya mage with a sharp glance. Perhaps he *had* heard the mutter. "If, however, the force of your weapon deactivates the Gate at your end, you will have to find another way back here."

"In other words," Firesong said, laughing, "we walk home."

:Not precisely.:

Heads snapped up all over the group, as even those who did not have Mindspeech reacted to that voice in their heads.

A Companion stallion emerged from the trees to their left, leading a group of four more, all of them young, all nervously tossing their heads, and all wearing saddles and halters. Not the fancy tack of a Companion on search for his Chosen, but the everyday stuff a working Companion used.

:Rolan would like you to relay the rest, Karal,: Florian said, as he nudged Karal's shoulder with his nose. *:He can Mindspeak with anyone he wishes to, but it takes a lot of effort, and this will be faster.:*

"Ah—this is Rolan, he's the Queen's Own Companion" Karal said hastily.

:These are four of the fastest and strongest of the Compan-

ions who have not Chosen Heralds, and they have been picked by Rolan out of the volunteers to serve as mounts for those who need them.:

"Unpartnered Companions volunteered to carry the humans of our group," Karal interpreted. "These are the best." He knew from his own experience that no horse could ever keep up with a Companion, and if somehow the others had missed that particular piece of information, they'd soon figure it out!

:Rolan has made assignments.: The stallion tossed his head, and a muscular male with a short mane and tail stepped forward and bowed to the Sworn Shaman. *:This is Kayka.:*

"Your mount is called Kayka, sir," Karal told that worthy, who bowed to the stallion.

"I am honored, Kayka." Lo'isha's tone made it clear that he meant his words, they were not just for politeness' sake.

Two mares with artistically flowing manes and tails tripped forward together, stopping in front of Firesong and Silverfox. *:Twin sisters, Senta and Sartra. Senta will take Firesong, and says—:*

"I can hear what she says, thank you, Florian," Firesong interrupted dryly. "And I assure you, I actually *do* know how to travel lightly. Remember? I came here with only what my *dyheli* friend could carry." He turned to the Companion and bowed to her as deeply as the shaman had bowed to Kayka, though with a touch more irony. "I am grateful for your assistance, Senta, and I appreciate your beauty."

Silverfox already had one hand on Sartra's shoulder, and appeared to be deep in mental conversation with her. The last Companion, another female, slim, with a long forelock half hiding her eyes, stepped shyly forward, and scraped at the snow in front of An'desha with one hoof.

:This is Idry,: said Florian. *:She is my younger sister, and was the first to volunteer.:*

An'desha smiled. "Then I shall be twice as glad to have her company, Florian."

"Well, that certainly solves your transportation problem,"

Elspeth said dryly. "If they can't get you there as fast as a gryphon can fly, it can't be done at all."

"Rrr, ssso we will rrracsse?" Treyvan asked, then gape-grinned. Hydona bumped her beak against his side.

"Excellent, I admit that I am very pleased," Sejanes called, "Now, can we get *on* with this?"

After seeing so many Gates opening over the past several days, even the heart-stopping magic of Gate-construction felt like a routine. Karal paid no attention to the goings-on, taking the time instead to make certain that his pack was secure and that Florian's saddle and halter were comfortable. It would be a long trek down to the bowl of the Plains with no place to stop on the trail, and anything loose could rub poor Florian raw. The others were taking their packs and securing them behind the saddles. Treyvan and Hydona already had their flying-harness on, and whatever gear they thought they would need was fastened to it. Jerven and Lytha, their half-grown youngsters, would be staying behind. According to Hydona, it was time for them to start serious fledgling lessons, and those were best given by someone who was not their parent.

Given what a full-time job those two were, Karal wondered if the two might not be using this as a chance for a vacation away from them!

He completed his inspection at about the same time that the mages made contact with the anchoring Gate in the ruins above the Plains. When he looked up, it was to see snow-covered heaps of tumbled stones below a sky so blue and clear it hurt to look at it, all framed in the arch of weathered stones on their side.

"Quickly, please!" Sejanes shouted. "We can't hold this all day, you know!"

Karal mounted, glad to feel a saddle beneath him again, and started for the Gate, but Treyvan and Hydona were already there ahead of him, dashing through with alacrity. He wondered why they were so eager, then remembered—Clan k'Leshya had settled there, in the ruins as well as in the old Vale! They were probably eager to see some of their old friends before taking the trek to Urtho's Tower.

He followed right on their heels, with An'desha behind him. He had never actually crossed large distances by means of a Gate before, and he braced himself for the unpleasant stomach-tumbling sensations of a Jump.

But there was nothing of the kind; he felt for a split second as if he was falling, and there was a strange darkness that was laced with fiery multicolored ribbons of power and light all around him. Then Florian's feet came to rest on the stone on the other side with a little jolt, as if the Companion had made a small hop over an obstacle in their path.

:Like that better than Jumping, do you?: Although Altra had not been with them on the Valdemar side, now he appeared.

"Much," he said shortly, as Florian moved out of the way for the rest to come through. Although snow lay everywhere, it was cleared away from the places that had once been streets in what looked like the ruins of a substantial town. Though still in ruins, there were signs of habitation here and there—places where walls showed signs of rebuilding, and farther in the distance, conical, shingled roofs poking up above the snow-covered piles of rubble. Just at the moment, there were gryphons flying in from every direction to meet their two. There were at least a dozen, but it seemed as if there were hundreds; gryphons in a group, Karal soon learned, were not quiet.

This was not a social gathering, however; the gryphons landed, had a brief conference while the rest of the party traversed the Gate, then flew off again. Without knowing where in relation to the Plains this ruin was, Karal had no idea which way they were going, but their flight was purposeful, as if they each had a task to perform.

The Shaman was the last through the Gate, and it closed behind him.

"The way isss clearrr," Hydona called from her perch atop a ruined wall. "The Ssssworrrd-Ssssworrrrn arrre all along it and will rrride with usss in rrrelays. Grryphonsss fly ahead to ssscout. The worrrrssst parrrt isss the trrrail down; icsssed, they sssay."

Lo'isha shrugged. "That is to be expected, but I am glad

our white friends have agreed to bear us. I am more confident with them than I would be with even the best Shin'a'in
stock."

Evidently he knew precisely where he was; Kayka set out
at a brisk walk, and the rest followed, except for Treyvan and
Hydona, who took to the air. Karal and An'desha took the
rearmost position.

There were gryphons overhead constantly; as the trail
wove in and around the ruined buildings, Karal became completely lost. He would have been certain that the shaman
was, too, but with all the help in the air, that was extremely
unlikely.

Soon enough, they turned another corner, and suddenly
there was nothing in front of them but blue sky. They had
come to the edge of the ruins, and before and below them lay
the Dhorisha Plains.

Karse was a land of mountains, so Karal was no stranger to
height—but it is one thing to look at something on a map,
and quite another to stand on the edge of a sheer precipice
and look down—and down—and down—-

Intellectually, he had known that the edge of the crater
that formed the rim above the Plains was hundreds of
lengths above its floor. Now he knew it with his gut, and he
gulped.

Florian seemed nonchalant. *:It's not that bad. Take a
closer look; there's a switchback trail going all the way
down.:*

He didn't really like the look of the trail any better than
the long drop. It was barely wide enough for a single rider;
they would have to go single-file the entire way, and may
Vkandis help anyone who slipped.

*:I'll see you at the bottom—unless you'd like to Jump
with me now,:* Altra said smugly. *:Feel like a Jump?:*

Thinks I won't take him up on it, hmm? "Sir!" he called
to the shaman, "Altra has volunteered to Jump us down, one
Companion and rider at a time!"

:I did not!: Altra cried indignantly, but it was too late.
Lo'isha turned to them both with a look of grave gratitude,
and it was not possible to back down without looking ungra-

cious and ungraceful. That, Karal knew, was something that Altra's pride would never permit.

"If you would be so kind, Firecat," he said in his deep, impressive voice, "I do not like the look of this trail. I would rather we did not lose anyone to something that could be prevented."

Altra grumbled mentally at Karal, but accepted the task with outward grace. *:Just for that, you can go last, when I'm tired,:* he added, as he jumped up on the pack behind the Shaman.

Then they were gone—and a tiny dot appeared against the snow far below them.

It took exponentially less time, even going down pair by pair, than it would have if they'd taken the trail. And even though Altra *was* tired when he got to Karal, and his control *was* a bit shaky, the resulting Jump was no worse than the ones he'd made getting out of Hardorn. That resulted in nausea, but not the gut-racking illness that had been the result of the flight from Tremane's study.

And when he "landed" beside the others, it was clear that the Shin'a'in had been there before them, breaking a clear trail through the relatively light snow so that they could proceed as fast as possible without worrying about getting lost.

When Karal looked up, he saw circling dots that were the gryphons. When he looked outward, he saw moving dots that must be the Sword-Sworn, riding a protective patrol ahead and to both sides of them. He'd wondered how they were going to manage without supplies, for no one had packed anything in the way of food or shelter and not even a Companion could cross to the center of the Dhorisha Plains in a single day; now it came to him. The Shin'a'in and the gryphons would take care of that, if they had not already.

Lo'isha looked about with satisfaction—even if his lips were a little white. "The trail is clear, the wind is at our backs!" he cried. "Now, let us *ride!*"

After the first day, Karal looked back on the grueling trip he and Ulrich had made from Karse to Haven with nostalgia.

Florian saved him as much as he could—and indeed a Companion's pace was blissful compared to that of a horse—

But this was still riding from an hour past sunup to far past sundown, in bitterly cold weather, without a break. Companions did not need rest the way that horses did, and the shaman saw fit to make use of that endurance.

The brilliantly blue sky of day became a huge black bowl studded with enormous stars by night. When the half moon rose, it flooded the featureless Plains with white light that had the effect of making Karal feel even colder than before. But the flatness of the Plains did have one advantage—they saw the fires and torches of their resting place from a vast distance away, as the only spots of warm color in all the icy whiteness. Just looking at the pinpricks of warm yellow gave Karal enough strength to hold onto Florian's saddle. His cold fingers had long since grown too numb for any pretense of holding to the reins.

When at last they reached the shelters, they found a single round felt tent awaiting them, with torches all around it, a fire in front of it, and black-clad Shin'a'in tending a stewpot over the fire. Karal fell out of the saddle rather than dismounting; he stumbled toward the tent, and Florian followed him right inside.

Evidently the Shin'a'in were prepared for the idea that the Companions should share their shelter; the tent, lit by three oil lamps suspended from the roof poles, was divided in half, with half of the floor covered in old, damaged carpets, with piles of hay and grain and leather buckets of water on top of the carpets. Treyvan and Hydona were already there, fast asleep, curled together in a single ball of feathers with no sign of limbs or heads. The other half had bright new carpets with bedrolls laid out neatly for them, in a semicircle with a charcoal brazier at their feet. It might not have been very warm by the standards of the Palace, but compared to the bitter cold outside, it was quite toasty. There was a Shin'a'in Sword-Sworn waiting inside, unsaddling and wiping down the Companions and throwing warm blankets over them as they ate and drank. Florian joined the others. As the last human inside, Karal found the others already wrapped up in their blankets, eating bowls of stew and sipping at mugs of something that steamed. Karal didn't know what it was, nor did he care. He took the last of the bedrolls, pulled off his boots and shoved his legs down into the warmth of the blankets, and accepted the bowl and mug handed to him with a murmur of thanks.

Then he ate as quickly as he could shovel the stew in with the aid of a piece of tough, flat bread. The tea had an odd, astringent taste, but it was curiously soothing to his raw throat.

As soon as he had finished both tea and stew, the same Shin'a'in took bowl and cup away from him. The others were already curled in their bedrolls for sleep, and he followed their example. The Shin'a'in blew out the oil lamps on his way out of the tent, leaving them in darkness.

At some point before he went to sleep, Altra appeared, lying beside him and half over him, creating a swath of heat at his back. The Firecat purred quietly and said just one thing.

:Karal . . . I'm proud of you.:

With that added comfort—in more ways than the merely physical—he fell instantly asleep.

The Shin'a'in woke them before dawn, and they broke their fast with more stew, bread, and tea. Then they were in the saddle again, and pushing outward.

The second day was a repetition of the first, as was the third. Karal's eyes grew sore from the reflection of sun on snow, and from the red eyes that met his every time anyone—except the shaman and An'desha—turned to face him, the others must be suffering the same. The cold, dry air made his lips crack and chap, and his throat sore. After the second day, Lo'isha gave them each a little vial of aromatic oil to moisten their lips with, and advised them that they might want to anoint their whole faces. Karal took him up on the suggestion; Firesong resisted at first, but by mid-afternoon, with his cheeks flaming from wind-chapping, he had given in and done the same.

Karal lost track of time; he was either riding or sleeping—too much of the former, not enough of the latter. The landscape they traversed was always the same; not quite flat, but close enough for a young man from the mountains, rolling hill after snow-covered, rolling hill, with scarcely a tree or a bush in sight except where they marked the passage of watercourses or the location of a spring. The cold numbed all of him, and he never was really warm except the moment that they awoke him. Firesong looked miserable, Silverfox looked resigned, and only An'desha and Lo'isha seemed to thrive.

But then, this is—was—his home.

The gryphons rarely appeared, and when they did, they were fixated on the goal and could talk of nothing else. At last—after how many days he could not tell, that goal loomed up on the horizon.

It was singularly unprepossessing, for something they had chased across half a continent—an odd, melted stub of silvery-gray rock, poking up out of the top of yet another rolling hill.

Then, when it didn't get any closer, he realized that it must be much larger than he had thought.

Then he finally spotted the tiny dots of more Shin'a'in swarmed about the base, and the equally tiny dots of two gryphons circling it, and he *understood* how large it was.

There was a long pile of something dark against the snow at the foot of the Tower—rich, turned earth. It looked as if the Shin'a'in had been digging for something.

The closer they got, the more his skin crawled. The Tower simply didn't *look* melted, it *had been* melted. The great force that fueled the Cataclysm had made the rock of the Tower run like liquid wax. And they were about to play with forces *worse* and more hazardous than the one that had done this, weapons that the Mage of Silence, who had created this, thought were too dangerous to use!

What am I doing here? he thought, aghast.

It would not be the last time he had that thought.

They rested and slept for what remained of that day and all the next night; it would be stupid, and perhaps suicidal to enter the Vault with their minds fogged with fatigue. But the moment the sun rose, so did they, and one of the Sword-

Sworn led them to the opening the Shin'a'in had been working on since this expedition had been decided on.

The old door to the Tower lay somewhere beneath several hundred tons of melted, fused rock. The Shin'a'in had taken a more direct route to the Vault beneath the remains of the Tower. There must have been hundreds of them working on it to get it done in so short a period of time.

They had burrowed down in a long slanting tunnel into the side of the hill supporting the Tower, straight to the ancient Vault wall. *That* was only stone blocks mortared together, and the mortar, after so many centuries, was old and weak. Urtho had never bothered to put any sort of armoring or defensive measures on the wall of the Vault—after all, anyone who got this far would still have to dig a hole in the full sight of the guards, the army, the Kaled'a'in, the gryphons. . . .

Not likely.

The Shin'a'in, with advice from the miners of k'Leshya, and additional help from the gryphons, had been working nonstop; together they had made an impressive tunnel, chipped out the weak mortar between the stones, and pried out enough of the latter to create an entrance fully large enough for Treyvan and Hydona, not to mention Florian, who insisted on coming below as well. The other Companions were perfectly happy to remain outside and rest, and Karal caught them casting many glances askance at Florian as he prepared to descend the precipitous tunnel with the party of mages. They all had lanterns, but the light didn't help the feeling of being trapped beneath tons of earth and stone. The tunnel itself had been shored up quite expertly, and for a moment Karal wondered where they had gotten the timbers.

The gryphons, of course. They must have flown them in from k'Leshya.

A formidable task, equal to the task of digging this tunnel.

Karal concentrated on keeping his breathing steady, reminding himself that as long as his lantern flame burned brightly, there was more than enough air down here for them all to breathe.

At least I'm not cold. There's no wind blowing. There's no snow-glare.

How much longer does this tunnel go on?

He hadn't begun by counting his steps, but he started at that point. Fifty . . . one hundred . . . one hundred and fifty . . . shouldn't they have reached the wall by now?

His chest felt tight; was the light a little dimmer? The flame of his candle a little lower?

:Karal. I'm right behind you.: The voice in his mind warned him, so when a head bumped against his thigh, he didn't jump and screech. *:It's all right. There's air, and if anything happens, I can Jump you out.:*

Immediately the invisible bands tightening around his chest loosened. Of course! Altra could get him out, even if the roof collapsed! He relaxed, and the flame in his lantern brightened again. Or perhaps it had never been dimming in the first place.

"We're at the Vault."

The shaman's voice, muffled by all the other bodies between him and the Shin'a'in, alerted him so that he didn't run into An'desha when An'desha stopped.

The line ahead of him shuffled forward, step by step. "Watch yourself," An'desha warned, as the light from his lantern caught on the regular shapes of stone blocks. "There's debris in the way."

An'desha moved forward and vanished into a hole a gryphon could barely squeeze through. There was a litter of stone pieces and other debris in front of the hole, as if it had just today been made. Perhaps it had!

He stepped over the edge of the hole, following the gleam of light—and stepped into another world.

The floor was smoothly polished white stone with a pattern, a compass rose of eight points inset in it, made of a rose-colored granite. This was a large, round room with white stone walls that rose in a conical shape to a point about two stories above their heads. Hanging down from the center by a silver chain was a large sphere of crystal, which shone softly in the reflected light from the lanterns.

Karal stared at it in awe. "What is it?" he asked. "A weapon? Something like a Heartstone?"

Firesong shook his head as he also stared; they stood in a loose circle with their mouths agape, gazing upward. Finally Treyvan laughed, and said, "Much sssimplerrr," and called out a word in a language that was not quite Shin'a'in and not quite Tayledras.

Obediently, the globe lit up from within. Karal cried out and shielded his eyes, but he needn't have bothered. The radiance was remarkably soft, and left only a faint afterimage that rapidly faded.

"It isss a lamp," Treyvan said superfluously.

Now that they could see clearly, they doused their lanterns and took a look around. This, obviously, was not the Vault itself, but probably a workroom to one side, for there was the dark gap of an open door in the wall. Firesong was the nearest, so he was the first one through it, where he stopped, just inside, blocking the door.

"Well," his dry voice echoed back, "it would be nice if I could see. What was that command?" Before anyone could answer him, he tried several versions of the word Treyvan had used, and finally hit on the right intonation. His form was silhouetted for a moment as the light flared to life, then dimmed to the twin of the first.

"I believe," the Tayledras Adept drawled, "we have found what we were looking for."

He moved out of the way, leaving space for the others to enter behind him.

Karal lagged back; for one thing, he was not sure he wanted to *see* what they were looking for. For another, he knew very well he wouldn't know what he was looking at!

So he allowed all the others to crowd in ahead of him, and trailed behind. He expected exclamations, but he heard nothing but a few whispers.

When he passed the threshold himself, he understood why.

This was a huge room, but practically empty except for four of the crystal lights suspended from the ceiling, and a single floating barge in the middle. Faint outlines in the ceiling above the barge suggested a door or hatchway there.

Around the periphery of the room were fifteen more doors, all of them closed.

Where were the weapons? Had all of them been taken away?

"The weapons must be behind each of those doors, one to a room," Firesong said authoritatively. "If *I* were holding dangerous objects, that's what I'd do with them. That way if you had an accident with one, it would be confined to the room it was in and not spread to the others."

"You begin to sound like a career artificer, Firesong," Silverfox replied. "That makes entirely too much sense."

Firesong turned to the nearest door on his right, and continued talking. "What's more, I'll bet the room we were in held a weapon that Urtho *did* use, and the reason that the barge is in here is to take large or bulky creations up to where you can—or could, I mean—move them out the doors."

"I wonder why this place even exists," An'desha said, as Firesong checked to see if the door was locked before he tried opening it. "You'd think that a force that would melt the Tower would destroy everything, wouldn't you?"

"Maybe because this was right below the event, none of the force went downward," Karal hazarded, trying to remember some of what he'd learned from the artificers.

"Perhaps the shields on the Vault disintegrated, but absorbed all of the force in the process," Silverfox guessed.

"Perhaps the Star-Eyed had something to do with it," Lo'isha said with great dignity.

"Perrrhapsss all of thossse rrreasssonsss, perrrhapsss none," Treyvan said with impatience. "Isss the doorrr locked orrr not?"

"Just stuck," Firesong replied, finally shoving it open. He spoke the word that lit the lamp and gave an exclamation of disappointment.

"Come look for yourself, but I don't think this one is going to do us any good," he said, waving them over.

Once again Karal held back, but on his own viewing, he was inclined to agree with Firesong. This room contained a conglomerate of bizarre parts, from coils of wire to animal skulls with jeweled eyes, all woven together in a crazed spider-web of colored string, ribbon, hair-thin wire, and raw-hide thongs.

"Good God, why *skulls?*" Karal exclaimed, revolted.

"Perhaps because they had been used in shamanic ceremonies and so now were attuned to power of a sort he needed," Lo'isha hazarded. "Not Kaled'a'in ceremonies, but Urtho made use of the magics he had learned from many peoples, and many peoples were his allies."

"I don't know about you, but I don't even want to touch that," Firesong said as he edged back outside. "I don't know what it does, and I'm not sure it would still do it at this point—and even if it did, how much of it would fall into dust if you brushed against it?"

"Trrrue," Treyvan said, taking care to tuck his wings in as he moved back outside. With one accord, they closed the door with the greatest of care and moved on to the next room.

By the time they were finished, they had eliminated eight of the fifteen possibilities. None were quite as bizarre as the cow-skull construction, but no one wanted to take any chances on them. Two were featureless boxes that had even Treyvan shaking his head in bafflement, one was an unidentifiable object that resembled nothing so much as a spill of liquid caught and frozen in midair. Two more were delicate sculptures of wires and gemstones that they were all afraid to touch lest they fall to pieces, and the remaining three Treyvan recognized from his litany as being simple weapons of dreadful mass destruction of life and property—not at all suited to their purposes, for there was nothing magical about the energy released when *these* things were triggered.

That left seven possibilities.

With each of the objects was a metal plaque, identifying how to destroy it, but nothing else about its nature, except the single line, "You cannot use this weapon without killing yourself. Neither could I. Be wise, and be rid of it." Each plaque was signed with Urtho's name and sigil.

They gathered rubbings of all these plaques, together with a crude drawing of each object and the number of the room it was in—counting the empty room as number one and going sunwise—and sat down together in the floating barge to discuss what they had.

"We have three days to decide which device and how to work it, one day to set up and practice, and that's all," Firesong warned. "If we don't succeed by then, working with the assumption that the waves going out can be made to match the speed of the ones coming in, the breakwater will go down. Irrevocably. Without that to break up the force, the next mage-storm through here might well trigger one or more of these things."

"Sssurely not—" Treyvan said, but he did not sound certain.

"Are you willing to stand around here and wait to see? I'm not," Firesong said bluntly. "Frankly, I didn't think we'd find more than one or two of Urtho's weapons existing; I never dreamed there'd be this many that were still intact. It seems to me that if we don't succeed here, we'd better evacuate the Plains *and* k'Leshya."

"I wish I didn't feel the same way," the shaman said with reluctance. "I had not expected to find so many lethal objects here either. If one or even two were activated, the Tower and the physical containments still here would probably keep the damage to a small area—but if three or more went—" He shuddered, his face white.

"Right," Firesong nodded. "And we are making a lot of assumptions about whether they'd 'go off,' for that matter. Some of them might be the magical equivalent of a slow acid, some might simply shred things randomly for a long period of time."

"Then let's get on with this and make a decision!" An'desha exclaimed, his nervousness evident in the high pitch of his voice.

But a few hours later, it was clear that they had another problem.

Between the litany and the instructions for disposal, it was possible to deduce what each of the remaining seven objects *did,* and they were able to eliminate three more of the seven. The trouble was, when they had ranked the remaining four in order of suitability, they came to another, unexpected snag.

The language that the k'Leshya *thought* was the purest Kaled'a'in, that they had cherished—they fondly assumed—as unchanged for centuries, was anything but pure and unchanged.

"Look, we have *three* words here that all mean 'explosive'!" Firesong burst out. "*Your* version of Kaled'a'in has two of them, Treyvan, *ko'chekarna* and *chekarna*, and from the destruction instructions I think we've got a third, *ri'chekarna!* So which is right? We have to know or we're likely to get our number one choice going off right in our faces!"

"I—do not know," Treyvan said helplessly. "The language hasss ssshifted. . . ."

"Languages do, over time," Lo'isha said ironically. "Your mistake was to assume that since the Kaled'a'in were among peoples that avoided change, your language and ways were immutable. We need a scholar in ancient Kaled'a'in—"

"Or someone with ForeSight, who could look at each of these things and determine which one we can use safely!" Karal said suddenly, as he looked directly at Florian and Altra.

The two looked at each other, as if they were consulting silently. The little group stared at both of them in an expectant hush. It seemed to take forever before Florian turned back to them, but it was Altra who "spoke," although his eyes were directed off past Karal's shoulder, as if he was concentrating on something.

:I cannot bring someone here in time. Florian cannot reach that far with his mind.: Karal's heart fell.

"I can't build a Gate that will reach that far," Firesong reminded them, "And neither can An'desha."

"Then we arrre rrright back to the beginning." Teyvan's ear-tufts flattened against his head. "Back to language, a ssset of verrrssse that hasss ssshifted meaningsss overrr the yearsss, and guesssesss which can get usss all killed."

"No—" An'desha corrected, his eyes half-closed in thought. "We do have more than that. Mage-Sight should tell us something about the power sources, and *that* should tell us if it's something we ought to avoid."

"It might tell usss otherrr thingsss asss well," Treyvan put in, his ear-tufts rising again.

"And let usss make the bessst transsslationsss we can," Hydona added. "If we have the choicssse between a devicsse with a good trrranssslation and one with a half trrransss-lation, need I sssuggessst which we usssse?"

Firesong rubbed eyes so tired and puffy they were mere slits. In the end, there was only one device they *could* use, and it was not their first or even second choice. Karal had spent the time making himself useful while the mages pondered translations and probed the devices with every tool available to them. Precious time was lost while they did so, but none of them were wasting any time either. They hardly slept, and ate only when Karal or Silverfox put food in their hands.

And in the end, the shaman himself used his powers, ill-suited as they were to such a task, attempting to help with a selection. His "inspired guess" matched the choice of the mages.

"There's only one problem," Firesong said glumly, eyeing the unprepossessing pyramid of silvered metal. "This thing is going to kill whoever activates it. According to Treyvan's litany and what I've gleaned from the destruction information, the rest of us would be able to get far enough away to avoid incineration, but not the person setting it off. It can't be set off magically, we don't have anyone who can move things with his mind with us, and when it goes, not even Altra would be able to Jump out in time. Assuming he had two hands with four fingers and a thumb each, which he doesn't."

"Unlessss—" Treyvan prompted.

Firesong shrugged. "I don't see where that could make a difference. The fatal flaw in this thing, and the reason Urtho never used it, is that there's spillover energy in the physical plane. *Incandescent, white-hot* spillover energy."

Karal looked from one to the other. "Unless *what?*" he prompted.

Firesong grimaced, and Treyvan answered. "Unless the perrrssson trrrigerrring it isss a Mage-Channel. He *might* be able to channel the ssspilloverrr enerrrgy to the enerrrgy-planesss wherrre it isss sssupposssed to go."

"Yes, well, there's just one little problem with that," Firesong snapped. "He stands even odds of getting burned out—if he succeeds—and he'll need to be completely shielded, *and* if he loses control, he'll *still* get killed along with whoever is shielding him! That assumes we *had* some-one who was tough enough to—"

He stopped, suddenly realizing that Karal had gone white as snow, and An'desha, Florian, and Altra were all staring at him. The muscles in his throat tensed as he swallowed.

"I'm a channel," he said, in a whisper.

Now Firesong stared at him, too, his mind whirling. "You're a fool if you think you can do this," he said harshly. "If you thought the Iftel border was hard, it's *nothing* com-pared to channeling this thing! You're not trained, you can't even *see* mage-energy—"

"But I am a channel," the young man persisted, though he was still pale and drawn. "And I've been told that channeling is instinctive, not learned."

"You're going to kill yourself!" Firesong shouted, unable to bear the tension. "You're out of your mind! *We can't help you.* You'd have to do this alone! The best we could do is shield you!"

"Is there any other choice?" Karal countered, looking each of them in the eyes. One by one, they each shook their heads. Finally, he came back to Firesong, who clenched his teeth angrily.

"Firesong—we all knew when we came here that we might not come back. We have all resolved in our own ways that we are willing to make sacrifices for even a chance of saving our homelands." Karal's facial expression looked like that of a boy ready to cry, but in the way he held his chin up and back straight, he acted like a grown man facing a moment of truth. "I know that if I have to give my life in this, I will be welcome in the Sunlord's arms."

How *dare* the whelp put him in this position? How *dare* he volunteer to get himself turned to a cinder before Firesong had a chance to get his own feelings straight?

"Damn you—" he began, but Karal interrupted him with a wan smile.

"I don't think your curse is capable of overriding Vkandis' blessing, Hawkbrother," he chided gently. "But if there is no other choice, I suggest you take it back anyway. I'm going to need all the help I can get."

"I take it back. But may *all* your children turn out like you!" Firesong exploded, unable to come up with a better "curse" to vent his feelings. He turned violently away and escaped to the empty chamber to pace. His gut was a solid knot of tensions, his neck felt as stiff as old rawhide.

How can he do this! He's right, but how can he! This is insane! An'desha will never forgive me!

Soft footsteps at the entrance to the chamber warned him that he was not alone.

"I have to, you know," Karal said quietly. "I had the feeling it might come to something like this. Altra kept saying he wanted me along for 'contingency'; I think he must have meant that there was an equal chance you'd have been able to use one of the other devices." A soft sigh. "The ForeSeers all said that the futures were so tangled they couldn't see past us getting here. There was always a chance that something else might have worked out."

"Maybe. If we had more time to study them. If I wasn't reasonably certain the wave front of the next mage-storm was going to get in *here* as well as everywhere else—this *is* the origin-point, after all. Hellfires! Where else would the energy go but here! And this place can't keep taking a battering without at least one of these devices going on its own!" He stopped pacing and turned to look into Karal's white and strained face. "I *do not want* you to do this!"

"I know," Karal told him.

"But if you're going to insist—by your gods and mine, I'm not going to stand around outside this place and leave you to do it alone." In this much, at least, he could assuage his own conscience. "I'll shield you—"

"We'll all shield him," An'desha said, coming up behind Karal. Firesong started to protest, then shrugged. It was their choice, too.

"All right." He took a deep breath and tried to reckon the time passed. "How much time do we have left? I know it can't be much."

"About half a day." Karal sounded steady enough. Maybe he *could* do it. "I've been keeping very careful track. Every mark we delay means the closer the wave front will be to Haven and the Heartstone there. Tremane's people can weather one more storm, maybe two—"

"But the shielding on the Stone might go down, not to mention all the other Vale Stones, I know, I know." He suppressed a wave of irritation at Karal for restating the obvious. He let his irritation show as he answered in a growl. "All right, then, if that's the way you all want it, who am I to argue?"

An'desha looked for a moment as if he might retort, but only turned back to the main room. Karal followed him, leaving Firesong to trail behind, feeling as if he had somehow lost an argument, even though there hadn't really been one.

They spent their remaining time in rehearsal for the moment. Aya chittered at him from atop the pack as Firesong rummaged deep into the side pocket. He noticed that he was not alone in surreptitiously going to his belongings for stimulants to keep him wide awake and alert; such things were dangerous and they would all pay later—if they survived this—but every mage knew there would be times when there were not enough hours to rest before a vital working, and carried a packet or two of such things. He even caught the shaman chewing a mouthful of something with an expression of distaste that told him it was not dried meat.

Tayledras stimulants had the peculiar quality of setting everything emotional at a distance, enabling Firesong to focus on the purely intellectual project at hand. The mental exercises that sharpened the mind came to him naturally, like a musician practicing his fingerings quicker and quicker. Diagrams of light shone against his lids as he concentrated, eyes closed—symbols for Vale, Veil, Heartstone, ley-line, shield, absorber, deflector, suspensor, buffer—current and anchor, circle and square, star and sphere—they all appeared and interwove. And it occurred to him, as soon as he felt that distancing of his inner turmoil, that there was a *reason* for that pattern in the floor of every storage chamber. The compass rose.

In his peculiarly exalted state, he leaped straight from flash of intuition to a plan, with no conscious reasoning in between.

"Look at this!" he said, as they entered the chamber for a final rehearsal. "Look, the device is in the exact middle of that inlaid compass rose—it can't be by accident! This is a shielding-circle!"

An'desha tilted his head to one side and frowned. "It doesn't look like anything in my memory—" he said tentatively.

"Of course it doesn't," Firesong interrupted impatiently. "Your memories are all of Urtho's arch rival, and if there was a way to do something the opposite of Urtho, you can be certain Ma'ar took it! The positioning is perfect, and I'll bet there's an amplification-effect when we set ourselves up and begin the shielding. Look here—the angle from point to point is a factor of eight, with eight points, and sixty-four marker triangles point in. Look at the cupping of those scallops around the center—I'll bet you all my silk that they're collectors. Check the angles of deflection from point to point, and they'll all line up to buttress each other."

An'desha looked at Treyvan and Hydona for confirmation. The female gryphon wagged her head from side to side. "It could be," she admitted. "Sssuch thingsss arrre known. Urrrtho wasss known forrr being rrresssourcssseful enough forrr sssixty men, beforrre brrreakfasssst. It would be in hisss ssstyle to put sssuch thingsss herrrre."

"Then you two—take North and South," he ordered, feeling as if this must be the proper configuration, though he did not know why. "Florian and Altra, East and West." That put all the nonhumans on cardinal points, which made a certain sense given what the gryphons had told him about Urtho and how he cherished his nonhuman creations. "Karal, stand in the center with the pyramid. An'desha, you go between Altra and Treyvan in the Northeast. An'desha, I'll be opposite you—"

But here he stopped, for there were only Lo'isha and Silverfox left, and both were shaking their heads. "I know nothing of shielding," the Shaman began—

Then, with a sigh and a rush of wings on a wind that existed somewhere other than *here and now*, the other two places were taken. Light filled the room, and Firesong's heart leaped straight into his throat.

The last pieces of the puzzle. They have had a hand in this, too—

Standing in the Northwest and Southeast were—

No—

Tre'valen—

"We have come to help in this," said one of the two creatures, part flame, part bird, and part man, with a face that had haunted his few nightmares since the moment he had found the lifeless body of the Shin'a'in shaman struck down by Mornelithe Falconsbane. *"We are still as much of your world as of Hers, and this is, after all, Her chosen land. She wishes it protected, as do we."*

Karal's eyes glowed with an emotion that Firesong could put no name to, but there was no mistaking the emotion on An'desha's face. It was pure, unleavened joy. And Firesong knew, truly, and with a settling of peace in his heart, that he had not "lost" An'desha to any human or any human arguments. There was no use arguing when someone heard the call of the Star-Eyed in his soul. That siren song was as unbreakable as any lifebond, and as enduring.

The other bird-human-spirit spoke. *"An'desha knows—we have been with you, aiding where we could—but the Star-Eyed helps only those with the bravery to help themselves. We have come of our own volition, and live or die, we stand beside you."*

Lo'isha was on his knee with his head bowed, and the creature who had once been Tre'valen, himself a shaman, gestured to him to rise. The shaman did so, but wearing an expression so awestruck that Firesong doubted he would say *anything* as long as the two Avatars were there.

But as Firesong turned his attention back to the circle, he realized he knew what that look in Karal's eyes was.

It was the look of someone who knows he is about to die, but whose faith is certain and confirmed and who is no longer afraid of the prospect. "Fey," some called it.

Perhaps, as Stefen bid him farewell in the mountains of the North, Vanyel had looked that way. . . .

But it was too late now to do anything about it. The last few moments were trickling away.

"Raise your shields!" he shouted, his throat tight, as he brought up his own. To Mage-Sight, each of them now stood within a glowing sphere of rainbow light, and as he had somehow divined, each point on the compass rose glowed as well. The light radiating from each of them reflected from the angled patterns outlined in the stone. It looked as though, if they survived this, he wouldn't owe anyone his silk.

"Link shields!" he cried out, before his throat closed too much to speak. There was a moment of faltering, then all of the shields formed into a thick ring of light surrounding Karal and the waist-high pyramid in the center. The young man closed his eyes and placed his hands carefully on two of the sides, fitting his fingers into the depressions placed there for that purpose.

But once again, as Firesong had guessed, older magics were activated by the energies of their shields. The design on the floor began to glow, sending up eight arms of light that pulled the shields with them, until they all met in a point, making a cone of radiance that echoed the conical shape of the walls around them. Instead of being merely ringed with shielding, Karal was encased in it, and the energy that he would release would be funneled straight up by the shields.

Precisely as it needed to be, to keep any harm from coming to the Plains outside.

Silverfox and Lo'isha watched anxiously; Firesong knew that the shaman would be able to see the energies they had raised, but the expression on Silverfox's face suggested that he, too, saw them, which meant that they were powerful enough even for non-mages to see. That meant he had been right; Urtho had built a mechanism of amplification into the design of the floor.

But there was no chance to gloat over this triumph of instinct and artistry over intellect and reason. It was time. He *knew* that, as if he were a water-clock and the last drop had just fallen.

"Karal, *now!*" he shouted, and Karal's face spasmed as his fingers closed convulsively on the trigger points of the device.

The center of the design exploded soundlessly into power. Karal was somewhere in the midst of all that—more power than any Heartstone, more power than Firesong had ever seen in his life, power that made Aya shriek and flee into the next room, that was so bright the shaman and Silverfox shouted and hid their eyes.

Somewhere in the heart of that inferno of energy, Karal struggled to hold it, to transmute it—he struggled—

And Firesong felt him failing. Not failing to *hold*, but failing in his grasp on the world, on himself, on his life. He was thinning, vanishing, evaporating in a little microcosm of his incandescent God. In a moment, he would be lost, and if anyone dared try to help him, the circle would break and they would all perish.

Over my dead body! Anger finally penetrated his drug-born and aloof indifference. Though—if instinct failed him, it might well be just that—

"Everybody! On my count, take human-sized steps forward, follow your compass point!" he shouted into the roaring silence. "*One! Two! Three!*"

The circle contracted around Karal, tightening in on him, and having the effect of focusing the energy he controlled as the rays' edges flanged and flared.

"*Four! Five! Six!*" They were all within touching range now, if they had all had hands. But that was not yet what Firesong's instincts cried out for.

"*Seven! Eight!*" They were practically on top of Karal

now—the pyramid was gone, completely, and Karal was as transparent as one of the Avatars, his head thrown back, his mouth open in a silent cry, surrounded and encased in a pillar of white-hot, ice-cold fire.

"*Nine!*" He reached out and seized one of Karal's arms—without prompting, each of the others did the same, except for Florian, who touched the young man's breast with his nose, and Altra, who reared up on hind legs and placed both paws in the middle of his back.

The light!

It flared up in his face the moment they all touched Karal, he closed his eyes, but it scorched through his eyelids and flung him physically back! He felt his hand discorporate, turning into vapor—he lost his grip on Karal's arm, and felt himself tossed backward through the air, to land against the wall and slide bonelessly and helplessly to the floor.

It was over.

He couldn't see; couldn't hear.

They had won—but they had lost Karal.

Firesong fell back into darkness as profound as the explosion of light, and all feeble remaining awareness left him.

Firesong wasn't unconscious for very long, but it was certainly the first time in his life that he had been knocked out by magic—and the searing pain in his head told him just what price he had paid for tampering with such powers. He wouldn't be able to light a candle for the next week until he healed—and the next day or so was going to be pure hell. But with a shiver of glee, he realized he was *alive.*

He couldn't move for a moment; couldn't even think past the pain except for that tangle of elation and grief. *We did it—I shouldn't have done that, he might have been all right if I hadn't told everyone to close in, it's my fault—*

And—oh, gods, but who else had they lost? He forced himself to roll over and sit up, forced his eyes to open, but they were watering so heavily he couldn't see. He wiped at them frantically with his sleeve, as Aya scuttled back into the room and settled against his side, crooning.

"What in the name of Kal'enel happened?" he heard the shaman croak.

But the voice that answered was not Silverfox—nor anyone else who had been in the circle.

"I haven't a clue," Karal said, in a weak whisper. "I don't remember anything but pressing those ten trigger points."

Firesong managed to get his eyes clear, and to his utter astonishment, they confirmed what his ears had told him.

Lo'isha and Silverfox were bent over Karal, helping him to sit up. There didn't seem to be much of him inside those black robes of his—he looked as if he'd been undergoing a thirty-day Vision-Quest fast. Both of the others were handling him gingerly, as if they felt he was as fragile as spun glass.

Well, Firesong wasn't feeling any too sturdy himself at the moment. . . .

But before he got a chance to build up even the faintest feeling of resentment, help arrived, pouring in through the tiny doorway, in the form of black-clad Shin'a'in Sword-Sworn, who quickly and efficiently gathered them all up and carried them bodily out through the tunnel and up into the scarlet light of the setting sun. He let his body stay limp, simply cargo.

The sunset was a crimson light enhanced a bit with a coruscating rainbow of mage-energy, covering the bowl of the sky, slowly fading as the day itself faded.

He let himself be ministered to, as Aya oversaw everything and scolded if they jostled him too much as they carried him, with the rest, into a warm tent. He was too weak to resist, anyway. It was all he could do to nod when they asked him if he wanted something to drink, and to accept the bowl of hot herbal tea—well dosed with painkillers that he recognized at the first sniff. Those would war unpleasantly in his stomach for a few moments with the energy boosters, but he knew which ones would win, and he was grateful. He drank the bitter bowl down to the dregs, and waited stoically for the roiling in his gut to cease. He gathered from the chattering that the area around the Tower had suddenly lit up like a tiny sun for a moment, though absolutely no physical effect other than the light had leaked over into the "real" world. Firesong had the feeling that not even that would have occurred if they had not interfered and kept Karal from evaporating. . . .

And if I had not—An'desha might have forgiven me eventually, but I would never have forgiven myself.

Not all of the effects of their counterstorm had been so benign, however. In ruins all around the rim of the Plains, the gryphon scouts were reporting odd collapses, disappearances of structures and parts of structures; nothing modern, but only those things dating from Urtho's time.

Including the Gate they had arrived through.

As he faded into drugged sleep, he heard Treyvan sigh, and Hydona make the observation that he was already thinking.

"Well," she said with resignation. "We shall surrrely take ourrr time getting back—but therrre will be a home to rrreturrrn to."